"You once told me that you can't remember who you want to be," Memphis said. She came in close, like the day we had first met. "There are always moments in life when we lose ourselves, but we're never lost. Not really. Sometimes we just can't see who we are, or who we have been, to the people around us—the ones we love, those who love us. Sometimes, you just have to remember that you made it this far. You can go a little longer."

"It's too late," I said. "Some sins just can't be forgiven."

Or can they?

A MESSAGE TO READERS

by Michael C. Haymes

AUTHORS ACROSS GENRES WORK hard to create the stories our readers enjoy. We have made you laugh, and we have made you cry. We have taken you to distant times and places, introduced you to fantastic worlds filled with wonders, and horrified you with terrors of the dark and lurking in the deep. We have guided you through mysteries that confound even the greatest detectives, dared you to dream of forbidden romance, and warned you to prepare for the coming apocalypse—including a pandemic.

We created and killed the ancient gods, crafted grand adventures for epic heroes, and entertained you with legendary villains who surely deserved their fate. We have led you through the rise and fall of empires, from deadly wars to glorious victories, and analyzed the historic impacts of dictatorships and democracies. We challenge you to understand perspectives beyond your own point of view, remind you that the hope of recovery is possible—and that love after death is within your reach.

Authors are the light cast upon the dawn of civilization. We have shaped the world around you as much as we now sustain it. The best of us drive you to be more tomorrow than you are today, but our work is now under siege as never before because of illegal downloads and pirated copies of books. When authors are robbed of our hard-earned income by such thieves, it is not just literary agents and publishers who are also cheated of their rightful profits—it is the very future of our civilization that pays the ultimate price.

Support your favorite authors.
Support independent bookstores.
Buy legal. Buy local.

REMEMBER WHO YOU WANT TO BE

REMEMBER WHO YOU WANT TO BE

a novel by

MICHAEL C. HAYMES

BRANCH HILL PRESS
PORTLAND ME USA

Portions of this work, in somewhat different form, have appeared in *Carvings in Stone, Downcity,* and *Widdershins.*

This is a work of fiction. Names, characters, places, and incidents are either products of the author's imagination or are used fictitiously. Any resemblance to actual events or locales or persons, living or dead, is purely coincidental.

Grateful acknowledgement is made for use of the following excerpts:

"Remarks by the President During Ceremony for the Signing of the Americans with Disabilities Act of 1990" by George H. W. Bush.

"2004 Democratic National Convention Keynote Address" by Barack Obama.

Branch Hill Press, LLC
91 Auburn ST 228
Portland, ME 04103

Hardcover ISBN: 978-0-578-90743-7
Hardcover LCCN: 2022913597

Paperback ISBN: 978-0-578-90744-4
Paperback LCCN: 2022913646

Ebook ISBN: 979-8-218-04206-6
Ebook LCCN: 2022913761

in Loving Memory of

Britany F.

1978 ~ 2006

“We know what we are, but know not what we may be.”

—Wm. Shakespeare

TABLE OF CONTENTS

INTRODUCTION

"I didn't give a shit. It's important in life if you don't give a shit. It can help you a lot. So, I didn't give a shit." —George Carlin

IT TOOK TWENTY-FIVE YEARS for me to write this story. That being said, it is impossible to acknowledge everyone who supported this project along the way. I did have a list once, but I lost it when my computer was stolen in 2010. It was hard enough to reconstruct the revisions, never mind trying to remember all those names. I ended up rewriting more than half the book. Besides, most of the people I want to thank are dead now.

After I wrote the dedication, it was ten years before I picked up a pen again. In the most miserable stretch of this literary marathon, I lost six people in three years. Half of them were suicides. The rest included two of my uncles and my grandmother, who, for reasons I will never understand, died on my thirty-fourth birthday. Eight years later, when I was almost ready to exhale, my father died the day before my forty-second birthday. At last count, my family has seven birthdays in March, including my beagle Autumn, with mine falling on the ides. After all that we've lost, it's less a time of celebration and more a moment of remembrance and reflection.

Looking back, I realize that this story would not have been possible without my grandmother. We became pen pals after my parents separated. I was just a seven-year-old kid who was often told that I "should be seen, not heard"—but Granny listened. That was her gift. Over the years, there were so many times she would share her wit and wisdom in ways that got me to see the answers I sought, as if they had been in front of me the whole time.

It was through those letters that I first learned to make sense of things that didn't make sense. Granny challenged me to see the world beyond my pain. She taught me that our lives consist of layers, that there is always more to our stories than we ourselves can see in the midst of our anguish, and that we can assuage our grief if we are but willing to take our eyes off ourselves long enough to find the words. While those letters have been lost to time, the experience instilled in me the power of language at a young age. That's when I first knew I wanted to be a writer. The results are now in your hands.

When I was a senior in high school, my father bought me an electric typewriter for Christmas. I was making progress at Natchaug, a mental health hospital where I'd end up spending twelve weeks recovering from my first suicide attempt. Since I was no longer at risk, time at home was my reward. I had been anxious about reentry, especially going back to school, but soon realized it didn't matter; you really can't go through something like that, not at that age, and then waste your life worrying about what other people think. I sure as hell couldn't. But I realize now that Dad was an optimist: that typewriter was more than a present; it was a promise. It was my father's way of telling me that I had more to do. He believed in me even when I didn't. I never would have finished this story if it hadn't been for him.

As much as Granny and Dad nourished and supported my talent for writing, my mother encouraged my passion for reading. When I was a kid, Mom used to take me to the Paperback Trader bookstore in Groton, Connecticut. She always had four or five of those big brown paper bags stuffed with books to trade, only to fill them all right back up again with more books. If I helped her carry them, and I was on my best behavior while she browsed, she'd buy me a comic book. To this day, Mom loves to tell the story about my two Superman comics. She had asked me, "Why do you want two copies of the same comic book?"

"One for upstairs, one for downstairs," I'd told her. That way, no matter where I went, Superman would always be with me. He was as real to me as the rising sun on a cold winter night. And still is. My mother got such a kick out of my answer that she did buy me those two comics. Truly, Mom had passed her love of reading on to me—and so much more.

Like my great-uncle and my grandfather, my mother, my older brother, and I are all late-deafened adults. In his senior years, as is common with age, my father became hard-of-hearing. We grew up in small towns that had no resources, and even less educational competence, for the deaf and hard-of-hearing. The technology that empowers access for so many people with disabilities today was the stuff of science fiction back then. Like the video calls we saw on *Star Trek*, speech-to-text conversion, instant messaging, hearing-aid compatible public payphones, telecommunication relay services, and amplified telephones were all centuries away to us. We never even knew about teletypewriters or caption decoder boxes until after the Americans with Disabilities Act was passed, even though such technology had been around for years. So, Mom would read from the time she got home from work until she fell asleep.

For us, there was an equality to books that we seldom encountered outside the written page (and have yet to see with ubiquitous clarity online). When I was in my twenties and my own deafness began to emerge, I realized that writing could bridge the gap between the hearing and the deaf—without, I hope, compromising Deaf culture. Literacy is the only requisite. Books themselves are never rude or inconsiderate; they don't interrupt or talk over each other. Paper has no frequency or pitch, the words don't mumble, and grateful authors never judge their readers—even though readers judge authors.

If a hearing person writes a bad book, as so many of them have done, only the most brutally honest critic will say, "Well, that wasn't so good." For deaf writers, the expectations are always higher because we know the odds are against us. Our challenges are not limited to merely breaking into the publishing industry. Hearing people still equate speech with language and intelligence, a myth as old as civilization itself, but that's always been a tale told by idiots.

If a deaf person writes a bad book, as so few of us have done, the hearing world will once again assume that we can't write. I have heard that crap all my life. So, I just stopped listening. I didn't give a shit. I *knew* I could write, but I never wanted to publish a good book. Greatness, to me, is a waste of time. And since I knew my best would never be enough, I was determined to do better.

A breakthrough in my writing process came in my second year of college. I signed up for a course on Shakespeare taught by Professor Charles Russell. Although I'd hated the legendary Bard in high school, and originally took the class just to fill out my schedule, Professor Russell was a great teacher who soon became my friend and mentor. That summer, I read Wally Lamb's *She's Come Undone* and decided I wanted to be a novelist. Before that, I only wrote short stories. Interestingly enough, Lamb would have been my high school English teacher had my mother not sold the house after the divorce, but it was Professor Russell who gave me the best advice about writing: "Get yourself into a critical audience."

Unfortunately, if great minds think alike, every idiot who knows a moron is a genius. It's easy to be a sage when you're surrounded by fools. Most people spend their lives gazing upon Olympus, dreaming of what might have been had they but the courage to climb. Some claim an ordained right to the mountain, infatuated as they are with power and prestige. I was always the one who wanted to reach the summit, to see the world from that legendary peak—to be the best writer I could be.

The elements I faced in my quest were merciless, much like *The Old Man and the Sea* by Earnest Hemingway: you seek the prize and hook it and try to reel it in but soon discover that your ambition has surpassed your talent so the experience you gain along the way as you kill it and lash it down and gut it and fight off all the predators, who only want a meal they didn't earn, ends up tempering your craft with a steel resolve until the glory of the great prize is but a distant memory and you're left with nothing but a tattered carcass. The journey was worth the destination only because it is over now, but the destination will never be worth the journey. It has taken too much, and I have traveled too far.

These characters have been with me now for half my life. I tried quite a few writing groups over the years but soon got so frustrated with all the compliments that I became my own worst critic. As a deaf novelist, I *had* to be harder on myself than any editor or critic could dare dream. For most of my life, I've seen hearing writers dictate deaf narratives time and time again, constantly confining our characters to their own misconceptions. But I never fit into a box, and I'm not about to start now.

Of the thousands of books that I had to read throughout my mainstream education, not one was written by a deaf author. I would like to think this story will change that, though I have no illusions. At best, I am cautiously optimistic. At worst, I remain wary that the hearing world will once again hijack our narrative. Nevertheless, people with disabilities—or, perhaps to put it more accurately, *people who have become disabled*—have a unique perspective on both the center and the margin. Having been born in the center, we've been shoved to the margin. I know how hearing people think because I was a hearing person. As my deafness evolved, I learned to put hearing ways behind me.

When I was a young man, I dreamed of winning awards and accolades as much as the next novelist. After twenty-five years in the margin, I am content to add this contribution for those who have been ignored for so long. Even the major publishing houses primarily constitute a hearing industry and, as such, remain largely uneducated about Deaf history and hard-of-hearing culture. Deaf writers have to be at our best just to get a foot in the door. But the more the hearing world told me that I couldn't do it, the more I wanted to kick that fucking door down.

And I have.

Applause is the noise that drowns out the message. The lessons get lost in the show. The charade swallows the gift. I'm not here for that. Love it or hate it, praise or criticize it, be as passionate as you must or as apathetic as you will -- that's all the same to me. But, above all, learn. For if my readers learn something, something good and true, honest and human, or just enough to keep going, then I will have accomplished everything.

-Michael C. Haymes
Portland ME USA
15 March MMXX

PART ONE

THE BEGINNING OF THE END

CHAPTER ONE

THE MAN WITH THE GREEN FACE

MY PARENTS AND I were waiting in line at the Stardust Drive-In when a mysterious stranger covered in a brown cloak stepped out of his car, walked to the front of the line, and insisted on seeing the film for free. When the girls selling tickets called in the troops, the stranger stepped back and took off his hood, revealing his snow-white hair and beard. Magically, like a wizard, he pulled a blue staff out of his long sleeve just as a man in black came around the corner with a few young guys who were all wearing white T-shirts and bell-bottomed blue jeans.

Once they had him surrounded, the stranger swung his staff like a sword and hit the man in black, who screamed out in pain. He swung a few more times, keeping the others at a distance, until the man in black grabbed a red steel rod by the ticket booth, twirled it around like lightning, and faced off against the mysterious stranger. They fought like pirates until the blue staff suddenly went flying into the darkness and disappeared. As they carried him away, that crazy old man shouted, "Don't give in to the dark side! Use the force! For the love of god, use the force!"

"This *Star Wars* must be one hell of a movie," a man in the car next to us said as the fiasco faded into the night. I got up on the seat of my father's Ford Fairlane and looked out the back window. There were cars as far as I could see. The Stardust Drive-In, the last one in southeastern Connecticut, had canceled all other shows just to meet the demand for the film. My mother thought we should see what all the fuss was about and talked my father into going on the only day off he'd had in months. One of the hippies sitting on top of a yellow Volkswagen bus took a swig, held up his brown-bag can, and shouted, "Hey man, down with that Vader dude, man!"

There was a gathering of hoots and cheers before the horns started. My mother lit a cigarette for my father. He grabbed it with his right hand, and I saw the word NAVY tattooed across his knuckles; it was the first word I had ever learned to read. After we finally got our tickets, my mother took me to the concession stand while Dad parked the car. Mom made me hold her hand so I wouldn't get lost. I could smell the buttery popcorn through the freshly mown summer grass. As we took a shortcut around back, I saw the man in black counting out cash to the mysterious stranger.

"Quite a show, boys," my mother said. The man in black jumped in surprise. He begged us not to say anything, and he gave us all the free popcorn and soda and licorice we could carry to keep quiet. When Dad met us at the concession stand and wondered why we got so many snacks, Mom told him what we had just seen as she handed him the tray of drinks. He put the bags of candy into his pockets. I asked my mother why the man got paid to fight. Taking the tubs of popcorn, Mom told me, "Things aren't always what they seem, Roger."

"What does that mean?"

"Hopefully," my father said, "you never will find out."

My parents held my hands as I walked between them. "Why?"

"Sometimes," my mother said, "the best kept secrets are best kept secret."

I had no idea what they were talking about, of course, and it would be years before I'd learn that every family has their secrets, that even a promise made in good faith can be disastrous when the truth comes to light decades later. But, that night, I was just a kid at the movies with my parents. We walked through the crowd of cars back to the Fairlane. People started honking again once the show started. Dad set up the speaker, wishing to god the bums in this town would shut up. South Brockton, he said, sure wasn't Poquanicut.

My parents had moved to Poquanicut from Elliott, Pennsylvania, in 1969. They bought a sky-blue house in the middle of a field of mud, which my father transformed into a yard of grass as smooth as a golf course. I was born a few months later, in January 1970. After his tour in Vietnam, my father got a job managing a gas station on the edge of town. When Dad left for work in the morning, he was clean-cut and smelled of Old Spice, but at night he always had a five o'clock shadow and reeked of gasoline. Dad would wash his hands, but the black grease lined his fingernails all week—until Mom made him do the dishes before they went out on Saturday nights. My father was supposed to have weekends off, but if something came up at the station he'd go back to work. Dad even worked late during the week to close up after the second shift got out at the United States Submarine Building Company, which we always called "the Boat," as if that were its proper name (also because, my father insisted, a submarine is *not* a ship).

The Cold War meant work, my father always used to say, and the Boat employed tens of thousands of New Englanders, sustaining even us. The busiest hours at the station were when the shifts changed; the commuters had to have their cigarettes and coffee and gas. When my mother and I stopped in to see my father, she always made sure there was a fresh pot brewing for the customers. She had filled a Thermos with that same coffee on our way to the Stardust Drive-In that magical summer night in 1977. I was seven years old and the screen was huge. I had never seen anything like those red and green lasers on television or at the drive-in before. How could beams of light hurt a person? Were those robots or people boarding that ship? What was that *thing* in black and why did it have a glowing sword? I watched in awe and fascination as a small band of rebels defeated an evil empire.

Despite my excitement, I fell asleep, in waves, on the way home. My stomach ached from all that popcorn and soda and licorice. As I was dozing off, I saw Mom lean over and set her head on Dad's shoulder. Soon, through the sound of thunder, I heard them arguing about turtles: Dad said that he just had shell shock, but Mom told him that he wasn't "the man with the green face" anymore and that the war was over. After that, I must have fallen back asleep.

I felt my father pick me up to carry me inside the house but woke up wrapped in my bedspread. I wondered where I was and how I got there until I saw the streetlight rain falling in shadows against my bedroom wall. The shouts and screams of my parents woke me up often in the middle of the night, especially after my father had too much drink. He started drinking a lot after his parents had passed away last year. We used to visit them at Christmas. They had a house in Philadelphia that was always so warm and cozy on those brutally cold winter days. Granny, who was bald, would make me hot French toast with bananas while Papa cooked the bacon; I can smell it. Mom told me that Granny had been sick for a long time with cancer. When she died, my grandfather lasted less than a day without her. During their funeral, I glanced up at my father, who had a blank look on his face, as if he could stare for a thousand yards. When I looked over at my mother, she had her head bowed and her eyes closed. I could recognize her voice through the crowd; I saw her lips moving as I curled myself up into a ball, reaching for something that I couldn't grab with prayers that I thought could.

> Hail Mary, full of grace, the Lord is with thee.
> Blessed art thou among women, and blessed is the fruit—

The storm outside cracked with thunder that I was sure had split the sky. The sheer force of the sound scared me half to death, silencing my prayers for the rest of the summer. My parents often shouted themselves to sleep, but I usually woke to the calm, quiet ones I knew—until my mother started working.

Mom got a job waiting tables at the Pizza Galley, which was in the center of Poquanicut. Lucy and Mac had leased the building to three businesses, including, besides the restaurant, a package store and a small market. Our neighbor, Grandpa Ryan (my mother's father), watched me the afternoons I got home from school and my parents were working. That summer, he took me to see a matinee of *Superman* at the new cinema in Rose City. The destruction of Krypton was devastating to my eight-year-old eyes. I had never seen so many people die like that before, and I was amazed that one boy could lose so much and still be so kind when he grew up. I was filled with joy, and even saw the smile on Grandpa's face when Superman saved the day, catching Lois and then the helicopter.

Most days, we would just stay home and make root beer floats. Grandpa would scoop the ice cream, toss it up in the air, and try to catch it with the mug. He always missed, but, like Charlie Brown trying to kick that football, he never stopped trying. It always made me laugh. Afterwards, we would play cards, usually versions of solitaire or games we could play together like match, blackjack, or go fish. My favorite was old maid. When we got down to the last few cards, Grandpa would always hold one card higher than the rest of his hand. He'd shake his head or raise his eyebrows when I touched a card that he didn't want me to take. One afternoon, when I had the old maid, I held my other card higher. When Grandpa reached, I smiled like a sly fox.

"Go ahead. That's your card," I told him through my giggles. Grandpa grabbed the old maid and I laughed. I snatched the last card from Grandpa's hand and showed him my pair. "I beat you!"

"You tricked me," Grandpa said in a sharp drawl. The hairs around his shiny, bald head were short like stubble. His goatee and mustache were gray. "I wanted the deuce. I thought I had the deuce."

I showed him my pair. "I got the deuce!"

Grandpa shook his head, smiling in silence as he playfully showed his disbelief. He had completely lost his hearing years ago, Mom had said, because of mastoid problems. Most of the time, my mother wrote things down for him while he responded in speech. Other times, it seemed, Grandpa could see what we meant. I was still laughing about the card game when my mother came home carrying two brown bags. Mom and May, a friend she worked with at the Pizza Galley, went grocery shopping together every other Friday. Walking to the kitchen, Mom nodded to Grandpa. He got up and headed outside.

"Roger, go help Grandpa bring in some bags," Mom said. Grocery shopping was a delight as long as I didn't have to go with my mother. The long walks up and down the aisles invited trouble, and if I got in trouble then my mother would take it out of my snacks. When she went by herself, I could just spy on the snacks I could sneak later—if I could sneak them later. Apparently, my mother caught on because the only snack she bought required electricity. This called for an extra special effort on my part.

"We got popcorn, Mom! Popcorn!"

"I know," she said. "Now you be careful with that bag. Don't drop it."

"Can we pop some?"

"Wait until your father gets home."

I knew what that meant.

I made my mother watch me shuffle cards after the groceries were put away. The deck came together in clumps and spilled all over the coffee table when I tried the bridge. Grandpa and Mom helped me pick them up. We played double solitaire, with Grandpa giving me hints, either by pointing or making funny faces, until Mom decided to start dinner. I was in the kitchen making card pyramids with Grandpa when Dad called to let us know he had to close the station again that night. The meatballs were simmering and the water for the spaghetti was boiling. I toppled my pyramid.

"Don't worry about it," my mother told him. "We'll save you some. I'll keep it warm for you. Love you too. Bye."

Mom hung up the phone, her cigarette smoke hovering in the air. She shut off the burners and leaned back against the counter. Grandpa started picking up the cards.

"Can we still pop some popcorn?" I asked.

"After we get back from bringing your father his surprise supper."

"We're gonna bring Dad a surprise?"

"As long as my dad lets me use his truck," Mom said, writing on his pad. Grandpa read her words and nodded. Mom told me to go wash up while she got things ready. I saw Grandpa smile behind his goatee as I hopped out of my chair.

My mother set the Crock-Pot full of meatballs on the passenger side of the truck beneath my feet. My job, she said, was to hold the rolls on the way down to the station and watch the pot around curves. By the time we got to Lucy's, water had built up under the lid, but the pot itself had never moved. I waited for my mother while she was inside the market. There was a poster of a woman in the window of the package store. She was holding two mugs of beer; her long blond hair and pretty blue eyes reminded me of my mother.

The red and white sign for MAC'S GAS could be seen from quite a ways away at night because it was the only light before Brockton, which was miles across the Poquanicut reservation. The parking lot of the gas station was dotted with oil, which had collected so much over the years that the pavement was cracked and worn. I could see my father sitting behind the counter inside the store. My mother parked at the far end. I got out of the car, walked inside, and set the rolls down on my father's paperwork. The Red Sox game was playing on the radio. Dad looked up and smiled.

"Hi, Dad," I said. "Mom and I brought you dinner."

"Hey, Roger. You brought me rolls for dinner?"

"Yup."

"Rolls," he said, opening the bag.

"Yeah. You know, Dad. Rolls."

He got a roll out of the bag and brought it to his open mouth.

"Dad, there're meatballs too!" I said just before he took a bite.

"Oh. Well, you didn't say anything about meatballs. Where are they?"

"Mom's got 'em."

Dad walked around the counter and met my mother at the door, who handed him the Crock-Pot. They kissed. After my father set it down and plugged it in, my mother sliced a roll and stuffed it with meatballs. Dad took half the grinder in his mouth in one bite. My mother and I split one while my father ate another. It was a cool, quiet night. I could hear crickets between passing cars. There were only a few customers while my mother and I were there, mostly people my parents knew from Poquanicut. Mr. Ridge, who owned a huge tree farm, asked my father about the oak he had planted a few summers ago (the one my father had warned me not to climb, but I climbed it anyway when nobody was looking). When Mrs. Johnson stopped in, my mother asked about Wednesday's bingo game. Mom went a lot less since she had started working but promised to try to make it next week. Mr. Gates came by just before we left. He asked if I wanted to sign up for Little League baseball next year. I was thrilled when my parents agreed to let me play.

My father loved the Boston Red Sox as much as he hated the New York Yankees. If Dad wasn't watching the games at home, he was listening to them on the radio at the station. A few years ago, he had even let me stay up past my bedtime when the Red Sox had made it to the World Series. I usually fell sleep because it got to be so late, but I woke up at the end of Game 6 and saw my father jumping and waving his arms like a maniac. When I looked at the television, I saw Carlton Fisk doing the same thing. Amazingly, the ball had stayed fair, and the Red Sox would live to die another day. Fisk had kept our hope alive, but Boston would lose it all the very next night. Sharing those moments with my father had made me a Red Sox fan too—and there was no going back. Baseball, for me, was a baptism of hope and despair, but through it all I was just a kid who loved the Red Sox because I loved my father. And I was delighted when Dad promised to practice with me before Little League started.

My mother and I left the station just after the second shift got out at the Boat. When the road was clear, the trip only took about ten minutes, depending on which one of my parents was driving. My mother drove a lot slower than my father. With so much traffic on Route 12, it could take anywhere from thirty to forty-five minutes to get home. Sometimes, the construction being done upstate meant delays, detours, and a really long ride. It was after my mother remembered the bridge work in Rose City that she cursed her timing.

The part of Route 12 that ran through Poquanicut felt like a roller coaster. The town had patched it together, but in winter the melting snow would seep into the cracks, freeze again, and split the road. Once the plows had cleared away the snow, potholes were everywhere. The years brought patchwork upon patchwork. It took forever to get home. Mom said that we could make the popcorn some other time because she was too tired. It was late and I had to get to bed.

But I couldn't sleep that night. The only thing I could think about was playing baseball in the spring. My pitching would break all the records in Little League, and I would lead the Boston Red Sox to their first World Series victory since Babe Ruth in 1918. People would stand up and cheer and scream my name and I would be famous. The only thing I had to do was wait for spring. In the meantime, my dreams made me hungry.

I got out of bed and quietly walked to the kitchen. The house was silent except for the downstairs television playing the national anthem. I turned on the kitchen light and saw broken glass on the floor. There were a few spots of tomato sauce on the counter. Opening the bread box, I got the bag of rolls and sat down at the table. Like my father, I took as big a bite as I could from the roll. I was chewing when a strange voice suddenly called my name. When I looked up, I saw Dad standing next to the refrigerator. He was holding a bottle of beer and blood was dripping from his wrist, falling onto the cream tile floor. I wanted to say something but was too scared. When he slapped me, I fell from the chair to the floor. My father, a giant, stood above me shouting until my mother flew into the kitchen. Mom set her hands on his shoulders, but Dad twisted away like a snake and almost stepped on me. He threw the rack of dishes across the counter and it hit the floor in front of me with a bang, shattering plates and bowls into tiny pieces all over the place. My stomach was on fire.

"That's it!" my mother, in tears, screamed. Dad pulled down his long sleeve. "You get yourself some help before you bring the whole goddamned house down! You almost hit Roger!"

"I did not!" my father growled. Crossing his arms, he took a seat at the table. I had crawled into a corner and was watching his chest rise and fall as he was breathing.

"The war is over," my mother said. "It's over! I can't live like this! We can't live like this! This isn't the way it's supposed to be!"

"Who the hell said your life is supposed to be anything?"

"We made a promise," my mother pleaded. "I know you're hurting, but I can't help if you keep pushing me away..." She held out her shaking hands and slowly walked toward him, but Dad just slumped in the chair. When he closed his eyes, it was as if he went elsewhere. Mom gently touched his cheek and suddenly my father's arm moved in a blur just before my mother fell to the ground in front of me.

"Go to bed, Roger!" my mother screamed, blood pouring from her nose. "Now!"

"Damn it to hell!" my father's voice echoed in the hall as I ran for my bedroom. I was scared to death. "You still don't get it, do you? Every night I close my eyes, I see it! I can still see it! I can't not see it! It's like a goddamned demon haunting my mind and I just can't not fucking see it!"

When I got to my bedroom, I quickly closed the door and hid under the covers. The shouting went on, as it always did, until the whole house was suddenly silent again. I couldn't possibly sleep so I listened for their voices, but soon all I heard was my father wailing like a wild, wounded animal. After a while, he settled down. I quietly crawled out of bed and met him in the hallway as he was coming out of the kitchen. His face was bright red.

"I thought I told you to go to bed," Dad said, wiping his eyes. There was a bandage around his wrist.

"I keep hearing loud noises."

"Your mother fell down a little while ago."

"Is she okay?"

"She's fine. She's sleeping. Everything's fine. Now, get to bed."

I walked back to my bedroom and fell asleep listening to the silence.

The house was often quiet after that night because my parents spent so much time working. Dad never did find the time to play ball or practice with me, and Mom had always left for the Pizza Galley by the time he got home so Grandpa had to bring me to my first day of baseball practice. I knew most of the kids from school. Mr. Gates stood by home plate with a clipboard in his hands, taking roll call. I waited for him to call my name.

"Roger Evans?"

"I'm right here, Mr. Gates," I said.

"Hey, Roger," he said. "You brought your grandpa too?"

"Yeah. He watches me until my dad comes home."

"Why don't you go out and play catch with some of the other kids while Mr. Wilson and I decide what positions everyone will play?"

Grandpa tapped me on the shoulder and pointed to the bleachers. I nodded to him before running out into the field next to Chris and James. We made a triangle in center field. Chris couldn't catch so James and I just played by ourselves. After a few throws, Mr. Gates came over to tell James that he was catching and that I was going to play shortstop. Once he finished announcing our positions, Mr. Gates had us run around the field as fast as we could. David, who was the smallest, started in the first position.

When Mr. Gates yelled for us to go, James and I collided with each other and fell down. I saw Grandpa get up off the bleachers and walk toward me. David had just passed first base and Billy was right behind him. I got up so fast and started running I almost tripped over my own feet. I could feel the ground pounding through my sneakers and felt the tightness in my legs as I passed the other kids. Dave tried to hit me when I passed him. Billy and I were running side by side as we rounded left field. My pace was getting awkward, but I was an arm's length ahead of him. Grandpa waved me home with a proud grin on his face.

"I don't have all day!" Mr. Gates yelled to the others, who were still jogging. James was sitting in the dugout with a blue icepack on his knee. I sat down on the bench beside him. My chest was burning.

"I never knew you could run that fast," Mr. Gates said.

"Neither did I," I said, gasping for breath. I spat on the ground. "I won."

"I didn't know we were racing," James said, laughing. "I thought it was just practice."

I was blind even to the world around me, somehow convinced that I could undo the series of events pulling my parents apart if I were just good enough. I watched the other kids do silly dances as they came to the plate.

When Grandpa brought me home, my father insisted that he join us for dinner. We ate at a restaurant just out past my father's gas station, on the Poquanicut reservation. Although the tribe ran Mrs. Pizza, they still lived without running water. Except for the fire and the jukebox, the candles on the tables were the only light. We sat by the window. After adding a log to the fire, the waitress came to take our order. Her long black hair flowed down her small back and her skin looked soft and smooth. I could see the fire reflected in her deep brown eyes. She was really pretty. My father asked for a pitcher of Michelob and three mugs. Dad always ordered one of the pizzas with strange-sounding names like "the Villager" or "the Coop." This time, Grandpa pointed out a weird pizza with eggs and hamburg, something the menu called "moussaka." Dad and Grandpa shared the pizza while my mother ordered the fettuccine alfredo. The waitress brought me a cheeseburger and french fries. The food was rich and fresh. When my father drew a slice of pizza, steam rose urgently between the clinging cheeses. His fingernails were clean. Grandpa savored the taste, biting small and chewing slow.

For the first time in a long time, my parents got along.

I was a fool to think it would last.

A few weeks later, I woke up after another long night of yelling and screaming and watched from my bedroom window as my father left for work. Grandpa was standing in the yard shouting, "…know that part of being a man means knowing how to treat a woman! That does not qualify!"

"I can't talk to you," my father said, opening the car door. "What difference does it make? I can't talk to anybody."

"Don't you ever do that again!" Grandpa shouted, pointing his finger at my father.

Dad was about to say something when he saw me in the window. He stopped a moment, and I saw his face turn red before he got in and started the car. I waved as my father backed out of the driveway, but he didn't see me that time. As the Fairlane roared away, I could have sworn Dad was just running late for work. When I got to the kitchen, my mother was sitting at the table with her head in her hands. I got a bowl from the cupboard and milk from the refrigerator. I was pouring Cheerios when Mom said that Dad left.

"I know. I saw him."

Mom looked at me for a moment. I was pouring the milk when I heard Grandpa come inside.

"No, Roger. He left. He's gone."

"I know," I said, taking a spoonful of cereal. "He went to work."

"He's not coming back," Grandpa said, coming into the kitchen.

I stopped chewing when a wave of panic swept over me; my heart skipped a beat. I dropped the spoon into the bowl and ran. For the first time in my life, I jumped the last three steps before flying out the screen door. The cool morning dew surprised my bare feet as I ran around the house, down the hill, and into the woods. The leaves crinkled and crunched when I tripped. I crawled under a nearby pine and started crying. Sunbeams echoed through the tall trees.

In the distance, I heard my mother call my name.

CHAPTER TWO

DACHAU, 1945

IT WAS GRANDPA WHO found me sleeping in the forest and carried me back to his house. The living room had a light-brown carpet with plastic walkways and the walls were covered with old photographs. It was filled with the scent of Grandpa's pipe, and the quiet made me comfortable. Laying on the couch, I wished I could be like Grandpa so I wouldn't have to hear my parents fighting all the time. Rolling over, I buried my face in the cushions and tried my hardest not to cry again but couldn't help it.

I thought I was alone until I felt Grandpa's hand on my shoulder. He squeezed tightly until I sat up and wiped my eyes. Once Grandpa had settled into his favorite chair, he told me something that I would never forget: "When a boy becomes a man, he must choose between the life he was given and who he wants to be. Remember who you want to be."

But, as a child, the life I had been given was the one I wanted—and it was the only one I'd ever known. Now, it was gone. There would be no more nights at the drive-in, no more family dinners, no more meatball grinders. After wiping my eyes again, I spent what felt like hours staring at an old black-and-white photograph of a soldier holding a young girl with short dark hair. She was wearing a raggedy outfit and had sunken cheeks with bony arms. The soldier had a short beard, and his gun was strapped over his left shoulder while he held the girl on his right. They were standing beside a crowd dressed like the girl, many of them sitting and eating. In the distance, a few soldiers had their weapons pointed at men in different uniforms, all of whom had their hands on top of their heads. When I looked more closely, I realized that the soldier holding the girl was my grandfather. Turning around, I saw him lighting his pipe as I pointed to the photograph.

"Nazi Germany," Grandpa answered, snuffing out the match. "Dachau, 1945."

I pointed to the young girl.

"That's your aunt, Carol," Grandpa said. He told me that he had found Aunt Carol during the last days of the war. She had spent her childhood hiding from the Nazis until they found her and sent her to that atrocious concentration camp. Living in fear, starving, and facing exhaustion and frostbite was all Carol had known until the day Grandpa's unit had liberated the survivors. He stayed with Carol as much as his orders would allow. When it had come time for him to ship out, Grandpa scratched his name and address down so that she could write to him.

By the time Grandpa got back to America, he thought that he would never see her again, but Carol had learned English while working with British and American volunteers at an orphanage for children displaced by the war. Grandpa would read her letters to the family after dinner, and they would all write back and put together care packages for her. Eventually, Carol came to America to live with her great-grandparents in New York. They were her last living relatives. When my parents got married in 1956, Carol had come to the wedding. It was there that she met my uncle, William, whom she would marry a few years later (though he died before I was born). "She was the one good thing I ever got out of that god-awful war."

I made pistols with my thumbs and forefingers, like a cowboy.

"No," Grandpa said sternly, shaking his head. "I've seen what those damned things can do. Had enough of that for one lifetime. Turned it in when my time was up. Haven't touched a gun since."

I pointed to the girl in the photograph and then down at the ground.

"She lives in Pennsylvania now," Grandpa told me. "Look, Roger, there are a lot of things we want to teach you, a lot of things you need to learn, but you're too young for that right now. Let me just say that the world can be a very bad place. And that's why it's so important to be kind to people, especially people who have been through such terrible things. My god, by the time your Aunt Carol was your age, she had already witnessed so many absolutely horrible things…"

As his voice trailed off, his eyes seemed distant. Looking at the photograph again, I wondered when I would be old enough to learn more about Aunt Carol. I knew, even then, that Grandpa was only trying to protect me, but I never could have guessed what he was protecting me from—or why.

"Well, that's enough for today," he said. "Want a soda?"

I nodded. He brought me a Coke with a glass full of ice. I drank it down in one shot and belched so hard I felt the fizz up my nose. Grandpa let out a great big belly laugh, and I laughed so hard at his laugh that I almost peed my pants.

"That one sure went down," Grandpa said, catching his breath. "How about we go to Green Field?"

I spent much of that summer playing ball with Grandpa. After my father left, my mother had to work six days a week at the Pizza Galley; they were closed on Sundays, like everything else. Mom had even stopped going to church, but Grandpa still took me every week. St. Andrew's, a small Catholic church made of stone and stained glass, had been built in 1672. It was there that I learned the story of Moses, whose mother had to hide him when he was a baby, but he grew up and became a great leader who freed his people from slavery. Grandpa would always take communion and get a copy of the sermon afterwards from Father Sullivan, who would type it up for him the night before.

Grandpa usually made supper for us, but once in a while Mom brought home something from the restaurant. The pizzas and platters were better than his pork chops, and I devoured those meals after spending all day down at Green Field. Grandpa had built a makeshift batter out of old plywood so that he could coach me through my pitches. Once I got my windup down throwing fastballs, he taught me everything from curves and cutters to screws and splits. After a while, he got behind the plate and made signs for the pitches he wanted me to throw. We already had some signs of our own, which came natural to us because Grandpa was deaf. My arm got strong that summer.

When James called one day, Grandpa suggested he come with us. I practiced batting while James, who had hit more home runs than anyone on our team, gave me tips because he knew I needed to work on my hitting. He also made fun of me like the other catchers had always done. It was so distracting that I didn't even swing at the first pitch, which was a fastball right over the plate.

"You'll never get this next one," James said. I swung and missed. "That was a nice hit…if you were aiming for the air."

"Shut up," I said.

Grandpa gazed intently at the signals James gave him. He threw a curve ball. I didn't swing; it was his hardest pitch to hit.

"I can't believe you didn't go for that one," James said. "It was right over the plate."

"It curved."

"You struck out looking," James said, throwing the ball back to the mound. "Grandpa, we caught him looking. That's the first out. Only two more and I'm up."

He pounded his fist into the mitt.

"Can't we just play?" I asked.

"We are playing. We're playing by the rules like Mr. Gates would want us to."

"All right," I said. "Get off my back."

I got so sick of James that I swung too hard with the next pitch and spun around with the bat, falling to the ground. I threw the bat against the fence. Grandpa picked it up and handed it to me after James helped me up.

"Knock it off," Grandpa warned. "Or we're leaving now."

"How am I supposed to hit if you won't leave me alone?" I said to James as Grandpa walked back to the mound.

"I don't mean nothing by it," James said. "All the catchers do it. You know that. If you let it bother you, you'll never get a hit. Just lean back, keep your balance, and shift your weight when you swing."

"How do you know so much about hitting?"

"My brother, Craig, taught me. If I can hit, you can hit."

I leaned on my right leg and held the bat in the air behind me. Grandpa hurled the ball and my grip tightened when I swung. The crack sent a sharp, stinging vibration up my arms. James got up and stood beside me as the ball sailed over the fence.

"You hit a homer!" James shouted as we exchanged high fives. "Radical!"

I handed him the bat. "Now it's your turn."

Grandpa handed me the ball as I walked to the mound. Once James got inside the batter's box, I watched for the signal from Grandpa. Winding up, I threw a fastball low and outside, just catching the corner of the plate. James didn't even move. "What the heck was that?"

"Fastball," I said as Grandpa tossed the ball back to me.

"You got to be kidding me!" James said. "Roger, did you hear that thing? It was like the air was on fire."

"Been throwing all summer." I watched again for the signal. Grandpa had taught me that the best pitchers mixed up the hitters, and he knew how to call them. This time, I threw a screwball that got away from me and went straight toward James's head. He hit the ground just as the ball slapped into Grandpa's mitt. He warned me to be more careful because I could hurt James.

"Don't get cocky," Grandpa said. "Just throw the ball, buddy. Just play catch. Just like I showed you."

"And don't kill me," James said, getting up. He brushed the dirt off his jeans.

After getting the ball back, I took a deep breath, closed my eyes, and cleared my head. Wiping my sweaty palm, I gripped the ball and wound up. James swung at my curveball and missed. The rest of the afternoon, I followed Grandpa's signs, striking out James again and again. The best he could manage was a few foul balls until, just before Grandpa said we had to leave, he hit a grounder into left field.

"That's it, I'm beat," James said. "Least I finally got some wood on that one. You know, Roger, you keep pitching like that you could go all the way. I ain't kidding. I hit more home runs than anybody, but I can barely get a piece of...whatever it is you're throwing."

We laughed.

When Grandpa dropped off James, I saw that his father was in the garage, drinking a beer and working on an old Mustang convertible. I only saw my father for a few hours on the weekend. We'd stop by Mac's after breakfast, but I hated waiting for him. My father bought Superman comic books for me to read, but I always finished them before he was done working. The customers kept interrupting so Dad would end up counting the same stack of twenties over and over. Nobody thought to ask Amos, the assistant manager, anything. I hated that too.

"I need gas," Grandpa said, backing out of the driveway. "We could stop by and see your dad, if you want to do that."

He turned toward me, but I only answered, "Okay."

Grandpa pulled over to the side of the road and turned off the truck.

"I need you to do something for me, Roger," Grandpa said. Opening the glove box, he took out a small pad and a pen. "Do you remember when I told you to write down what you want to say because I'm deaf? Well, when I ask you a question like that, just nod or shake your head. If I can't see you, just tap my arm. Okay?"

I nodded.

"Do you want to stop and see your dad?" Grandpa asked. I nodded again. I really appreciated Grandpa asking if I wanted to see my father, instead of us just going like Mom would have done. "Thanks, buddy. Now, if there's anything else you want, anything at all, just write it down like your mom does or use one of our signs. Okay, buddy?"

I nodded. Grandpa smiled and rubbed my head. I took the pen and pad.

—Can I get somthing to eat? I'm hungry.

"How about a fluffernutter when we get back?" Grandpa asked. I was so happy I just smiled. And Grandpa understood. He started the truck. "All right. Now, let's go and see your dad."

The station was busier than usual for a Thursday afternoon because Labor Day weekend was coming. My father, whose graying temples I noticed from a distance, was pumping gas on one side of the island while Amos worked the other. They both wore change banks on their belts, little steel columns of coins that made counting change easier. I was always amazed at how fast my father could push the release buttons and get the customer's change correct. When Grandpa's truck drove into the lot, my father nodded to us and hurried over to a Jaguar. Amos was opening the gas tank, but it looked like the driver was giving him a hard time. As the car in front of us drove away, Grandpa pulled up to the pump. I got a closer look at the driver of the Jaguar. He wore gold chains with a brown leather jacket and white polyester bell-bottoms; he looked like Vinnie Barbarino on drugs. When Grandpa rolled down his window, I heard some of the conversation.

"Don't worry about it," my father was saying. "I'll take care of it."

"I should hope so," the man said. "Your boy here couldn't figure it out."

Amos took a deep breath. It looked like he wanted to say something, but he just started pumping the gas. My father walked over to Grandpa's truck.

"Rough day?" Grandpa asked.

My father shook his head. "You just get back from Green Field again?"

"Yeah," I said. "James went with us. He couldn't hit anything, though."

"You was pitching?"

"Yep. And I hit a home run off Grandpa too."

"That's terrific, Roger," my father said. I sensed that I had finally earned his approval. "I asked Amos to open tomorrow morning so we could get together. Why don't we go down to Green Field so you can practice some more?"

"Really?" I said. I wanted to believe him.

"Sure. We could go to a movie afterwards—" Amos asked my father if he had any change. Dad released the handle on the pump but left the hose in Grandpa's tank. He held up a finger, telling Grandpa to wait a minute. Back at the Jaguar, Dad realized that neither of them had enough change. The customer had to wait while Dad went inside for the money.

"That's just great!" the man complained. "It's not like I have to be anywhere. I could just stay in this thriving fucking metropolis forever because nobody has ever seen a C-note before!"

"He told you he'd be right back," Amos said calmly.

"Just what I need," the man said. He scoffed in disgust and started pacing, facing away from me, and I couldn't hear what he was saying until he turned back around. "…with a fucking attitude!"

Amos punched him in the face and walked away. The man fell to the ground and never said another word. Dad came out of the store just as Amos's car squealed out of the lot.

I spent the next afternoon watching the Red Sox game on TV with Grandpa, waiting for my father to call. After Amos quit, my father explained that he had to open the station but added that he should be done by two o'clock. At three-thirty, I realized my father had lied to me. After my parents separated, Mom worked just as much as Dad, but at least she did what she said she would. I had wanted to go to Green Field and hit a home run and please my father so that maybe he'd come back. My stomach jumped when the phone rang. The dial tone was a disappointment; it must have been a wrong number. During a commercial, I wrote on Grandpa's pad, asking him if he had ever got married.

"Of course," Grandpa said, laughing. "I married your grandmother."

—Did you get divorsed?

Grandpa shook his head. "Your grandmother passed away, like your uncle, William. You spelled 'divorced' wrong. It's with a 'c,' not an 's.'"

—Why?

Grandpa shrugged. "Well, I don't know. That's just the way it's spelled."

His belly laugh was contagious. After giggling a moment, I took the pad and asked what happened to Uncle William. Grandpa took a deep breath. "It was his time."

I made our sign for *curveball*, which meant I didn't understand.

"Best answer that never satisfied anybody," Grandpa said. "See, when your uncle passed away, it…well, it just broke your grandmother's heart. She died a few days later, before you was ever born. It was a tough time for Carol and your mom. They're twins, you know, your mother and your uncle. Born twelve minutes apart. Your mother, she was first. Anyways, a few years later, Jake's parents passed away. Things just fell apart for them from there. That, and the war. It's nothing you did, Roger. Nothing you did at all."

—Whose Jake?

"Your father."

When Mom came home, Grandpa told her that I had asked about Uncle William. Sitting across the room, I couldn't see what my mother was writing, but after reading the note, Grandpa gave her back the pad and said, "You know that's not my decision."

"He was your twin brother," I said to Mom.

"And my best friend," she said.

"What was it you asked Grandpa?"

"That is not your concern," my mother told me. She tore the page out of the notepad and got up and walked away. Grandpa patted my shoulder, like he always did, before he went home. Mom was in the shower when my father finally called. Dad said he'd be leaving shortly, just as soon as he got cleaned up a bit. I told my mother when she came downstairs. She was in her blue bathrobe and had a pink towel wrapped around her head.

"Is he going to feed you?" Mom asked.

"I don't know. I guess."

"How about I heat up some macaroni so you can eat before he gets here?"

"Okay."

I hated leftovers, but my mother insisted that I eat something. She was still heating up the macaroni when my father showed up. I left her scraping it back into the bowl. It was too late to go to Green Field, so we went out to eat at Ponderosa.

My father rented a small apartment on the third floor of the Riverside complex. It had two bedrooms but mine wasn't furnished yet. I slept on the couch. The next morning, when I looked out the window, I could see the Poquanicut River just beyond the trees. Inside, empty pizza boxes, beer cans, and napkins were scattered all over the kitchen and living room. I searched the cupboards for a trash bag and started picking up the garbage, rinsing and packing the cans into a brown bag because I knew my father would want the nickels. When I got back from the dumpster, Dad was in the kitchen making French toast for breakfast. "Did you clean up?" he asked.

"A little."

"You didn't have to do that," he told me. He seemed to be embarrassed. "I'm just not settled in yet."

"I know," I said. He gave me a paper plate with three slices of French toast, chopped bananas, and a plastic fork. There was bottle of syrup on the table. Once Dad realized that he didn't have any orange juice, he gave me glass of water and said that we needed to go shopping. After breakfast, we spent the rest of the morning at Rose City Plaza. We stopped first at Zayre, a huge department store that had everything. Aside from my new bed, Dad bought a vacuum, a popcorn maker, a hamper, a couple board games we could play, and stuff for cooking and cleaning. We had lunch at McDonald's and then went grocery shopping at Price Rite. Everything he bought we already had at home. The whole day was just a reminder to me of what my family had lost.

When we got back to his apartment, Dad hauled the bed upstairs and started putting it together while he had me bring in the rest of the bags. By the time I was done going up and down all those stairs to the third floor, my father had finished the bed and was putting away the groceries. He told me to pick up the clothes and towels scattered in the bedroom and bathroom. I filled the new hamper. My father's razor was next to a cake of shave soap, worn to a small circle in the center of the mug. I could smell his Old Spice until I noticed the popcorn.

The popcorn popper Mom and I used at home doubled as the bowl we ate it from. Mom would pour the kernels into a pool of melted butter. After setting up a big glass bowl over the pan, she would let me turn it on. I'd watch and wait with my mother as the kernels popped. When they were done, Mom shut off the pan, flipped it, and we had a full, fresh bowl of popcorn. Last week, she let me wear the potholders and flip the pan. My father's new air popper poured the fluffy kernels into a bowl, which was overflowing onto the counter. I snatched them when Dad wasn't looking. I'd never tasted popcorn so warm and fresh.

We played Monopoly and ordered a pizza after I bought double hotels for Boardwalk and Park Place. The rest of the properties I owned had at least one house. When we left for the Pizza Galley, I realized that it was after six o'clock and Mom had already gone home. The ride in the car was so quiet I got the courage to ask my father why he had left. In the silence that followed, he became a fragile man. The dark circles under his eyes stood out against his wrinkles when he squinted. I thought he was going to cry when I realized I wanted to desperately. He parked the Fairlane.

"Well, I just…I guess I just don't love your mother anymore," Dad said, getting out.

A few minutes later, he came back with the pizza. I could smell the pepperoni through my stuffy nose.

When my father brought me home on Monday night, I found Mom sitting on the couch, slumped over a photo album on her lap. An opened bottle of wine was on the coffee table, next to an empty glass. I called her name, but she didn't answer. Slowly, I took the album off her lap. It was filled with old black-and-white photographs from the time Mom and William were kids. Every year, they got a chocolate cake for their birthday and blew out the candles together. I also saw a few photographs of Grandpa and Grandma, Uncle William and Aunt Carol, and my parents on their wedding day. They looked so happy when they'd cut the cake together. When I turned the page, I saw a photograph of Uncle William graduating college. There was a wire leading to his ear. My mother lifted her head and lit a cigarette. Her bloodshot eyes sagged through the hovering cigarette smoke. I had never seen my mother drunk before, and I barely recognized her slurred words. "You look just like him."

"Who?" I asked. "William?"

Sitting up, my mother closed the photo album and set it aside. "You start school tomorrow. I went out and bought you some new school clothes."

"Where are they?"

"Upstairs on your bed," Mom said. I turned to leave. "Aren't you going to thank me?"

Reluctantly, I gave her a hug. Her breath made me sick. "Thanks, Mom."

"Did you have a good time with your uncle?"

"Uncle?"

"Your father."

"It was all right," I said. She put out her cigarette. "We played Monopoly and made popcorn."

"He has a popcorn popper?"

"Yeah."

"Oh. But you like Mom's popcorn better, don't you?"

"Not really. Ours comes out all greasy and burned. Dad has one of those air poppers that pops the popcorn into a bowl. It's neat. Plus, all the dead kernels stay…Mom? Mom, what's wrong?"

She had passed out. When I shook her shoulders, Mom fell to her side, on top of the photo album. I thought she was dead until I saw her breathing. I considered getting Grandpa, but I knew Mom would be mad if I woke him up. Instead, I grabbed her clock, some pillows, and a pile of blankets. I set the alarm, laid the blankets over her, and made the recliner my bed.

If Mom needed me, I had to be there for her. I just had to.

The next morning, I slept through the alarm. Mom woke me up just in time to get ready for school. The alarm clock and blankets I had brought down for her were gone. That was the last time I ever saw my mother like that. From the top of the stairs, she called my name again.

"Roger!" I turned and saw James walking with two other kids, Jeff and Matt. It was recess, and I was playing dodgeball with Ed, who had just moved to

Poquanicut. The ball hit me so hard that my head bounced against the wall. I saw stars after I fell.

"Hey, Roger," Matt said, squatting down beside me. "We found something we want to show you."

"What is it?" I asked, still dizzy.

"A vine," James said. "Just behind the swing set. You can get up on the rocks and swing real high! Let's go!"

When Mrs. Simonson, our fourth-grade teacher, turned her back to talk to some of the girls, we snuck into the woods. There was a path that led to a small clearing in the forest, with one side surrounded by a slope of stone and a vine dangling from some part of the trees above. Matt grabbed the vine and climbed up the rock.

"Watch this!" he said as he swung over our heads. Matt waited until he had stopped completely before climbing down to let me try. I took a deep breath and launched. The ground passed beneath me as the wind blew in my face. I flew so far out that the leaves of the trees on the other side brushed against my arm. When I glided back, I set my foot down on the rock.

"I told you he'd do it that way," James said.

"Do what what way?" I asked.

"Swing back instead of stopping like Matt always does."

"So," Matt said. "I don't give a care. I like swinging till I stop."

"He's chicken," Ed said.

"I am not."

"You are too."

"Am not."

"Are too.

"Am not!"

"Then go again and swing all the way back here," James said.

"I don't want to," Matt said.

"Because you're chicken," I said.

"No! You swing!" Matt shoved the vine in Ed's face, and everybody watched as climbed to the very top of the rock and swung. A branch snapped and fell when Ed hit the trees on the other side. Swinging back, Ed let go of the vine and jumped onto the rock. I was about to swing again when I noticed Matt was laughing at something. Jeff pointed to the wet spot beneath Ed's belt. Ed stood there for a moment until he realized we were all looking at him.

"What?" Ed asked. He looked below his belt. "Oh, that. I can't help it."

"You can't?" I asked. "How come?"

Ed explained that when he was younger one of his testicles had gone up into his stomach and had to be removed. The operation had damaged some of the nerves, and he ended up with no feeling in his urinary track; he just went. Ed told us that he could feel number two, but not number one. Matt's face was red from laughing so hard. Jeff was grossed out and told Ed to leave before he peed all over everybody.

"He's not going to go on anyone," James said.

"You need diapers!" Jeff said through his giggles. Matt was hysterical.

"I ain't wearing no diapers!" Ed shot back. "Not now! Not ever!"

"He can't help it," I told them. "He had a problem when he was younger, and he can't help it. Why don't you guys just leave him alone?"

"Yeah!" James said. But Jeff and Matt were already laughing like they had never seen anything so funny. Ed climbed down the rock.

"I can't help it!" Ed shouted, crying as he walked out of the woods.

"Crybaby!" Matt called after him.

"At least Ed can swing," I said.

"At least Matt can stand," Jeff said as he pushed me off the rock. I heard them arguing as I tumbled to the ground. When I got up, James had Matt in a headlock and kept kicking Jeff away from him. I grabbed the vine, climbed to the very top of the rock, held as tight as I could, and swung. I knocked down Jeff and Matt just as Mrs. Simonson made her way into the clearing.

James and I had inside recess for a week for beating up Jeff and Matt. The first couple of days we couldn't pick up a pencil without asking Mrs. Simonson for permission. After a while, she let us build pyramids with the class math cards on our desks but made us move to the floor after we had got up on our chairs to place cards on top. James and I built one so high that she let us leave it up for the rest of the class to see after recess. James knocked it down just as everybody settled in their seats.

A few weeks later, Mrs. Simonson passed out notices for open house. My mother made arrangements to have the night off so she could go. She borrowed Grandpa's truck and we drove to McDonald's in Rose City for supper. I waited in the library with Tim and Dave, who were brothers, while our teachers met with our parents. Tim suggested we play TV tag.

"You're it!" Tim said as he tagged me and ran. I quickly reached for Dave, but he twisted away running. I had to try to tag one of them before they sat down and called out the name of the TV show.

"*The Muppet Show*," Dave shouted as he sat. I stayed close, waiting for him to get up again. Tim taunted me at the other end of the shelf, so I ran after him.

"*Little House on the Prairie*," Tim called out, sitting. Dave ran past me. I went back and forth between the two of them, chasing one and then the other. They watched more TV than I knew what to do with.

"*Three's Company*."

"*Six-Million Dollar Man*."

"*Hardy Boys*."

"*BJ and the Bear*."

"*Incredible Hulk*."

"*Super Friends*."

"'Just a Bill.'"

"That's not a show," I said to Dave, trying to get Tim to come closer so that I could finally tag someone.

"*Dallas*," Tim said, sitting.

"*Dallas*?" I said. "You watch *Dallas*?"

"Our mom does," they both said at the same time. I quickly turned around, tagged Tim, and ran.

"*One Day at a Time*," I said, tripping myself to safety. The fluorescent lights stared at me as I caught my breath. Tim and Dave sat down next to me.

"Did you see it last week?" Tim asked.

"We watched it with Mom and Dad," Dave said.

"I was talking to Roger, you dummy."

"Just because you and Roger are in the same grade doesn't mean—"

"Will you shut up already? God, little brothers can be such a pain."

"I missed it," I said. "What happened?"

"Schneider had to have an operation done on his ear because he was going to go deaf if he didn't."

I had seen that episode. I had watched it with Grandpa a few months ago, but we missed the rerun last week. When I had asked Grandpa about getting an operation, writing on his pad, he frowned and shook his head, telling me that he didn't want to be a damned robot. Now, as Tim and Dave talked about the show, I realized how much I missed my father; we would have watched that show together. My memories faded as a frightening thought hit me: if my parents couldn't stay together, what else would I lose?

My mother was pleased with my performance in school, except for the vine incident. The last anyone knew Ed had transferred to Russell Elementary

School in Brockton Heights. When a sheet of paper fell from the folder my mother was carrying, I picked it up for her. Mrs. Simonson told Mom that I was becoming a perfect gentleman. I was smiling when we left the school that night.

Outside, autumn leaves crinkled as they danced in the evening wind. It was the first sign that the holidays were coming.

CHAPTER THREE

A SUNRISE AT MIDNIGHT

THE BRISK WINTER WIND stung my face as Grandpa and I browsed the pines for the perfect tree. The untouched snow crunched beneath our feet after we left the main trail, trampled as it was with the tracks of Christmas-tree shoppers. I made fists inside my mittens and envied Grandpa's gray-and-red pinstripe gloves that gripped the orange handle of his saw.

Despite the cold, I enjoyed the long walk through the Ridge farm. Every year, Grandpa and I went farther into the forest to get our tree. My mother wanted a small pine. I held the tree while Grandpa sawed at the trunk. The weight shifted when he finished, and the needles pricked my arms. Grandpa carried the tree back to the parking lot, where Mr. Ridge tied down the branches and told us to pay his wife. Mrs. Ridge, who was also my fifth-grade teacher, charged us five dollars: a buck a foot. I paid for the tree with the ten my mother had given me.

After Grandpa and I got home and set up the tree, we strung cranberries on some of my father's old fishing line. His pole was still in the garage with a bunch of tools he had left behind. Most of them were scattered across the bench, cold and coated with dust. I shifted through them until I found the fishing line. By the time May dropped off Mom, Grandpa and I had yards of cranberries for the tree. I gave Mom her change, and she said that the tree looked wonderful. Grandpa put on the lights while Mom brought out boxes of decorations. The gold tinsel glimmered in the light from the fire. We had a Styrofoam Frosty the Snowman that I had made in first grade and Grandpa's wood carving of Santa Claus. I could see my reflection in the ornaments as I set them on the tree. At the bottom of the box, I found an embroidery that read "Jake & Mary First Christmas 1956." I set it up in the center of the tree while Grandpa and Mom watched. Every year I expected my mother to say something about it. She never did.

Mom got her camera and took a picture of Grandpa lifting me up so that I could put the star on top. He grunted when he set me down and said that I was getting heavy. When the lights came on, the rainbow array glowed around us as the front window reflected the entire tree. My mother wrapped a red blanket around the stand and then passed out mugs filled with eggnog. Grandpa left after he finished his drink. My father had called that night to make arrangements to pick me up on Christmas Eve. Dad wanted me to be ready at six-thirty because there was someone that he wanted me to meet on Christmas morning. My mother agreed but said that I had to be back by nine o'clock. Like last year, I was supposed to spend Christmas Eve with my father and Christmas Day with my mother.

It always seemed simple enough.

My father got a plastic tree about eighteen inches tall that came with its own set of lights and a crooked star. "I guess the box was too small," Dad said, trying to straighten the star. He bent and shook that tree like a man possessed. After setting it up on top of the television, Dad got a green towel from the bathroom and placed it under the tree. When the corner of the towel fell in front of the screen, my father tried to yank it away, but the tree came with it. He unwrapped the towel, tossed it into the bathroom, and set up the tree again. It fell before he sat back down.

"Oh, for crying out loud!"

"I'll get it, Dad," I said. I set up the tree, but it leaned to the left. When I held out my hand, it stayed slanted at that strange angle. That was the first time I had the patience to do something my father couldn't. He opened another beer while I started watching television. "Can I stay up and watch the specials, Dad?"

"I don't care," he said, settling into the couch. A dozen beer bottles had collected on the coffee table before Dad brought out my Christmas presents. He set them on the floor. "Santa had to leave them in the closet this year. He was in a hurry. You can open—"

I was about to tell him that I was too old to believe in Santa Claus when he misjudged where the couch was and fell to the floor trying to sit down. I thought it was funny until he started kicking and screaming. He flung one of my presents against the wall and threw a beer bottle across the room. Some of the beer got in my eye, and I started crying because it really stung. He told me to open my fucking presents.

"It's not Christmas yet."

"I don't give a shit! I bought the damn things, now open them!"

I picked up a present and opened it with tears falling from my eyes. It was a pair of gloves, the kind I had told him I wanted. Only now, I didn't want them. I didn't even want to be there, but I opened those gifts one at a time just like my father told me to do. When Dad finally went to bed, I picked up the wrapping paper and beer bottles and went back to my spot on the floor. I prayed he'd get hit by a truck and die as I cried myself to sleep.

The next morning, I felt my father shake my leg several times, but I was still too scared to get up. When Dad yanked off the blankets, I knew I couldn't pretend anymore. I sat up and saw the sun rising behind him. He was a giant. "Why didn't you wait for me before you opened your presents?"

I rubbed my eyes. "You told me to open them last night."

"I what? I did not tell you to open them last night."

"Yes, you did. You sat right there on the couch and watched—"

"I did not. Do you know what my father would've done if I opened my Christmas presents early?" He waited for me to answer, but I didn't know what to say. "My father would have skinned me alive if I didn't wait. Is that what you want me to do to you?"

"No," I answered quietly.

"Start picking up," he said. "You're lucky I don't send those presents back to the North Pole."

"Dad, there's no such thing as Santa Claus."

"Would you just start cleaning up? We're going to have company."

I hated him; I thought of ways to kill him myself because I didn't want to wait for the truck. Dad put on a pot of coffee and started washing the dishes. At eight-thirty, I tried telling him that I had to be home at nine, but someone knocked on the door.

"I need you to get into the bedroom."

"Dad, I have to be home at nine!"

"Just get in there," he said. He pushed me in and closed the door. A moment later, I heard him say, "Okay, right here. That's good. I'll bring him out."

I stepped back when the door opened.

"Now," my father said, closing the door behind him. "There is someone I want you to meet. You have one more present to open, and this time I'm going to watch you." He was about to leave, but I didn't move. I could feel snakes swirling in my stomach. "What's wrong?"

"I'm not moving," I said. "I'm not going anywhere, and I'm not meeting anyone."

"What? What is wrong with you?"

"You told me to open my presents last night. I didn't want to because it wasn't Christmas yet, but you told me to open them."

I was so scared I thought he was going to hit me, but I could see the shame in his eyes as he realized what he had done.

"Roger, I…might have told you to open your presents last night. The truth is, I don't remember. Sometimes, I drink too much and I do things I just can't remember doing. And sometimes, there's other things I remember too much…"

"What things?"

"It's not important," he said. "If that's what happened last night, I want you to know that I'm sorry. It won't happen again. I promise."

My father would have given me the world if it would get me to behave that morning, but I believed him because it was the first time that he had promised me anything. Dad covered my eyes and led me into the living room. He removed his hands and started to say something, but I was already tearing the shiny gold wrapping paper off the huge box. I screamed in excitement when I realized I had my very own TV.

"It's black and white," Dad said, picking up the wrapping paper. "Should be small enough to fit on top of your dresser so you can keep it in your bedroom."

Maybe things weren't so bad after all. Maybe my father would keep his promise. I gave him a hug. "Thanks, Dad."

"I guess he likes it," the woman said. "Merry Christmas, Roger. I'm Dorothy."

"Merry Christmas!"

Dorothy was short compared to my father. She had long auburn hair and green eyes, and she was wearing a red sweater with large white snowflakes and a green midi-skirt. She was younger than my father, but it was obvious he enjoyed her company—and the egg casserole she brought for breakfast. While we ate, Dorothy shared some of her Christmas memories. She had grown up in a small town in North Carolina. Dorothy didn't like spending the holidays away from home but hadn't yet earned enough money to return. She lost her job when the accounting firm she worked for closed. Mac had hired Dorothy so he could retire in a few years. She lived at Riverside, two floors down from my father. We left at ten-thirty. When we arrived at the house, Dorothy thought our tree looked terrific before the big storm window, which reflected the lights.

"We got the tree from the Ridge farm," I said. "Me and Grandpa—"

"Grandpa?" Dorothy asked, turning to my father. "I thought you said—"

"He's my mother's father. Everybody just calls him Grandpa. Even Dad. Right, Dad?"

"That's right," my father said, opening his door. "Let me get that TV for you."

Dad carried my new television set while I gathered my presents. As we hauled everything to the house, I realized that I spent more time with Grandpa than I did with either of my parents, and even my mother leaned on him. After the divorce, Mom was worried about keeping the house. She worked full-time at the Pizza Galley but couldn't afford a car with a mortgage. My father took the Fairlane, so Grandpa had to drive Mom to work while, most of the time, she found her own ride home. Mom could barely keep up with the bills and so got me into the habit of shutting off the lights whenever I left the room. When Grandpa and I watched TV, there was only one lamp on in the whole house. Even our clocks had to be wound.

"You're late," Mom said. From the bottom of the stairs, I could see her basting the turkey in the kitchen. "I told you I wanted him home at nine."

Grandpa came to the door as my father rolled his eyes. "I'll see you on your birthday, Roger."

"Okay," I said.

"Looks like Santa was a busy man last night," Grandpa said. He took my TV and headed for my bedroom. I hung up my coat and put away the rest of my stuff but took the Rubik's Cube into the kitchen. My mother was peeling potatoes, and Grandpa started slicing celery. As I began playing with my Rubik's Cube, Mom warned me not to take it apart to because it might break if I tried to get the colors in place that way. I already knew that so I didn't say anything. I just kept turning my Cube as the logs in the fire snapped and cracked between the roar of the flames. After dinner the amber embers glowed against the bricks and out across the room. I finished my second slice of peach cobbler while Mom and Grandpa played chess. I slouched in my chair.

"What's wrong, Roger?" Grandpa asked, handing me his pad.

I shrugged and set down the pad. All day long I had waited for my mother to give me a gift. I thought for sure she had something for me when Grandpa gave me the chess set.

"I know what he needs," Mom said as she got up and left the room. She returned a moment later with a small wrapped package and handed it to me.

Grandpa shared her smile as I slowly opened my present. It was a deck of cards with portraits from American history. I hugged my mother and removed the cellophane. People I had read about in school were on the cards: Washington and Lincoln, Grant and Lee, Harriet Tubman and Susan B. Anthony. Grandpa got a kick out of "Uncle Sam" Wilson being the joker. We played blackjack until ten o'clock, when I told Mom that I was hungry again.

After New Year's Eve, I quit trying to please my parents. My father wanted me to be with him, my mother insisted that I spend the night at home with her. I went back and forth between them over the phone because they still weren't speaking to each other. After ten minutes of "Tell your father..." and "Ask your mother..." I finally settled it on my own.

"Look, Dad," I said. "I spent Christmas morning with you this year so I'm staying here."

My mother gave me a thumbs up.

"Well," my father said. "Can I still see you on your birthday?"

I suddenly felt sorry for him. I agreed that we'd get together for my birthday, which was January twenty-third. I felt guilty because my parents couldn't settle things themselves. It was like pleasing one meant disappointing the other, and there was no middle ground. I hated it. No matter how hard I believed I could keep the peace between my parents, things just never worked out.

Outside, the snow drifted in the cold wind.

Once some of the snow had melted, Aunt Carol drove down from Pennsylvania for my eleventh birthday. It was the first time I could remember meeting her, but I knew that she wrote letters to Mom and Grandpa all the time. My mother had taken the afternoon off to clean the house while Grandpa split logs for the fire. I had to haul in the wood and clean my room too. When we took a break for lunch, Mom told me about Grandpa finding Aunt Carol during the war, but she warned me not to say anything because Carol didn't like talking about it. The memories were just too painful. Some experiences, Mom said, are beyond judgment. My mother also made it very clear that I was not to ask about Uncle William either. After lunch, Grandpa put some logs into the fire and we finished cleaning.

When Aunt Carol arrived the next day, she dropped her suitcases at the door, raced up the stairs, and threw her arms around me. "Oh, Roger! My

Roger! Our Roger!" She was hysterical, and she hugged me so hard and so long I nearly suffocated. After wiping her eyes, Aunt Carol turned to Mom and said, "Oh, he is so handsome!"

"He is," my mother agreed. "It's good to see you again, Carol."

"Thank you for having me," Aunt Carol said. She had, like me, smooth black hair and hazel eyes. Her smile was beaming, and she had an old rosary around her neck. On her left hand, she wore a gold wedding band and a diamond engagement ring. "Oh, Roger…you've gotten so big!"

"I have?"

"You were just a baby the last time I saw you."

"I was?"

She smiled, caressed my cheek, and said to Mom, "He looks so much like his father."

"I do?"

"Let's get you settled," Mom said, grabbing a suitcase. She headed down the hall. When Aunt Carol reached for her other suitcase, I saw that her hands were shaking.

"Let me get that for you, Aunt Carol."

"Are you sure?"

"Yeah," I said. "You're our guest."

She smiled, but her eyes were still watery. "You've become such a fine young man, Roger. Your mother is so very proud of you."

"Thanks," I said. "Grandpa wanted you to know he's taking a nap."

"Is he feeling okay?" she asked as we walked down the hall. Her suitcase was heavy.

"Yeah," I said. "He always takes a nap after church."

"That's right," Aunt Carol said. "It's Sunday. Do you like going to church?"

"It's kind of boring," I said. "But the story of Moses was really something."

"So, you know his mother hid him when he was born?"

"To protect him, yeah," I said. With trembling hands, she wiped her eyes again. "You okay, Carol?"

"Oh, I'm fine," she said, taking off her coat. Mom gave her a hand and hung it in the closet. "I'm fine. It…it's just been such a long drive. And I guess I had too much coffee. I can't wait to see Grandpa again. You know, he has been as much a father to me as he has to your mother."

"Well, we're all family."

"Yes, we are," Mom said.

"He has turned out so well," Aunt Carol told Mom.

"He has," Mom said. She smiled, but her eyes seemed sad.

Aunt Carol took a deep breath and said, "And how is your dad doing?"

"Okay, I guess. He might be by tomorrow for my birthday. At least that's what he said."

"He'll be here," Aunt Carol insisted. "He will. Just watch."

To my surprise, Aunt Carol was right: my father actually showed up on time. Dad was as happy to see Aunt Carol as my mother had been. They talked, quietly, at the doorstep while I got my coat and said goodbye to Mom. I was getting in the car when I saw Dad give Aunt Carol another hug. They waved to each other as we backed out of the driveway.

"How long have you known Aunt Carol?" I asked.

"Years," Dad answered. "Last time we saw her, you was just a baby. No, that's not right. It was just after the funeral."

"Whose funeral?"

"My par—your grandparents."

"I remember that but not meeting Aunt Carol."

"She didn't stay for very long," my father said. "Just came to pay her respects. Lord knows she's seen her share of funerals."

I spoke with Aunt Carol later that night after my father had brought me home. It turned out that my mother and father not only went to the same high school, they were in the same grade. Aunt Carol, who was five years older, was my mother's maid of honor and Uncle William was Dad's best man. And when Aunt Carol and Uncle William got married, Mom was maid of honor and Dad was best man. They were all really close in those days. That was also the night I saw Aunt Carol light candles and whisper songs of prayers. I couldn't understand the language, but she had a beautiful voice, like a sunrise at midnight, casting brilliant colors across the horizon, illuminating seas and landscapes while dispelling the darkness. When she was finished, Aunt Carol kissed my forehead and told me that, no matter what happened, I would always be loved; by that time, I had forgot to ask her about my grandparents' funeral. It was probably better that I didn't say anything. That afternoon, my father had seemed relaxed and looked well rested. The air ahead was clear, the ride calm. Patches of snow coated the fields and the roads. The sand drifted into the wind behind us. When Dad passed the Riverside complex, I asked if we were going to Mac's.

"Just for a minute," Dad said. He had told me over the phone that we were going to his place, but now I had visions of spending my birthday listening to my father talk about our new president, Ronald Reagan. When we got to the station, Dad set the Fairlane in park but left the engine running. Amos waved on his way out to the gas island. I watched as Dad walked into the station and picked up the phone. A moment later, he was back inside the car and we were on our way to his apartment.

"I thought Amos quit," I said.

"He quit because he thought I was going to fire him."

"He punched that guy, though. I saw him."

"I'd never fire a man for defending his dignity."

"What do you mean?"

"Well, there's some things you just don't do," my father told me, "and there's some words you just don't say, like that word that guy called Amos that day. There is a whole horrible history behind that word—slavery, lynching, segregation. Rape. List is damn near endless. Besides, Amos is a veteran. We look out for each other."

"A veteran like you?"

"He's Army," Dad said. "I'm Navy."

"What did you do in the Navy?"

"I was a SEAL."

"What's that?"

"Stands for sea, air, and land," Dad explained. He looked at me and shrugged. "It just pretty much means I did a little bit of everything."

"By sea, air, and land?"

"That's about it," Dad told me. The few times my father did mention his military service, he always made it seem like it wasn't a big deal. I wondered why until I remembered Aunt Carol hiding during World War II. If the memories she had were too painful to talk about, maybe my father's experience in Vietnam was painful for him too. When we finally got to the apartment, Dad parked by his building but told me that we had to go to Dorothy's place because that's where my birthday present was. Once I opened the door, I was thrilled to see my brand-new BMX bike.

"Awesome!" I shouted. When the three of us hugged, Dorothy kissed my cheek.

"I'm glad you like it," she said. "Your dad picked it out. He called a few minutes ago to make sure I finished putting it together. It was a close call, but…we did it. I made meatloaf for supper, if you haven't eaten yet."

"He can have some," my father said. Dad always announced my appetite without asking me how I felt or what I wanted. He opened the fridge and grabbed a can of ginger ale. Dorothy glanced at my father, then looked at me.

"Roger?" Dorothy said. "Would you like some meatloaf?"

When Dad brought me home on Sunday night, he took my bike down to the garage. I went upstairs and set the clock radio Aunt Carol had given me for my birthday on top of my nightstand. Sitting on my bed, I frantically turned my Rubik's Cube, trying to get the colors back into place. Once I was done, I went down to the garage and rubbed a small drop of oil into my new baseball glove, which had been a gift from Grandpa. The leather was still tough, but I had a few months to break it in before spring. If I put the glove under my pillow every night, it would be perfect. Back in my room, I got in my pajamas and turned on the clock radio until I found a good station. I recognized the song because I'd heard it playing at Mac's a million times; it was called "If I Can't Have You" by Yvonne Elliman. She had a beautiful voice. My room became a stage as I lip-synched in front of thousands of invisible fans. I got so caught up in the song I hadn't noticed that Aunt Carol and Mom were watching. They applauded my performance. "Bravo!"

Embarrassed, I shut off the radio. "I didn't see you."

"We just came to say goodnight," Aunt Carol said.

"Roger," Mom said, picking up my Rubik's Cube. "I thought I told you not to take this apart. It could break if—"

"I didn't take it apart."

"You mean you solved that puzzle by yourself?" Aunt Carol said.

"Yeah," I said. "Why?"

But they just looked at each other. Then, at me.

I spent most of my February school vacation with Dorothy because my father had to work. When Dad left the apartment Saturday morning, I was scaling a mountain of Froot Loops while Dorothy sat at the table in her bathrobe. She could work out of the apartment, she said, and spent most of the morning talking on the phone and drinking V8. Papers, files, and books were scattered across the table. When Dorothy had a moment, I asked when my father would be home.

"He ought to be here by lunch, Roger," she said, rubbing her eyes.

"Oh," I muttered. "What are you doing?"

"I do a little bit of everything."

"Like what?" I asked.

"Well," Dorothy said, setting me up on her lap. "I just calculated payroll for the week and now I have to finish formulating a buying plan for Mac based on his estimated income taxes."

"Oh."

"And I had a V8."

"I could've had a V8!" I said, slapping my forehead.

"You'd rather have a V8! Aaaarr!" I squirmed in Dorothy's lap as she tickled me, laughing out loud. She quit when I told her to stop. "Are you okay?"

I nodded. I was still trying to catch my breath when my father's call came. We were supposed to go places and do things, but he always spent so much time working. I should've known better than to believe him.

"I'm sure he'll be here as soon as he can," Dorothy said. "I know it's been pretty busy down there on Saturdays lately and Paul has the flu. Roger…"

"He always breaks his promises! I hate him!"

"Roger, listen to me," Dorothy demanded. I tried to run away, but she grabbed me. "Roger, listen. Listen! Why don't we get dressed and go ice skating? Isn't there a lake around here somewhere?"

I nodded.

"Do you have a pair of ice skates?"

I shook my head.

"Well, don't worry," Dorothy said. "We can fix that."

She called my father to get directions and drove all the way to Zayre in Rose City to pick up a pair of skates for me. Although James and I had rode our bikes to Ledge Lake before, I had never seen it in the winter. The old road had been plowed and sanded for the folks who went ice fishing on weekends, but the lake was as empty as the blue sky above today. There was a small trail on the steep ledge that separated the ice from the dead trees. The wet snow from the last storm had frozen solid in the polar vortex, creating a smooth surface. The brightness was blinding in the sunlight. I hardly recognized the place.

Dorothy glided gracefully out onto the lake. Her speed amazed me while I struggled just to keep my balance. At the far end of the lake, she went into a turn backward and came out step by step. She jumped and spun; I fell. Dorothy hefted me up and gave me a lesson on balance and turns, demonstrating her father's famous "glide-and-push" technique that she learned when she first started. We skated together. Dorothy steadied me, smiling as I picked up speed. After I told her that I'd be okay on my own, Dorothy flew out across the lake. I practiced turns until I caught sight of her again.

She started spinning faster and faster. Her auburn ponytail flew out while she arched her back and became a blur against the landscape. I had only seen women in the Olympics move like that. Behind Dorothy, a deer came into the clearing, walking slowly along the ledge of the lake. Her winter coat was a blend of brown and white fur. She was so precious, beautiful, and delicate. I listened as her deep, sharp breath froze in the brisk air. When she stopped and stared at me, I held my breath. She perked her ears.

The thunderous crack of the shot toppled the deer instantly. I fell down, frozen with fear. Steam rose as the hot, dark blood of the deer poured out onto the frozen lake, breaking the ice. The boom echoed into the forest as the giant hunters stepped out of the forest. One of them knelt, grabbed the legs of the deer, threw it over his shoulders, and disappeared back into the woods. The other hunter walked over to Dorothy, who was lying still on the ice. He picked her up, and I just knew he was going to kidnap her. When the hunter turned, he saw me for the first time. I stared at the wind-burnt skin outlined by his camouflage mask. His eyes were dark, his voice deep. "You're Jake's boy, aren't you?"

I was too scared to answer. The hunter carried Dorothy over to me and set her down.

"Listen," the hunter said. "Me and my buddy tracked that deer for some time and I…I just wanted to make sure your lady friend here is okay. I can see that she is…I'm a doctor. She'll be all right."

The hunter walked into the forest and disappeared. I crawled over to Dorothy and tried to wake her up. When I shook her, I saw a small cut on the bump on her forehead. She had to be dead, and I was so alone and so scared that I started to cry. My hands wouldn't stop shaking. I stared at the blood on the lake.

For a long time, I thought the hunters might return.

After we got back to the apartment, Dorothy took a hot bath while I huddled up under a blanket on the couch. I couldn't sleep and I didn't want to be alone. Why would a doctor try to take Dorothy like that? Who would try to shoot a deer with two people so close? How could he know my father if Dad didn't hunt? The station, I realized, Dad was always at the station. He was there right now, probably filling up the hunter's car with regular unleaded. Did Dorothy get shot like the deer? Is that why the hunter tried to carry her away? Dorothy? Dorothy, wake up. Please, wake up. Dorothy, there is blood all over the lake and I want to go home. Why can't I stop shaking, Dorothy? She sat down on the couch next to me. Her hair was still damp, and she was wearing a white bathrobe. There was a bandage on her forehead. She pulled a blanket over us.

"I called the state police about those hunters," Dorothy said. "They told me they would 'look into it.'"

Still in shock, I could barely hear her.

"Are you all right, Roger? Listen, the shot just startled me. I lost my balance and hit my head on the ice. My father used to hunt all the time with my brothers. Sometimes, people get careless. But it's all right, okay? No one got hurt. Your father said he's leaving now."

When I closed my eyes, all I could feel was the instant before the gun went off—that deceptive, deadly peace. Dorothy wrapped her arms around me, set my head against her shoulder. The slow and steady rhythm of her heartbeat soothed me as I drifted off to sleep.

James slept over the Saturday after Dad and Dorothy brought me home. She had explained to my father what happened at the lake like it wasn't important, telling him that we went ice-skating and a deer got shot. Dad said that hunters usually stay away from Ledge Lake this time of year. (I didn't tell them about the doctor; the more I thought about it, the less real it seemed.) Once I told James what happened he wanted to go see the blood, but Grandpa wouldn't let us. Instead, we built snowmen and got my baseball bat out of the garage.

James hit three home runs before I had the chance to bat. He was winning seven to nothing, so I was anxious to even the score. I missed the first pitch. The second hit me in the leg.

"Watch it!"

"Oops," James said. "Snowman on first."

"James," I said. "The snowman is first. And second. And third."

"I know," he said. "But since we're playing baseball in February, I thought I could say 'snowman on first' instead of 'ghost-man on first' like we do in the spring."

We laughed. Our love for baseball had driven our creativity to new heights. With the snow so deep, a real baseball would be buried until spring after the first pitch, but with snowballs we didn't have the problem.

"What are you worried about?" James said after he threw another pitch. "I won't hit you again. At least not on purpose like you did me."

"I'm not worried, and it wasn't on purpose," I said, laughing. He knew I was lying. The snow was perfect for packing and I couldn't resist. I'd nailed him square in the head with my first pitch, and he vowed revenge. I swung hard with the next pitch; the snowball burst into pieces. James ducked and covered his head as the snow sprayed over him.

"Avalanche," I said, which meant I had hit a home run. "Seven to two."

"What are you trying to do, bury me?"

James packed another snowball. I bunted. The snowball fell to the ground in front of me, so I dropped the bat and ran. The snowman that was first base got hit in the head with the snowball that James threw. I bolted for second base. Since he had to make another snowball, I knew I'd make it. I was almost to third when I saw him charging at me with a handful of snow. We toppled the snowman that was third base, losing our balance and falling over each other.

"You're out!" he shouted triumphantly.

"I know," I said, trying to catch my breath. I was sweating underneath my coat. Aunt Carol called us in from the top of the porch. We helped each other up.

"I can't wait to play real baseball in the spring."

"Yeah," James said. "You don't have to worry about destroying the bases..."

We laughed so long I thought we'd never stop. The late winter afternoon had turned the sky and the snow a deep, menacing blue.

By the time we got inside, I forgot who won.

CHAPTER FOUR

AMERICAN SIGN LANGUAGE

THE STARDUST DRIVE-IN CLOSED its doors one autumn afternoon and never shined its silver screens again. A chain-link fence barricaded the entrance, as usual when it closed for the season, but it remained rusted and unlocked the following spring. Overgrown brush covered the ticket booths while grass began breaking through the pavement until the land was leased to the Great Atlantic & Pacific Tea Company, which built a huge supermarket on the land. Before long, there were a host of small specialty stores. It was my first glimpse of changes to come.

In the spring of 1981, Grandpa and I enrolled in a basic sign language course. It was part of the Brockton County Adult Education Program, which included Poquanicut. Mom insisted that I go with Grandpa, and she called to make sure I was allowed. The class was in the evening so it wouldn't interfere with Little League.

"It's past time you two learned," Mom told me. "I've about had it with writing things down all the time."

Grandpa and I arrived early for the first day of class. He told the woman at the welcome table that I was his grandson and that he was deaf, but she kept shouting as if he could hear. "What class are you here for? I NEED...TO KNOW...WHAT CLASS..."

What an idiot, I thought. I couldn't for the life of me understand why she was shouting when Grandpa had already told her that he was deaf. A few people stepped in front of us. "We're here for Intro to Typing."

"You're in room 112," the woman said, pointing. "Down the hall, on the right. Next?"

One by one, the woman called the other people to the table and told them where to go. It was like Grandpa and I weren't even there.

"The hell with this," Grandpa said. He stepped forward and grabbed the registry from the woman. "I've waited long enough."

Her mouth dropped open.

"We're in room 227, Roger," Grandpa said. "Let's go."

"You know, young man," the woman said as we started walking away. "Your grandfather is really rude."

"Yeah? Well, you're a moron, lady. He told you he's deaf. All you had to do was show him the book and point to the room number. Or write it down."

She was still staring when I turned around and followed Grandpa. Inside the classroom, the desks were arranged in a half-circle. After Grandpa and I had taken our seats, a woman wearing a black turtleneck came in and pulled a chair forward to face the front of the class. Her long blond hair had a light, blended shade of gray. We watched as she leaned back against the chair and said, "Hello, everyone. My name is Lisa, and I would just like to say that both of my parents were born deaf. I was signing before I could speak. Is there anyone here who has had previous experience with American Sign Language? Nobody? All right, then. This is a beginner's course so we're all going to start in the same place."

She passed out sheets of the manual alphabet.

"We are going to begin at the beginning. This is *A*," Lisa said as she made a fist. The class did the same. "*B*... *C*... *D*..."

Grandpa grinned as he made the letters. I realized that sign was something he really wanted to learn, and Grandpa drank the information in as if he had been parched for years; it seemed to be a refreshing experience for him. When we finished, Lisa took us through a review. I made a *P* when we got to *K*.

"Wait a minute," Lisa said, walking over to me. "This is a *K*. That is a *P*. Just think of it this way, keep your *K* up while you *P* down."

The whole class burst out laughing—except Grandpa.

As Lisa went on with the review, she noticed that Grandpa made an *A* when we got to *S*. Walking over to his desk, Lisa knelt down and said, "That's the first letter. This is an *S*."

Grandpa looked at his hand. "Am I doing something wrong?"

Reaching over, Lisa pointed out the *A* on his sheet and Grandpa's eyes lit up. Getting her purse, Lisa took out a sheet of paper, wrote something down, and gave it to Grandpa. After reading the note, Grandpa nodded, set the paper on the corner of his desk, and tapped it to get my attention.

—See me after class.

As the class went on, Lisa had us spell our names to the person beside us. Grandpa watched as I made the letters. *R-o-g-e-r.*

G-r-a-n-d-p-a. When he finished, Lisa came over to his desk, pointed to herself, and spelled her own name. With questioning eyes, Lisa asked Grandpa, in speech and sign, "*What's your name?*"

B-y-l-l, Grandpa spelled slowly. Lisa, kneeling beside him, pointed to the sheet. Grandpa took a look and spelled, *B-i-l-l.*

Lisa rubbed his shoulder. They were both staring at each other and smiling. Finally, getting up, she leaned back against her chair and said, "I think that about wraps up our first class. I have some practice sheets for everyone to use, which I'm sure will help."

She gave a stack of sheets to Grandpa and motioned for him to take one and pass them down. He did.

"Okay," Lisa said. People were getting up and putting on their coats. "Be sure to get a copy of your homework. While those are going around, I would like to point out that this will be easier for some than for others. But we are all here to learn, not to criticize each other. Have a great night, and I'll see you next week."

A few people talked to Lisa before they left, but she seemed eager to see Grandpa. When everyone else was gone, Lisa said and signed, "*I guess you two know each other?*"

"Yeah," I said. "He's my grandfather."

"*So how do you communicate?*"

"I write stuff down for him," I answered. "Or we just use our pitching signs."

"*Pitching signs?*"

"From baseball," I told her. "Like, fastball means 'now' or 'quickly.' Curveball is 'surprise' or 'confused.' Breaking ball means 'pay attention' or maybe sometimes 'watch out.'"

Lisa grabbed her pen and pad and started writing.

—I'm glad you're here. Do you have any experience with Sign?

"Thanks," Grandpa said. "And no, I don't. For the most part, Roger here has gotten used to writing things down. We have a few signs of our own that we use, though. Works out well for us."

We read as Lisa wrote.

—It's great that you have someone to practice with. It will help you a lot. A lot of LDAs (late-deafened adults) try it, but soon give up because it's such a commitment. Children tend to pick it up easily, but it can be difficult for adults because they get set in their ways.

"You can't teach an old dog new tricks," Grandpa said. "Fortunately, I'm not a dog."

Lisa laughed out loud and Grandpa grinned. She was staring at him with a beaming smile, her eyes sparkling.

"My hands don't quite work the way they used to," Grandpa said. "Got a touch of arthritis, and the doctor always wants me to take it easy. Surgeon had other ideas. Wanted to put one of them damn radios in my head. Implants, I guess they call 'em. For my ear, you know? But I don't care what that damned fool says. I told him, 'God made me this way. If you have a problem with that, take it up with him.' Besides, I want to do this. I want to learn. Guess I've gotten stubborn in my old age."

I could hear the determination in Grandpa's voice. Lisa took the pad and started writing.

—I'm sure you'll do just fine. This class is an intro, but if you really want to learn sign, I'd suggest meeting Deaf people whose first and only language is Sign. I am a CODA (child of Deaf adults) so I was signing long before I could speak. Why don't we see how the class goes (seven more weeks) and then we'll discuss it further? You're stubborn in a good way!

"Looks good to me," Grandpa said.

—See you next week!

"Yes," Grandpa said, smiling. "I definitely will see you next week."

Over the next few months, Lisa often went out of her way to work with me and Grandpa. Each class, she made up a word list of the signs we would be learning. While everyone got the lists, Lisa watched closely to make sure Grandpa and I were following along. If Grandpa got lost, he would ask Lisa where we were, and she would point to the sheet and demonstrate the sign for him.

Grandpa and I practiced every day, finger-spelling the words we didn't know. There were times it was difficult for me to sign what I wanted to tell him, but Grandpa was as patient with me as Lisa had been with him. A few times, I got so frustrated that Grandpa told me to write. He always stayed after class to sign with Lisa and, if I'd had to write something down that week, Grandpa would save the paper and ask how to sign what I had written.

On the last day of class, after everyone had left, Lisa invited us to join some of her deaf friends for dinner at Lums in Rose City. As she introduced us, George and Julie both stood to welcome us. George wore a dark-blue suit with a colorful tie. His salt-and-pepper hair was thinning; he looked older than my father but younger than Grandpa. As we sat down, I saw that Julie had a few gold rings with bright, sparkling jewels. She wore a white blouse with a blue skirt and her curly dark hair had blond highlights.

Nice to meet you, Grandpa signed. *I hope she…explained we don't know a lot of Sign.*

That's okay, George signed. His hands flowed as he made signs I didn't even recognize. When I looked at Grandpa, he was asking George to repeat. He signed slower and Grandpa asked him to finger-spell some signs. As I watched George sign, I realized that he was spelling the words then making the signs and watching to make sure we understood. *Lisa told us that you're i-n-t-e-r-e-s-t-e-d…interested…in learning Sign. Where do you live?*

Poquanicut, Grandpa replied. *And you?*

Rose City, Julie answered.

Easy to remember, Grandpa signed. When the waitress came, Lisa translated what George and Julie wanted to eat, but Grandpa just told the waitress what he wanted. When I asked for a hamburger, in speech and sign, Julie smiled. She signed slowly and carefully but I still couldn't understand everything. I asked Julie to repeat herself.

It's wonderful that you are learning Sign with your grandfather.

I think we are…b-e-t-t-e-r now. I'd had to finger-spell.

Better, Julie demonstrated. I followed her hands as she made the sign. She continued courteously, facing Grandpa. *We were born deaf. You became deaf late in life, right?*

Grandpa nodded. *My grandson helps me a lot, but I w-i-s-h I'd started years ago.*

Julie smiled and put her hand on my arm. At first, it surprised me, but it wasn't long before I felt welcome. They were both teachers at the American School for the Deaf in Hartford and had met at Gallaudet University in Washington, DC, years ago. After the waitress bought our food, Julie asked George if he wanted to try the lobster. George nodded, smiling as she fed him. As the meal went on, I realized that everybody was eating without talking, but it wasn't that awkward silence I had sensed all those nights at the dinner table between Mom and Dad. This felt relaxed, even natural. With Lisa interpreting, George and Grandpa made plans to help Grandpa enclose his porch, which I knew he had been planning for a while. After the waitress took our plates, Julie asked Lisa if she wanted something, but I couldn't tell what it was.

"*No dessert*," Lisa said and signed. The waitress was slowly walking to our table, carrying a slice of chocolate cake with a candle on top. Lisa had her back toward the waitress. "*I couldn't eat another bite.*"

The waitress set the cake in front of Lisa, who blushed and laughed out loud. When the waitress started singing "Happy Birthday," Grandpa and I followed as George and Julie signed. I think I finally learned the song when it was over. Reaching over, Lisa gave Julie a hug and then turned to Grandpa.

"*Did you know?*" Lisa asked, smiling.

"*How could I?*" Grandpa said with a shrug. *I just met them tonight. Happy birthday.*

Thank you, Lisa signed, wiping her eyes. She gave Grandpa a hug and kissed his cheek.

How did you know? I asked George and Julie, motioning toward the cake. I was hoping they would understand that I was asking how they had told the waitress that it was Lisa's birthday. They did.

Writing, Julie answered. *I wrote a note and gave it to the waitress.*

I write a lot for Grandpa, I signed. *Before we learned Sign.*

"*You're doing very good*," Lisa said and signed. "*Keep practicing.*"

I have a good teacher, I signed. *How... o-l-d are you?*

Twenty-nine, Lisa answered, looking away. She took a bite of her cake. With questioning eyes, George pointed out something behind our table. When Lisa turned around, George quickly held up an open hand and made a zero. Julie playfully punched George, who made the sign for *50* again just before Lisa turned back around. She looked at everyone. *What's going on?*

Nothing, Grandpa signed. *Like the cake?*

Lisa fed a piece to Grandpa. I could tell he really liked it. When Julie smiled and made a sign I didn't recognize, Lisa motioned for her to stop.

"*What does this mean?*" I asked Lisa, making the sign. Grandpa was watching.

"*Sweethearts*," Lisa said and signed. She seemed embarrassed and hesitated. "*They think your grandfather and I are sweethearts...*"

"*You're twenty-nine*," Grandpa said and signed, "*and I don't date older women.*"

Over the next few weeks, George, Julie, and Lisa would usually stop by Grandpa's house on the weekends. Lisa had given Grandpa a couple of TTYs and caption decoders, one each for his house and ours. The TTY looked like a typewriter but had a small screen that displayed the words. Grandpa could use that instead of a phone. The caption decoder put words on the TV screen;

he wouldn't miss anything that way (as long as the shows were captioned). When I first started to use captioning, my eyes strained to keep up with the words. Grandpa would watch and read all evening. He was glued to the television that first night, watching *Happy Days*, *Laverne & Shirley*, *Three's Company*, and *Soap*. Grandpa used to just watch baseball games—and sometimes a show I wanted to see when we were at his house—but with captioning he could enjoy everything. Access had opened up a whole new world for him.

What will they think of next? Grandpa signed when a commercial came on. Most of them weren't captioned. I pointed out the TTY. *Tomorrow. Lisa is going to call the phone…people. Company. Do you want some popcorn? Then you make it! I want to watch TV!*

He was still up when I had gone home to go to bed.

As the days grew warmer, Lisa and Julie would get an afternoon barbecue going while Grandpa and George spent most of their time working on the porch. I would practice signing with everybody, getting better every day, as the porch evolved from a skeletal frame angling off the roof of the house to a full enclosure, complete with windows. When Grandpa was working on the roof and George was putting in the screens, the two of them would end up making all kinds of noise just trying to get each other's attention because they couldn't see one another; they had finally settled on "shave and a haircut." Lisa explained that they could feel the vibrations of the pounding hammers in the wood and that some deaf people had a little residual hearing.

After lunch, Grandpa would take me to Green Field for baseball practice; if I had a game, though, Grandpa and Lisa would stay. I loved seeing them stand up at the back of the bleachers and applaud, shaking their hands above their heads whenever we scored. At my last game, even Mom got into the habit of shaking her hands above her head. My father, of course, was nowhere to be found.

Dad had said he'd be at the game as soon as he picked up his new truck, but he never showed up on weekends at all anymore. It felt like my father didn't want anything to do with me. I had hit three home runs that season, but Dad had missed every single one of them. I had watched the other fathers cheer for their kids whenever they made a play or got a hit, but my father was never there for me. And I really missed him.

We were behind four to nothing in the bottom of the third inning. James had tried to tell Mr. Gates about my pitching, but he didn't want to hear it. Instead, he put his son on the mound every season. It was disappointing to stay at shortstop but at least I could play. Mr. Gates also had a new rule about not eating candy during games, which seemed to keep everyone from playing their best. Everyone except James, that is. I caught him sneaking a Milky Way bar behind the dugout.

"How'd you get that, Jim?" I asked. "You know you're not supposed to—"

"I went to the concession stand while Mr. Gates was yelling at Chris," James answered. He gave me a quarter. "Go and get a candy bar. It'll give you energy. I saw Grandpa in line too. Who's he with?"

"Lisa," I said. "She teaches sign language, but me and Grandpa are learning a lot more now because our friends George and Julie come over so much. Lisa just hangs out a lot with Grandpa."

"Why are they holding hands?" James asked. I didn't know what to say. "Hey, I got to go. I'm up."

James hit a double batting cleanup and drove in two runs. I stayed behind in the dugout until Grandpa and Lisa had left the concession stand. James was right: they were holding hands. When they went back to the bleachers, I snuck a Go Ahead bar just before it was my turn to bat. After a few practice swings, I dug my sneakers into the dirt at home plate and leaned back like James had taught me. (Mom couldn't afford to get me cleats or a batting glove.)

"Don't worry about this one, Steve," the catcher called out to the pitcher. "He won't hit anything."

I tried to ignore him, but the chants of the other Yankees were really getting on my nerves. "Batter can't hit…can't hit…can't hit…swing!"

The umpire dramatically stretched out his call. "Steeeeerike!"

I kept control of my swing, but the umpire made me feel like I was playing for The Bad News Bears. The catcher didn't help. "Maybe we should get a Wiffle ball for him! We don't want him to get hurt!"

I saw James take a lead from second base. Matt, who had walked, was at first and ready to run. I tightened my grip as the pitcher wound up. The chants faded with the crack I heard and felt when I swung. I watched the ball drop over the fence before I reached first base. As I rounded second, I saw Mom, Grandpa, and Lisa shake their hands above their heads and sign, *Wonderful!* James and Matt gave me high fives. The rest of my teammates swarmed out of the dugout, sharing our triumph. My home run gave us a one-run lead. As I touched home plate, the catcher lifted his mask and spit at my feet. I kicked it back at him and said, "Yankees suck!"

In the dugout, I looked at the bleachers for my father but couldn't find him anywhere. I sat on the bench and kicked and spat in the dirt.

In the last inning, our efforts paid off. We kept the Yankees from scoring any more runs, holding our lead. After Billy struck out, I saw a brand-new blue and gray Ford F150 park on the other side of the fence, just behind first base. My father, who was wearing sunglasses, opened the door and stepped out. Dad sat down on the bleachers, but he didn't even wave to me. John flied out to centerfield and, on the very next pitch, James caught a foul ball. There were two outs now. Brian smashed a line drive over my head and just out of my reach. I jumped to catch it, but my landing was awkward, and I fell back onto the grass. I saw the ball fly across the sky just before Chris helped me up.

"Are you all right, Roger?" Chris asked.

"Fine," I said, brushing the dirt off my uniform.

Mr. Gates was furious. "Get the hell up and pay attention, will you? Or we're all going to lose! We got one out to go!"

I saw my father shake his head.

When Eric came up, I knew he was the last hope the Yankees had of winning the game. My stomach tightened with the next pitch. Ball. Brian stole second base. With two outs, I knew he'd run on anything. I watched the next ball snap into James's mitt.

"Steeeeerike!" the voice of god boomed over the field. That was the nickname we gave the umpire because he was so loud. "Steeeeerike!"

My palms were sweaty, and my heart was pounding.

Eric swung. The ball hopped once, twice, and right into my glove. I tagged out Brian as he tried to run past me and threw the ball with everything I had toward first base. Tim jumped as the ball flew over his head and shattered the windshield of my father's new truck.

"You're out!" god shouted.

The crowd went wild as the Red Sox jumped for joy. We threw our gloves into the air and mobbed each other. Huddled up on the pitcher's mound, we screamed our ceremonial victory chant.

Yankees! Yankees! Ra ra ra!
Throw em in a trash can! Ha ha ha!

Back at the bleachers, I saw my father sitting completely still as the crowd swarmed onto the field. A few people patted him on the shoulder. The parents were cheering and screaming as if they themselves had won the game. I saw my father get in his truck and leave.

James's brother, Craig, rushed through the crowd in his bell-bottomed blue jeans. His long hair and beads were flying all over the place. As Craig lifted his brother up onto his shoulder, James raised his arms in triumph but fell backward. Craig grabbed his feet and started spinning him around. Laughing like a maniac, James kept screaming for help as Craig teased him. "Are you having fun yet? Are you? Are you having any fun yet?"

Finally, Craig set James down in the grass. Craig himself was so dizzy he could barely stand. He helped James get back up as Mom made her way through the crowd.

"What about Roger?" James said, still stumbling. He fell down again but said, "He hit that homer we needed. You got to get him too."

"That's right," Craig said, coming toward me. "If you're Jimmy's friend, that makes you family!"

I knew there was no way I could ever get away from Craig, but I ran anyway. I had just made it into the outfield when he grabbed my shirt. He threw me up over shoulder and spun me around, just like he had done with James. The bleachers, the fences, the dugouts, and the people all became a blur as Craig spun me faster and faster. It was so much fun I wished I had a brother. By the time Craig set me down, I could feel the Earth moving. I had never had so much fun in my life. Mom, of course, was worried.

"That's enough, boys," she warned, approaching the outfield.

"He's all right," Craig said, catching his breath. "He just…he played a great game."

"Yeah," James agreed. "We couldn't have won without him."

"Come on, Jimmy," Craig said. "I have to get the car back before Ma freaks out. By the way, Roger, that was a nice hit."

"Thanks," I said, getting up. "We really needed that home run to win."

"I wasn't talking about the home run."

"Look at it this way, Roger," James said. "At least your dad got the game ball."

Mom took me to Mrs. Pizza to celebrate with Grandpa and Lisa. It took her a while to get used to using an interpreter—she kept saying, "Tell him…" and "Ask him…" or "See if he wants…"—but Lisa patiently explained that if Mom had something to say to Grandpa then she should just talk like she was addressing him. "*And I'll take it from there, okay? It also makes things easier for us.*"

"But I still don't understand why he doesn't want to learn to lip-read."

"*Everyone reads lips to a certain extent,*" Lisa said and signed, after translating what Mom had said. Grandpa was watching. "*Hearing people just don't realize it until they are in a noisy environment, like a stadium. But even the best lip-readers will tell you it's an inexact science. And most deaf people just prefer sign language. Many of them don't feel left out in the Deaf community.*"

As I watched Lisa, I realized it was difficult for me to pick up on what she was signing because I could hear her, and her voice was distracting.

"*You should learn sign language, Mom.*"

"*I'm sure it would be easier for Bill if you—*"

"Roger, why don't you go play that new arcade game they have," Mom said, handing me a quarter. "Go on. I'd like to talk to Grandpa and Lisa for a minute, okay?"

"Okay." I went around the corner and found the video game machine. I had never played *Pac-Man* before, but everybody knew you just had to eat the dots and avoid the ghost monsters until you ate the big blinking dots. After that, the ghost monsters changed color and you could eat them until their color changed back. As the opening jingle played, I realized I could hear some of the conversation Mom was having with Grandpa and Lisa. The machine I was playing was in the other room, but it was still right next to our table.

"...having a hell of a time since the divorce," Mom was saying. The ghosts got me. "I work sixteen hours a day, and I just don't have the time or the energy right now."

As I ran from the ghosts, I heard Lisa say something about picking up sign language here and there. I thought the ghost was going to get me, but I ended up passing right through it and ate the last of the dots. When I glanced over at the table, I saw that Lisa was signing while she spoke. "*...easy with George and Julie and me around. He really has learned a lot.*"

"Do you have children?" Mom asked.

When I looked over, I saw Lisa shake her head.

I ate a big blinking dot, but the last ghost changed back sooner than I had expected. My game was over. When I went back to the table, the waitress was serving our pizza. She still had the same long dark hair; somehow, she was more beautiful than the last time I saw her. Grandpa set a slice on Lisa's plate and took one for himself. Lisa sprinkled parmesan cheese on her slice. Mom asked me which one I wanted.

"The biggest one."

"The biggest one?" Mom said, digging into the pan. "I guess winning all those games made you hungry. Here you go, honey."

After dinner, Grandpa went with Lisa to meet George and Julie at the bowling alley, like they did every Saturday, so Mom brought me home in

Grandpa's truck. She tried to scold me for throwing the ball at Dad's truck, but she kept laughing about it. "There's something I don't understand. Why did you throw the ball to first base…if there were already two outs and you tagged…that other kid?" She was laughing so hard tears were streaming down her cheeks. I tried to answer, but her laughing made me laugh. When we got home, Mom demanded I call Dad to apologize. I didn't take her seriously until she threatened to ground me. I really didn't want to talk to my father after what I had done but a phone call was better than apologizing in person. Dorothy picked up halfway through the first ring.

"Roger, hi! I just got in. How was the game?"

"We won."

"Oh, that's terrific! How did you do?"

"I hit a home run."

"Really? That's wonderful! Did your dad see it?"

"No," I said, turning away from Mom. "That's kind of why I'm calling. We finally beat the Yankees in the last game of the season, but Dad missed my home run. He never calls. I never see him anymore. All he cares about is his job and now his stupid truck."

"That's not true, Roger. He really thought he would be there before the game started."

"He wasn't," I said. "He got there the last inning."

"It must have taken longer than he thought to get his truck."

"Yeah. About his truck…"

"What about his truck?"

"I threw the ball too high and it smashed the windshield."

"Roger!"

"I didn't do it on purpose," I said. "It was an accident. I called to apologize."

Dorothy promised to talk to my father and to tell him that I was sorry.

By the end of the summer, Dad still hadn't called.

In August, Mom let me sleep over at James's new place in South Brockton. His parents had to sell their house in Poquanicut because of the strike at the Boat and, according to James, their income wasn't half of what it had been. James's mother was now in a mental hospital, but his father spent most of his time rebuilding his Mustang. We skipped breakfast, so Jim made blueberry pancakes for lunch. Late that night, after his father had finally passed out, James and I went back downstairs to finish our game. He was down to three dollars in Monopoly money when he surrendered the last of his property. I started putting away the pieces while James got some sodas.

"Jimmy," a voice called. I looked around the empty apartment. "Hey, Jimmy!"

"Yeah?" I answered.

"Is Dad awake?" the voice asked. James came back with two glasses of soda. When I pointed to the window, James pulled back the curtain.

"What's going on, Craig?"

"Nothing," Craig said. "Listen, these guys tied me to a tree and poured screwdrivers down my throat."

I had visions of high school students with glasses full of tools.

"Are you all right?"

"Sure," Craig said. "I told Dad I was spending the night at Daryl's. But, listen. I don't want you to think I did this on purpose or that I'm like Dad. We just wanted to have some fun, but things got out of hand. I didn't even know there was going to be vodka until they were pouring it down my throat. It's not my fault."

"I know it's not your fault," James said, his voice breaking. "Is there anything I can do?"

"Nah. Just be cool. Who're you?"

"I'm Roger," I said. "We met before. At the—"

"He's not gonna turn me in, is he, Jimmy?"

"Nah. Roger is cool."

Craig's breath made me want to vomit. I stepped back from the window and sat on the couch. My hands were shaking when I picked up my soda. I turned on the television but kept the volume low so I wouldn't wake James's father. Once the picture came up, I saw a bunch of people, who looked like they were on a groovy spaceship, singing and dancing and playing music. The credits at the end revealed that the band was called The Buggles; the song was "Video Killed the Radio Star." After the performance, I realized it was some new cable channel called MTV Music Television. James closed the curtain.

"Is he all right?" I asked.

"He'll be okay," James said. "My dad is just giving him a hard time right now."

"I hardly see my dad at all anymore," I said. "I hate it."

Someone howled outside. We peered through the curtain and saw a car driving away.

"There goes Craig," James said.

It was late so we shut off the lights and television and tried to sleep. I got the floor because James wanted the couch. I lay in the darkness for a long time thinking about what drinking did to people. “You know, Jim, people do different things when they drink.”

“Drinking ain’t got nothing to do with it,” he said. “My mother don’t drink, but she’s got so many people living inside her head she’s a different person every damned day. Some days, she’s a whole lot of people.”

“What do you mean?”

“Just different people,” James said. But I couldn’t understand how one person could be a lot of people. “They all have different names, different voices, even different handwriting. I never know who she’s going to be or when. The doctors say she’s got multiple personalities in her head. It’s like one minute she’s nice and the next she’s fucked up. There are other times she fucks everything when it happens too, even me. That’s why she’s in the hospital, so they can fix her.”

“Your mother fucks you?”

“I didn’t say she fucks me! I said, ‘She fucks everything up.’ Look, just forget it, all right? She’s crazy. She’s so fucking crazy. Like I said, she’d be better off drinking. Besides, Craig doesn’t usually do this.”

“You mean he did before?”

“A couple times. It’s no big deal. You should see my dad.”

“You should have seen mine…” I told James about the night my father hit my mother, and we both agreed that our lives were going to be different. We weren’t going to divorce our wives or sell our homes or be bad fathers. Jim wanted a son, but I wanted at least three kids. Maybe four. I was so sure I was going to finish the life my parents had started. I was going to do things right.

It was all so simple, especially since I didn’t know anything about it.

The next Saturday, Dorothy called me so early that I was still in my pajamas and my mother hadn’t yet left for work. Mom had just stepped out of the shower when I asked her if I could go to Mystic Aquarium with Dad and Dorothy. My excitement surged when Mom asked how long I would be there.

“For how long?” I asked Dorothy.

“All day.”

Mom agreed but wanted me to let Grandpa know. I got dressed and as I was walking over to his house, I saw Lisa’s car in the driveway. I knocked, then banged, until Grandpa opened the door.

Don’t knock, Grandpa signed. *Push the doorbell and the sun…*

What? What sun? I don't understand!

Not sun, Grandpa signed. *L-i-g-h-t-s. The lights flash when you push the doorbell.*

Grandpa signed slow enough for me to understand him, which usually wasn't so hard because we signed all the time now—unless Grandpa was exhausted; then he would speak. It was difficult, I think, for Grandpa to learn Sign at his age. He had spent decades talking, wasting words, and his hands and fingers did not move as easily or as freely as mine. Still, Grandpa was determined to learn; and against the odds of age and arthritis, he did. Every so often, though, Grandpa and I had a misunderstanding. Just last week at the hardware store we met an elderly deaf man who had grown up on Martha's Vineyard. He had to finger-spell some signs because Grandpa and I were not nearly as fluent. The man had also used some different signs for words we already knew. Later, Lisa explained that deaf people have different accents. She also reminded us that Sign has its own unique set of rules, including grammar and syntax, but if I had to write a sentence, it was in English. Otherwise, I would finger-spell the words I didn't know. I watched Grandpa press the doorbell and saw a few lamps flash inside the house.

Like that, Grandpa demonstrated. I saw a light flash behind him.

How did you know I was knocking?

Lisa heard you, Grandpa answered. *What's going on?*

Dad and D-o-r-o-t-h-y want me to go to the a-q-u-a-r-i-u-m with them today. Mom wanted me to tell you before I left.

Okay, Grandpa signed. *I'm going to help George with some things today. We're going to build some furniture for the porch tomorrow. Want to help?*

I shook my head. *Why is Lisa here?*

Sweethearts, Grandpa signed, smiling. He pointed to something behind me. I turned and saw Dorothy pulling into our driveway.

I have to go, I told him.

All right. See you later.

My mother, dressed in her work uniform, came out of the house as I was walking to Dorothy's car.

"You behave today," Mom said. "I want you home in time for supper."

"I know," I said. "I'll be home on time."

I waved goodbye to Grandpa. When I got in the car, Dorothy asked me if I knew sign language.

"Yeah," I said. "Me and Grandpa took a class, and we've been signing a lot with George and Julie and all their friends. They're in a bowling league."

"How did he lose his hearing?" Dorothy asked, backing out of the driveway.

"I don't know," I answered. "Mom said it was because of mastoid problems. It was before I was born. Isn't my father coming with us today?"

"He'll meet us there. Is that okay?"

I was excited to spend the day with Dad. *Okay.*

"Roger, is that all right?"

I tapped her arm. "*Okay.*"

She smiled and mimicked my movements.

Dorothy had certainly come to know her way around Connecticut. She crossed Route 12 next to Lucy's and took the back roads to Route 17. From there, she picked up Interstate 95 in Brockton to get to Mystic. The lights inside the aquarium were dim, but the exotic fish were swimming in tanks glowing in fluorescent light. We arrived early for the show so we could get seats up front. When the dolphin flew up into the air to touch the ball, we got drenched in the splash. Dorothy squealed with laughter and licked her lips. I could smell the saltwater. With her arm around me, Dorothy pulled me close as the dolphin jumped, and the water washed over us once more. I felt like a kid who had never gone to sleep listening to his parents scream at each other. When the hostess came around asking for volunteers, Dorothy shot her hand up.

"Here!" Dorothy called to the hostess. "Here's a volunteer!"

"Hi," the hostess said. She knelt before me. Her damp hair had been set back from when she had come out of the pool. I had never seen a woman so well defined as the hostess in that wetsuit; there was something about her that gave me tingles. "What's your name?"

"Roger."

"Hi, Roger. I'm Katie. Would you like to come with me to meet Meridian?"

"Who's Meridian?"

"She's a seal."

"Sure."

"Good luck, Roger!" Dorothy called, smiling and waving as I left.

There was so much light in front of the stage that I had no idea where Dorothy was sitting. I kept looking for my father too, wondering if he had arrived yet. Katie introduced me while I watched Meridian swim. When the seal surfaced and came up onto the stage, Katie gave her a fish. Picking up the rings, she told me to watch closely as she threw them one by one. She gave Meridian another fish after she'd caught the last ring.

"It's your turn, Roger," Katie said, handing me the rings. Her voice echoed through the microphone. "Just throw them one at a time."

I tossed the first ring so far to the left that it landed in the pool. The whole audience laughed. I felt Katie's cold, damp wetsuit against my back when she reached around to show me how to throw the rings. "It's all in the wrist," she said, demonstrating. Her voice wasn't going through the microphone. Katie told me to throw the ring on the count of three and, as she snapped my wrist, the ring flew through the air just before Meridian caught it.

"Just like that," Katie said, setting her hands on my shoulders. "You can do it, Roger."

I counted to three, tossed the ring, and watched as Meridian quickly swooped down to catch it just before diving into the pool. A moment later, Meridian surfaced with three rings around her neck. The audience clapped. After giving Meridian a fish, Katie smiled and clapped then escorted me off the stage. Dorothy was waiting for me.

"That was great!" Dorothy said, giving me a hug. "I always wanted to see a seal up close like that. What was it like?"

"I don't know. I guess I was kind of scared at first, but she was real friendly."

"Let's go have a look at the dolphins."

Dorothy set her hands on my shoulders and leaned over me as we watched the dolphins swim in the glowing blue water behind the glass. They flowed so gracefully.

"They look so different down here."

"Yeah, they do," Dorothy agreed. "Hey, are you hungry? Why don't we go to McDonald's for lunch?"

"But we have to wait for Dad."

"He has to work today."

"You said he'd meet us here."

"Roger..."

"You said he was coming."

"...that's not what I meant."

"What are you talking about? Why did you say he was coming when you knew he had to work today? Why?"

"Roger, it's all right. Let's go to McDonald's. I'll get you a Happy Meal. They come with a toy, you know."

The thought of getting a Happy Meal made me sad. I was too old for those toys now anyway. More than that, I was mad at Dorothy for lying to me about spending the day with my father. It was like a stain that tainted all the fun I'd had at Mystic Aquarium. Worse, she tried to make up for it by taking me to McDonald's.

The ride to the restaurant was filled with that awkward silence, the one I had always felt between Mom and Dad but never with Grandpa. When we got to McDonald's, the lunch lines were long. I watched a young kid hold on to his father's leg as they walked up to the counter, and I knew I was never going to have a normal family. After getting our food, Dorothy and I made our way through the crowd to an empty booth in the corner. I sat facing the wall.

"I thought we'd never make it," Dorothy said. "So many kids here... children."

She dumped her french fries out onto the tray. Dorothy glanced around the restaurant and ate her fries one by one, like a robot. I got a Batman & Robin PrestoMagix in my Happy Meal. Every time something caught Dorothy's attention, she'd smile and tell me to take a look. I would turn around, but I never could figure out what she was talking about. All I could see was a bunch of kids. I finished my cheeseburger and started on the french fries. When I looked up, Dorothy was in tears. "It's my fault...all my fault..."

Confused, I stopped chewing. "What?"

"Ever since I was a little girl, I've wanted to have a baby of my own," she said, crying. I glanced around the restaurant and saw that people were looking at us. "And I love your father...so much, but he can't have any more kids now because of the war. He was injured, and...after all these years, it caught up to him. It was my idea to take you to the aquarium. I knew your father wasn't coming, but I didn't know you'd be so mad at me when you found out. I just wanted you all to myself. Just for one day..."

I watched her walk to the bathroom. Somehow, I lost my appetite. The more I thought about it, the more I couldn't understand why Dorothy had just decided to start crying in the middle of McDonald's. It was embarrassing watching all those people stare. The only time I had cried in public was when my mother smacked me for trying to juggle oranges at the supermarket. I just wanted to lay down on the floor and cry, but Mom wasn't having it. She yanked me up and said that there was a time and a place for my tears—and Price Rite wasn't it. After wiping my hands, I threw away the food wrappers and my PrestoMagix. The restaurant got quiet after the parents and kids had left. Dorothy was silent for most of the ride home.

"I had a good time today," she finally said. "Didn't you?"

I shrugged. "I guess."

"Are you okay?"

Okay, I signed angrily. She saw it.

Dorothy laughed, but before long I couldn't tell if she was laughing or crying. She pulled over to the side of the road and wiped her eyes.

"I'm okay. I'll be okay, anyway." She blew her nose. "I just need some time to get myself together. I'm sorry I broke down at McDonald's like that. Seeing all those kids just…Hey, do you want to go to Mystic Seaport next weekend?"

"I can't."

"Why not?"

"Because Grandpa needs me to help build furniture for his new porch."

That was the first time I lied because I didn't want to explain the truth.

CHAPTER FIVE

THE BRIDGE

IN THE SWELTERING SUMMER heat, I sat sandwiched between Grandpa and Mom while we took an eight-hour trip to Elliott, Pennsylvania, to visit Aunt Carol for two weeks. I had helped Grandpa load the suitcases and the cooler onto the bed of the truck before he tied everything down. His old pickup ran pretty well. Traffic crawled through New Haven, but New York was impossible. I had never seen so many cars in all my life. The buildings were stacked next to each other like Legos, and the city was so crowded we actually had to drive under four buildings in the Bronx. I kept wondering if they were going to fall on us. The humidity in the city was unbearable. As we approached the George Washington Bridge, Grandpa smiled and said, "It's coming up!"

"This is where you were born, Roger."

"I was born in New York?"

"You were born here," Mom said. "Right here, twelve years ago. God, it's hard to believe you're going to be thirteen in six months! Less than six months now."

"That's it," Grandpa said, pointing to the deck of the northbound side. "Right there!"

As we passed the second tower, Mom explained that Dad had got a job down at the Boat after getting out of the service. Grandpa and Aunt Carol had come along to help us get settled, but my mother said that I couldn't wait until we got to a hospital. A fierce blizzard had stopped the city in its tracks, including traffic on the bridge. Scared of getting stuck, and with me in a such a hurry, Dad pulled over and ran through the snow into the city to get help. Grandpa kept the car running while Aunt Carol delivered me. Once Dad had found a plow, the driver got ahold of his dispatcher on the CB radio, who called it in. "But we were on the northbound side and the ambulance from New York couldn't cross the barrier, so they had to send one up with a plow from Jersey to clear the way."

"I was born on a bridge?"

"Right on the George Washington Bridge," Mom said. Grandpa paid the toll in Jersey. Ahead of us, traffic was finally moving again. "Grandpa had the heat blaring, and he gave us his T-shirt so we could clean you. Your father left his coat to help keep you warm."

"Didn't he get cold?" I asked.

"The cold didn't bother him, because of his Navy training," Mom said. "It could be seven degrees, but he could move like it was seventy degrees. Finally, the ambulance came, and we got you to the hospital. I'll never forget that day. Neither will your Aunt Carol."

"How come?"

"You were just beautiful," she said. "So beautiful. My son, at last."

Mom set her arm around me and kissed my head. The traffic cleared for good once we got into Pennsylvania. The clouds danced in shadows across the deep, distant shades of the forest, down through the valleys and up the mountains. It was amazing. For lunch, we stopped at a diner called The Way to Go. A line of people stretched out the door. There was no way I could wait that long.

"*Where's the bathroom?*" I asked. Grandpa had got me into the habit of signing whenever I said something with Grandpa and Mom around. I also had to interpret for my mother because, she had said, she didn't have the time to learn sign language. It was so hard to interpret all the time; I didn't know nearly as much Sign as Mom seemed to think I did so I would often go back to spelling out words. If Grandpa knew the sign, he would show me as I went along; when I finished, he would have me repeat the sentence in Sign, which always helped me remember. When I asked again where the bathroom was, Mom told me to go inside and ask a waitress. I made my way through the crowd and found the end of the line leading to the men's room. There was only one stall free when I got inside. When I was done, there was a man sitting in a wheelchair waiting to use the stall. His chest and arms were huge, like an Olympian. "Thanks a lot, kid."

"I'm sorry," I said. "It was—"

"Sorry didn't do it. You did." The man closed the door to the stall behind him. When I thought about it, I realized that I had noticed the handicapped sign; I'd just never thought about what it really meant before. My face was burning with embarrassment, but I was relieved that Grandpa and Mom had a table. Mom asked me what I wanted to eat.

"*I'm not hungry.*"

"Roger, you need to eat."

"*I'm not hungry. Really.*"

"How about a tuna salad sandwich?"

I shrugged. When the waitress came, Mom told me to ask Grandpa what he wanted.

"*Mom wants to know what you want.*"

Grandpa decided to tell the waitress himself and asked me to interpret what she said. He insisted on doing as much as he could by himself, but my mother kept wanting to do things for him. I knew it would be easier for everyone if Mom would just learn Sign, but instead I was stuck between them. After we had finally finished eating, my mother gave me a twenty-dollar bill to pay for the meal. I forgot the receipt on the table. Mom called my name and said, "You can't pay the bill if she doesn't know how much it is. Go get the receipt. I guess your father never taught you anything."

I bit my lip and paid the bill. My mother seldom missed a chance to put my father down.

Back at the car, I asked Grandpa when we would get to Aunt Carol's house.

Soon, he signed, handing the keys to Mom. *Maybe four more hours.*

I crawled into my cramped space and tried to sleep.

The heat and the highway made it easy.

I woke up as Grandpa was getting out of the truck and saw Mom meeting Aunt Carol on the concrete steps. The houses sloped up and down the mountains in Elliott. The hills and the yards were so steep that there were no driveways; every car was parked on the street. Getting out of the truck, I grabbed my suitcase and one of the bags my mother had brought, the one she had insisted stay on the floor after I had tried to move it. It was a relief to finally stretch my legs in the cool twilight. Aunt Carol took my mother's suitcase and gave me another one of her suffocating hugs. She still wore her old rosa ry—and she was still such a beautiful woman, but she had somehow gotten smaller. Grandpa and I brought in the rest of the suitcases while my mother, who had driven most of the rest of the way, sat slumped on the couch. Mom was exhausted; she told me that working for a living could do that to a person and if I wanted to wait on tables for sixteen hours a day, I could be her guest.

"Oh, lighten up, Mary," Aunt Carol said. "He's been in the car all day too. He probably couldn't move the whole trip because you insisted on crowding him with all that luggage."

Mom rolled her eyes. Grandpa sat in the recliner.

"How did you know?" I asked.

"Woman's intuition. That, and mothers can be quite insistent."

"Carol, don't start. We just got here, for heaven's sake. The next thing you know you'll be selling him insurance."

"Actually, Jake made sure—"

"Carol!"

"Won't youse stop bickerin'!" Grandpa growled. "I'm gonna go deaf, you don't shut up!"

Aunt Carol, Mom, and I all looked at each other; we thought the man had lost his marbles. It wasn't until Grandpa burst out laughing that we got the joke. Aunt Carol was the first one to catch her breath.

"*Sorry, Daddy,*" Aunt Carol said and signed. *We didn't want to leave you out like that.*

"I may be deaf, but I ain't dead," Grandpa said in his deep, sharp drawl. My mother rolled her eyes again. "I like what you've done with the place. Looks good."

Aunt Carol smiled. "*Thanks, Daddy.*"

"I was born in this house," Mom told me. "Your great-great-great-grandfather built it in the eighteenth century. That's why there are no driveways. It's been in the family ever since. Carol bought it from Grandpa when we moved to Connecticut."

"*I was born on the George Washington Bridge,*" I told Aunt Carol, spelling out *G-W-B* and making the sign for *bridge*. I was getting better at using shorthand by watching Grandpa and George.

"*I remember that day!*" Aunt Carol said and signed, smiling. Her eyes were filled with joy. "*You wouldn't stop crying until I held you for the very first time. You looked right into my eyes, like you'd known me your whole life. I was so exhausted, but you were just this little bundle of joy...*"

Her hands stopped as her voice faded. She seemed sad for some reason.

"*When did you learn sign language?*" I asked.

"*When I learned you and Grandpa were learning*," Aunt Carol answered. *I just finished Sign Language II last semester. Now, I volunteer at a deaf retirement home in Pittsburgh. They taught me a lot.*

It was tough for me at first too, Grandpa signed. *But I wanted to learn. And I think if we listen over the next few weeks, we'll do just fine.*

"Let me get you something to drink," Aunt Carol said. Getting up, she looked at Grandpa and made the sign for *drink*.

"I'll have an iced tea."

"Decaf," Mom said.

A few moments later, Aunt Carol set Grandpa's tea and Mom's decaf down on the table. I got a glass of blueberry Kool-Aid. It reminded me of the summer when James and I had made some Kool-Aid while jumping our bikes over a ramp we had built. James had tried to flip his bike but ended up breaking his arm. Grandpa had rushed him to the hospital. When James was finally released with his arm in a cast, the first thing he noticed was my cherry Kool-Aid mustache; it had been there all day, but nobody had said anything to me about it. I carefully sipped my drink, wondering what James was doing hundreds of miles away. Grandpa decided to go to bed after Mom told Aunt Carol about the showdown at the diner.

"Well, that's enough for me," he said as he got up. "See you in the morning."

See you tomorrow.

Goodnight, Aunt Carol signed.

Grandpa walked up the stairs slowly.

"Does he speak often, Mary? Besides when he's exhausted?"

"No," Mom answered. "When his audiologist suggested he learn to lip-read, Grandpa told him and the speech pathologist to go to hell."

"He never did like doctors."

"Grandpa and science are like oil and water," Mom said.

"I hate science," I said.

They looked at me.

"What?" I asked. "What?"

Those two weeks in Elliott went by so slow I thought I was going to lose my mind. Aunt Carol and Mom would usually go shopping or just out for a cup of coffee after Grandpa had made breakfast. I got stuck doing the dishes. One morning, I caught Grandpa reading the newspaper out loud while I was laying on the floor and watching TV. When I turned around, he stopped. I went back to watching *The Munsters* until he started doing it again.

Why are you talking? I asked. But he ignored me. I tapped his foot to get his attention. Looking up from his paper, Grandpa raised his eyebrows, pleading innocent. *Why are you talking and reading?*

"Practice," Grandpa said. "If I'm going to keep it, I've got to use it."

But George and Julie and Lisa and me—

Grandpa nodded. *But some people don't know Sign.*

I knew he meant Mom. I thought for a moment how to sign what I wanted to ask Grandpa but ended up having to write.

—Does it bother you that she doesn't want to learn?

No sooner had Grandpa set the pad down that I realized I could have signed *annoy* instead of using the word "bother."

"Come on," Grandpa said, getting up. "Let's get this place in shape before the girls get back."

Outside, Grandpa got the lawn mower, a ladder, and a pair of gloves out of the old shed. I started mowing the lawn while Grandpa went into town to pick up a few things so he could tune Aunt Carol's car. The hills in the yard were so steep I had to get down on my hands and knees to drag the lawn mower up, and I almost lost control going down. When he got back, Grandpa told me to mow side to side so I wouldn't struggle. It was a lot easier, but my arms got so sore. Grandpa set up a ladder against the house and cleaned out the gutters. He had just finished raking up the leaves when I had the lawn done.

"Rake the grass later," Grandpa said, taking off his gloves. *What do you want for lunch?*

I made our sign for *fluffernutters.*

"This is western Pennsylvania," Grandpa said. "I doubt anyone within a thousand miles knows what a fluffernutter is. Settle for a root beer float?"

He could tell I was excited about having a root beer float for lunch. I didn't even have to say anything.

Let's go, Grandpa signed. As we came around the house, Mom and Aunt Carol were just getting out of the car. Grandpa tapped my shoulder and quickly signed, *Don't tell them about lunch! Get in the truck!*

Aunt Carol set down her shopping bags and asked, "*What's going on?*"

"We're just going to get some things to tune up your car tomorrow," Grandpa said, getting into the pickup.

"Did you eat, Roger?" Mom asked as Aunt Carol signed *eat* questioningly.

"We're all set," Grandpa said, starting his truck. "Had a great big breakfast for lunch and just polished off some fluffernutters. See you kids later."

"There's no fluff in Pennsylvania!" Mom shouted as Grandpa drove away.

A few miles down the road, Grandpa said, "That was close. If your mom knew we were having root beer floats for lunch, she'd never let me live it down."

At a stoplight, I tapped Grandpa's arm. *Why did you say we ate breakfast for lunch?*

"Because I'm a bad liar."

The night before we left, Mom went to bed just after Grandpa, but Aunt Carol and I stayed up late again to watch TV. I always enjoyed the conversations we'd have afterwards. Tonight, there was a rerun of *The Jeffersons*. George was looking for the people who stole Louise's ring and had tracked them to their hideout, where he ended up delivering a baby. Afterwards, the leader of the gang returned the ring. When Carol got up and shut off the television, she asked me what I had learned.

"Bad people can do good things."

"And good people can do bad things," Carol added, sitting back down. She let out a long sigh. "That's what makes us human."

"Grandpa always tells me to do my best."

"He raised his kids the same way," she said. "Of course, I'm sure all that was easier before the war."

"What do you mean?"

"It's like you said," she told me. "Bad things happen to good people. Good things happen to bad people. And that's just the way it goes. The challenge is to keep your integrity when the people around you have none."

"Like George helping the people who robbed him."

"Exactly," Carol said. She sipped her tea. "I've been meaning to ask how your father is doing."

"I don't see him much," I said. "Not since I smashed his windshield."

"You smashed his windshield?"

"During a baseball game," I said. "I threw the ball too high to first base. He missed most of the game anyway. Dorothy said it was because he had to get his truck."

"He wrote me about Dorothy," Aunt Carol said. "How do you get along with her?"

"She's okay, I guess. It's just…"

"What?"

"Things are just different now that Dad's not around."

"Different how?"

"I don't know," I said. "Mom's just hard on me sometimes."

"Sometimes, a mother has to make very difficult decisions to protect her child. That doesn't mean she loves you any less. It actually means she does love you—and very much."

I shrugged. "I guess."

"Well, anyway…Grandpa is really glad you're learning Sign with him."

"What made you want to learn Sign?"

"Grandpa always treated me like I was his own daughter," she said. "Besides, I know William would have learned."

"How come you and Uncle William never had kids?" I asked. Immediately, her face turned pale as her back straightened. Her body became a statue, like she was standing at attention. I wondered what was wrong until I remembered Mom warning me never to ask about Uncle William. "Aunt Carol, I'm sorry, I—"

"What?" she said as her body relaxed. "Oh. Well, we tried. Tried for years. And then, one day…well, one day, you came along, and…I'm happy being your aunt. It's better this way. It is. It's better this way."

"Are you all right?" I asked.

"I'm fine," Aunt Carol said. "It's time for you to go to bed. You've got a long way to go tomorrow."

"Okay," I said. Getting up, I gave her a hug. "Goodnight."

"Goodnight," she said. "And don't forget to write me when you get home, okay?"

"I will," I told her.

She gave me another hug, kissed my cheek, and held on to me longer than I expected.

"I love you," she said. "Please remember that, okay?"

"Love you too, Aunt Carol."

It was past ten o'clock when I went to bed.

My mother woke me up at dawn to help Grandpa load the car. I was eager to get home, but I still wished I had learned more about Uncle William. As we left, I told Aunt Carol that I'd write her as soon as I got back.

It was the first promise I broke.

"Phone!" my mother said, shuffling her keys into the door. She raced up the stairs while I hauled her luggage inside. Mom gasped a hello, then said it was for me.

"Who is it?" I asked, trying to keep my balance as I carried a suitcase up the stairs. Somehow, my mother brought home more suitcases than she had taken with her.

"It's Jim."

"Hey, Roger," James said when I finally got to the phone. "How was your trip?"

"It was all right. We just got in, just now. Man, it's good to be home."

"I…I wouldn't be so sure."

"Why is that?" I asked. I heard him take a deep breath. "Jim?"

"Craig is dead."

A wave of shock rolled through me.

"What?" I asked. "How? What happened?"

The night we had arrived in Elliott, Craig's father let him borrow the sedan on the condition that he pick up his mother from work. Although the strike at the Boat had ended a year and a half ago, they were stuck with a load of debt from his mother's time in the mental hospital. After being discharged, she had been doing well enough to get a job. When Craig never showed, his mother had to walk home alone in the dark and the rain. The police were already at their apartment when she arrived. They had found Craig's body crushed in the car in the woods off Interstate 95 and suspected he'd been driving drunk. "There is nothing left of the car. Nothing at all. We still have the Mustang, though, so that's good. My father said we might get another sedan…"

"Jim, I…"

"The funeral was the following Wednesday."

"Are you okay?"

"Shit happens."

"Do you want me to see if you can come over? Tomorrow?"

"That'd be cool. Call me. When you know for sure. I got to get the hell out of this place."

The line went dead. I hung up the phone and walked into my mother's bedroom. Mom was sorting through her opened suitcases. I sat on the bed and told her what had happened to Craig. She gave me a hug.

"I know you wanted a day to settle into things once we got back, but I was kind of wondering if Jim could come over tomorrow."

"Sure," Mom said. "Let me see if Grandpa can pick him up."

She grabbed a pen and pad and asked if I was okay.

"It's Jim I'm worried about," I said. I was unpacking my clothes when I heard Grandpa yelling. Looking out the window, I saw him in the front yard following Mom, who was walking toward the house. I ran outside as quickly as I could.

"Mary?" Grandpa called. "Mary!"

Mom turned around and faced him. "Is it so difficult to just read? Can't you see—"

"Taught you how to wipe your ass, now you think your shit don't stink!" Grandpa shouted. "Don't you realize the name you answer to is the one I gave you! The language you speak is the one I taught you! Have you forgotten that I named the whole world for you! I did that! Me! I'm your father, goddamnit! You wouldn't so much as know what a tree was or how to pick up a fork or get behind the wheel of a car were it not for me! I taught you how to drive! Both of you kids! You and your brother! I carried you five miles when you broke your leg camping! Worked my ass off for years building submarines and delivering mail just to put a roof over your head and food on the table! Do you think because I can't hear that I'm helpless? I taught you the same goddamned language you now use to condemn me! So, for Christ's sake, *sign*!"

His furious hands flew as his fingers circled.

My heart was pounding in my chest. Never in my life had I seen Grandpa so angry. All the way to Elliott and back I had done my best to translate for the both of them.

"Can't you see this is important?" Mom said to Grandpa. She was in tears.

"Mom," I said. "He can't hear you."

"I know he can't fucking hear me! Ask him *why he has to make things so*—"

I was translating when Grandpa cut me off, demanding that I stop. *Sign! Or we have nothing to say!*

Mom moved her hand slowly, and we all knew. I was shocked to realize, finally, what it meant to Grandpa that Mom hadn't learned the language her own father needed when he had taught her the language she used every day. Defiant, Grandpa waited. After a few minutes, Mom went inside the house. With trembling hands, I explained to Grandpa what had happened to Craig and asked if he could pick up James tomorrow.

"Aw, Christ," Grandpa said. He took a deep breath and let it out slow. "When it rains, it sure as hell pours..."

The next afternoon, I went with Grandpa as he dropped Mom off at the Pizza Galley. The tension between them was thick. It wasn't until Mom got out of the truck and signed *thank you* to Grandpa that it finally cleared.

"*You're welcome*," Grandpa said and signed. "*See you later.*"

See you later, Mom signed to Grandpa. He smiled.

Grandpa drove out of the parking lot, heading toward South Brockton so we could pick up James. I tapped his arm and asked, *Think Mom will learn Sign?*

"She'll get there," Grandpa said, shifting gears. "I taught her one language already. She can learn another. I ain't giving her a choice this time, either."

While Grandpa took his truck in for an oil change, James and I waited at the arcade. He had clearly mastered *Galaga*—and the art of profanity.

"Check this shit out, dude. They're going to steal my ship, but I'll get it right back. I can still blow that shit up!"

A moment later, he was fighting with two ships.

"Smart move, Jim."

"Damn straight. Shit. I'm dead. Your turn."

I had never played before. James kept giving me hints, like he used to do at baseball practice, but now it seemed more like he was telling me what to do. I made it past the first level, but I died before I had the chance to kill anybody on the second level. When James cruised through the next three levels, I realized that he had died on purpose the first time. James blamed the machine when he kept getting killed.

"Fuck that! That goddamned joystick is all fucked up! I beat this fucking game before, Roger!"

I couldn't believe how angry he was. "I'm sure."

"Don't believe me?"

"I said I did believe you. Relax. It's only a game. And besides, you did a hell of a lot better than me."

Profanity is addictive.

"That's because I used to come here all the time with Craig. I need a cigarette."

I followed him outside. "You smoke now?"

"Why not?"

"I don't know. Lung cancer, maybe?"

"Fuck that shit. Cancer is for old people. Let me know if anyone is coming."

He walked behind the building. I followed him part of the way but wanted to watch for Grandpa. I couldn't believe how much James had changed. It wasn't just that his voice was deeper or that he was taller—I knew he'd stayed back a year in school—but he was so angry now. "How you doing, Jim?"

"I'm fine," he said. "I mean, my brother is dead, my father is just a goddamned drunk, and my mother is such a fucking psycho she's out there with fucking Pluto. We were just starting to get ahead when she had to go back to that fucking nuthouse last week."

"She went back? What happened?"

"She just snapped," James said, taking a drag. "Bitch just totally fucking snapped. I counted seventeen different fucking personalities between the time the cops told her what happened and when they finally got her in the car. Other than that, it's all good. Everything's cool. Don't sweat it, dude."

He laughed like he didn't want to believe it. I saw Grandpa's truck pull into the lot.

"Grandpa's here," I said. "Can we talk later?"

"Why not now? He can't hear us."

"Because he's my grandfather, and I'm not going to be disrespectful. I do know sign language, you know."

"You speak sign language?" James asked, crushing out his cigarette. We went back into the arcade through the side door so we could go out the front. James said that no one would get suspicious that way. When he made mocking gestures with his hands, I grabbed his arm.

"I don't 'speak' sign language. I said I *know* sign language. There's a difference. A big difference."

"Chill out, dude. Shit."

"And watch your mouth around my mother."

"Dude, will you chill out already?"

"All right. But I'm serious. Don't swear around my mother."

We got in the truck. Grandpa stopped for gas at Mac's. My father was inside the station counting cigarettes, which meant that he was changing shifts. Kristine pumped our gas while Grandpa got his coffee. James and I searched the coolers for something to drink. I apologized for snapping at him earlier, but James told me not to worry about it. We set our sodas on the counter beside Grandpa's coffee. My father rang us up and pointed to the total on the register.

"I got gas," Grandpa said.

"Pay Kristine," my father said, pointing to the pumps. "You have to pay Kristine for the gas."

Grandpa shook his head in frustration. I tapped his arm.

Pay her for the gas.

I could feel my father staring at me.

"I always pay inside when I get a coffee, Jake. You know that."

My father sighed, took the money, and gave Grandpa his change.

"When did you learn sign language, Roger?" my father asked.

"*I learned a long time ago. Why?*"

Dad watched me sign, and I could sense the distance between us.

Come on, Grandpa signed, holding open the door. *We have to go. Tell him to call you later.*

Okay, I signed. But I didn't. I figured if my father never bothered to call me then, I wasn't going to call him. Besides, I didn't want to see Dorothy.

"That was cool," James said as we stepped outside. "How do I thank him for the Coke?"

"If he's not looking directly at you, wave your fingers or tap his arm to get his attention, then sign *thanks* while indicating the Coke."

James followed my instructions.

Grandpa smiled. "*You're welcome.*"

On the way home, my T-shirt stuck to my back in the humid summer heat. When I saw the construction crew ahead, I took a long drink from my Coca-Cola. The state had widened Route 12 to ease the traffic from the Boat. A steamroller was leveling the pavement, and the stench of the hot tar hung in the air. Grandpa drove slowly through the steam. He rolled up his window when we got close to the noise.

Thanks, I signed.

Grandpa smiled and rubbed my hair.

We shared something my parents couldn't possibly understand.

James brought his Atari and a bunch of games with him. He connected it to my TV because Grandpa was watching the Red Sox game in the downstairs den. We played *Pac-Man* before moving on to the other games. When Mom brought us a large Hawaiian pizza, James ate slice after slice while playing *KaBOOM!* I went into the kitchen to get some more Coke.

"How is he doing?" Mom asked. She was sitting at the table, eating a salad and flipping through a book.

"We're just hanging out now, playing Atari. It's almost like nothing happened."

"It will," Mom said. "It'll come out somehow. It always does. Just remember, Roger—you can help him, but you can't save him. That part is up to him."

"I know," I said. But, really, I didn't. "What are you reading?"

"It's the student handbook for Rose City Community College. I signed up for the fall semester."

"You're going to college?"

"Well, you don't expect me to wait on tables for the rest of my life, do you?"

"Hell no," I blurted out. I realized what I had said after I had said it. My mother set her fork down and gave me that look she had. It was sometimes a contest to see how far I could press her without getting into trouble, but I didn't want to push my luck with James here. When Mom went back to eating her salad, I knew I was safe. I put the Coke back in the fridge and started walking to my room.

"'Hell no,'" I heard my mother say. "My thoughts exactly…"

I heard that unmistakable "kaboom" in the hallway and I knew James had lost.

"My mom's going to college."

"My mom's in a nuthouse," James said, tossing the joystick to the floor. "And I'm dead."

James had another piece of pizza while I finished the last slice. After Mom told us to get to bed, we listened to her footsteps go down the hall and into her room. Once James heard her door close, we went right back to playing video games with the sound off. *Missile Command. Asteroids. Space Invaders.* James wanted a cigarette after he got bored playing *Pac-Man* again.

The night air was cool. I could hear crickets chirping as we walked out into the yard. My mother's bedroom was on the other side of the house, but I was still scared we'd get caught. There was no wind. I looked across the yard and saw Grandpa's house sitting in the darkness. The tip of James's cigarette glowed like a lightning bug. He pointed out all the constellations after we sat in the grass. I heard James open a can of soda that he must have brought with him.

"You know," James said, taking a sip. "Craig fucking loved astronomy. We used to stay up all night and watch the stars before we moved. We tried it in South Brockton, but there's too much light from the highway and the Boat and shit. It's nothing like Poquanicut."

"There's no place like Poquanicut."

"Yeah, right," James said. The lightning bug dove into the grass and disappeared. "Did you know Craig was going to join the Air Force? He was all set to go in and everything. I still have his letter of acceptance."

"Really?"

"He thought it would get him started on being an astronaut," James said. "That's what he really wanted to do, you know, go up in space. He used to tell me stories all the time about having his own starship, like Captain Kirk on *Star Trek*. I still can't believe he's gone. God, I can't take this shit no more!"

James started crying. Then he leaned back in the grass and bawled his eyes out. I laid back beside him, wondering what I could possibly do to help. The stars were burning brightly all the way across the sky, from the roof of the house to the tall, dark shadows of the surrounding trees. Finally, I said, "At least now you know how bad drinking can be, Jim."

"There was still a full six-pack left in the car," James said, his voice breaking. A bright orange light started flickering against the distant trees. When I sat up, a rush of adrenaline shot through my bloodstream as I realized the pile of dry grass had caught fire.

"Holy shit!" James shouted. We sprang up off the ground and frantically tried to put out the fire. James stomped on the edge while I kicked dry grass on top of the flames, hoping to smother the fire. Smoke rose from beneath the grass. I was still stomping the pile when James started screaming. Flames were rising up his leg. I tackled James to get him away from the fire. He kept screaming as I slapped his leg several times before the cold water hit us. As the last of the flames got doused, I saw my mother standing in the yard with the garden hose, still shooting water at the pile of dead grass.

I was watching Johnny Carson on *The Tonight Show* when the door to my room flew open. The contest was long over.

"I want to know what happened tonight!" Mom demanded. "Who started that fire?"

"I don't know," I said. But it had to have been James's cigarette. "Is Jim okay?"

"He's going to be fine," Mom said. "You were both lucky. Very lucky. But you had better know something because somebody started that fire. Do you realize you could have burned the whole house down if I hadn't checked on you two?"

I stared at the hole in the knee of her jeans. "Yeah."

"Now, I want to know where that beer came from."

"What beer?"

"Answer me!"

"I thought it was soda," I said quietly.

"Bullshit!" Mom snapped. "You're grounded for a year. No baseball, no TV, no phone calls, and no more sleepovers after tonight. I'm taking James home tomorrow as soon as Grandpa gets up. He is sleeping downstairs tonight. And don't you ever play dumb with me again!"

Mom took my TV and James's backpack with her. I watched the door close as I shot my hands at her. *Fuck you!*

Later that night, James came into my room with his backpack. He opened a pack of Marlboro and lit a cigarette. I wanted to say something to him about smoking in my room but sensed things would be worse if I did. James leaned against the open window and blew smoke through the screen.

"You know, your mother ain't gonna let us hang out no more," James said. His voice was cracking. "South Brockton sucks. You can't go anywhere without seeing some piece of shit drunk or on drugs. And they always want money. Always. If they ask for coins, you know they drink. Cash, it's drugs. I swear, if we never fucking moved, none of this would have happened. Craig would still be alive if my father never sold our house! I swear, I hate him!"

"It's not his fault," I said. "You know, Jim, you really shouldn't—"

"I fucking hate him!" He was seething with rage, but it wasn't long before he started crying again. Then, I couldn't tell if he was angry or sad. "God, I miss my brother…my father is such a fucking asshole for selling that house! And my mother is a fucking psycho! I swear, I'd rather die than see that fucking bitch again! I'd rather fucking die!"

I didn't know what to say; I just stayed awake for as long I could, listening to him cry.

CHAPTER SIX

THE COLD WAR

GRANDPA AND I WATCHED as news of the nuclear alert spread throughout the country. The day we feared had arrived. In a panic, people poured into the grocery stores to get as much food as they could while following the news reports on the radio as the war escalated. The nuclear missiles shot up into the sky, leaving trails of smoke. We stared in horror as the whole world was suddenly coming to an end before our eyes. The bombs flashed in blinding light. Seconds later, houses collapsed, buildings disintegrated, and stalled cars filled the highways as mushroom clouds roared like thunder, vaporizing millions of Americans in a nuclear holocaust.

"Mother of god!" Grandpa said when a commercial came on. "Hell on Earth and in the backyard!"

I had to watch *The Day After* as part of a homework assignment that one of my eight-grade teachers gave me. I was supposed to take notes on the movie and discuss the Cold War in an essay. Halfway through the film, I'd forgotten all about the assignment. Later, when I was in bed, I kept getting up and looking out the window at the night sky to see if any missiles had been launched. The moonlight glowed across the yard. Was I going to die instantly, or would the radiation slowly kill me? I got up and found my mother doing her homework in the kitchen.

"What's wrong, Roger?"

"I don't know," I said. "Do you think there's going to be a nuclear war sometime soon?"

"Is that what's on your mind? Come here," Mom said, holding her arms out and giving me a hug. "Look at me. It's not going to happen. Okay? I promise. I know you're worried, but it's only a movie."

"But it could happen."

"It won't."

"How do you know?"

"Because sometimes you just have to have faith, Roger."

"Faith in what?"

"In the love that all parents have for their children," she said. "Just because governments don't get along doesn't mean people have to hate each other…" Mom told me about the air-raid drills she had endured growing up in the Fifties, hiding under her desk at school or dropping to the ground when they were outside. The closest we came to nuclear war, she said, was during the Cuban Missile Crisis, but President Kennedy had forced the Soviets into a shameful retreat. She went on about President Reagan and the Cold War until I told her I wanted to go back to bed.

The next day, I started writing my essay on the bus ride to school. The bumps made my chicken scratch worse, and I couldn't concentrate anyway. Last week, James told me that he had to get a part-time job helping the fishermen down on the dock because his father was out on disability. He had got carpal tunnel working at the Boat and needed surgery on his wrists to repair the damage. It was going to take several months to get his strength back, and the payments from his temporary disability insurance were so low that James had to contribute now.

While the Boat paid for his father's procedure and rehabilitation, his mother's constant stints in the mental hospital over the past few years had maxed out their personal medical insurance. They couldn't afford her psychiatric care anymore, including her medication. It was hard to imagine how James could handle all that, but he never complained. He said that he loved working on the dock because it got him out of the house—and kept him out of trouble. As I considered what James was going through, my essay didn't seem so important anymore, but I finished it during study hall.

Mom had put me to work while I was on restriction. I did the dishes, cleaned the house, and learned how to cook and do laundry. I also mowed the lawn and shoveled snow. Grandpa and George had showed me how to change the oil and tune my father's old lawn mower. One day, I filled a bucket with soap and water and got a rag from the garage. The bright red paint shined beneath the layers of grass and dust. Except for a few nicks and scratches, it looked brand new. I mowed Grandpa's lawn as well and raked the grass on weekends. I'd usually finish just in time for dinner and then would watch the ballgame with Grandpa. Mom wouldn't let me play that year. I knew there was no way I was ever going to make it to the Majors anyway. My dreams of winning the World Series had been reduced to watching the Red Sox on television. In the eighth inning, Grandpa got a call on his TTY. After the light flashed a few times, he sat down and started typing. When the commercials were done, he motioned for me to come over and read and type.

Who is it?

Aunt Carol, Grandpa answered.

I had never used his TTY before. I sat down and read HELLO QQ in green letters on the tiny screen then asked Grandpa what it meant.

"QQ is question," Grandpa said. "GA means 'Go Ahead,' which means it's your turn to type. My TTY doesn't have punctuation so don't worry about that."

HI, I typed. Grandpa pointed out the GA key. I accidentally pushed it twice.

GAGA

I KNEW YOU WOULD BE WATCHING THE RED SOX GRANDPA ALWAYS LOVED THEM EVEN WHEN HE LIVED IN PA THE IMPOSSIBLE DREAM OF 67 GOT HIM HOOKED HOW ARE YOU QQ GA

OK GA

YOUR MOM TOLD ME ABOUT THE FIRE WHAT HAPPENED QQ YOU NEED TO BE MORE CAREFUL YOURE LUCKY YOUR MOM PUT IT OUT BEFORE IT GOT TOO BAD GA

IT WAS A ACIDENT GA GA

I KNOW HONEY I SENT YOU BOTH NEW TTYS AND TELECAPTION BOXES SO GRANDPA CAN WATCH TV AT YOUR HOUSE AND YOU CAN CALL HIM IF NECESSARY LATEST MODELS GA

THANKS AUNT COARL

YOU THERE QQ GA

GA SORY GAGA

BY THE WAY IM STILL WAITING FOR THAT LETTER YOU PROMISED QQ GA

I MEAN T TO SEND ONE BUT SO MUCH HAPPNED GA

I UNDERSTAND HONEY BELIEVE ME LIFE HAS A WAY OF DOING THAT TO US ALL TELL YOUR MOM I CALLED I LOVE YOU GA OR SK

Turning to Grandpa, I asked him what SK meant. He got up and looked at the screen.

"That means you can end the call by typing 'SK,'" Grandpa told me. "Or you can type something else. That's why she typed 'Go Ahead' or 'Send Kill.' SK is like saying goodbye."

I CAN WRITE YOURLETTER DURING GAME LOVE YOU TOO AUNT CAROL SK

After the ballgame, Grandpa asked if I wanted to go bowling with him. Being around native signers had helped a lot because he had learned so much. In a lot of ways, and especially compared to how much I didn't know, Sign seemed to come naturally to him now. When he reminded me of how important it was to keep practicing, I decided to go with him.

Once we got inside the bowling alley, the first thing I noticed was all the noise. The place was filled with the constant bangs and slams of the balls spinning down the alleys and hitting the pins. Every lane was taken up, and I had never heard so much racket in all my life. Grandpa found George and Julie practicing in one of the lanes. They were signing with some people I didn't know. After Grandpa waved to get George's attention, he motioned for him to wait. Grandpa's hands moved so fast I couldn't see what he had told George, and I wasn't standing in front of him. Grandpa held up his key chain and pointed to the lockers. George nodded and got his bowling ball the instant it popped up. I watched him toss it down the lane. It looked like the ball was going to go in the gutter, but it was spinning so fast it hit the number-one pin dead on for a perfect strike. He kissed his wife to celebrate. Waving to get my attention, Julie smiled and signed, *Wonderful to see you again!*

Thanks, I signed. *Good to see you too.*

Where are Grandpa and Lisa? she asked. I looked around, but I couldn't find them anywhere. With a questioning look on her face, Julie pointed to the lockers. I walked down one aisle of lockers then crossed over into a perpendicular set. It soon felt like I was lost in a maze and, after wandering around for a while, I gave up on trying to find them and just wanted to get out. Turning the corner, I saw Grandpa with Lisa. He had his hands around her waist, and I watched as Lisa crossed her arms against her chest and pointed to him.

They kissed.

Grandpa and Lisa always had a thing for each other, but until that moment I hadn't realized just how important Sign really was: you could do anything, even fall in love, if you knew the language. I left before they saw me, wondering just how many opportunities had been lost to people who limited themselves to speech. As I turned a corner, I bumped into a tall man with dark hair who asked, *Do you know sign language?*

A little, I answered. I had seen him with George and Julie. *My name is Roger. You?*

Hi, the man signed. *Nice to meet you. I'm L-a-r-r-y. We have been looking for you.*

I was lost, I explained. *I have never been here before.*

Come with me, Larry signed, smiling. *We'll go back.*

When we got back to the lane, Grandpa and Lisa were signing with George, Julie, and a woman I didn't recognize. Grandpa waved as I walked down the steps. Larry introduced me to Maggie just before she got up to bowl. When I sat down, Grandpa asked if I wanted something to eat. I shrugged.

What's wrong? Grandpa asked.

It's noisy, I signed. The sound was pounding in my ears like a massive wind tunnel. It was actually painful.

"Hadn't noticed," Grandpa said, laughing. Lisa smiled and playfully tapped his arm. Looking at me, Grandpa signed, *Come on. Let's get something to eat at the restaurant.*

By the time we left the bowling alley that night, I had a headache.

Later that spring, I had a dream that I got lost in a forest and was trying to find my way out. The trees were laughing at me because I didn't belong. When I saw a tall tree on fire at the end of horizon, I started flying like a phoenix longing to be reborn. As I got closer, I realized that although the tree was on fire, it wasn't burning. Suddenly, I felt an incredible urge to get to that tree, and I started flying as high and as fast as I could. I flew so high that I almost touched the sun, then I went into a steep dive, heading straight for the flaming tree. Voices echoed in the darkness as I fell. Were my parents fighting again? Was it James? I could still hear the voices when I woke up, and then I realized that it was the voices that had woke me. The hall light was blinding as I opened my door. There was a man talking in the kitchen, a voice I didn't recognize. "...think I've been doing? I know I missed weekends and birthdays and holidays, but it was the only way. I never missed a payment for his child support or your alimony. And I still sent them Superman comics for him."

"So, you think he's just going to welcome you back with open arms?" That was my mother's voice, but who was she talking to? "You abandoned him, Jacob! You can't just expect him to—"

"Listen," another woman's voice said. "Why don't we all just calm down and think about why we're here. Was it like this years ago? You're going to wake him up if you keep shouting, just like you probably did back then."

"I doubt that," the man said.

"He is definitely a heavy sleeper," Mom added.

I stepped into the kitchen and saw Dorothy sitting between Mom and an old man.

"Are you sure?" Dorothy asked, nodding in my direction.

"Roger..." the man said as he looked at me. The deep wrinkles stood out against his dark eyes. His hair and whiskers had turned gray. His hands were so dry that the skin had cracked and scabbed. He was my father.

"Hi," I said.

"Come sit down," Dorothy said. Her auburn hair was longer, and she was wearing a little makeup. She pulled a chair. "Sit by me."

"How are you doing in school?" my father asked.

"Fine," I said, sitting down. "What's going on?"

Mom grabbed a cigarette and looked through her books and papers for some matches. My father took out his Zippo and lit her cigarette. The way Dorothy was watching them, I thought something was wrong. Mom looked away, inhaling deeply, before Dad snapped the lighter shut.

"Well," my father said. "I'm going to buy the station from Mac next year when he retires. Your mother is still in school, and since you don't get an allowance, I thought it'd be a good idea for you to come work for me."

"As long as he keeps up his grades and the work he has to do around the house," Mom added. "And if he wants to."

"Sure," I said. "I'll do it."

My father smiled, leaned back in his chair, and lit a cigarette. Mom rubbed her temples and told us that she needed some air. As she stepped out onto the porch, Dorothy asked Mom where the bathroom was, but the screen door slammed in her face. My father told Dorothy to go down the hall, first door on the left.

"When are you done with school?" my father asked.

"Next month," I said. "I think it's the fifteenth or sixteenth."

"And then you'll be going into…eighth grade?"

"Ninth. I'm starting high school."

"You're starting high school? My god, I can't believe it! High school! Well, anyways, you can start the weekend you're done with school. That'll give you some time to get used to things before you go back. Then we'll cut your hours down—"

"How much money am I going to make?"

"Ask me that again sometime. I want you to put that money away for your college tuition. That's why your mother agreed to this. She'll have the house paid off soon and she doesn't want to have to mortgage it again for you to go to college."

"Is all my money going in the bank?"

He leaned toward me. "Think of it as an investment."

"That's not fair."

"Yes, it is," he said. "Now, listen to me…" But all I could think about was that I was going to be working for nothing. My father went on about the opportunities I had that he didn't, how he had worked hard and saved for years to buy the station. "…because your mother and I want you to go to college and make something of yourself. Do something you enjoy."

"Whatever," I said, half listening, hoping I'd make him angry. He stood. There was a hole in the knee of his jeans and his boots were filthy, but his white T-shirt looked brand new.

"Trust me," my father pleaded. "Just this once."

Dad leaned over and gave me a hug before he left. The muscles in his back were as hard as a rock, and his whiskers brushed my cheek. Dorothy appeared in the hallway.

"Are you going to pick me up next weekend or is Grandpa gonna bring me?"

"I'll pick you up. I'll call to let you know when. Your mother wants to talk to me about some things before you start. I'll see you later." Dad walked past Dorothy and down the stairs. Dorothy gave me a hug and kissed my cheek; her lips were wet.

I heard the front door open and close.

"Are they gone?" Mom asked from the porch.

Wiping my cheek, I said, "Yeah."

"Took her long enough."

My father was supposed to pick me up at eight o'clock in the morning on the weekend I got out of school, but I forgot to set my alarm the night before and overslept. It was strange waking up and seeing my father leaning over me, telling me to get up and at 'em. Mom was standing in the doorway. In all the years since they divorced, I never thought I'd see the two of them sitting down and having breakfast together again. It was Mom's idea. She made French toast with bananas. Dad got a bottle of syrup from the refrigerator. It had been set upside down because it was almost empty. "Do we have any more?" he asked.

"I do," my mother said, shutting off the stove. She grabbed a plate full of steaming French toast. "Left cupboard. Second shelf."

They tried to move around each other but kept getting in the way. "Sorry."

"Behind the rice," my mother said. Dad got the syrup and settled into the chair across from her. For once, I sat at the head of the table.

"No bacon?" I said.

"Not today," Mom said. But I swear I could smell it.

We ate in the same awkward silence we used to share at dinner. The quiet reminded me of being with Grandpa and his deaf friends, but that silence was completely different; it was peaceful compared to what I always sensed between my parents. I was sick of the constant tension. When Mom asked us how the French toast was, my father nodded between forkfuls.

"We never did this before," I said.

"We used to."

"I just thought I'd make something special," Mom said. "And your father got here before you woke up. What's wrong, Roger?"

"Nothing," I said. But as I watched my father finish eating, I saw him screaming at me to open my Christmas presents. If he ever pulled anything like that again, if he ever yelled at me for no reason, I was not going to just sit back and take it. I was going to fight back. When Dad asked if I was ready, I took his leftovers and told him, "Not yet."

He looked at my mother and asked if I always ate so much.

"Only lately," Mom said. "And he's already outgrowing most of the clothes I got for his birthday. I doubt I'll survive another growth spurt."

"If you need more—"

"We're doing fine," my mother said. "Besides, you know I don't want him spoiled. He'll never learn to appreciate anything, and one day he'll have to work for what he wants."

I put my father's hat on his head and told him that it was time to go. The inside of his truck smelled like cigarette ashes and old coffee. I rolled the window all the way down and watched the morning mist drift by. The sides of Shetucket Street were lined with grass and weeds, and the trees had grown out so much that the dirt road was completely covered in the early morning shadows. There were a couple of older kids at Lucy's, waiting for the market to open. I knew I didn't have time to hang out anymore. I was a working man now. "Hey, Dad? What am I going to be doing?"

"Well, for now, just a few odd jobs. I want you to be able to handle the outside of the place before the inside. Then you'll move on to the groceries, the cooler, the register. We'll see how it goes, but today we're just going to work on the lot."

When we got to the station, my father filled a bucket with gasoline and gave me a sponge and a putty knife. I followed him to the far end of the lot. Dad soaked the sponge in the gasoline, squeezed it out onto the pavement, and scraped up a spot of gum with the putty knife. Handing me the sponge and the knife, Dad told me that the gum came off just like that.

"How much do I have to do?" I asked.

"Well," my father said, getting up. "I'd like to get the whole lot done today so we get it sealed tomorrow."

I looked out across the lot and past the pumps. There had to be a million spots of gum. "Dad, this is impossible."

"No, it isn't," he said. "You know, your uncle used to mow lawns when he was your age. He'd send the money to your Aunt Carol to help her come to America because her great-grandparents didn't have a whole a lot, not at their age. It wasn't much, but he always said a lot of a little bit makes a big difference. Now watch…"

He dunked the sponge and squeezed until it was empty.

"Now, that's five spots you can do right now, and that won't take more than a minute. You just have to do things one step at a time. And make sure no one smokes around here. They shouldn't anyway, but if they do then we're going to have fireworks early this year. This is enough of a fire hazard as it is.

Don't forget to rinse the pavement with that hose over there before you do too much. I'll be inside if you need me."

I knelt and started scraping the gum. The skin on my hands dried instantly because of the gas, and the scrapes I got on my knuckles stung like crazy. After the sun came up over the trees, the gooey gum was hard as hell to get off. What right did my father have to make me do this anyway? I wasn't getting anything for it. Cars came and went all day at the pumps. People stared and snickered. One guy thanked god that he wasn't me. After my father finished pumping gas for a customer, he rinsed the lot with water. I had forgot. I knew he was going to be mad at me, but I didn't care.

"You're almost finished," my father said. "Why don't you take a break and get a soda or something. You hungry?"

"I don't have any money," I said, looking around the lot. I hadn't realized how much I had done; my anger gave me energy.

"Well, if you want something, just ask for it."

I dropped the sponge into the bucket and went inside. Kristine was behind the counter, waiting on some customers. My father said that he was going to take me to Bonanza for a late lunch, just as soon as he found his keys. Dad looked around the station while I grabbed a bottle of fruit punch. Kristine told me that I was all set, and she asked how my first day was going.

"It's boring," I said. "What am I scraping gum up for anyway?"

"He wants to seal the lot tomorrow," Kristine said, ringing up a man's coffee. He had a full-grown, graying-blond mustache and some whiskers. There was no filter on the end of his cigarette, and his fingertips had calloused burns. Kristine asked if he would like anything else.

"Pack o' Luckies," the man said, tossing crumpled ones onto the counter. He held out a pack of Big Red. "Hey, kid, you want a piece of gum?"

I saw what was left of his teeth when he laughed.

"Be nice, Charlie," Kristine warned. "It's his first day, and he's Jake's kid. Roger, this is Charlie. Charlie, Roger."

He had a firm handshake. "Roger that, Charlie."

"Don't let him bother you," Kristine told me. "He's been working the graveyard shift down at the Boat a little too long."

My father came out of the backroom and asked if anybody had seen his keys.

"Did you leave them in the truck?" Kristine asked.

"I have no idea," my father said. "I can't find them anywhere. Roger, do me a favor. Go see if my keys are in my truck."

I finished the fruit punch and threw away the bottle. The keys were sitting on the floor mat of the truck. Grabbing the key chain, I noticed the Alcoholics Anonymous chip and wondered if my father was still drinking. The chain revealed that Dad had been sober for at least a year, but it was probably longer because it was nicked and scratched. I read the serenity prayer on the back before I went inside.

"I don't believe it," my father said as I handed him the keys. "I've been looking all over for them things. Let's go eat. Your mother wants you home by five. Hey, Kris, tell Paul to finish scraping the lot when he comes in. If he gives you a hard time, just tell him that he can do it between cars."

We were on our way out the door when Charlie stopped us.

"I heard this joke from my best friend," he said. "But I can't remember where she got it from..."

"You have friends?" I asked. Kristine roared with laughter.

"How does it feel, Charlie?" my father asked, smiling. He started laughing too.

"Aw, get the hell out of here," Charlie said. "Go and eat."

As we pulled out of the station, Dad looked out across the lot and said that I had done quite a bit. I tried to see what he meant, but everything looked the same to me. Dad drove past the Riverside complex and took Route 12 to Rose City, chain-smoking the whole way. When we got to Bonanza, he ordered two Cokes and Texas Toasts for starters.

We glanced over the menu. My father ordered a T-bone steak and skipped the soup of the day for extra fries. He made me get a Salisbury steak with a baked potato and mixed vegetables. When I was all grown up and had gone to college, I could eat whatever I wanted, but until then I had to eat what was good for me. Dad lit another cigarette and blew smoke out of his nose. Sealing the lot was going to be a job for the both of us, he said, but things were slow on Sunday, so he was sure we'd get it done.

"I don't care what I do," I told him. "As long as I don't have to scrape up gum anymore."

"Everybody's job is important," my father said. "Don't ever put somebody down because of their job. Running that station wouldn't be possible without someone to balance the books, order from the vendors, or pump gas and smile. And that's just the tip of the iceberg."

"I guess I just had a bad day."

"That's another thing," Dad said. "If you're having a bad day and you're working with people, hide it. Otherwise, you'll go hungry."

The waitress brought our food.

"Can I eat now?" I asked. My father frowned. Midway through the meal, a tall man with one eye came into the restaurant and smiled at me as he walked over to our table. He wore a black leather jacket, and his dark hair was long in the back but short on the sides and the top. My father called him Patch.

"Did he survive his first day?" Patch asked, nodding toward me.

I wondered why a man I didn't know knew so much about me.

"Oh, yeah," my father said. "He's actually better than that turkey Mac hired last week."

"The one you were telling me about?"

"Yeah. If that guy was a musician, he wouldn't know his bass from his oboe."

They laughed, but the joke went right over my head. Dad told Patch he would be at the meeting tomorrow night. Patch grabbed one of my fries, winked, and left. My father later told me that Patch was a veteran who had become his sponsor with Alcoholics Anonymous, someone who had been where my father was now and knew what he was going through. On the way back to Poquanicut, I realized my father had become even more of a mystery to me. The divorce was just the first piece of the puzzle I would have to sort through to find him. The next day, while we were sealing the lot, Paul kept asking questions he should have known.

"Hey, Jake, where's the dipstick? Hey, Jake, does oil go in the tank or the engine? Hey, Jake, is this that brake fluid thingy?"

Moron.

By the end of the day, I was calling my father by his first name.

CHAPTER SEVEN

1984

POQUANICUT IS SUCH A small town it has no high school. The students who went to Poquanicut Plains Middle School got divided between Rose City Academy and Brockton High School. Most of the kids I knew went to Rose City, but I got stuck at Brockton. It didn't take long to figure out which kids were from what part of town; like every high school, you could tell how much money their parents made and where they lived based on their clothes and haircuts.

Preppies and surfers came from the mansions in Brockton Long Point; nerds, punks, and nobodies split the duplexes of Brockton Heights; head-bangers and trailer trash had the projects of South Brockton; while skaters, rockers, and outcasts came from Brockton. Jocks came from everywhere, but every student had a clique. Being from Poquanicut, not really knowing any-body, I often felt like an outcast.

The only people I knew were James and Tim, but we were all in different classes that year. James was hardly ever there anyway. Every time he got suspended for fighting or skipping class, he acted like it was a vacation. When I got home from the station, Grandpa always made sure I finished my homework before I went to bed. I had done well enough in middle school to take college-prep classes, and Jake had cut my time at the station down to three hours a day except on Friday and Saturday nights. Sundays, I had off. My first-quarter grades were good enough that Mom let me keep working.

The only problem I had was with Mr. Wright, my English teacher, who had embarrassed me in front of the whole class because of a homework assignment. I was supposed to choose a passage from Shakespeare, write it out, and highlight the accented and unaccented syllables. Mr. Wright read my paper out loud in a condescending, mocking tone before the whole class. Most of the students ended up laughing at me because of his performance. When he was finally finished, he announced, "Now, I don't know what you think you did, Mr. Evans, but this nonsense here is most certainly not iambic pentameter."

"If you say so."

"You are never going to amount to anything if you can't hear, Mr. Evans."

A rush of anger shot through my bloodstream.

My grandfather is deaf, I signed, looking directly at him in defiance. *He can do anything you can do. And he can do it better than anything you ever do.*

He sent me to the principal's office for what he said was obscene gestures. I gathered my books and, as I left the classroom, I was the one laughing at him.

The last bell rang when I was in the hallway, so I just went to my locker and then got on the bus, which dropped me off at the station. (Mr. Wright, for whatever reason, never said another word to me about that afternoon.) It was tough working and going to school, but I learned to make the most of my time. I usually did my homework in my history class because we never learned anything. Mr. Rollins had gone through chapter one of our textbook in September, but that was it for the whole year. He was even sleeping at his desk one day before class started. Other times, he would talk about sports or music. The battle between heavy metal and rap music was heating up and everyone thought their music was the best. Tim and Junior were the frontrunners.

"At least we don't spin on our heads on the streets for nickels," Tim said. His hair was long, and his jean jacket had patches of Black Sabbath, Iron Maiden, and a host of other bands I didn't even recognize. One girl actually thought he worshiped the devil, which I thought was funny because I knew his parents made Tim and Dave go to church on Sunday mornings and Wednesday nights.

"That's 'cause your hair's so long and dirty ain't nobody wanna clean up the mess," Junior retorted. He had a flattop, and his scalp was visible through the small, shaved streaks of lightning on the sides of his head. Junior had to be the coolest kid I ever met. He got along with everybody, and he even treated an outcast like me like I was one of the gang. The class laughed as Tim and Junior went back and forth. One day, they caught me at my locker.

"Who's better?" Tim asked. "Run-DMC or Aerosmith?"

"I don't know," I said. "I listen to jazz."

James had left a cassette at the house. After I had played it once, I couldn't stop listening to it.

"Jazz?" Tim said.

"John Coltrane," I told them, shutting my locker. "*A Love Supreme*."

"That's cool," Junior said. "You're all right, Roger."

"Man," Tim said as they walked away. "That kid is into some heavy shit."

"Word."

It was the first thing they had agreed on all year.

Homecoming and the dances came and went. I heard stories about what was going on, and it seemed like everybody was going out with somebody except me. All I did was go to school, study, and work. Besides sealing the lot, Jake and I had painted the parking spaces and the curbs around the gas island. (He had to set up cardboard borders after I had left strings of paint around a space.) After he had fired Paul, Jake let me pump gas and showed me how to check the fluids on cars, which I had already learned watching him work. He almost cleaned my clock after the handle on the pump got stuck and I accidentally sprayed gas all over a car.

"Can't you do anything right?" Jake said angrily. "It was a good thing they had their windows up or they'd sue for sure."

"It was an accident," I told him. I had snakes in my stomach. Jake had grabbed me so hard one of the snaps on my raincoat broke. I didn't want to work for my father anymore after he lost his temper. I only stayed at the station because I didn't want to walk all the way home in the rain. Grandpa could give me a ride to Fleming's tomorrow; I could apply for a job there. Jake took the next car and told me to stay inside and finish cleaning the windows. Tim and Dave got out of the car and came inside.

"Hey, Roger," Tim said. "What's going on?"

"Not much," I said. "Just today's my last day."

"Why?" Dave asked. "Don't you like your dad?"

"Shut up," Tim said, punching Dave in the arm. "Mom said it's none of our business, remember? You do this stuff and then you wonder why I don't want to hang out with you anymore."

They must have thought Jake was still drinking. Things always get around in small towns and Poquanicut was no exception; it's one of the reasons I like living in silence. I rang up the drinks for Tim and Dave, but Jake stopped them before they got back in the car. I sprayed the window just as Dorothy's car drove into the lot.

"Did you ring in those sodas?" Jake asked.

"Yeah," I answered. He hadn't shown me the register yet. A motorcycle roared up to the pump. I put my raincoat back on and waved to Dorothy as she was going inside. I motioned for the rider to cut the engine; the quiet was a relief. Setting up the hose, I asked the man how much he wanted.

"Hurry up and fill it," the man said. "Aren't you a little young to be pumping gas?"

"Isn't this a little too much rain to be out riding a motorcycle?"

"Wise ass," the man said with a chuckle. I put the hose back. The man gave me a five-dollar bill and slowly rode away. I rang up the gas inside the store and asked Jake what I was supposed to do with the change.

"It's yours," he said. "So is all this..." He reached inside his pocket and pulled out a handful of bills and coins. People left tips all the time, but Jake only kept them if no one else was working because he was the boss. I counted nine dollars and twelve cents in tips. Jake said that was pretty good for one afternoon, but it was going to be a while before I was ready to work the rush from the Boat. He sat down and put a new roll of paper into the adding machine.

"What's the most you've ever made?" Dorothy asked.

"About fifty," Jake said, punching numbers. "That was right before the strike started. One time I actually ran out of gas 'cause there was so many cars."

"I remember," Dorothy said, rubbing his back. "Are you ready to go, Roger?"

"I thought Grandpa was going to bring me home."

"Doesn't he have bowling tonight?" Dorothy asked.

"Only on Saturdays," I said. "But they practice on Thursdays. Today, he gave Larry a ride to pick up his car. Somebody hit it at the bowling alley last week."

"Did he find out who did it?" Jake asked.

"No," I answered. "They went to get something to eat after bowling. They asked around, with Lisa interpreting, but nobody saw anything."

"That's hard to believe," Dorothy said.

"Probably just some jerk who doesn't have any insurance," Jake said. "At the very least, he should have left a note."

"Maybe he knew it was Larry's car," Dorothy said, "and he was a sore loser."

Grandpa got to the station just as I had finished mopping the floor. Dorothy waved as Grandpa came inside the store. Stepping outside, Jake nodded to Grandpa, who held the door open for him.

How are you doing? I asked.

I'm tired, Grandpa signed. He looked it. *Ready to go?*

I nodded and put the mop and bucket in the backroom. It was filled with all the supplies Jacob had left over from the station's makeover. I bought a bottle of Diet Pepsi Free for Mom and paid for Grandpa's coffee. Getting tips, I decided to pay for my sodas and snacks myself, despite Jake's insistence that I didn't have to. It was one small way I could get back at my father for the things he had done. Rejecting his money meant I could reject him. On the way home, I asked Grandpa how it went with Larry's car.

"Could have been better," Grandpa said. "Larry has full coverage on his car, but the mechanic still wanted him to pay for it. We knew his insurance company had already sent the check for the repairs. They always think we don't know a damned thing."

When we got to the stoplight, I asked, *Why do they think you don't know anything?*

"Because hearing people are stupid," Grandpa said. "My deafness is only a problem when hearing people make it a problem."

By the time we got home, I had completely forgot that I had wanted to quit; I just collapsed on my bed and fell asleep. When the headlights from the car pulling into the driveway woke me, I sat up in bed and peered through the window. After several seconds, my mother got out of the back seat. I heard a laugh after she leaned into the driver's side window. Walking to the house, my mother turned and waved as the car pulled out of the driveway. I slumped back in bed and glanced at the glowing green face of my clock radio. It was after two-thirty! What was my mother doing staying out so late? I heard her in the hallway and pulled sheets over myself. Mom opened the door, but I didn't move until I sensed her hovering over me.

"Hi," I said, pretending I just woke up. Her blouse was wrinkled and untucked. In the light from the hall, I could see that she was exhausted.

How was your day? she asked. Mom had got into the habit of signing with me, though we often went back and forth between using speech and ASL.

"I get tips now. There is a bottle of Diet Pepsi Free for you in the fridge, and I got some donuts for me and Grandpa tomorrow."

Grandpa will like that.

How is school? I asked.

"George Orwell sure had some strange ideas about the future. *Nineteen Eighty-Four* is nothing like 1984."

That's weird.

Are you getting along with your father?

She started playing with my hair.

"Pretty much," I said. "He just expects me to know everything."

Nobody knows everything, Mom signed with her free hand. "You need a haircut."

"I'm going to let it grow," I said. She gave me that look. "Not too long though, Mom."

"Better not," she said, leaning over and kissing my forehead. "Get some sleep. I want the grass cut by the end of the week."

I dropped back into bed. She closed the door on her way out.

One summer morning, I was mowing the lawn when James raced down the driveway on his bike and collapsed on the grass. I made him move so I could finish the last three rows. He sat on the porch steps and lit a cigarette. After I shut off the mower, he asked, "How come you got to do this shit?"

"I have to," I said, pushing the mower into the garage. "If I don't, Mom won't let me work at the station. How did you get here anyway?"

"I rode."

"You rode your bike all the way from South Brockton?" I asked. James always had the guts to do crazy things like that. In a way, I envied him for it. "And your father let you?"

"He don't care what I do," James said. "He ain't never cared about me. Besides, it's only thirty miles."

"How is your mother doing?"

"Same as always," James said, taking a drag from his cigarette. "Most of the fucking time she don't even recognize me. Last night, she was acting like a little girl who wanted to run away from home. She said something about monsters coming into her bedroom at night. It's always some stupid shit like that."

"How are you doing?"

"I'm fine," James said. "The doctors say it's another one of her personalities. They say it's got something to do with her childhood. She had some bullshit trauma so her fucking brain created these alternate personalities in her mind to separate herself from it somehow. They say it's rare, but it happens. She's so fucked up. Half the time she don't know the difference between me and my father."

"How the hell do you even deal with that?"

"I don't know," he said. "I guess it's like having a mother and yet not having a mother."

James flicked his cigarette out into the grass. Remembering the fire, I stomped out the ash with my foot. "Don't do that again."

"You want to go to Ledge Lake?" he asked. "I need to cool off."

"Sure," I said, pulling down the garage door. "You want something to eat first?"

James practically inhaled the food.

I left a note for Grandpa. I hadn't been to Ledge Lake since Dorothy took me skating and that deer got shot. I pedaled hard, as if the wind in my face could blow away my anxiety about James's world falling apart. Maybe that was why he had stayed up all night riding: so he could forget his dead brother, his enraged father, and his mother slipping further into madness. I was ahead of James when he yelled for me to stop. Riding back to where he was, I saw two people at the end of the road walking toward us. James had set his bike down and was sitting in the grass. He poured water from his bottle all over his head. I asked if he was all right.

"This was stupid," James said. "I should just go back to your place and crash."

"We're only about halfway there. We could still go back."

James looked down the road. The people I had seen walking were girls close to our own age. I didn't recognize them, but they were smiling about something. They both had long hair and there were towels around their necks.

"The brunette is mine," James said. He took a drag from his cigarette.

"Girls ain't property, Jim."

But he ignored me.

"Going for a swim?" James called out to them. He took another drag and blew a smoke ring. I could tell he was trying to be cool, trying to impress the girls. The brunette was the older one of the two. I couldn't tell if they were wearing any makeup or not.

"Isn't there a lake or something around here somewhere?" the brunette asked.

It was James's idea that we give them rides to the lake, and he talked the brunette into going with him. She stood on the bolts of his back tire and held on to his shoulders. They left me and the other girl standing by the side of the road. James told us we'd miss the fun if we didn't hurry. The brunette laughed.

"Well," I said. "He was tired."

"Hold this," the girl said, handing me her towel. She pulled her thick red hair back into a ponytail. She was wearing cutoffs and a black half-shirt. "Who was tired?"

"Jim. My best friend."

"I'm Allyson, but my friends just call me Ally. My sister's name is Rachel."

"Roger," I said. "But my friends just call me Roger."

She laughed. At the end of the road, James and Rachel were waving us on. Allyson got on my bike and put her hands on my waist. I didn't know her or her sister because they had just moved to Poquanicut. Their father, an engineer, used to work for Narragansett Nuclear Dynamics in Virginia, but the Boat had outbid them for the latest contract. The rivalry between Narragansett Nuclear Dynamics and the United States Submarine Building Company went back decades. Allyson's father had to change jobs, but she had just started high school and didn't want to leave her friends. Her mother had told her that she didn't have a say in the matter, and Allyson hated her for it. When we got to the lake, we couldn't find James or Rachel anywhere.

"Maybe they got lost," Allyson suggested.

I shook my head. James had been to Ledge Lake a dozen times. He had moved to South Brockton, but there was no way he would forget where the lake was. Allyson and I called for them a few times, but there was no answer. I took off my shoes and socks and shirt.

"They're around," I said. "Jim is just fooling around."

"With my sister?" Allyson said as I jumped into the lake. The water was cool. I came up in the middle of the lake and swam away from her. When I looked back, she had taken off her shorts and was wearing a bikini. She held her half-shirt as she walked into the water. I looked for her after she dove in, but I lost track when the wind blew over the water. In the distance, I spotted Rachel walking down the hill through the forest to the lake and asked where James was.

"He's coming," Rachel said. "He was right behind—"

Allyson suddenly surfaced before me and pushed me under by my shoulders. The water went up my nose and got in my lungs. I came up coughing, with Allyson swimming away and laughing.

"Very funny," I said, splashing water at her. "Very funny!"

I swam after her. James came out of the woods and told me to go for it. I put my hands on Allyson's shoulders and pulled her back toward me. She was floating, holding down her shirt, but I saw the strap of her bikini on her shoulder.

"Don't," Allyson said, breathing through her mouth. "Please don't."

When I saw her light-green eyes, I let go.

"What the heck?" James shouted from the ledge. "Why didn't you dunk her, Roger?"

"He didn't do it because he didn't want to do it," Rachel said.

"So? She dunked him. It's only fair."

"Shut up, Jim," I said, walking out of the lake.

"You're a square. You know that, Roger. A square."

"What's it to you?" Allyson said, coming out onto the old boat launch.

"Nothing," James said. "Nothing at all."

James opened his backpack and took out a small radio. As Eddie Van Halen's "Eruption" blasted through the speakers, I tried not to watch Allyson put on her shorts. Rachel started searching through James's pack. I wondered why he had brought so much with him, even a change of clothes. When Rachel asked James where something was, he pulled a small plastic bag from his sock. There were three joints inside. Before I knew it, James had lit one and handed it to Rachel. He lit another and held it out to me and Allyson.

"She won't do it," Rachel said. "She never did before."

James said she didn't have to do it if she didn't want to.

"I'll do it if Roger does it," Allyson said. She smiled when I looked at her.

"So what makes Roger so different?" Rachel asked, inhaling deeply.

"I don't know," Allyson said. "Because he didn't dunk me."

"Whatever," James said. "Take a drag already."

I inhaled as deeply as I could and coughed so hard I thought I was going to vomit my lungs. James told me to ease up and hold it in. Allyson and I passed it back and forth until James gave us a paper clip. The four of us all shared the last one. The sun was shining and the sky was blue and I was right up there with everything, higher than a kite.

"Sex, drugs, and rock and roll," James said. "It don't get no better than this."

I was on Pluto.

"You wasted?" Rachel asked.

We looked at Allyson.

"I don't know," she said. "Maybe I am. I forgot."

I think it was Rachel who suggested we play truth or dare. I don't remember much about who said what, but I'll never forget the first time I kissed Allyson. We were by ourselves at the ledge of the lake; she wouldn't do anything with them watching. I put my hands on her neck and closed my eyes. My heart leapt.

"Come on," Allyson said, jumping into the lake.

"What?" I asked. "What are we…doing?"

She threw her shirt up onto the boat launch.

I jumped in the water.

I couldn't sleep that night any more than James could ride all the way back to South Brockton. I knew Mom didn't want him around, so James ended up sleeping in my closet. My mother had class that night and probably wouldn't be home until after ten. At nine-thirty, I shut off all the lights, ready to pretend I was asleep if Mom checked on me. My closet was on the same side of the room as the door so the chances of Mom finding James were slim. I'd even hid his bike in the woods behind the house. By the time I'd got back inside, James was sleeping.

I was exhausted, but I couldn't stop thinking about Allyson. I had given her a ride to Three Streets Circle, where Thames Avenue, Quinebaug Court, and Shetucket Street converged. There were no houses around the circle. Rachel had insisted on walking the rest of the way with Allyson. They lived in the second house on Thames Avenue. After we kissed again, Allyson gave me her phone number. I said it to myself over and over again as James and I rode back to the house. The buzz was beginning to wear off, and I was starting to get a headache. My ears were ringing. Nothing had really sunk in yet.

"You really like Allyson, don't you?" James asked.

"Oh, yeah," I said. "Oh man, do I. What's the deal with you and Rachel anyway?"

James shrugged, raced ahead. "She just ain't my type."

Allyson and I had fooled around all afternoon at the lake. It was the first time I had ever touched a girl and the first time a girl had ever touched me. Allyson seemed to be as curious as I was; she had even dug her nails into my back while giving me a hickey on my chest. As the headlights moved across my room, it dawned on me that Allyson and I probably would have gone all the way if we'd had more privacy. I heard a door slam and peered outside. Mom was walking backward toward the house, looking at the car and yelling at the driver, whom I couldn't see.

"You know these summer sessions are a pain, and you know I've got a term paper to write! It's after eleven, and I've got to open the Galley in the morning so get off my back!"

"Then next week you can find your own ride!" a man's voice shouted. The car roared out of the driveway and down the street. I was waiting for my mother at the top of the stairs when she got inside.

"Men..." Mom muttered, closing the door. She was surprised to see me. "Why aren't you asleep?"

"You woke me up," I said. It was a white lie. "Who was that?"

"Just...someone I used to go out with after class. Please just go to bed."

"Is everything all right?"

Mom sat down at the kitchen table and rubbed her temples.

"I don't know," she said. "I don't know how I can keep this up. I think going back to school was a mistake. I'm so close to finishing, but I just don't know how much more of this I can take. What was I thinking?"

I could tell she was stressed, holding back tears.

"You were thinking you didn't want to wait on tables for the rest of your life."

"You're right," Mom said. She suddenly seemed relieved. "That is what I was thinking. Thank you, honey."

We hugged.

"You'll make it, Mom. You always do."

"Go to sleep," she said. "I have a term paper to write."

I was still awake when Mom went to bed. Restless, I couldn't stop thinking about Allyson and what that afternoon had meant. She had trusted me because I hadn't dunked her. Was love based on trust? Was that why my parents got divorced, because after my father hit my mother they couldn't trust each other? And why did Dad hit Mom? Was it just because he was drunk or was it because being drunk brought something out of him, like the demons in his mind? Was it his memories of the war? I checked to make sure James was asleep before I got my bike out of the garage.

The night air was cool, but there was no moon to light my way; I followed the stars through the tall trees, and I could smell the humidity collecting on the grass as I pedaled down Shetucket Street. The houses were on one side of the road, and the porch lights flickered between the passing trees. Even when Allyson and I had kissed, it felt like there was something missing, something I couldn't quite place. When I reached Route 12, I knew it'd be crazy not to go back. The trees were clusters of darkness, and the open road was gray on either side of me. I rode with no hands between the double-yellow lines, pedaling while flapping my arms like a bird—or a phoenix. There was nothing everywhere.

I was looking for the red and white sign for MAC'S GAS when I saw the neon sign for EVANS FOOD & FUEL. The green letters of the logo glowed in the night: our last name was up in lights. I rode around the clean, vacant lot until I saw a car coming. I shot across the street and pushed my bike into the woods. The sky was purple in the east. The car drove by.

Looking at the station from a distance, I realized how much it had changed since I had started working. Sealing the lot made it look like it had just been paved. I could see the curbs and parking spaces we had painted in the neon glow. We had even power-washed and painted the store and built the box, a small shelter Dad had wanted for the gas island so he didn't have to run back and forth to the store during the rush. He had wanted every nook and cranny covered. I was on my way out of the woods when another set of headlights came around the corner. Pushing my bike back behind the trees, I saw crimson clouds east of the dark-blue sky. It was amazing.

The truck slowed down as it approached and turned into the station. I wondered what on earth somebody was doing here so early, but then I saw my father get out of his truck, unlock the front door, and go inside.

"You close at midnight and you're here at sunrise?" I whispered. "Dad, that's crazy."

The sky was orange. I had to get out of there. I waited for Jake to go in the backroom then I hurried out of the woods and started pedaling as fast as I could. A few cars passed me. I thought I was safe until I realized a set of headlights had pulled up behind me. I kept riding, but it was obvious someone was following me. When I heard my name, I circled back.

It was Patch. He was wearing one of those muscle T-shirts, and his arms were covered in tattoos.

"Everything all right?" Patch asked.

"Why wouldn't it be? I just got up early and wanted to go for a bike ride. That's all."

Patch took a long drag from his cigarette and offered me a ride home. I put my bike in the trunk and got inside the car.

"Did you know your dad tried calling you yesterday?"

"No," I answered. "It was supposed to be my day off."

"He didn't need you to work."

"Well, what did he want then?"

"Did you know your buddy, Jim, ran away from home?"

CHAPTER EIGHT

THE BREAKFAST CLUB

I LIED TO PATCH. I told him that I had no idea where James was or where he might have gone. Patch gave me a big speech on the way home about doing the right thing, but I knew better. If I said anything, my parents would want to know everything. I'd be grounded for the rest of my natural-born life if they ever found out I had smoked dope. And I couldn't get Allyson in trouble for something James had done. I had to call her later tomorrow—today, I realized; I forgot I had stayed up all night. Patch dropped me off at Three Streets Circle.

The sun was just above the horizon, and a cool wind blew across my face as I pedaled home. I knew James's father must have had something to do with James running away. He had called the station looking for James and Dad had tried to get ahold of me. That was how Patch had found out. But why would James run away and not say anything to me about it? It didn't make sense. I raced down the driveway, into the garage, and waited for my mother to leave. After I heard Mom close the front door, I went upstairs. James had a lot of explaining to do. But what if something was wrong? What if something had happened to his mother or his father got hurt? I decided to call the station and told Jake that James had just showed up.

"He did?" Dad said. "Well, tell him to get home. His father was looking for him all day yesterday."

"All right." When I turned around to hang up, James was standing right next to the phone, smoking a cigarette.

"You turned me in, didn't you?" he said.

"What are you talking about? Your father called my father, and I told him you were here."

"You told him that I just got here."

"So."

"So, are you that worried about your own neck that you just had to turn me in? What the fuck, Roger!"

I told James about my running into Patch, that I had lied at first but changed my mind because I thought something might be wrong. "Why don't you tell me what's really going on, Jim?"

"Why do you always do what people expect you to do?"

"What are you talking about?"

"You cut the grass, you work for your father, and you always have your homework done. You can't think for yourself. Give me a break."

"Don't turn this around on me. Why didn't you just tell me in the first place that you ran away? What's so bad you couldn't even talk to me about it?"

"We still friends?"

"Yeah."

"Best friends?"

"Yes!"

"So, if you promise not to say anything…"

"I promise I won't say anything. Just tell me why already," I said. James took off his shirt and turned around. His back was covered with dark bruises and welts. "Holy shit! Jim, you …your father did that to you?"

"He got mad at my mother again," James said, putting his shirt back on. "And he took it out on me. Besides, where do you think I got the weed from? Why do you think he's looking for me? I had no place to go so I came here. And you turned me in. Shows what I know."

"You know I wouldn't have said anything if I knew what was going on," I told him. "There has to be something we can do!"

"What can we do? You tell me what the hell I'm supposed to do!" He screamed and punched the wall several times. "I mean, what do you think they're really going to do? Send me to foster care to live with some strangers? A fucking group home? Fuck that!"

He grabbed his backpack and left. I was so tired that all I wanted to do was go to sleep and wake up from this nightmare. It wasn't real. I found James out back, tears streaming down his cheeks. He threw his bike out of the woods.

"Maybe we could talk to my mom and see if—"

"Your mother would never let me stay here," he said. "Besides, it's not your problem. But I swear to god, one day I'm going to get away from here forever!"

I didn't know what to say.

James was still crying as he rode up the driveway and disappeared down the street. My head was heavy from the humid summer heat. I walked back to the house, fighting my exhaustion, knowing I had betrayed him again.

I tried calling Allyson when I got up, but nobody answered. Grandpa was in the kitchen with Lisa making spaghetti and meatballs for supper.

Who are you so anxious to call? Grandpa asked.

Her name is A-l-l-y. We met yesterday. She wants me to call her... What?

Grandpa was grinning behind his goatee. He shrugged his shoulders slightly. *Nothing.*

I need a shower. Dad will be here soon.

Mom was home by the time I got out of the shower. Grandpa hardly ate anything for dinner. I asked if he was all right. Shaking his head, he picked up his fork and twirled his spaghetti for a few moments. Lisa gently touched his arm.

What's wrong? Mom asked.

I'm tired.

Do you want to take a nap before bowling tonight? Lisa asked.

Grandpa nodded. Mom waved her fingers to get his attention. *Maybe you should take it easy the next few days.*

He agreed. As we sat there at the dinner table, with everybody signing as Grandpa responded in speech, I realized I was happy. There was no tension between anybody anymore, no awkward silence filled with words unsaid. We could finally communicate as willingly as we wanted. It was liberating. This is my family, I thought, and it's not so bad after all.

Want me to stay with you? Lisa asked Grandpa.

He shook his head. "I'm just *tired*."

When we finished eating, Lisa wrapped up Grandpa's plate and put it in the fridge. I heard Dad honk the horn from the driveway. I told Grandpa that I needed to go.

I got some ice cream this afternoon at Waldbaum's, Grandpa signed. He was grinning behind his goatee. *Let's make some root beer floats tomorrow!*

I smiled. Grandpa was the one person I could always count on for a good time.

I love it when you flip the ice cream and miss the mug! I signed.

Tomorrow, I'll catch it! Watch me!

You always say that, I signed, laughing. *And you always miss! I love you, Grandpa.*

I love you too, he told me. *See you later, buddy.*

Dad asked about James when we got to the end of Shetucket Street. I told him that James had left right after I called this morning. The less I said, the better off I was. I looked out the window at the passing trees.

"Did you sleep last night or today at all?" Jake asked.

"I'm fine." This was supposed to be the big day I was going to work the rush from the Boat, but I was too drained to worry about it. In the past twenty-four hours, everything had changed. It was bad enough that Craig had died, worse that Jim's mother had come undone, but his father beating him like that…it was no wonder James had tried to run away. But what was he supposed to do? I wondered what I would do if my father still drank. He put out his cigarette when we got to the station. I waved to Rob at the island before going inside; he never said much of anything to anyone, so I wasn't surprised when he didn't wave back. Jake and I were stocking the cooler when he asked how I thought things were going for James.

"I know ever since his brother died he's been having a hard time at home. He thinks they never should've moved."

"Oh, no kidding," Jake said. "Selling that house was the dumbest thing they could have done. It was their most valuable asset. Hell, they were probably paying two-fifty a month for that sucker and that apartment has got to be four-fifty."

He was so predictable, always thinking about money. I opened a case of New Coke and started putting the cans on the shelf. "You have an apartment."

"Not for long," Jake said. "They're making the whole complex into condominiums by the end of the year. I'm going to buy mine and get it paid off as soon as I can. God, I can't wait for them to go back to old Coke."

"How do you know they're going back to old Coke?"

"They made the announcement last month," he said. "New Coke doesn't sell. In fact, I read that if it had been a success, then Pepsi was going to come out with Pepsi Supreme, which probably just would have had one less gallon of sugar per thousand cans or something."

"No shit," Charlie said at the threshold. "The whole country would have gone to hell in a handbasket if we lost Pepsi too. Hey, Rob wanted you to know that he already split and there's a car out here."

I grabbed a change bank from behind the counter, strapped it around my waist, and went outside. The stars were starting to fill the twilight sky. There were two girls in the car, and the back seat was filled with all kinds of bags. “The Beautiful Ones” by Prince and the Revolution was blaring on the radio.

“How much tonight?” I asked over the music, taking off the gas cap. The girl shut off the radio.

“Fill it,” the girl said. I realized it was Rachel the moment she realized it was me. “Roger! What are you doing here?”

“I work here,” I said. “Or wasn’t that obvious?”

“Ha ha,” Rachel said.

Allyson asked why I was at Evans if I worked at Mac’s.

“My father bought this place from Mac,” I said, setting up the hose. “You know, I tried calling you before I left, but there was no answer.”

“We went shopping at the mall,” Allyson said.

“Our father is trying to make it up to us for having to move. Our mom’s gonna be mad.”

“They just use us to get back at each other.”

“And we’re caught in the middle.”

“So, we get to get all this stuff.”

“Oh,” I muttered, nodding. “Okay. Anything else tonight?”

“Yeah,” Allyson said. “Um…would you…I mean, I was thinking—”

“Do you want to go to the movies with my sister?”

“Wasn’t I supposed to ask?” I could feel the heat on my face. She had actually asked me out and I blew it.

“It’s the Eighties,” Rachel said. “You can do whatever you want.”

“Have you seen *The Breakfast Club*?” Allyson asked. I told her I hadn’t. “We found out it’s still playing at the Old Towne theater at the Diamond Mall. Want to go?”

“All right. Yeah, sure. I’d love to.”

“How does Friday sound?” Rachel suggested. “That way I can bring you. I’m meeting some of my new friends that night anyway.”

“Sure,” I said. “I’ll call. I have it off. Be right back.” I stepped into the box and rang in their father’s credit card. It was all happening so fast. After I gave Rachel the charge receipt, Allyson motioned for me to come closer. I walked around the car and leaned in to give her a kiss. My heart was pounding.

“Hey!” Charlie shouted. “None of that risky business in this town!”

He had scared the living daylights out of me, and I hit my head on the roof of the car. Allyson said she’d see me later. Still laughing, Charlie got into his old, wood-paneled station wagon and left. Inside the store, Jake asked about the girl.

"I met her at the lake yesterday," I said, walking back to the cooler. "We're going to see a movie Friday."

I was getting good at avoiding his questions. After the cooler was done, we went outside and waited. Jake lit a cigarette and told me to take off my change belt. There wasn't going to be any time to count out loose coins, and people usually didn't want to bother with them anyway. He'd dropped the gas orders I had done that day and gave me twenty-five dollars in ones and fives. Five or six cars flew past the station. It was ten-thirty.

"Here they come," Jake said. "Get to the box. I'll be inside if you need me. If they want coffee or soda they'll come inside. There should be enough cigarettes in the box. The big thing is to fill them up and get them out of here as soon as possible. Go and good luck."

The glow from the headlights of the oncoming cars lit up the trees on the side of the road. Traffic was a river. So many cars flew past the station that I began to wonder if I anyone would stop. I looked at Jake inside the store and shrugged my shoulders. He pointed out a car turning into the lot. I motioned for the driver to pull to the forward pump. A middle-aged man I'd never seen before rolled down his window and said, "So you're the one Jake's always bragging about..."

Rush was nuts. I kept giving people the wrong brand of cigarettes, and I had to run all four pumps at the same time. I'd finish two cars and two more would pull up. Jake was just as busy inside the store. There were lines of parked cars. Four guys would get into a car to leave and somebody else would be waiting for the space. Some people even parked on the side of the road. They'd get their cigarettes from me at the box and somehow drive back out into traffic. It was a miracle there were no accidents. I kept mixing up the cash and credit card sales, but the people were unusually patient. (I told one guy that I put someone else's gas on his MasterCard. He laughed when he found out it was nineteen cents more than what he actually got.) It seemed like it would never end, but at one o'clock the last car pulled away and Jacob shut off the outside lights.

"Did you survive?" Jake asked.

"Barely," I said. "Right now, I just want to go home and go to bed."

Some nights, I can still see him smiling.

On Friday, the day of my big date with Allyson, I got out of bed at about ten o'clock. I had never worked so hard in such a short time, but I had made enough in tips over the past few days to buy dinner before the movie. After I showered, I smothered my cheeks and chin with soap and borrowed my mother's razor to shave. (It wasn't like I could use my father's.) I nicked my chin, and it took forever to get the bleeding to stop. I still had a tissue on the cut when the laundry was done.

I was spending so much time doing my chores and working at the station that I never did anything else. It'd be nice to have some fun for a change. After folding my clothes, I decided to call Allyson. She said that Rachel would be by at about four o'clock. Mom had left work early to study for one of her exams. I introduced Mom and Allyson before leaving.

"What time will you be home?" Mom asked.

"After the movie," I answered. "Probably ten. Maybe eleven."

"Did you eat?"

"We were going to get something at the mall."

"Where's your jean jacket?"

"I left it at the station last night. I'll see you when I get back."

Rachel made me and Allyson sit in the back, but Allyson didn't say much until we were by ourselves. We decided to get hand-rolled pretzels before the movie and ordered dinner from Arby's. Once we got our food and sat down, Allyson made a surprising confession. "I can't do this."

"Can't do what?" I asked. "Did you want to get the pretzel first?"

"No," Allyson said, laughing. "That's not it. It's just…my sister made me ask you out. It's not like I didn't want to go out with you. It's just…I was hoping you'd ask me."

"I was going to," I said. "I really was. Why did she do that?"

"Ever since Rachel had a boyfriend, she's wanted me to have a boyfriend. And I guess I was hoping you'd ask me because…"

I could tell she was just as nervous as me. "Because why?"

"Because…that way I'd know if you really like me."

"I do," I said. "I really do like you. Tell you what, why don't we just start over? My name is Roger."

"But your friends call you Roger."

"Yes, they do."

"Ally." She smiled as we shook hands.

"Okay, great. So, what do you say we go to the mall and see a movie and maybe get something to eat at Arby's? We could get some roast beef sandwiches and some fries and maybe even a hand-rolled pretzel?"

"Okay," Allyson said, still smiling. "Sounds like fun."

"And we're here already," I said. "See that?"

"Hey, it's the Eighties!"

"And we can do whatever we want, right?"

"Absolutely!"

After we ate, Allyson and I got our pretzels and walked from one end of the mall to the other and just talked. She said that Mom was nice; she wished her own mother showed that much concern for her. I told Allyson that Mom was working and studying to be a nurse, and she couldn't believe it. Her mother, she said, didn't do anything but cook, clean, and complain. When we got back to the food court, I saw Tim and a group of headbangers walking toward us. Most of them had made my freshman year miserable.

"Well, well," Steve said. "Look who we have here."

"Hey, guys," I said. They were upperclassmen out of South Brockton. They all had long, wild hair and were wearing faded jean jackets with patches of heavy metal bands and that satanic crap. The fruit appealed to them, but only because it was forbidden. As they gathered around us, I suddenly found it odd that so many teenagers trying to be so different could look so much alike. "What's going on?"

"Nothing much," Glenn said. He put his arm around Allyson and pulled her up against him. She elbowed his rib cage and stepped away. "Hey, we hardly know each other, babe."

"Her name is Ally," I said. My stomach was in knots. "And she's with me. Or haven't you figured that out yet?"

"He hasn't figured that out yet," Tim said.

"Don't," Glenn warned, turning to Tim. "She's just playing hard to get."

"No, I'm not," Allyson said. But Glenn grabbed her arm and pulled her toward him; she winced. "Stay away from me!"

I punched Glenn's forearm as hard as I could and stepped between them. "Part of being a man means knowing how to treat a woman. That does not qualify."

I could feel everyone staring; it was as if the entire mall had stopped moving and someone had put a spotlight on the two of us. Glenn's long, wild hair was intimidating; he was taller than me but a lot skinnier. His whole face was covered in acne. "You want to start something?"

"You've already done that," I said. "She told you to leave her alone. So, leave her alone."

"You think I'm afraid of you?"

"Do you think I'm not afraid of you?"

My response caught him off guard as he realized that I could see through his tough talk. Our staring contest lasted for an eternity. We measured each another in the silence, waiting to see how far the other was willing to go.

Once I was certain that he wasn't going to do anything, I stepped closer and took a deep breath, all without taking my eyes off his.

"Come on, Glenn," Steve said, slapping his hand on Glenn's shoulder. "It ain't worth it."

"You're lucky I'm hungry," Glenn said. "Later, twerp."

I watched them walk away. Allyson held my arm. "What a jerk."

"Why did you stand up to him like that?" Tim asked. "They could've killed you."

"So, what was I supposed to do?"

"You did the right thing, Roger," Allyson said. "Thanks."

"Look, Roger," Tim said. "The right thing ain't gonna matter when Glenn comes looking for you at school next month. It's only a matter of time. You signed your death warrant today."

"What are you doing with those guys anyway?" I asked.

"I'm trying to get a band together," Tim said. "They said they could play, but they suck."

"Next time pick somebody who won't be collecting Social Security when they graduate," I said.

"No kidding," Tim agreed, laughing. "I'm heading to Ron's Guitars. Maybe I'll find somebody who can play over there. Want to come?"

"We got plans," I told him.

"We should go," Allyson said. "The movie starts soon."

We tried to get in to see *The Breakfast Club*, but they wouldn't let us. Instead, we got tickets to one of those PG-13 movies, went separately to the snack bar, and snuck in to see it anyway. I usually chose the middle of the theater, but Allyson insisted that we sit in the back. Once the movie started, she began teasing with the popcorn, holding out the bucket then quickly snatching it away the moment I reached for it. It was funny the first time, but I got annoyed when she just kept doing it. After a while, I gave up and decided to watch the film. Allyson put her head on my shoulder when Bender climbed over the table to confront Andy. I set my arm around her and gently kissed her head. My heart was racing as I waited, listening to her body and reading her movements to see if she wanted to go further.

She fed me a piece of popcorn.

After the movie, we held hands and walked through the mall as the stores were closing. Rachel had told us to meet her at the car, but she'd parked at the other end.

"That was a great movie," I said.

"Yeah, it was," Allyson said. "It's almost scary."

"What do you mean?"

"Do you think our hearts will die when we get older?"

"I don't think it's inevitable," I said. "I guess it all depends."

"On what?"

"On who you want to be."

Facing me, she stopped walking. "And what do you want?"

Stepping toward her, I set my hands on her neck. Her eyes were glowing with anticipation. I was just about to kiss her when somebody screamed, "Can we fucking go already?"

We turned and saw Rachel by the food court, waiting with a few other girls.

"God, I swear she ruins everything!" Allyson said.

"No argument there."

"Make sure she lets me walk you to the door when we drop you off. If she says anything, just tell her we'll only be a minute."

"Why me?"

"Because she won't argue with you the way she always does with me," Allyson said. She was right. When we got to the house, I asked Allyson if she would like to say goodnight. Rachel didn't say a word as we got out of the car and walked to the front door.

"I had a good time tonight," I said.

"I had a wonderful time," Allyson said. I felt fireworks when we kissed.

"You want to go the lake again?" I asked, hopeful.

"Yeah," she said. "Yeah, I do. I really do. I'll call to let you know when I can."

Inside, Mom was sitting on the couch, smoking a cigarette and waiting.

"You're late," she said. "Did you have a good time?"

"It was great."

"Good. Now get some sleep. You have to work tomorrow."

"I know," I said, heading for my bedroom. "Goodnight."

"By the way," Mom called. "Grandpa picked up your jean jacket earlier today. It's on your bed."

I tossed it on the floor, flopped down on the mattress, and went right to sleep.

A few days later, Allyson called and asked me to go to Ledge Lake with her. I should have been exhausted from working so much, but I had this mad urge to see her again. We set our bikes against the trees along the ledge of the lake. Allyson spread the blanket out along the old boat launch, and the lake behind her was a deep, dark blue. She looked great. I took off my shirt and sneakers but didn't go in the water. We started kissing and touching each other all over. When Allyson moved my jean jacket, three condoms fell out of the inside pocket.

"Where did you get these?" she asked.

"Honest to god, Ally," I said, blushing. "I don't know where they came from or what they're doing in there."

"You mean, they're not yours?"

"I…I never got them. I don't know how they got in there."

"Well, where did they come from?"

"I told you. I don't know."

Allyson put on her shirt and walked to the end of the launch. I buried my face in the blanket.

"If there's someone else," she said, "the least you could do is tell me."

I got up. "Someone else? No, there's nobody else. I told you I don't know—"

"Then how did they get in there?" she snapped.

"I swear, I don't know! I left my jean jacket at the station the night we went to the movies and somebody picked it up later. I've never even…"

She looked at me. I went back to the blanket and sat down, ashamed. A few moments later, Allyson sat with me.

"You've never done it before, have you?"

"No," I said. "I don't even know why I brought that jacket on a day like today."

"I've never done it either."

"You haven't?"

Allyson shook her head and pulled her T-shirt over her legs. "I guess I just wanted my first time to be perfect."

"Sorry I messed it up," I said. "It could've been anybody, but it wasn't me. You've got to believe me. I didn't know anything about them until just now."

"I do believe you," Allyson said softly. "But why would someone do something like that?"

"Beats me."

"Maybe they just want us to be careful."

"Maybe they thought we were going to do it anyway."

"Maybe we should."

"You serious? You still want to?"

The wind blew her hair in waves when she nodded, smiling. She was so beautiful. We kissed, slowly. I was so excited that I started shaking.

After a moment, I stopped and asked, "You okay?"

"Yeah," she whispered. "Thanks for asking. Are you?"

"Yeah," I told her. "Yeah, I am. It's just hard to believe it gets better…"

Over the next few weeks, I got working the rush down to a science. I stopped mixing up the sales and started getting the cigarettes right. I knew what the regulars wanted. If they parked on the side of the road, I'd toss their cigarettes to them and they'd hand me the money while I was pumping gas. Weekends got to be so busy that I would usually just stay with Dad and Dorothy. One Saturday, the station was so busy it was crazy. The new submarine was about to head to sea, and thousands of people had come to see First Lady Nancy Reagan christen the boat that afternoon. The governor, our senators and representatives, the first selectman of Poquanicut, and the mayors of Brockton County all made it a point to attend the ceremony. The state police had even reassigned officers to help with all the traffic and people. James, Tim, and Junior had come to stay at the house that night so we could all go swimming at Ledge Lake tomorrow afternoon. They got sodas and snacks, hanging out while I worked the rush. I always looked forward to the last car pulling away at the station, when Dad would shut off the outside lights. Just when I thought it was over, Dad told me to empty the trash while he stocked the milk and soda.

"Again?" I asked. "We just did the cooler before rush."

"I know," Jake said. "But I try to sleep in on Sundays, so Kristine opens tomorrow. Won't take but a minute. You have the whole day off tomorrow."

After I took out the trash, I went to the cooler to help Jake. As I started stocking the milk, I asked him why he doesn't work at the Boat. He kept stocking the soda cans, tossing them from one hand to the other as I filled the racks.

"I used to," Jake said. "That's why your mother and I moved to Poquanicut. The Ridgway Company was closing down—"

"The Ridgway Company?"

"You know that old building by your Aunt Carol's? The one across from the railroad tracks? That's where it used to be. They made generators for the old submarines."

"How come you quit the Boat?"

"I didn't want to spend my whole life working for someone else. That, and I really didn't like the way they did things. How did you do in tips tonight?"

"I don't know," I said. "I haven't rung any of this in yet."

I emptied my pockets onto the counter. Ever since Allyson and I started going together, I put extra effort into getting better tips. Jake started shifting through the cash, sorting the bills. I went outside to get the readings off the pumps.

"Sucks that the only place to hang out in this town on a Saturday night is gas station built in the Fifties," James said. "Can we get out of here already?"

"In a minute," I told him. "These readings are the last thing I have to do."

"You were moving like a racehorse, Roger," Tim said. He tossed his empty soda bottle into the trash can I had just emptied.

"No kidding," Junior agreed. "That was some serious power ballet shit."

"I got tired just watching him," James said.

"Just another day, guys," I said, getting the last reading. "Wait here while we lock up."

When I got back inside, Jake had rung in the gas totals and was finishing his paperwork. He had counted fifty-six dollars in tips.

"Looks like you did good tonight, son."

"Thanks."

"You did real good. In fact, I wanted you to know I'm—" The ring of the phone cut him off. He answered it. "Evans. Yeah. He's right here. We're leaving shortly..."

After a moment, he hung up the phone and turned toward me. His face was red, like he was about to panic.

"What is it?" I asked. "Jake, what's wrong? Dad?"

"You...your grandfather was shot and killed in South Brockton."

CHAPTER NINE

ONLY AS GOOD & ALWAYS AS BAD

THE NIGHT RAIN POUNDED against the windshield as Dad drove down the dark highway. We were finally on our way to Pennsylvania for the funeral. Since getting the news, time had come to a standstill for me as the hours that followed felt like days, and the days felt like weeks. I had cried so hard and so much, my heart was numb from exhaustion. I couldn't eat, and I barely slept. The weight of it all had become a fog, and I felt trapped in my grief as I tried to absorb what had happened, but it was impossible for me to process the reality of my grandfather's death. The shock lingered for days, then weeks. Months, and years. The best friend I'd ever had, the greatest man I'd ever known, had been murdered—and the details that emerged that night would turn my nightmare into a living horror story.

It had been too late that night for Dad to take everybody home so Tim and Junior rode in the bed of the truck with James and me back to the house. The wind whipped my long hair as I gazed upon the stars in the night sky. I felt small, as if I were seeing the universe for the very first time. Tim, like an idiot, started talking about Jesus. He was so religious he claimed he wasn't religious at all but instead had a personal relationship with the divine (which I found laughable).

As we rode in the truck, Tim said that god has a plan for everybody, that good things always come out of bad things. When I told him that was a pretty shitty fucking plan, he got defensive, as if my shock and grief were somehow an assault on his faith. Amid the never-ending agony of losing somebody you love, religion is the salt poured into thousands of fresh wounds that were once such precious memories. Hearing the fairy-tale promise of eternal life before the unbearable, undeniable reality of such a horrendous death only compounded the impossible weight of my grief. Tim's words hit me like bullets; he knew I was wounded too, but he just kept shooting. It wasn't until James told Tim to shut the fuck up that he finally stopped preaching.

When we got to the house, Dad stopped by the side of the road. There was a police car in the driveway, and Dad ordered us to wait while he took a look at the house and the yard. Another car flew past us and parked on the lawn next to the cruiser. Immediately, Lisa got out and raced inside the house, followed quickly by George and Julie. After Dad parked his truck on the other side of the cruiser, closer to the house, we all jumped out. Once I got up the stairs and into the living room, Mom and Lisa embraced me. We stood there, frozen, for so long I began to feel suffocated. Tim and Junior were beside James, but Dad stood before the two police officers. George and Julie sat with Lisa, who had positioned herself to translate. One of the policemen took his hat off and introduced himself as Officer Burke, adding that his partner was Officer Samno. The first thing I noticed about them was that they had guns. Burke, who had a shaved head, was older than Samno, but they both looked a little young to be policemen. As my mother set her hand on my arm, I felt her trembling. She looked exhausted, and her eyes were bloodshot.

"Too late to take them home," Dad told Mom as he nodded toward my friends. "Figure we can sort that out later."

"We can figure it out later," Mom repeated. "They can call who they need to."

I'm so sorry, Julie signed as Lisa translated. Her eyes were sad, welling up with tears.

We found out after your mother called Lisa, George signed.

"Why are you waving your hands around like that?" Samno asked. He had his hand on his gun. I froze, like a dead man. He stepped toward George and Julie and stuck his finger in their face. "Stop waving your hands around! This is—"

"Sit down, Rambo," Dad told him.

"It's Samno," he said, turning around.

I heard someone, probably James, try to stifle a laugh.

"*They're deaf*," Lisa said and signed. "*I'm their interpreter.*"

"*You don't know sign language?*" I asked.

"Why would we?" Officer Burke said defiantly.

I shook my head. "Mom, what…*what happened?*"

"We're still in the process of conducting our investigation," Officer Samno announced as Lisa translated. He had taken his hand off his gun and was now fidgeting with his hat in his hands. Samno had short, bright blond hair and glowing blue eyes. For some reason, he kept blinking. "From what we've been able to piece together so far, it looks like he was just in the wrong place at the wrong time. Is there anything you can tell us?"

"*He had to get brakes for his truck this morning,*" Lisa said and signed. "*We were going to meet for dinner before bowling. When he didn't show up, I tried calling—*"

"And he didn't answer," Burke injected. "South Brockton, that's a tough neighborhood. Unfortunately, these things happen all the time down there. Busy day with the christening too. You Navy?"

He pointed out my father's tattoo. When I looked at Dad, I could see a great darkness in his eyes, but he stood as cold as a mountain. "Chief."

"Submarines, I take it?" Samno said.

"SEAL."

"Holy Christ," Burke whispered under his breath. He was surprised I had heard him, but he just turned back toward my father. "Your knuckles are flat."

Looking down at his hand, Dad made a fist. I had never noticed it before, but Officer Burke was right: my father's knuckles were so flat his hands looked like hammers when he closed his fingers. James and Junior looked at each other.

Dad said, "Vietnam, '67."

"And I'd bet you'd love to tell me," Samno said. "But then you'd have to kill me…"

I saw a great big wad of white gum in his mouth when he laughed. White fucking gum. It did nothing to hide the stench on his breath. The site of that man disgusted me, and the sound of his roaring laughter filled me with a maddening rage rising in my chest like a tsunami after an earthquake on the ocean floor.

"Would everybody please just sit down?" my mother snapped. "You're all standing around acting like a bunch of dropouts on graduation day! I feel like I can't breathe!"

James, Tim, and Junior all sat on the floor. Lisa took the loveseat across from George and Julie on the couch while Jake settled into the recliner. Looking around, I waited to see where Burke and Samno were going to sit. I felt like a stranger in my own home.

"Need some air, ma'am?" Officer Burke asked.

Samno stepped toward my mother. "I'd be happy to step outside with—"

"Will you just shut the hell up for two goddamned seconds and let me talk to my son?"

Samno's face turned red. Even I knew not to push my mother this far, but he still wouldn't sit down. Or shut up. "With all due respect, ma'am, that kind of language—"

Mom shot him a look that could melt the polar ice caps. "Two. Seconds."

"Ma'am," Burke said. "I apologize for—"

"Sit down," Dad commanded. He spoke like he was giving orders to a new recruit. When the officers looked at him, my father met their gaze with steel in his eyes. "If there is a perfect example of how not to do this, you two turkeys are it."

"You ever lose anyone under your command?" Burke asked.

"I knew better before the first," Dad said. "And I never made excuses after the last."

"Last year, we almost—"

"Every day is almost," my father said. "The only easy day is yesterday. I also have five years sober, which means I can smell that clown from across the room. Now, sit down."

The sound of his voice sent a chill down my spine. My father had sucked all the air out of the room, and it had finally shut them up. As Burke and Samno slowly sat down, I felt my pounding heart echo in my head as a drop of sweat fell down my chest. I looked at Lisa, who seemed to be having as much trouble as I was trying to make sense of this mess.

"Mom," I managed to say. "I don't…This is…I just…"

She sighed, took a moment to compose herself. "Take all the time you need."

Passing the stairs, I saw Dorothy and Charlie coming inside the house. I wanted to say something to them but felt paralyzed. I could see in their eyes that they knew, but I just turned away as they started coming up the stairs. With trembling hands, I locked the bathroom door. As I splashed ice-cold water on my face, I craved the sensation. I wanted to feel something, nothing, anything but this impossible pain. My whole body began shaking. The tsunami was coming. Even as I tried to hold it back, the agony of my anguish grew in grunts and growls until I was seething so much I felt like my head was going to explode. It was exhausting.

When the wave of my grief had finally rolled back, I held myself up against the wall, my hands on either side of the mirror. I had whiskers. As my bloodshot eyes stared back at me, a burning rage rose from deep inside of me.

It wasn't just that Grandpa was gone, and it was no longer that he had been shot, but those officers, like Tim and his religion, had turned my nightmare into a horror story straight from hell. I wanted to beat that man to a pulp for laughing—until I remembered what Grandpa had told me years ago.

> "When a boy becomes a man, he must choose between the life he was given and who he wants to be. Remember who you want to be."

I wasn't yet a man, but I still had a choice. Our circumstances may shape us, but we do not have to let them define us; we have the power to remember who we want to be. Realizing that my father had pointed out that those two assholes were a perfect example of what not to do had somehow eased the burden; at least I knew I wasn't the only one who felt betrayed. I washed my face with soap and water and dried off. Reaching for the door, I saw that my hand was still trembling. I didn't want to go back out there, but I knew I couldn't hide forever. Taking a deep breath, I ran my fingers through my sweaty hair and opened the door, knowing that things couldn't possibly get any worse than they already were.

And I couldn't have been more wrong.

As it turned out, Charlie had learned about the shooting down at the Boat. Word had traveled fast with the First Lady in town, and it wasn't long before he had put it together. After seeing Grandpa's rusty, old pickup truck at the scene, Charlie soon realized that Grandpa was nowhere to be found. After work, he went to the condo to wait with Dorothy so that he could be there when we saw the eleven o'clock news. A television crew out of Hartford had come to Brockton that afternoon to cover the christening, but they ended up reporting Grandpa's murder as well. As I walked into the living room, I saw that Burke and Samno were standing, again, with Dad and Charlie beside them. I had never seen so many people at the house. I wanted all of them to leave, for things to go back to the way they had been before this night from hell.

"You okay, Roger?" James asked. I shook my head once and looked away from him.

"This is it," Charlie said as the picture came up on the television. I sat down on the couch next to Mom. "You should see me in there somewhere."

On the television, I saw Charlie standing behind the reporter, who was interviewing a witness. He was about Grandpa's age, with the same white hair, but he was clean-shaven and wearing sunglasses. It took a moment for the captioning to come up, but I caught his name on the screen: ADM. JOHN PATRICK "BULL" WELLINGTON (RET.)

"...only tell you that as a retired officer, and certainly as a private citizen now, I have a responsibility to honor the truth. I was in line behind him. He paid for his brake shoes, took the receipt, and then stepped aside to inspect them as I was buying my fuses. The clerk took the box and threw it away. So, he put the receipt and the springs in his shirt pocket and carried his brakes. He smiled when I opened the door for him. That's when I dropped my keys. Once I stepped outside, I saw him on the sidewalk, heading south past the intersection. A moment later, I saw the officer come into the intersection, also facing south, with his service weapon drawn. His cruiser was parked east on the side street—no siren, no lights. I heard him shouting, 'Drop it! Drop your weapon! Drop the knife!' He fired off four rounds and the gentleman fell down. Shot him in the back. Just like that, he was gone. Just like that."

"Oh...my...god!" Dorothy said.

What does that mean? I asked. "*What does that mean?*"

"Means you don't question an admiral," Dad said.

"Especially in Connecticut," Charlie added. "Christ, ain't this the shits?"

"Is there anything you can tell us about why he may have ignored the police officer's commands?" the reporter asked. Again, I saw Charlie appear behind her on the television.

"*He was deaf!*" Lisa screamed at the television. "*He wasn't ignoring anybody!*"

Burke and Samno turned red as cooked lobsters.

"Well, if you hear a policeman shouting 'drop your weapon' and you know you're not carrying a weapon, you have no reason to believe that officer is talking to you. I certainly know he wasn't carrying a weapon. Even from where I was standing, I could see clearly it wasn't a knife. He was just walking down the street. I saw the whole thing. It's tragic, just tragic. Later, on the scene, I gave the officer-in-charge my statement. Said he'd be in touch. I told him I'd never tolerate such a lack of discipline under my command. He sure seemed like a decent fellow. Friendly, had a nice smile. I hope—"

Dad shut off the television and turned toward the officers. "Time for you to leave."

"We're still in the process of—"

"Get the fuck out of my house!" my mother screamed. Jaws dropped, worlds collided, and entire galaxies disintegrated before her fury. She had screamed so loud my ears were ringing—and my heart was pounding so hard I felt the vibrations echo in my feet.

When I stood up, Dad immediately set his hand on my shoulder and pushed me right back down onto the couch. Mom, taking my hand, slowly shook her head. I was trembling as Dad and Charlie escorted the officers outside. Dad was walking behind them while Charlie took point. After I heard the screen door close, I just sat there, in shock, listening to my body tremble as Lisa wailed.

"Holy shit!" James finally said. "Holy fucking shit!"

On that hot summer night, the truth had stopped the Earth cold.

It was after one o'clock when Lisa left with George and Julie. Mom and Dad agreed to call an old friend in Elliott to be there for Aunt Carol. They didn't want her to be alone when she got the news. I didn't want to hear it again, not again, so I stepped outside with Tim and Junior. The humidity felt like soup. Dorothy had made a pitcher of iced tea (or "sweet tea," as she called it) and put on a pot of coffee while Mom sat at the table with Dad and everybody else, trying to decide what to do and when to take everybody home. Once James got back from the bathroom, the four of us walked out into the backyard and sat down on the hill in the grass. The stars glowed across the night sky as the tall trees stood cloaked in shadows.

"This can't be real," I said. My heart weighed a ton. "This is...I just saw him. Jesus, I saw him every day of my life. And now...now, I'll never see him."

"I can't believe it either," Tim said. "Police don't shoot unarmed citizens. It's illegal."

"Laws don't change hearts," Junior said. I tried to ask him what he meant, but Tim and James started arguing.

"It has to be a mistake," Tim said.

"Burnt toast is a mistake," James said, lighting a cigarette. He was sixteen now and could buy his own. "A fucking cop shooting an unarmed—"

"They don't just go around killing people," Tim shot back.

"You are so fucking naive."

"Okay, fine," Tim said. "So, one police officer makes a mistake and they're all bad?"

"Guys, stop," I said. But they kept arguing—and the more they argued, the more I got enraged. It was like Grandpa's whole life had been reduced to a sound-bite on a goddamned talk show. I kept trying to ask Junior what he meant, but Tim and James got so heated they were shouting over each other. I couldn't even hear half of what they were saying, but they had my blood boiling.

"Jesus, you still don't get it, do you?" James shouted. "Cops serve and protect cops before they ever serve and protect us. They got that fraternal mentality. Even the so-called good cops are guilty 'cause they empower the corrupt ones by their silence."

"I'm telling you," Tim said. "It has to be…I mean, did he have a gun or something?"

"Dude, you just saw the news," James said. "How fucking stupid do you have to be to not understand something you just saw with your own eyes?"

"Guys, cool it," Junior said, trying to keep the peace, but the shouting match had just gained another voice.

Finally, I had enough.

"Will you guys just shut the fuck up!" I snapped. James started to say something, but I wasn't having it. "Shut the fuck up! I mean, shit! You fucking guys are acting like you know my grandfather better than I do, like you know more about my experience than I do. You think because you have an opinion that the whole fucking world wants to hear it? Have a little fucking dignity, would you? The greatest man I have ever known is dead! Dead! The least you could do is show an ounce of fucking decency instead of spewing your goddamned bullshit opinions like some fucking cultist on a no-good, goddamned daytime fucking talk show!"

I knew that there were crickets chirping, but I could only hear my ears ringing.

"Feel better, man?" James finally said.

"Fuck you."

"Thought so," James said, smiling.

Tim said something, but I didn't hear it. "What?"

"I said, 'I'm sorry.'"

"Yeah? Well, I've been trying to ask Junior a question for ten fucking minutes, but you fucking guys just kept going on, making snap judgments about everything you know nothing about. You didn't know him like I did. Nobody knew him like I did. Nobody."

The humidity had completely soaked my T-shirt; it was hotter than hell, but I was freezing.

"What was your question?" Junior said. He was calm, cool. When I asked what he had meant about laws not changing anything, Junior told us about the time he had gone to Texas to visit his family. The schools had been integrated by that time, he said, but nothing had changed because of redistricting. While it had become illegal to segregate public schools, there was no law that required whites to live in the same neighborhood as blacks. When his aunt and uncle had first moved into the neighborhood, they had endured endless harassment from their white neighbors until another family moved into the same neighborhood. Within a few years, all the white people had left. "They call it 'white flight' down there, stupid white people so damned scared they leave as soon as we start showing up."

"So, the law changed," I realized, "but the people didn't."

"It's all the same as it ever was," Junior said. "To see that place…man, you'd never even know Dr. King had a dream."

"What does all this have to do with…with tonight?" James asked, glancing at me.

"You remember all those civil rights films we saw in school?" Junior said. "White police officers beating and dragging and hosing my people. Siccing vicious dogs on us, chewing apart girls and grandmothers. You think all that changed just because a couple laws got passed? I mean, you guys think because it doesn't happen to you that it never happens to anybody. Happens to us all the time. This is just the first time I ever heard about it happening to a white person."

"Don't forget, he was deaf," James said. He lit a cigarette and handed it to me. "And those fucking cops don't know sign language."

My mind was reeling. "Junior, how did…How do you even deal with all that?"

"I got my people," he said. "There's a reason we call each other 'brother.' We stick together. Shit, man, even if our parents don't give us the talk, we get it from each other. We all know."

"Jesus fucking Christ," I whispered. He had opened my mind.

"Welcome to my world, man," Junior said. "Welcome to my world."

I spent the next few days (or maybe it was weeks) at the condo with Dad and Dorothy while Lisa stayed with Mom. Once my mother had identified Grandpa's body, she made arrangements to fly to Pittsburgh with Lisa because Grandpa had wanted to be buried with Grandma and Uncle William. Mom had insisted that I drive out with Dad, and we stopped at the house before leaving so I could pack. I took my time getting my clothes together; it felt like the whole world was moving in slow motion. When Dad went to the station to fill up, I called Allyson. Her mother answered and told me to hold on a second.

"I haven't heard from you," Allyson said. "I thought you forgot about me."

"I'm sorry I haven't called. I just…it's just a lot has happened."

"I know," she said. It took me a moment to realize she thought I was talking about us. I honestly didn't know how to tell her about Grandpa until she said, "Can you believe tomorrow is the first day of school?"

"Not really," I said. "I have to go to my grandpa's funeral."

"Oh, my god! I'm so sorry. What happened?"

Hearing her ask that question made me feel the sharp, stabbing answer.

"He…he went to South Brockton to get brakes for his truck," I managed to say, "and a police officer shot him."

"Oh, my god!" Allyson said again. She started talking about her uncle in Wisconsin, who was a cop. He had told her that police were trained to avoid confrontation; they would never shoot somebody without a reason. She asked if Grandpa had a gun. Or were the police after somebody else? Had Grandpa got caught in a crossfire? Or ignored the officer? She had so many questions I felt that burning rage rise inside me yet again as I realized that Allyson was more concerned about what had happened than she was with what I was feeling. Finally, I told her that I didn't want to talk about it. "Well, you know I'm here for you," she said, "if you want."

The sound of her words hung in the air, like she was making a demand. I did want to talk to somebody, but I sure as hell couldn't talk to her.

"Look, Ally, I just…I have to finish packing. We're leaving for Pennsylvania any minute now. I'll call you when I get back, okay? Promise."

"I wish there was something I could do for you," Allyson said. "You don't think this kind of thing ever happens to you. It's usually just something you see on the news. You know, I always used to see my pop at Christmas, and, well, sometimes on my birthday, but I don't think he'll make it this year because we're in Connecticut…"

I wanted to scream. "Ally, I…really have to go."

After finally getting off the phone, I went back to packing as her words echoed in my head. Jesus, did she even believe me? How could I expect her to be there for me if she was so…so centered? It was as if Grandpa wasn't a person to her, like his whole life had been reduced to a single moment. Going to the kitchen, I glanced at the clock on the stove. It was taking Dad forever to get back; he probably had to make sure Dorothy and Amos could handle things while he was gone. I was trying to make a fluffernutter when the phone rang. Thinking it was Allyson, I answered and said, "The funeral is in three days. I told you I have to finish packing!"

"Excuse me?" It was a man's voice.

"I'm sorry," I said. "I thought you were somebody else. Who—?"

He said something about calling from the office of an attorney or some kind of general, but I didn't hear him because he had been talking over me. "Is Mrs. Evans home?"

"She's not in right now," I said. "Can I take a message?"

"Is this Mr. Evans?" he asked.

"Yes," I said. "I am Mr. Evans."

"I'm calling to confirm your appointment next week regarding the incident in South Brockton. We hope to—"

"Incident? Incident!"

"Mistake?"

"Motherfucker, burnt toast is a mistake! When you forget to add the fucking fabric softener, that's a fucking mistake! When a police officer, a police officer who gets paid—who gets fucking paid!—to protect the public shoots and fucking kills an innocent, unarmed, deaf, private citizen who happens to be a World War II veteran that liberated Dachau, that ain't no goddamned 'mistake,' you stupid fuck! Fuck you and the horse you rode in on, you mother…fucker!"

I slammed the phone down several times trying to hang up. When the receiver fell to floor, I stopped and closed my eyes, holding out my hands to keep the rising, raging tsunami at bay. After a few deep breaths, I picked up the phone and went back to making my fluffernutter. My hands were shaking so badly I couldn't spread the damned fluff. The bread came up in clumps until finally I just mushed the mess together and rolled it up into a ball. Once I sat down, I pushed the ball of bread away because I still couldn't eat.

All I could think about was Grandpa. He could throw a perfect strike across the plate but would flip a scoop of ice cream and always miss the mug. No matter how many times he'd tried to catch that ice cream he never could get it. That was always the joke, like Charlie Brown trying to kick that football. Grandpa had never given up on anything, though. He was a brave man. He had learned a whole new language in his old age and even fell in love again after losing his wife and son. As I sat there staring at my fluffernutter, I remembered the day Grandpa had explained to me to write things down. "If there's anything you want, anything at all, just write it down. Okay, buddy?"

You love fluffernutters, I signed. *Why did they kill you? Why why why!*

The doorbell rang. I wiped the tears from my cheeks.

"It's open," I called, thinking it was Dad. I was getting a paper towel to blow my nose when I saw her coming up the stairs. "Ally, what…what are you doing here?"

"I rode my bike," she said. She was out of breath and sweating. "I…I'm sorry about your grandfather."

"Ally, look, I…I'm leaving as soon as…"

She put her hands on my neck and softly kissed my cheek, but I stood as still as a stone. After a moment, she asked me again what happened.

"Ally, I just told you."

"But, did he have a gun or something?"

"Obviously, if he shot him."

"Oh, my god! Your grandfather shot a cop?"

"What are you talking about? What the fuck are you talking about? No, my grandfather didn't shoot a cop! He didn't even have a gun! I already told you that!"

"Well, there has to be a reason! Police just don't go around killing people!"

"This one did," I snapped. "I already went through this shit with Tim. Look, I…Ally, I just told you I don't want to talk about it. We went over this. We just went over this. We literally just went over this! I already told you, he wasn't armed. Besides, a witness saw the whole thing. A witness who happens to be a retired admiral. You want to argue with an admiral? Be my guest. All I know is a goddamned cop murdered my grandfather in cold fucking blood, all right? End of fucking story! Jesus!"

"I'm sorry."

When Allyson realized what she had done, she started crying. So, of course, I held her in arms. She had come to comfort me, or so I thought, but instead I was the one who had to comfort her.

And I hated her for it.

The pounding rain had finally let up as Dad pulled into The Way to Go. The restaurant looked completely different coming out of the dark, dense fog. There were only a few truckers inside, drinking coffee and smoking cigarettes at the counter. We took a seat in a booth. Dad hadn't said much of anything since we left Poquanicut. When I got up to go to the bathroom, he asked me what I wanted. "In case the waitress comes."

"Midnight Special," I told him. "French toast, home fries, eggs, and bacon. Anything to drink but New Coke."

Inside the bathroom, I splashed water on my face again as my tears burned my bloodshot eyes. I hadn't eaten anything since Dorothy had made me a meatloaf sandwich two days ago. Or was it three days ago? I was so hungry it was painful, but my appetite was gone. Running my fingers through my hair, I pushed the button on the electric air dryer and held my face above the hot air. Cool tears glided along my temples, but the pain would not be washed away. Back at the table, Dad was reading a newspaper and eating. I wondered how he could be so cold; he hadn't shown one sign of anguish whatsoever. But why should I be surprised Dad didn't care that Grandpa was gone? He never cared about anything anyway.

"One of your teachers stopped by the station before we left," he said. "Mr. Lamb, I think it was. Said his first name was Wallace. Something like that. Anyways, he knows what's going on and that you won't be in school for a couple of days."

"Okay," I said, playing with my food.

He folded the newspaper and set it down. "You really should eat something."

When I told him I wasn't hungry, he pulled the old I-paid-for-it-so-you'd-better-eat-it bit.

"Fine," I said, reaching for my Velcro wallet. "I'll pay for it."

"Roger, that's not the point. You need to eat."

"Don't you even care what happened?"

"Of course," he said calmly. "But I'm still your father and I still have a responsibility."

"I know, eat." I told myself that I was only going to have one bite of French toast, but finally getting food in my stomach gave me the urge to fill it. The syrup smelled delicious. When I finished eating, I decided to ask my father, "Does this… this ever get any easier when you get older?"

"Nope," he said quietly, shaking his head. "Truth be told, sooner or later you learn some things just don't make sense. That I learned a long time ago."

"What do you mean?"

He lit a cigarette. "I have been through the fire before."

"In Vietnam?"

"That's not important," he said. "Besides, you have enough going on right now."

"Dad, come on. I mean, I've seen these old photographs of you and Mom and you both seemed so happy. So, what happened?"

"You really want to know?"

"Yeah, I really want to know."

He took a drag from his cigarette and twirled the end to a point in the ashtray.

"I have the same nightmare every night," Dad said. He told me about his last mission in Vietnam. He was under fire while running through the jungle, heading to the extraction point, when the booby trap went off. He wasn't sure who had tripped it, but it was either him or First Class Petty Officer Alan Aaron Anderson from Effingham, Illinois, because they were the only ones who had survived the mission. The explosion had shredded the skin on my father's leg, and he still had shrapnel in his body because of it. That, he said, was why he never wore shorts. When Dad reached Anderson, he realized that the explosion had shattered the back of his skull. "I was holding what was left of his brain in my hands."

"Jesus."

"We used to call him Trip," he said, taking a drag from his cigarette. "Short for triple-A, after his initials. His eye sockets was hollow. And every night…every night those empty eyes…they stare back at me. Hollow eyes filled with darkness. They just get bigger until they swallow me and…"

"And?"

"And then I wake up."

"How did you get out of there?"

"Wasn't easy," he said. "Explosion gave away our position. Few seconds later, had a gun to my head. They wanted a prisoner. I was the only one left. So…"

He looked down at his tattoo.

"That's how your knuckles got flat," I realized.

He nodded. "I disarmed them and…and then I beat those men to death. Smashed their skulls just like that explosion had shattered Trip's skull. By that time, of course, I'd had enough of that whole goddamned war. Hell of a thing."

"Hell of a thing," I repeated. As we sat there, I took a cigarette from his pack and lit it. He never said anything about my smoking. As the buzz hit, I felt a sense of relief. I realized that my father was still fighting his own battle, even though the war had ended long ago. The front lines were now the memories of the horrors he had endured, and as a child I had seen his trauma consume him. "Any regrets?"

"Losing my men," he said, sipping his coffee. "That and by the time you do what it takes to be a hero, you don't want to be a hero."

"What do you mean?"

"The Navy wanted a commitment," Dad said, "and I gave them a commitment. Nobody ever told me that I would lose the family I had enlisted to support and protect in the first place. Wasn't until your grandfather opened up about his time in Europe that I realized I wasn't alone. That war had haunted him too. So, he put me in touch with a group of veterans, guys who had their own horror stories, like I got mine. Unfortunately, by that time, it was too late. Your mother had filed for divorce and your life, as you knew it, was over."

"I think that was the beginning of the end."

"After this, probably," he said. "I suppose I got off lucky with the divorce, though. Not just because I deserved worse, but..."

"What?"

"Well, few weeks ago, there was an article in the newspaper about how three times as many veterans have committed suicide since the war ended than actually got killed in combat. You believe that? They're still killing us..."

I suddenly remembered the night I saw blood dripping from his wrist, falling onto the cream tile floor in the kitchen. I was scared to death to ask, but he knew what I was thinking.

"Oh, I'm all right," Dad said. "I still have flashbacks, but that's about it."

"Flashbacks?"

"A loud noise will bring back a memory. Fireworks. A storm. Storms do it. It's—" He stopped talking when the waitress came by to check on us. Dad just stirred his coffee, his black coffee, and told her we were fine. After she left, I realized that he had avoided her on purpose. "People don't need to know everything."

"Including women?"

"Especially women," he said. When I asked what he meant, Dad told me about the first time I had gone stomping off to my room as a child. My mother was furious because I had left the table, but Dad wanted to know what was wrong. Before he could ask, though, my mother got up, dragged me back, and scolded me for leaving. She was so upset she had even berated my father for being concerned about me. "That was the first time I saw my life through your eyes 'cause my father used to do the same thing to me when I was that age."

"How old was I?"

"You was four."

"Sneakers," I said. The memory had just emerged. "I had new sneakers. I remember how strange they felt strange on my feet because they weren't broken in yet. I was walking down the hall, crying, and...and my shoelace was untied. And I remember thinking that I should tie it because I could trip, but I didn't care. I didn't care if I got hurt..."

"Because you were hurt and you thought nobody cared," Dad said. "You know, your mother always had a habit of scolding me whenever I tried to do what I thought was best. If I didn't do something exactly the way she did it, she'd treat me like I was useless. Stupid, even. I tried to stop it. Tried to stop it that day you went storming off to your room, but…man, she'd just let me have it. We learn at a very early age that if something is important to us, it... it's just not important to the people around us. We have to be there for them, but they're never there for us. Not in all the ways that matter, that would help."

"Is that why you never talked to Mom about it? About the war?"

"We're taught not to talk about it," he said. "Far as she was concerned, the war was over. She didn't understand what it did to me. That just made it that much worse. Compounds the pain, the trauma, the memories. When the people you try to talk to about your pain just add to it, sooner or later you learn it's just easier not to say anything. Less painful, less of a hassle. Starts when we're young. Boys don't go stomping off to their rooms because we're angry. We do it because we have already learned that nobody listens to us, and that…that's why we're angry. A lifetime of being ignored can have toxic side effects."

The weight of his words pressed upon me as I thought of Allyson's reaction. I had needed to talk about Grandpa, but when I tried, she'd just driven me to silence. My problems and my feelings obviously didn't matter to her. If I wasn't going to get better unless I talked about it, how could I talk about it if she didn't listen? It was all so hopeless. I still couldn't process what had happened to Grandpa, much less my father's lesson or his confession. Like Junior, he had overloaded my mind.

That was the first time I began to understand the duality of human nature, how my father had been the vicious drunk who broke my mother's nose as well as the wounded veteran whose nightmares never went away. He had been born with the potential to be angry and cruel but also loving and kind. The more I thought about it, the more I realized that was true for everybody.

But the war had twisted my father. It wasn't just his trauma that drove him to drink, but also the limits and expectations in which my mother had imprisoned him. Unwilling to see the depths of his pain, my mother had confined my father to a dungeon of isolation. She had wanted their life to be the way it had been, but after the war that was impossible. Like me and Allyson, my father couldn't talk to my mother about what was haunting him either. But the divorce had forced my father to face his demons on his own, and, to his credit, Dad got sober and started counseling and attending Alcoholics Anonymous meetings.

Until that night, I had only seen my father as my dad; I hadn't realized who he was, much less what he had been through, before I was born. For so long, I had condemned my father as the monster he was instead of the man he had become. He was still my father, but he had been a son, a husband, a best friend, and a Navy SEAL as well. He had his own burden to bear, just as I now had to bear the burden of Grandpa's death. When we were ready to go, Dad gave me money to pay the bill so he could use the restroom. I forgot the receipt on the table, but he handed it to me at the register.

"You can't pay the bill if she doesn't know how much it is," he said. "Didn't your mother ever teach you—Roger, what's so funny?"

"She said the same thing about you the last time I was here," I told him, still laughing. "I don't know why you ever got divorced. Between the two of you, I never learned anything."

I woke up at sunrise, shaking off yet another nightmare, when we finally got to Aunt Carol's house. Dad hadn't said much of anything since the diner, and the endless interstate drifting through the darkness had consumed me. My nightmares haunted me all the time now, like demons in my mind. I could never remember them, but always I woke up feeling that same terrible moment I'd known just before that deer had been shot at Ledge Lake. That same feeling lingered as I thought about what my father had said last night. Nightmares, I realized, were inevitable.

Aunt Carol, with tears in her eyes, came down the concrete steps and gave me a hug, rocking me gently without a word. Dad gave her a hug and said that he needed to get to bed. Mom and Lisa were still sleeping. After we brought the suitcases inside the house, Aunt Carol made a pitcher of iced tea and got a couple of glasses. We sat down on the front porch. She was wearing a pair of blue jeans and a white V-neck; it was the first time I had seen her in short sleeves. There was a small tattoo on her left forearm, a faded series of numbers. She had salt-and-pepper hair now but still wore her old rosary.

"How are you holding up?" Aunt Carol asked.

"I guess I'm still trying to process it," I said. "I mean, I…the one person who was supposed to protect him made a deliberate decision to...to kill him."

"A badge is only as good as the one behind it," Aunt Carol told me. "And a man in uniform can be as bad as any man can be. Man or woman. As good, as horrible. Horrifying. A badge, a uniform, a flag…such things are only as good, and always as bad, as those who wield them. People don't change just because they put on a uniform or wear a badge or carry a flag. Those things, for better and for worse, just accelerate our character, but often reveal the darkness of who we are."

I wanted to ask her about the Holocaust but remembered my mother's warning. I had read *The Diary of Anne Frank* in school and my English teacher had shown us a film about the Holocaust. For as long as I live, I will never forget seeing hundreds of skin-and-bone dead bodies lying naked in the concentration camps, being buried in massive graves. At the very least, I had come to understand why Aunt Carol never wanted to talk about her experience. It was difficult enough for me to understand what had happened to Grandpa, but the pain of six million Jews, including her own family, being systematically murdered was light-years beyond my comprehension—and my judgment. Slowly, I reached across the table and gently set my hand upon hers. Aunt Carol squeezed so hard her knuckles turned white, like she couldn't bear the thought of letting go.

As we sat in the early morning stillness, I looked out across the street. At the base of the mountain stood the Ridgway Company, where Grandpa and Dad used to work. The old brick building, once the center of economic life of Elliott, was closed and shuttered. A car drove by on the street below us. As the sound faded, the silence grew peaceful. My left ear started ringing.

"It's so quiet here."

"Sometimes I get up early just to hear the birds sing," Aunt Carol said. But I couldn't hear them. "It relaxes me. I used to listen for them when I was a child. That's how I knew we were far from the war. Are you hungry?"

"Not really," I told her. "We stopped at a diner."

"How did that go?" she asked. Somehow, Aunt Carol always had a way of knowing things without my ever telling her. It was weird.

"I don't know how he does it," I said. "I mean, I'm still in shock, I think, but there are times it seems like it's just another day to him…"

"Don't compare," Aunt Carol said, shaking her head. "It is foolish to compare."

When I asked her what she meant, Aunt Carol said that Mom and Uncle William had shared the same womb at the same time, had the same birthday, and so many of the same experiences. But they were still different people who had to interpret those events, and that led to each of them having different memories of the same experience. Grief, she said, was like that as well. Nobody has the same relationship with the same person, even if they share the same experiences. "Nobody grieves in quite the same way because nobody ever loves the same person in quite the same way," she said.

"I guess I never thought about it like that before."

"The world is a pretty big place," Carol said, sipping her tea. "And it is a fool's errand to presume people must think and act or believe as you do. The only people who won't change are the ones who want everybody else to change."

When she let out a long sigh, I asked, "Have you been sleeping?"

"I'm fine," she said. "I just…I wanted so much to protect you from these horrors…"

"Aunt Carol, you didn't have anything to do with what happened."

Wiping her eyes, she inhaled sharply as her body became stiff again. After a moment, she exhaled and took another sip of her iced tea. She pointed out the Ridgway Company.

"Your grandfather used to run that place," Aunt Carol said. "He was the youngest of five children. They've all passed on; his brothers were lost in the wars, but his sister had tuberculosis. That's why he went to work so soon. He started when he was seven years old, just after the United States had entered the First World War. He'd run errands for the plant manager in town, getting stamps, mailing invoices, counting stock, that sort of thing. By the time he took over, he knew exactly what they needed before they needed it. He kept it all in his head. Everything."

"That's where they made batteries for the old diesel submarines, right?"

She nodded. "He grew up during World War I and helped his father make moonshine during Prohibition. Later, he endured the Great Depression. That's why he saved every penny he could. He never even bought a car until he moved to Connecticut. Kept that old pickup running for years…"

"The same truck he has now?"

"Same truck," she said. "After the attack on Pearl Harbor, he got drafted when William and Mary were barely out of diapers. They sent him to Europe—"

"That's where he found you."

"—and when he got back home, he worked three jobs. He delivered newspapers in the morning, worked all day at Ridgway, and then he'd deliver the mail. After the Navy transitioned to nuclear power, the plant closed, and he became postmaster. He was deaf by that time, of course, but he was the only one in town who knew the job. People knew they had to write things down for him."

"Did he ever have any trouble?"

"Every week some moron would make a fuss about him being deaf," she said. "But he put up a sign at the counter telling people to turn on a light switch he installed that was connected a lamp in the back. That way, he'd know when he had a customer. He'd just point to the sign and hand them a pencil and a piece of scrap paper. A lot has changed over the years. When he was born, all these streets were made of brick, filled with the horse and buggy, but he lived to see a man set foot on the moon."

"Hard to believe," I said. "Horse and buggy to a man on the moon..."

"Imagine what your children will live to see."

"Can you tell me more about him?"

"He always thought he'd stay in Elliott," Aunt Carol said. "Because his great-grandfather built this house, but he retired and moved to Connecticut after you were born. If things had gone differently, you would have grown up here in Elliott."

"You mean, if the plant had stayed open?"

"That's one way of looking at it," she told me. "But it has been said that one never really has a choice because nobody truly knows the outcome of any decision until the consequences arise. And now...we know. I don't think I ever really understood that until just last week..."

As tears welled up in her eyes, I asked, "Aunt Carol, are you going to be okay?"

"I tried," she said. "I swear, I tried..."

"It's going to be okay," I told her. But I didn't believe it—and I knew she didn't either; I just knew that, somehow, we both needed to believe it. Reaching over, I gently wiped away a tear falling down her cheek. She smiled.

"Your mother is so proud of you," she told me. "She knows you will be a good man."

The hot air rose from the blacktop like a fog as we made our way into the funeral home. My T-shirt was sticking to my back, and I felt like my tie was choking me. Aunt Carol had bought the suit for me the other day, and she ended up getting me some new school clothes as well. Mom and Dad wanted me to escort Aunt Carol while they went in with Lisa. The cool air inside the funeral home was a welcome relief, but the sudden change in temperature made me dizzy.

Old black-and-white photographs of Grandpa had been placed upon tables at the entrance. They told the story of his life. As a child, his smile had been filled with joy, and I saw that same hope when Grandpa and Grandma cut their wedding cake and when Mom and Uncle William were kids. As Grandpa got older, though, I could see that the seasons had pressed upon him through the wars, the loss of his brothers, his wife, and his son. I stared at every photograph, wanting to memorize every detail. The hall was lined with Polaroid photographs of me and Grandpa. On my first day of kindergarten, in 1975, I looked ridiculous wearing plaid pants and that great big belt, but I still had a huge smile on my face standing next to Grandpa. We both looked so happy I couldn't believe that kid was me.

"I'm so glad he finally had that," Mom said.

"What?" I asked.

"Had the chance to be there for you," she said. Mom told me that Grandpa had always left for work by the time she and William had to get up for school, and he was still there when they got home. After I was born, and Mom saw Grandpa out there every day waiting for the bus to pick me up and drop me off, she realized just how much he had wanted to do that for his own kids. Being a grandfather made up for all the time he had lost being a father. "It was really something, seeing that."

"We should get in there," Aunt Carol said. As Mom and Dad made their way into the parlor, I saw Lisa laughing with an old man. He was wearing a military dress uniform and only had one arm.

"You must be the grandson I heard so much about."

"The one and only."

Lisa introduced us. "Roger, I'd like you to meet Sergeant Ziminsky. He's retired."

"Call me Frank," the man said, holding out his stump. He seemed surprised to see it. "What the hell? When did that happen?"

Lisa laughed. "You were just telling me about it."

"So I was. That's right! Old Wild Bill and me, we took the same bullet. Nicked his temple and made me a lefty."

"Did you really forget what happened?" I asked.

"Course not. Didn't anybody ever tell you that laughter is the best medicine?"

"Not lately," I said. "How in the world did he get the nickname Old Wild Bill?"

"Because he was so wild over there it was enough to make us old."

"It's time," Aunt Carol said, nodding toward the parlor. As we walked in, I saw the casket surrounded by flowers and covered in an American flag. In the center, upon the casket, was that same black-and-white photograph of Grandpa and Aunt Carol, taken the day he had found her at Dachau. It was the one I had seen so often at Grandpa's house. I was relieved to know that he would be remembered as a hero, one who had saved the life of a little

Jewish girl from the horrors of Nazi Germany—and he had loved her as his own daughter.

"He always said you were the best thing he ever did over there," I whispered to Aunt Carol. Tears welled up in her eyes as I kissed her cheek.

Most of the people had already sat down, but there were two empty seats next to Mom and Dad—front and center reserved just for us. Mom was sitting with her head down, crying quietly. Dad put his arm around Mom, who leaned into him. Watching my father comfort my mother as she cried on his shoulder, I realized that despite all the anger and arguments they'd had, my parents still came together when they really needed each other. The love they shared for Grandpa had somehow brought back their love for each other.

Maybe being a family meant being there for each other when you have to endure a pain greater than the suffering you've caused. Maybe my mother had forgiven my father after all. Maybe my parents really did still love each other, but that love had simply taken a different shape through the years.

And I loved them both. I did.

Looking around the crowded room, I realized that everyone here had known Grandpa at one time or another. As I slowly led Aunt Carol to her seat, I could feel the muscles in my back tensing up. Lisa reached for my hand, and I could feel her shaking.

"Why?" I whispered. I didn't think anyone had heard me, but Sergeant Ziminsky had said that it was Grandpa's time. I turned around and said, "It was his time?"

"Best answer that never satisfied anybody."

The sun was setting as the guns exploded in Grandpa's salute. The shock echoed through me like a thunderbolt. My whole body trembled. After the second volley, I closed my eyes and imagined Grandpa walking to his truck, carrying his brake pads. I felt his plea in his pain as the bullets struck his back. He fell, helpless and alone, as confused as he was horrified. Now, the same violence that took him from me was being used to salute his life. As the smoke slowly drifted away, and people started to leave, Mom handed me the folded American flag that had been over his casket. "He would have wanted you to have it," she whispered, kissing my cheek.

A chill as cold as ice ran down my spine.

It was all so much, it was just too much.

Taking a deep breath, I held the flag against my heart and ran my fingers along the edge of the casket. In the distance, I saw Mom and Carol talking to

Sergeant Ziminsky and a few other people. Dad was walking to his truck. I paused a moment and stared at Uncle William's gravestone, which was right next to Grandpa and Grandma's. At least they were, in some way, together. *Goodbye, buddy.*

Somebody put their hand on my shoulder.

"Are you going to be all right?" Lisa asked.

Pushing the tsunami back, I took a deep breath as we started walking. "Nope."

"It takes time," she said. "George and Julie send their condolences. They wanted to be here, but they had to go to their daughter's wedding in Washington, DC."

"I wish my mother had learned sign language sooner," I said. "They were times they were so isolated because of it."

"Hearing people have a lifetime of habits that they learned just as surely as they ascertained their ability to speak," Lisa said. "You know that when someone becomes deaf like your grandfather did, everyone is affected. Sometimes it's hard for people to accept. Communication makes everything possible—television, space shuttles, vaccines…you name it. Your grandfather was a great man because he had the courage to learn to live with his deafness. He never denied who he was becoming but accepted and embraced it."

"Yeah," I said. "He was the best. I'm really glad you could make it, Lisa."

"I had to be here," she said. *First time I saw him I felt like a little schoolgirl who had a crush. He was so handsome. I loved him so much. I never thought I could after losing my husband, but…I loved him.*

I know, I signed. *And I know he loved you too.*

Lisa leaned against my shoulder as her grief rose. I held her as she soaked my shoulder with her tears. After a few moments, she composed herself. I invited her back to Aunt Carol's house, but she had booked a late flight back to Connecticut that night. Dad held the door open for us as we got in the limousine with Mom and Aunt Carol. Parked cars lined the sides of the streets around Aunt Carol's house; she had invited everyone over after the funeral. After dinner, Dad and I were in the living room trying to watch TV, but Mr. Rosten and Sergeant Ziminsky fought like the Hatfields and McCoys.

"Hey, Frank," Mr. Rosten said. "You remember what the 49ers did in the Super Bowl, don't you? As god is my witness, they'll do it again."

"Montana got lucky and you know it!"

"Don't be such a lousy loser! They won, didn't they? You're not stupid enough to think Chicago's gonna do it this year, are ya?"

"I'll bet you my Social Security that it comes down to New England and Chicago! And Chicago's gonna kill 'em!"

"Only if William 'The Refrigerator' Perry swallows a vat of beans before kickoff!"

I couldn't stand listening to them anymore, so I went into the kitchen to get something to drink. Mom, Aunt Carol, and a few other women were sitting at the kitchen table drinking coffee. I got a jug of orange juice from the fridge.

"…don't know yet," Aunt Carol was saying. "We're still waiting to hear from the attorney general."

"General?" I said, getting a glass. "Somebody called about that before we left."

"Was it the attorney general?" Mom asked.

"I don't know. He just said he was calling from the office for a general or something. He might have said he was an attorney. I thought it was Allyson…"

"Why didn't you tell me?" Mom demanded.

"What did he say?" Aunt Carol asked.

"He said he wanted to talk about the mistake in South Brockton."

"Roger, what did you tell him?" Mom asked.

"I told him burnt toast is a mistake."

Mom couldn't believe it. "You told the attorney general burnt toast is a mistake?"

"Well, isn't it?"

"What else did he say?" Aunt Carol asked. "What else did you say?"

"I don't know," I said, pouring a glass of orange juice.

"Roger, I need to know," Mom warned. I could tell she was getting upset. "Now, think. What else did he say? What did you tell him?"

I was so thirsty I drank the whole glass. "Well, I may have told him to go fuck himself."

"You what!" Mom shot back in shock.

"And the horse he rode in on. What?"

"Well, he is a politician," Mrs. Rosten said. "Why, I've wanted to tell them that for years."

"That's true," Mrs. Ziminsky agreed. "After all, they certainly deserve it."

Mom was furious. "You told…you actually told the attorney general for the state of Connecticut to—you better not be serious right now, Roger!"

"Why?" I asked. When Mom got up, Aunt Carol told her to use the upstairs phone as she flew through the living room and marched up the stairs. "What? Well, who is he? What's going on?"

"It's nothing you need to be concerned about, Roger," Aunt Carol told me.

"I don't even know what's going on," I said.

Mrs. Ziminsky started to say something when Aunt Carol cut her off. Soon, they were both interrupting each other, and then all three of them started talking over one another so much that I couldn't hear what any of them were saying. I was pouring another glass of orange juice when the men roared. That got the women's attention.

"My goodness," Mrs. Rosten said. "They've been fighting like that for years."

Aunt Carol said she was surprised they hadn't killed each other.

"No kidding," Mrs. Ziminsky said.

"Aunt Carol, please don't let me end up like those old fogies."

She spit up her coffee and the other women laughed so loud they drowned out the men. Mrs. Rosten put her hands on my cheeks and kissed me. Her puckered lips looked like plastic.

"You hear that, boys?" Mrs. Rosten called. The men suddenly shut up and turned toward the kitchen. "Roger says he doesn't want to end up like you two old fogies!"

"Aw, get the hell outta here!" Mr. Rosten shouted. "I got underwear older than that kid."

"So do I," Sergeant Ziminsky said. "And I'll bet that kid don't know his bat from his balls!"

"Show's over, boys," Aunt Carol said in exasperation. She got up and grabbed their coats. "It's a long way back to Connecticut, and they're leaving in the morning."

Mr. Rosten called her a party pooper.

Before dawn, Dad and I loaded our luggage into his truck. Aunt Carol had got up to cook breakfast for us and made us brown-bag lunches while Dad was in the shower. Mom, still sleeping, had a late flight that evening. As Carol gave me a hug, I didn't want to leave because I knew Grandpa wouldn't be there when I got home. I slept most of the way, the endless interstate consuming me yet again.

When I finally got back to Poquanicut, I took a deep breath and let it out slow. The house smelled different, the stale scent of Grandpa's pipe still lingering in the air. As I walked through the living room, feeling the furniture and the rug beneath my bare feet, I remembered all the good times Grandpa and I had had together—playing cards, watching the Red Sox, going down to the baseball field, learning Sign, making popcorn, fixing things up—it was like I could still sense his presence around the house. I slumped in his chair, set the recliner back, and then quickly got up; Grandpa had never let anyone sit in his chair. After making a root beer float, I held up my mug and gave a toast. *Here's to you, buddy.*

The tears burned my eyes.

Later, when I was unpacking, Allyson called. I stretched the telephone cord from Mom's room to mine so I could finish.

"I'm glad you're home," she said. "I wanted to apologize for the way I acted."

"Don't worry about it," I said. "This…it's just difficult for everybody."

"It is," she said. There was a pause. "I'm really sorry, Roger…"

"Don't worry about it," I told her again. There were two boxes of condoms stuffed inside my suitcase. "Guess what I just found?"

"What'd you find?"

"It looks like someone invaded my privacy again in the name of AIDS prevention."

"Birth control," Allyson insisted. "Why would they worry about HIV, or AIDS, when you've only been with me and I've only been with you? Unless you've had a transfusion of tainted blood or you're sharing needles like they mentioned in that health class at school last year. But maybe they don't know we've only been with each other."

"I doubt that," I said. "I mean, if somebody went through all this trouble, it's a good bet they know what else is going on."

"Do you want me to come over?"

After what happened last time, I honestly had to think about it for moment. In the end, I decided I didn't want to be alone. "Okay."

"You still don't know who is doing it?" Allyson asked.

"I know it's not my grandfather," I said. "I guess we're down to my mother and my father. But this time it might have been my aunt. I don't know. Maybe this is what the tooth fairy does when you get older."

She laughed. We met near the house being built on Three Streets Circle. The leaves of the trees were cloaked in the shadows of the night and the stars in the deep-blue sky were starting to come out. Allyson said that Rachel could give me a ride to school in the morning, as long as I was ready on time, and that she was also going out with Tim. They had a math class together and had spent the whole day at Brockton Long Point. Allyson hated being home when her parents were fighting. She thought for sure they'd be divorced by now, but they just kept arguing with each other. Allyson didn't want to live like that.

"Let's talk about something else," she said, holding my arm. "How was the funeral? Are you okay?"

"I don't want to talk about it," I said. "It's all I've thought about the past few days. Or weeks. Or whatever it's been. I don't even know."

"As long as you're sure," she said.

"I am."

"Okay," she said. "Well, I heard they found the *Titanic*."

"Yeah, I saw that in the newspaper. It was, what? Two miles down? I bet they'll do a documentary about it, probably a movie-of-the-week too."

Allyson tugged my arm; we stopped walking. "Let's say they do make a movie about *Titanic*. Let's go see it together, even if it's twenty years from now…"

"Ally, I'll be thirty-five," I said. "That's so old."

"So what! I want you to promise me that we'll go. Whatever we're doing, wherever we are, we'll forget about it for one night and go and see that movie!"

"What if it's awful?"

"We'll go anyway. Because it makes a hell of a lot more sense than spending your life screaming at somebody you're supposed to love, doesn't it?"

"Okay," I said. But I knew it didn't matter; it was just what she wanted to hear.

"God, I don't want to end up like my parents!"

"You won't," I told her. We sat down on the hill behind the house. It was dusk, and the constellations were beginning to take shape. The yard, like everything, seemed smaller. "It's hard to believe he was just here…"

"Who?" she said.

I couldn't believe she had asked that. "Never mind."

"Okay," she said. Moving closer, she set her hand on my leg and rubbed it. When she tried to kiss me, I leaned back. "What?"

"Nothing," I said. "I just…this isn't a good time."

"What do you mean?" she asked, moving away. "Don't you find me attractive?"

"Of course I do," I told her. But I could tell she was mad. "I told you, this just isn't a good time."

She folded her arms. "Well, why did you ask me to come over? You were the one who told me you had more."

"Ally, I was unpacking my suitcase when I found them. We were on the phone, so I mentioned it. It's been an impossible week. I just...I mean, I'm just not ready for...for that yet. Not yet."

"I thought you were always ready."

"Well, that's your problem," I said, getting up and walking back toward the house. I couldn't understand how she couldn't understand that I had just buried my grandfather. Turning around, I saw her in the darkness, still sitting in the grass. "You know, I needed a friend tonight."

A few moments later, she came into the kitchen and sat down at the table as I was pouring a glass of Pepsi Free. "I can be a friend," she said.

But I didn't believe her, not after the way she had treated me again; I just wanted, needed to believe her. And that's how it happens. In the vulnerability of our grief, we seek any port in a storm, even if we know such a precarious dock puts us at greater risk of drowning in our pain than navigating the winds and waves on the open sea, facing the tempest directly. In the short time we had been together, Allyson had made it clear, twice now, that how I felt wasn't important to her—which meant I wasn't either.

After that, I knew to keep my distance.

In October, when Dorothy brought me home from work, there was a car in the driveway next to Grandpa's old truck. Mom and an older woman were sitting at the kitchen table, drinking coffee and talking. When my mother saw me, she gathered up the papers and told the woman that they were finished for the night. On the way out, Mrs. Walker introduced herself and said that she worked for Century 21. Mom closed the door behind her.

"You're not selling the house, are you?"

"Not this one," Mom answered. "Carol and I talked about it and decided it would be best if we sold Grandpa's house. The property taxes, the maintenance, and trying to rent it would just be too much. I'm sorry."

Mom went to the kitchen and poured herself another cup of coffee. It was a homework night.

"Do you really have to sell the house?" I asked.

"Honey, please," Mom said, sitting down at the kitchen table. "It's just not going to work. The taxes alone are almost twice as much as when he bought the place. I am going to need your help cleaning and moving the stuff out. It would take too long for me to do it by myself. And I just don't want to have to do it by myself."

"Can I have his couch?" When she asked why I wanted it, I told her, "I just do."

Mom agreed to let me have Grandpa's couch, but she insisted I wait for Dad so that he could help move it. I kept reminding him, but he was too busy running the station or going to see his lawyer. After Mrs. Walker set up the FOR SALE sign, I decided to move the couch myself. Inside the house, I could still smell Grandpa's pipe, but it wasn't the warm, comforting scent I had discovered the day Grandpa had found me in the woods; it was stale and damp from the autumn rains. Lifting and turning the couch one end at a time was slow, but it wasn't as heavy as I had imagined. I thought taking the legs off to get it through the sliding glass door would make things easier, but it got stuck anyway. I had to yank and turn and pull until I finally got the damn thing out.

"What a pain in the neck," I said. It was a crisp autumn night, but I was covered in sweat. I slipped on the steps inside the house and the couch landed on top of me. My leg was stuck, and my muscles were so exhausted from the strain I couldn't get out.

I struggled and cursed and screamed.

The storm door opened behind me. My mother was standing next to a bald, middle-aged man with a scruffy beard and glasses. Twisting beneath the couch, I looked out across the yard behind them and saw the car upside down in the driveway. It was the same one that had brought my mother home so late after class. When Mom took a deep, furious breath, I knew my natural-born life was in her hands.

"Guy," she said, "I'd like you to meet my son, Roger."

"Can I help you with that?" Guy asked. He lifted the couch so I could finally get out.

He moved in six months later.

CHAPTER TEN

BULLIES

I DIDN'T EXACTLY SIGN my death warrant the night I stood up to Glenn at the Diamond Mall, but, at the time, being bullied every day in front of the whole school was humiliating. The hostility between us grew for months before I finally snapped. Glenn's torture routine consisted of yanking my ponytail, knocking my books out of my hand, and tripping me in the hall. Tim and Junior told me to ignore him—until Glenn shoved me into the showers while I was getting dressed for gym class.

"Why don't you sit this one out?" Couch Siegel suggested when I showed up soaking wet. The only good news was that my street clothes were still dry. I could see everybody laughing and snickering as I took a seat on the bench beside James. He rarely, if ever, got dressed for gym. Coach Siegel thought he was lazy, but I knew James didn't want anyone to know about his father beating him.

"What happened to you?" James asked. "The plumbing stop working at your house?"

"Very funny," I said. "You know what happened. I can't stand this shit anymore."

"So, do something about it," James said. Nobody had ever stood up to Glenn before so he thought he could do whatever he wanted. If I wanted to fight, James would make sure nobody else interfered. James was smaller than me, but he insisted that size didn't matter. All he had to do was kick Steve and John in the balls and they'd both be down on the ground crying for their mothers. James promised that if I started something, he would be there to finish it. After all, we were best friends.

Despite the humiliation I had endured, I was willing to forget the shower incident—mostly because Allyson kept telling me between classes that I was a better man, which I knew was just her way of telling me to stay out of trouble. Glenn was constantly trying to get to me, she said, but I didn't have to stoop to his level. If Allyson didn't care what people thought, then why should I? Unfortunately, high school never was that simple. If I didn't do something, I'd be nothing. But Glenn was older than me, and I was afraid of him. Walking down the hall, I suddenly lost my balance and fell on top of Allyson. Looking up, I saw Glenn and Steve running away laughing. "Enjoy your shower?"

Allyson winced in pain when she tried to get up. I started picking up her books. "Son of a bitch! Are you all right? Ally, are you okay? All right. Stay here. I'll be right back!" I kissed her cheek and sprinted down the hall through the crowd. My rage rose as I ran, but it wasn't just Glenn. I was mad at everything and everyone, from Mom and Dad to Burke and Samno. And that laugh. That stupid fucking laugh Samno had that night. Grandpa's life had ended so goddamned carelessly, like he was nothing to nobody, and I hated the whole world because of it.

Grandpa had meant everything to me. And I'd had enough of it all. Everything.

When I caught up to Glenn, I kicked his books out of his hand and shoved his head into a locker as hard as I could. As he turned around, I punched him square in the jaw and he fell down. Within moments, a great big goose egg formed on his forehead. As the crowd quickly gathered, cheering me on, I felt the power of my rage. It was like a drug, the high and rush of it all, but all of that faded once I saw the truth in his eyes. It wasn't just that he was surprised by what I had done, and it was more than the pain I had caused him; he was afraid—of me. And it was then, as I saw the pain in his pleading eyes, that I realized I had become the monster I'd wanted to defeat.

I finally beat him. And I hated myself for it.

People kept yelling for me to hit him, or for him to fight back, but I just offered Glenn a hand and helped him up.

"This is a four-year school," Mr. Shuster, the notorious shop teacher, said. "You have already been here for five years, Glenn. Unless you want to make it six, I would strongly suggest you get to class."

Mr. Shuster hovered like a vulture as Glenn picked up his books. He walked past me without saying a word and disappeared into the crowd.

Rachel dropped me and Allyson off at the station after school. Dad hadn't put out the new schedule yet, so I wasn't sure when I had to work. Dorothy was behind the counter, pushing numbers into the adding machine between customers.

"Jake around?" I asked.

Charlie came in and poured himself a cup of coffee.

"He wanted to get some sleep before the rush," Dorothy said. "It's really been wearing him down lately."

"Well," Charlie said. "Looks like 1986 is turning out to be a memorable year. The Patriots lost the Super Bowl, the space shuttle blew up, and Jake finally got some sleep."

"Ally, meet Poquanicut's resident comedian, Charlie."

"How ya doin'?" Charlie asked, shaking her hand. "When was Christa McAullife's last meal?"

I shook my head. The jokes about the *Challenger* disaster had spread faster than the photograph of the Y-shaped explosion. Everyone had heard them, but the ones Charlie made up were the worst.

"When was her last meal?" Allyson asked. "I don't know."

"Launch time. Ya get it? Launch time?"

"Please," I said. "No more jokes."

"We don't laugh because it's funny, kid," Charlie said. "We laugh because there's nothing we can do—except go on living. That's really all any of us can do."

"Good point," I said. "Dorothy, do you know if Jake needs me to work tonight? I've got exams coming up next week."

Dorothy rang up Charlie's coffee. "Why don't you take the afternoon off and study?"

"Are you sure?" I asked.

"I can give Rob a call and see if he wants to come in and work," Dorothy said. "Jake and I can handle the rush. I'll cover for you."

"I've got to study too," Allyson said. "We can see each other this weekend."

"I was just going to suggest that."

"I can give you two lovebirds a lift," Charlie said. "Least I can do for my captive audience."

"'Captive' being the operative word," I said as we stepped outside.

"I think I taught you too well, kid," Charlie said, getting into his old wagon. He dropped off Allyson and brought me home.

I hated being home when Mom wasn't around. Guy had taken over the downstairs den. After disconnecting Grandpa's TeleCaption box, he spent all of his time watching stock car races, football, hockey, or the news. The man just never did anything else—except work at the Boat. Mom was in her last semester of college, but Guy had dropped out in December. When he finally got out of Grandpa's chair in the middle of the night to go to bed, Guy always left the television on. Mom would have given me a hard time about wasting electricity, but Guy was supposedly paying the bill.

He thought his money entitled him to do whatever he wanted. He wasn't rich, but his income was substantial compared to my mother's tips and wages. Although Mom had started grocery shopping again, she never had the time to cook. I was living on hamburgers and school lunches—unless Allyson and I went out to eat or Dorothy brought something for Jake and me at the station. Guy ate nothing but TV dinners, and the downstairs den was a cesspool of moldy trays and empty beer bottles. He came upstairs to get something to eat. As usual, he looked disheveled, had not shaved, and just flat-out stank.

"This place is a pigsty," Guy said, pouring his cereal. "Why don't you do your mother a favor and clean it up?"

"Because I'm not the one who made the mess in the first place. Why can't you just pick up after yourself?"

"Because I work all day," Guy said, getting the milk.

"So," I said, following him downstairs. "My mother and I both go to school and work. And some nights I don't get home until midnight. You're not the only one who lives here."

"You want to pay the bills?" Guy asked, settling into Grandpa's chair. "Be my guest. You ain't even been in the real world yet."

Guy never really ate cereal; he just sort of slurped it.

"So, where have I been all this time? And what were you doing when you were sixteen? Perfecting a career as a couch potato? We don't need you! We got by just fine before—" Guy sprang from his chair and shoved me into the fireplace. The corner of the bricks stabbed my back. He punched me in the head so hard I fell to the ground and didn't dare move. As he started screaming, I couldn't have feared god more than I did that man. "…one word to your mother and she throws me out then I'm gonna kick the living shit out of you! I don't want to have to come home to this shit! Got it, kid?"

I nodded. There was a hammer pounding inside my head, a darkness calling my name. I heard Guy slam the front door, and his car roared down the street. The throbbing in my head echoed. I was in too much pain to even move. Mom woke me up later.

"What are you doing down here?" she asked, kneeling beside me. It was dark outside, and I was cold. "What happened?"

"I just…I got into a fight after school. It was nothing."

Mom helped me get up. We went upstairs and into the kitchen. She examined the lump on my head and got some ice. "Why did you fight? You know how I feel about fighting."

I was too scared to tell the truth. "I tried to ignore him, but he kept bothering me. He's been doing it since the first day of school too. He pushed me into the showers before gym, and he tripped me and Ally in the hall. What was I supposed to do?"

"I hope he'll leave you alone after he gave you that bruise."

Mom went to her bedroom. I followed but stood in the threshold, holding the ice on my forehead.

"How come you never asked me how I felt about Guy moving in with us?"

"Isn't there anything I can do without having to ask your permission first? The world doesn't revolve around you, Roger."

She tossed her earrings into the jewelry box.

"Don't you think I know that? I've known that ever since Dad left. You never even told me what was going on. I was just a kid, and I am still just a kid. At least, I'm trying to be. Why the hell should you care—"

"Watch your mouth," Mom warned, pointing her hairbrush at me. She started brushing her hair furiously. "Sooner or later, you're going to realize that even the best intentions often yield the worst results. When that happens, your life is going to be everything you never wanted it to be. After that, you've got two choices: you can compromise and accept what your life has become, or you can remember who you want to be and get to work on building the life you wanted in the first place. But you just might not know what you want until you lose what you have. And, unfortunately, there are a lot of things you're going to learn that I can't teach you."

"What does that have to do with Guy?"

Mom let out an exasperated sigh. "Why can't you just try to get along with him?"

"Because he…he…"

"What? Jesus, what did he do that's so terrible?"

I didn't know what to say. "Nothing."

"Nothing? Then get to bed. It's late."

I must have stayed awake half the night staring at the ceiling, wondering what had happened to my mother.

On Friday, teenagers filled the buses while Allyson and I waited in the parking lot for Rachel. Allyson always had stacks of books to bring home, but I managed to do my homework in study hall, at lunch, or during whatever free time I had throughout the day. Most of the time, Allyson stayed home and studied while I was at work. She worried constantly about her grades, which I couldn't understand because she always did so well. Across the lot, I saw Bill's Jeep trying to give Steve's Chevette a jump. Glenn was connecting the cables.

"God, I don't want to go home."

"I know," Allyson said. She was the only one who knew what Guy had done. "That's why I asked you to come over before you go to work. I got my license, but my parents won't buy me a car until I'm eighteen. How come you never signed up for driver's ed?"

I told her that my parents wouldn't sign the papers I needed to get my license. They wanted me to wait until I was eighteen because they thought I would be more responsible. I had been saving for a while to get a car anyway because I knew Jake would never let me touch his truck. Steve started kicking and screaming at his Chevette. He shouted every curse word I'd ever heard—and even made up a few of his own.

"Hang on," I said. "I'll be right back."

"Don't," Allyson warned. "They haven't bothered us since Mr. Shuster—"

"I just want to check something out," I told her. Once Steve stopped pounding the Chevette, I reached inside the car, switched on the headlights, and checked to see if they were on. They were. I heard somebody make a comment about the battery not being dead. There was a click when I tried to start the car, but the engine wouldn't turn over. I put the key in the on position and grabbed a big screwdriver from the back seat.

"Better not mess up the car," Steve said.

"Cool it," Glenn said. "He works at that gas station. He might know something."

Looking under the hood, I braced the screwdriver against the starter and lifted. The Chevette roared to life.

I handed Steve the screwdriver and said, "You need a new starter."

As I was walking away, I heard Glenn call my name. "Thanks, man. That was pretty cool."

"Don't mention it."

"How did you do that?" Allyson asked when I got back. "Why did you do that?"

"It was the right thing," I told her. "Besides, next time it might be me."

Tim and Rachel were talking as we approached the car, but he turned and left. I could tell Rachel was upset about something. "Let's go already," she demanded.

"Everything okay with you and Tim?" I asked, opening the door.

"It's fine," Rachel said. "I'm meeting him at the lake after I drop you two off."

Allyson told me about videocassette recorders on the way to her house. She could now rent movies on videocassette or record television shows on blank tapes. Somehow, Allyson had programmed her VCR to record *Miami Vice* so that we could watch it together. "We have four. My dad says the VCR is going to make movie theaters a thing of the past."

"Didn't they say the same thing about newspapers when radio was invented?" I asked. "And radio when television came along?"

"Probably," Rachel said, looking at me in the rearview mirror. After turning onto Three Streets Circle, she pulled into the driveway. No sooner had we got out of the car than she backed out and gunned it down the street.

"Show-off," Allyson remarked. I didn't say anything but took her books so she could check the mailbox and unlock the door. After getting some Tab, we went up to her bedroom. The theme from *Miami Vice* started playing as the opening sequence came up on the TV screen. I sat on the floor and leaned against Allyson's bed so her Michael Jackson posters wouldn't be staring at me. When I saw her fast-forwarding through the commercials, I decided having a VCR would be pretty cool. We were almost done with the third episode when Allyson paused it and sent me downstairs to get some more soda.

Rachel was crying in the kitchen. Surprised, she quickly grabbed a tissue and wiped her eyes.

"Hey," I said. "What's going on?"

"Nothing," she said.

I got the bottle of Tab from the fridge. "Want some?"

"Yeah," Rachel said. I poured her a glass. She took a sip as I set up the ones for me and Allyson. "Thank you."

"Don't mention it."

"How long have you known Tim?" she asked.

"Forever," I said, putting the soda bottle back. "We've been in the same grade since kindergarten. Why do you ask?"

"He broke up with me today," Rachel confessed. "Just now. At the lake."

"Sorry to hear that," I said, sitting down. "Did he say why?"

"You don't know?" she asked.

I shook my head.

"He's gay."

It took me a moment. "What?"

"He likes men."

"I know what it means," I said, chuckling. "I'm just surprised."

"You've really known him your whole life and you didn't know?"

"No, I didn't know," I said. "Did he...did he say anything else?"

"He made me promise not to tell anyone. He said that even his family doesn't know. I literally just picked out my dress for prom! I bought our tickets and everything!"

"Look, Rachel...I'm no expert, but I've known Tim for a long time. He's always wanted to do the right thing, even if...even if he can't do it in the right way. Or the best way."

"Like when your grandfather was killed?" she said.

I felt like I'd just been poked with a hot coal. Taking a deep breath, I fought to keep my composure.

"He told me what he did, all that preaching," she continued. "He really regrets that, you know. He also said that was the first time he started questioning what he'd learned from church."

"Like they say, 'It's better to be an honest sinner than a false saint,'" I told her. "I don't know anything about that. I just know that the world is a pretty big place. He respects you enough to tell you the truth. Maybe he figured he owed you that. As far as I know he hasn't told anybody else, not even me. It's really...it's none of my business anyway. But you know what his parents are like. I mean, if they knew..."

"They'd rain hell from on high."

"Exactly," I agreed. "I think this is one secret we have to keep—until Tim decides otherwise."

"Yeah," she said. "You're right. I really thought you knew. God, you should have seen him when he told me. He was so scared. I wanted so bad to be there for him, but I just didn't know what to say."

I heard a door open and Allyson marching down the stairs. "Here we go..."

"Don't worry," Rachel said quietly. "I can handle her."

Allyson came into the kitchen.

"I should have known," she said. "It doesn't matter where we are or who comes over, you always have to be the center of attention. You know he has to work tonight. You know I hardly see him outside of school. Is it too much to ask for us to have some time to ourselves?"

"Oh, relax. We were just talking."

"Tim broke up with her today," I said to Allyson. She got a bag of Doritos out of the cupboard. "I just wanted to make sure she was all right."

"Why did he break up with you?"

"Oh, you know how I can be," Rachel said. "He thinks I'm too bossy."

"I could have told him that," Allyson said. "Come on, Roger. She'll be fine. Don't forget my soda."

She went back upstairs.

"Talk about bossy," Rachel said. She looked at me. "Thank you."

"You know, there's bound to be a couple guys going stag at prom," I said. Getting up, I grabbed the sodas. "Who knows? You might get lucky."

"Yeah," she said. "You're not mad at Tim for what he said when your grandfather died?"

I shrugged. "It's just a moment. Besides, I kind of had other things on my mind. Still do, I guess. I don't know. It's no big deal."

Allyson shouted my name impatiently.

"Good luck," Rachel said.

"Keep going," I told her. "You'll get there."

When I got to the bedroom, I gave Allyson her drink and settled back into my spot on the floor. She pressed Play.

"Watch," she said. "This is the good part."

A lunatic tore down a wall, and there was a corpse inside.

"Damn," I said. "That's messed up."

"I told you it was just like 'The Tell-Tale Heart,'" Allyson said. She had mentioned the story a few days ago at school, but, until I saw the dead body buried behind the wall, I couldn't possibly imagine what Edgar Allen Poe could have in common with Don Johnson and Philip Michael Thomas. There are so few original stories.

Allyson asked if I wanted to watch a movie.

"I should be going," I said. "Can you give me a ride?"

"Sure," she said. The first time Allyson brought me to work, she thought my starting at noon meant that we had to leave at twelve. Jake had chewed me out for being late. Ever since then, if Allyson was taking me to work, I made it a point to tell her that my shift started an hour before it began. My father had always insisted that if I wasn't early, then I was late.

When I got to the station that evening, Dad was outside having his traditional cigarette before the rush. I barely recognized him in the fluorescent lights with his long gray hair and beard. The wrinkles on his face had deepened; he looked like he was sixty.

"You're early," Jake said. "You start at eight."

"Well, it's after seven," I said. "Besides, 'if you're not early, you're late.' Can I have one of those?"

He handed me a cigarette from the crumpled pack he kept in his pocket. I got a buzz from the first drag.

"Slow for a Friday night," he said. "Won't be for long, though. I had a chance to get most of the stuff inside done earlier. Baseball season starts soon. You want to play?"

"I haven't played ball since Little League."

"I know," Dad said. "But if you played now, well, you could probably get a scholarship for college." Jake said that he would cut my hours down, but I needed the money because I wanted a car. He took a long drag from his cigarette and told me to think about it. If I got a scholarship, that would be something I could earn all by myself. "You can take pride in accomplishing something like that."

"Can't I take pride in what I do here?"

I thought my father would finally be proud of me, but it was like hitting that home run for the town championship—he had missed it completely.

He tossed his cigarette into the ash can before going inside. "Wax the pumps."

I finished my cigarette and got a bucket from the backroom. We were probably the only gas station in Connecticut that washed and waxed our pumps. Dad did his paperwork and waited on customers while I washed the hoses and pumps between cars. I was waxing the last pump when Dorothy stopped by with a lasagna. She wanted me to have some while it was still warm, but I finished my work first.

"Are you done?" Jake asked.

"Almost," I said, carrying the bucket into the backroom. I emptied the water and washed my hands. The phone rang; it was Mom. Grandpa's truck had broken down in Rose City and she couldn't get it started. Mom had called Guy, but he just gave his triple-A membership number (and probably went back to sleep). It was going to be a few hours before the tow truck arrived; all my mother could do was wait. I could hear distant thunder between the cracking static; Mom must have been using a payphone.

"Do you know what's wrong with the truck?" I asked.

"I don't know," Mom said. "Why didn't you come home after school? You know I wanted to talk to you."

"How come Guy can't go out and get you?"

"Holly is with me," Mom shouted over the static. "Everything is going to be all right. I'm calling be—"

The line went dead. I hung up the phone and got some lasagna.

The storm hit Poquanicut just before the rush. My raincoat kept me dry, but my jeans and boots got soaked. People were running around in the rain, trying to get their cigarettes and coffee or their bread and milk. I didn't have to wash any windows, but I must have changed a million wiper blades. When Dad shut off the outside lights, the rain glowed in the streetlights. Standing in the empty lot, watching the pouring rain, I knew that whatever happened, my family would be all right.

My mother was still in Rose City riding out the storm when I got home, and all of Shetucket Street had lost power. I tripped over something in the hall, cursed quietly beneath my breath. The last thing I needed was to wake up Guy in the middle of the night. Besides, I was too exhausted to deal with anyone. My whole body ached from working so much, and all I wanted to do was go to sleep. I banged my head against something when I flopped down on my bed. It screamed and shoved me onto the floor.

"What the fuck are you doing?" a girl's voice asked.

The lights came back on with the power. There were posters of heavy metal bands and half-dressed muscle men on the walls. A bunch of opened boxes were sitting on Grandpa's couch. I didn't even recognize the black-and-white checkered sheets, but some girl with purple hair had been sleeping in my bed.

"What the fuck are you doing?!"

"What are you talking about?" the girl said. "My dad said I could have this room."

"You mean to tell me that...Guy is your father? You know what? I don't care what he told you! This is my room, and I'm keeping it!" I ripped a poster off the wall. The girl jumped on my back and started screaming, pulling my hair, and scratching. I ignored her and tore the posters off the wall. With the purple-haired heavy-metal girl still on my back and beating my head, I grabbed a box and threw it out into the hall. It hit Guy at the threshold.

"Dad! Stop him!"

"None of you even belong here! Hey, what the f—"

Guy grabbed my T-shirt and threw me out into the hall. It was my own stuff I had tripped over. Guy was screaming. "...trying to get some sleep around here and now I got to deal with your shit again! You knew damn well she was coming!" He picked me up and started carrying me down the stairs. I kept punching his side, screaming that I never knew.

"Tough shit!" Guy shouted, kicking open the front door. "If you can't be civil, you can sleep outside!"

Guy threw me out onto the lawn, into the thunderstorm, and slammed the door. The ice-cold rainwater ran down my back as I slipped on the grass trying to get up.

"You can't do this!" I screamed, banging on the locked door. "I live here! I…I've always lived here!"

A light came on downstairs. I ran around the house as fast as I could, but the back door and the garage were already locked. Guy shut off the lights and disappeared in the moving shadows. Looking up, I saw the silhouette of the girl standing in my bedroom window. She shut off the light and disappeared.

Dropping to my knees, I clenched my fists in the freezing rain and screamed.

CHAPTER ELEVEN

GAME 6

THE BRILLIANT RAYS OF the rising sun filtered through the tall trees along Shetucket Street. The scent of a crisp morning after a rainy night soothed my exhaustion. It had been too cold and wet last night for me to wait outside for my mother. I ended up punching in a window to Grandpa's old house and spent the night inside. When I had turned on the light, I half expected to see him at the top of the stairs, smiling down on me. I could sense his presence around the place, and I'd had to remind myself that he was dead.

My heart jumped when the power went out again. Feeling my way around, I went up the stairs and into the kitchen. After finding an old flashlight in the drawer, I checked the rooms just to make sure nobody else was around. Mom and I had cleared out most of Grandpa's old furniture, which we had donated, and there was nothing left in his bedroom. The cold rainwater on my clothes made me shiver but being in a dead man's house after midnight by myself scared the shit out of me. I shut my eyes tightly and took a deep breath, swallowing the fear and the pain as I closed the bedroom door.

No sooner had I taken a few steps down the hall than my tsunami of grief came roaring back. I stumbled against the wall and fell to my knees, crying and screaming like a wild, wounded animal. Grandpa's whole life, all that he was, was gone—stolen in a single moment by a careless, thoughtless, stupid fucking cop who believed a goddamned badge allowed him to do whatever the fuck he wanted with a goddamned fucking gun.

"They were supposed to protect you!" I screamed, wailing. "They get paid to protect you, not to fucking kill us!"

Burning with rage, I clenched my fists so hard my forearms shook violently as my whole body trembled. Finally, exhausted, I collapsed on the floor.

My ears were ringing.

As I closed my eyes, the cold and the darkness consumed me.

I woke up shivering, my clothes still drenched from the storm. Feeling for the flashlight, I found it and made my way downstairs. Mom and I hadn't done anything with the garage. All kinds of tools, rakes, shovels, and a hose set up on the walls with nails. A bunch of boards sat on sawhorses, and Grandpa's toolboxes had been left open. There was a stack of dry wood against the wall next to a small pile of sticks and newspapers. I found some dusty matches sitting on the workbench and got a fire going in the den. As I was gathering more wood from the garage, I found an old cardboard box beside the logs. My name was on it, and it was dated for 23 January 1988, my eighteenth birthday, and Grandpa's last gift to me. I carried it inside and, by the light from the fire, marveled at my own handwriting on the top piece of paper.

> —Never again! We won't need to write anymore!!!

> —I know! Do you think Mom will want to learn Sign?

The box was filled with hundreds of papers Grandpa had saved from thousands of conversations. There were dates on some of the ones that didn't have my handwriting. Grandpa had clarified others in his own way.

> —I know you're not the Bionic Woman, but I really think you should consider getting an implant.

> —(Surgery is an entree short of cannibalism.)

There were a host of notes and letters from my mother. I wanted to read them, but I was freezing. After getting undressed and grabbing a blanket, I hung my wet clothes on the mantel to dry. The flashlight was going dim so I shut it off and read some more of my mother's notes by the flickering light from the fire.

> —Would you mind taking Roger to baseball practice? I tried to get tonight off, but May couldn't switch.

—Jake is working late tonight. Can I use your truck to bring him dinner? Thanks, Daddy. I made meatballs. Help yourself. Love you, Daddy!

—Are you sure this is what you want? I thought getting an implant would make things easier. I meant for you!

As I read her notes, I wondered how Mom and I had got to this point. It just didn't make any sense. Why didn't Mom tell me about Guy's daughter moving in with us? Was it because she knew how I would feel? Because she knew I couldn't stand him? I set my mother's notes back in the box and took out the photo albums.

The pictures gave me a visual history of my grandfather's life, from when he was a baby sitting on his father's lap to his wedding day and his enlistment during World War II. I also saw pictures of Grandpa and Grandma with Mom, William, and Aunt Carol. They had been a family, but tragedy would take a toll upon them all after William and Grandma had passed. I stared at a photo of his headstone.

WILLIAM OSCAR RYAN, JR
MARCH 10, 1938 ~ OCTOBER 20, 1969

Nobody had ever told me that William had been named after Grandpa. It must have been hell for Grandpa to bury his son and lose his wife just a few months later, but Grandpa had always been strong—or, at least, he'd had the courage to keep going. Maybe I could too.

I also found an old scrapbook that cataloged everything from the days of the horse and buggy to the man on the moon, just like Aunt Carol had said. I couldn't believe Grandpa had lived to see so much or that he had lived through so much: World War I, the Roaring Twenties, the Great Depression, World War II, Korea, the Cuban Missile Crisis, the Moon Landing, Vietnam, the Civil Rights Act, and now the space shuttle. Grandpa had witnessed history, which I could only read about in school textbooks. I missed him so much, but I realized he had lived a full life. Setting the scrapbook aside, I fell asleep watching the flames dance in the fireplace.

The sun was just above the horizon when I reached Route 12. It was a balancing act hauling Grandpa's box up on my shoulder and walking. The whole town was still asleep. I was wondering if anybody would drive by when Mrs. Johnson picked me up in her new Cadillac. She offered me a ride and asked where I was going.

"To the station," I said, getting in the car. "Jake wants me to clean the shelves today and I want to get started early."

I only lied because it was none of her business.

"Why couldn't your mother give you a ride?"

"The truck broke down last night," I answered. "And I just have a few things to take care of at the station."

Somehow, facing Dad made my getting thrown out more real.

"What are you doing here?" he asked.

"Guy threw me out last night," I said, carefully setting Grandpa's box behind the counter. I rang in a pack of Marlboro. Lighting a cigarette, I saw Charlie's old Ford station wagon sputter into the lot. That damned thing was ugly as sin; even the fake wooden side panels were peeling. When Kristine came out of the backroom, Dad told her to go see if they needed more cigarettes for the box.

"It's nine o'clock in the morning," Kristine said. "The next rush isn't until four."

"Just check anyway," Dad demanded. "Can you do that?"

She passed Charlie on her way out.

"His daughter took my room," I said. "I got home last night and there she was, sleeping in my bed. I didn't even know she was supposed to be moving in."

"Your mother never told you?"

"Never said a word. He threw me out in the rain last night and locked the door."

"And your mother let him do that?"

"The truck broke down last night," I explained. I had left after Guy had taken Mom to work that morning. There was no point in trying to explain to her what had happened; Mom would just take Guy's side anyway, like she always did. My head was still reeling from the shock of coming home and finding my whole life upside down.

"Now you know how the three bears felt when they found Goldilocks," Charlie said.

He chuckled, drank his coffee. Dad had Kristine watch the station while we went back to the house to get my clothes. Holding the box, I pushed open the door with my back and asked Charlie if he could ever say anything funny.

"President Reagan turned seventy-five a few months ago."

"Yeah? What'd he have to say about that?"

"He said…uh, shit. What the hell was it he said? Oh, yeah. He said it's only twenty-four Fahrenheit. Hey, it ain't that funny."

My stomach was killing me from laughing so hard.

"Celsius, you moron! Celsius! Seventy-five Fahrenheit is twenty-four degrees Celsius!"

"Well, Charlie," Dad said. "At least you finally said something funny."

"Hey, it worked," Charlie said.

When Dad and I got to the house, I charged through the front door and headed straight for my bedroom to clean out my closet. The girl wasn't around so I started gathering my clothes until Guy showed up. He was, of course, drinking.

"What the hell do you think you're doing?" Guy said. He chugged his Schlitz.

"Getting my stuff."

"You can do that when your mother gets home," Guy said. Dad appeared behind him.

"He can do it now," Dad said. Surprised, Guy turned around. "And you can wait outside until he's done."

Dad followed Guy down the hall. When I saw them through the window, Dad directed Guy to stand on the far side of the yard, away from the house and driveway. Most of my stuff was already in boxes so I hauled them outside and into the truck bed. On my final trip, I took a long, last look around my room before ripping the posters off the walls. I yanked the black-and-white checkered sheets off the bed, flipped the mattress, and threw her clothes all over the place. Some bitch I didn't even know had ruined my life.

"Thanks, Guy," I said, stepping outside. I was still trying to catch my breath. Dad was standing between him and me. I was lugging my clock radio with the last of my clothes. "Tell your daughter I said hi."

"Her name is Maureen," Guy said, pointing his finger and marching toward me. "She's at a friend's house. And if I ever see you here again, I'm gonna kick the living shit—"

He fell down when Dad punched him square in the back of the neck. "Don't ever threaten my son again."

I put the last of my stuff into the bed of the truck.

When we drove away, Guy was still lying motionless on the ground.

Dad and Dorothy had plans to go out that night. While Dad was in the shower, Dorothy went on about how much I was going to love living with them.

When Riverside converted to condominiums, they had bought a two-bedroom unit so there was plenty of room. They even had cable television with all the movie channels, which was terrific. As Dorothy went on about HBO, I was still wondering why my mother hadn't told me about Maureen. What did I do to deserve losing my room? Or, for that matter, getting thrown out of the house?

"How could your mother do that to you?" Dorothy asked, putting on her earrings. "I just don't get it."

"You're not the only one," I said, lighting another cigarette. "I wish I could just…go someplace and forget everything forever."

"You'll always have a place with us," she said. "Are you sure you're going to be okay by yourself? We could cancel."

Dorothy smothered me with kindness. When I was a child, I had appreciated the acknowledgement, but as a teenager I just wanted to be left alone.

"I'll be fine," I said. "Really. I'll watch MTV."

"Are you positive?"

"Honest. I want my MTV. Really, I do."

Cable television kept me up half the night. There were so many movies I wanted to watch that I kept flipping channels back and forth between *The Terminator* and *Rocky IV*. *The Empire Strikes Back* was also on, but I dozed off when Luke was running from the abominable snowman. Nobody was home when I woke to the ringing phone.

In the kitchen, I found the machine Dorothy had been telling me about at lunch, the one that somehow answered the telephone for you and allowed people to leave messages on a cassette tape. I counted the four bright red blinks again and again, torturing myself as I wondered if my mother's voice would be on the tape. I really missed the house, and I wanted to sleep in my own lumpy bed. But, I reasoned, the messages were probably just from Rob or Kristine, who were working the rush. When I pushed the button, the machine beeped each time a new message was played.

> "Jacob? This is Mary. Elaine stopped by the Galley and said that she gave Roger a ride to the station this morning. I assume he's with you. Could you have him call me? I'd really like to talk to him. I'm at work. [Beep.] I'm calling for Roger. Again. There are some things I'd like to explain. About last night. Call me, okay? [Beep.] Does this stupid thing even work? It's me again. Look, just…can somebody please just tell me where my son is? I just got home, and

> his clothes are gone. Nobody knows what happened. I'm worried sick. [Beep.] This is…is…goddamnit, Jacob! I don't know where you are or what's going on, but I want to talk to my son!"

I picked up the phone but stopped dialing halfway through the number. Guy might answer, I thought. Besides, what could Mom possibly say that would change things? I was watching MTV when Dad and Dorothy got home. It was almost midnight.

"Didn't you sleep?" Dorothy asked.

"Some," I said. "But I told you I wanted my MTV."

"Is this that stupid music channel?" Dad asked. MTV had this mysterious power to enrage parents, which saved me the trouble of doing it myself. "Well, shut that damn thing off and get to bed."

"No messages," Dorothy said, checking the machine. "Anybody call?"

"No," I said. "Nobody."

I secretly delighted in punishing my mother for what her boyfriend had done. And I thought I could avoid her for the rest of my life—until she showed up at the condo the next afternoon. Opening the door, I saw a different version of the woman I had known. Her hair was down. She was wearing a brown leather coat with a white shawl and her black dress had sunflowers. There were circles under her eyes.

"What do you want?" I asked, leaning against the threshold. It was just my luck that Dad and Dorothy were at the station. I had spent most of the morning sorting out my stuff.

"To talk to you," my mother said.

"So. Talk."

"May I come in?"

I heard the door close behind me as I went into the living room. Sitting on the couch, I ran my fingers through my long, snarled hair as I held back tears. Mom sat beside me, but I couldn't look at her.

"You know, when your father left, Carol thought I should sell the house so we could move in with Grandpa. And everybody, even Grandpa, told me that there was no way I could possibly keep up with the mortgage on my own. All my life I've depended on someone else for something: my husband, my father…Guy. But, do you want to know why I kept the house all these years, honey?"

"Do you realize he threw me out in the rain? I came home from work and his daughter is sleeping in my bed!"

"That's why I called…"

"And you never said a word to me about it!"

"Honey, I know—"

"So, I smashed in a window and spent the night in Grandpa's old house! And he's dead, Mom! He died for nothing because of some stupid fucking super-cop!"

"Honey, I'm so sorry," Mom said. "I know it's the only home you've ever known. That's why I kept it. But it's true—I made a mistake. Please, forgive me."

My mother had thrown Guy and Maureen out of the house that morning. She didn't want to have to depend on anyone anymore, and Guy had become too much of a compromise to bear. As it turned out, Maureen wasn't supposed to move in until next month, but Guy had mixed up the date. He told my mother before she left for work on Friday. Mom wanted to tell me after school, but I never came home. And when she had tried calling me from the college, we got disconnected. "But I think we've been cut off for a long time. The truck is fixed, and I straightened up your room. You can stay here if you like, but please don't hold this against me. You're all I have, honey."

When I didn't say anything, she got up to leave.

"Mom?" I called. She turned around. "Can we make some popcorn?"

"Yeah," Mom said, smiling. She gave me a hug. "Of course, we can."

We spent the rest of that weekend cleaning the house. I threw away bags full of TV dinner trays, scrubbed moldy dishes, and hunted for silverware. Mom washed the windows and swept the steps while I moved the furniture and vacuumed. We even rearranged the downstairs den. The furniture had been in the same place since my parents had bought the house, but Mom wanted a change. After all, she said, if she was going to celebrate her newfound independence then she might as well go all the way. We moved the couch across the room.

She said something, but I didn't hear it. "What?"

"I said, 'What do you think?'" Mom asked. "Is the couch better over here or what?"

"I like it," I said, lighting a cigarette. "It's different."

Mom sat down and lit one of her own. "Do you realize that all these years I've wanted this couch right here? You would think that after your father left, I'd have just done it then. I mean, all I had to do was pick it up and move the thing. Now, I can't believe I was so scared to move one lousy couch. This is freedom!"

"It's a couch, Mom," I said. Rubbing my back, she told me that I'd understand one day. "Can I ask you something?"

"Sure."

"It's about Dad. You and Dad, I mean."

"What's on your mind?"

"Did Grandpa find out what was going on?" I asked. "Or did you tell him?"

"He knew something was wrong the night your father broke my nose," she said. "He saw it the next day after I got home from work. I told him I'd slipped in the kitchen. The problem is, I made excuses about it because I was afraid of your father—and I was afraid of what Grandpa would do to him if he ever found out. Part of me was also ashamed."

"Ashamed? Why?"

"Well, I guess the simple answer is, when you have a family, you want to keep that family together," she told me. "When you're young, you think it's going to be Sundays at home with apple pies and anniversaries, birthdays and holidays, your graduation, your wedding…all those rites of passage that I thought we would share and remember forever. But I tried so hard to keep us together that I couldn't see just how bad it had become. I tried to get your father to stop drinking. It took me a long time to learn just how powerless I really am. Everybody is. Anyways, one night when we were arguing, your grandfather came over, and…that was that."

"So, Grandpa threw him out?"

"He did a little more than that," she said. "God, I was scared to death."

I took a drag from my cigarette. "What did you do?"

"I spent the night sleeping on your bedroom floor, right by the door. That way, if something happened and your father opened it, I'd know immediately. It was the only way I could protect you."

"I don't remember that at all," I told her. "Just the morning he left."

"He came by about a year later," Mom said. "I think it was in March or April. The divorce was about to be finalized. I had the papers for him to sign. He showed me his chip, ninety days sober, and said that he wanted to try again, but I couldn't do it. I was afraid he'd fall off the wagon and that next time you'd be the one who got hurt. Besides, I knew he was already spending time with Little Miss Kansas."

"She's from North Carolina."

"Well, whatever," she said. "Anyway, he said they weren't serious, but they certainly are now. I'm surprised they lasted this long."

"I remember the first time I met Dorothy," I said, putting out my cigarette. "That was the Christmas I stood up to him about his drinking."

"That's a burden you never should have carried."

"Well, he quit," I said. "And if he had ninety days sober in March or April, it must have been that day. It had to have been that day. Or close to it."

"The important thing is you're all right," Mom said. "That's all I care about."

I lit another cigarette and asked if she really could keep up with the mortgage on her own.

"Not much choice," she answered. "I'm graduating soon, and I've already got a job lined up at the Southeast Hospital. It's going to be tough for a while, but the sale on Grandpa's house should be finalized in a few weeks. Have you heard from Ally?"

"Yeah," I said. "She wants me to go to the mall with her next weekend. I think she just wants me to carry all her stuff."

Whenever Allyson made the honor roll, her father gave her a credit card to go shopping while I ended up lugging her bags around the mall. When she made Student of the Month in May, I knew I was in for another long afternoon. Allyson caught me looking at a jean jacket in the window of the Levi's store.

"Why don't you get it?" Allyson asked.

"Nah," I said, walking away. "That's all right. Maybe some other time."

"Are you kidding?" Allyson said, tugging on my old jacket. "Look at this thing, all faded and frayed."

"I'm not running the rat race."

"That race isn't worth running," Allyson said. She pulled out a compact mirror and put on some more lipstick. "It's for rats. But you should get it. It would look really good on you."

"My mother is graduating soon," I said. "I think I'd rather get something for her."

"I can get it for you."

"That's okay," I said. Allyson said that she wanted to prove just how much material things didn't matter to her, which I thought was funny because she put the jacket on her father's credit card anyway. When I told her to take it back, she tore up the receipt. I wondered why she didn't care about the rat race but still got so much stuff. When we got back home, Mom told me that Grandpa's house had been sold. She asked Allyson to stay for dinner and we had spaghetti and meatballs. After we ate, Mom taught Allyson how to play canasta while I folded my laundry. My room was clean, but there were still a few pieces of paper on the walls from Maureen's posters. Pulling them off, I realized it wasn't Maureen's fault that her father had messed things up. She had been just as shocked as I was when I came home that night. But that's the thing about being a child of divorce and alcoholism—you just never know what to expect. Uncertainty is the only certainty.

After my clothes were put away, I sat on Grandpa's old couch and went through one of the photo albums. The pictures were like finding a treasure filled with gold.

"Hey, Roger," Allyson called from the kitchen. "Come on."

"Hurry up," Mom insisted. "The popcorn is ready."

Closing the photo album, I put it back in the box.

I could always look through the rest later.

After I moved back home with Mom, I could sense that my father was disappointed. He seemed distant at the station, and our talks before the rush had been reduced to details about the place. He had decided to buy milk and eggs from the Ridge farm and bread and donuts from the R&R Bake Shop in Rose City. The station was a local business, my father had said, and he wanted to support local businesses. I would listen to him talk, wondering why he was always so distant. Maybe he had hoped that I would stay at the condo with him and Dorothy. Maybe he was worried about another Guy coming back into our lives. Or maybe, just maybe, he had hoped to spend more time with me outside the station.

When the Red Sox made it to the World Series that year, Dad changed the entire schedule around at the station so we could watch it together. Every night before the game he'd order two large grinders from the Pizza Galley for dinner. Dad always added layers of banana peppers to the top of the finely shredded lettuce, doused with vinegar and garlic oil, and sprinkled with salt, pepper, and oregano. In New England, a grinder is not a grinder until you pack it with potato chips, which we both did handily. With Dwight Gooden, the Mets were a force to be reckoned with, but we had hope because our guys had serious hitters in Rice and Evans. We'd heard rumors about Wade Boggs and his superstitions, but like Dad had said, "The man can wear a garter belt for all I care, as long as we win."

"What's a garter belt?" I asked.

Dorothy stifled a laugh as she was eating her salad. She quickly regained her composure as her left arm disappeared beneath the table.

Dad tried to explain. "Well, it's…Well, who cares? As long as he hits, and we win."

For some reason, Dorothy stopped eating and left the room. And that was the last time she ever tried to watch a ballgame with me and Dad.

"So anyway," Dad said. "Clemens is our answer to Gooden. He struck out twenty last spring—"

"—and he pitched three perfect innings in the All-Star Game," I added, unwrapping my grinder. "But those Mets play some serious ball. Dad, do you really think this is The Year?"

"The Year," as we called it, was the season Boston would finally break the Curse of the Bambino, which had become as much a part of New England folklore as Lizzie Borden and the Salem witch trials.

"I sure hope so," Dad said. "So many times, we almost had it. I figure something's got to give. You can't always almost have it, right? I just wish to god it wasn't a New York team."

Our nerves were raw all week long, but the Red Sox took the first game by a run. We were on fire the next night because Clemens was facing off against Gooden. The "duel of the decade" never came to pass though, with Boston blasting Gooden for six runs and Mac pulling Clemens early. That, my father said, was the nature of the baseball beast. The only statistic that matters in October is the last game. After five games, the Red Sox had a 3-2 series lead.

All we needed was one more win.

And then, Game 6.

We lived and died with every pitch. Boston struck first, but the Mets tied it in the fifth. It's always at that moment, just when you think everything is going to work out for the best, that your enemy takes his swing. So, back and forth it went. Every time the Red Sox scored, it seemed the Mets had an answer. It was fucking torture.

"We'll get 'em, Dad," I said. "There is always hope."

"Broken hearts begin with hope," he said. He was staring at the television, tapping his fingers against his knees. It went to extras. After taking a two-run lead in the tenth, we jumped up and down, screaming like maniacs, and even woke Dorothy up—but we didn't care.

We were thrilled to death. We had it. We finally had it. And there I was, watching the Red Sox win a World Series championship with my dad. Smiling, he looked at me and said, "You're going to remember this, Roger. You'll remember this night forever…"

I was proud to be his son.

In the bottom of the tenth, the Red Sox got two easy outs against the Mets. The next batter got two strikes against him. Jim Rice was in the outfield, smiling like a kid at Christmas. His present this year would be a World Series ring. For us, the end of our agony. The pride of a championship we'd waited for all our lives.

One strike.

It didn't happen. We couldn't get it. I was dying.

We started to sweat after two lined singles, but Bob Stanley's wild pitch had us cursing when New York fucking tied it again. Next, in the most torturous at-bat in baseball history—a full count with four fouls—Mookie Wilson hit a slow dribbler to first.

Buckner.

We sat there for what felt like hours, staring at the roaring crowd at Shea Stadium. What had once been so promising—one fucking strike—had become an epic collapse.

An impossible nightmare. The nature of the beast.

The Curse of the Bambino.

CHAPTER TWELVE

WALT DISNEY WORLD

"THIS IS SO COOL," Allyson said, pulling up to the McDonald's drive-thru in her father's BMW. "By the way, have you heard anything from Jim?"

I shook my head. James had dropped out of school in October of our senior year, and he ran away a few days later. When his father had called the station, I told Dad that I didn't know anything; James had just disappeared. He had always talked about getting away from his father, especially after his mother had been admitted again. One afternoon at school, while Mr. Lion was going over Chaucer, I had told James that if he didn't like living at home then he should do something about it. Mr. Lion caught us talking and called on me. I didn't know what to say.

"Well," Mr. Lion said. "For those of you who are paying attention, the rules of mathematics do not apply to the English language. More than one negative in a single sentence was used for emphasis. Isn't that right, Roger?"

"Absolutely," I said. "You got it."

I never meant for James to run away.

"Hurry up," Allyson said. "What do you want? I'm freezing."

The February wind was howling, and it was snowing.

"I'm not really hungry," I said. "I'll just have a Quarter Pounder, some fries, some of those chicken things, and...let's get a chocolate shake."

"And you're not hungry," she said, shaking her head. She ordered a Filet-O-Fish and asked for an extra straw. We always split the shake.

"So, what's the big secret?" Allyson asked, parking the car. "Where are we going?"

I was digging in the bag for my food. “It’s a surprise.”

Allyson asked if I wanted to drive. On my eighteenth birthday, I had taken the day off from school to get my driver’s license and to register for the Selective Service, but I didn’t want to drive the BMW in the snow. I took a huge bite out of my Quarter Pounder.

“How can anyone eat so much?” Allyson asked.

“I haven’t had anything since lunch,” I told her, grabbing a handful of french fries. Allyson put our straws in the shake. When we were done eating, I reminded her that we still had to go back to the station to pick up the deposit before Kristine closed. “So, we should get going.”

“How can I get us there if I don’t know where we’re going?”

“I’ll let you know,” I said. Once we crossed the border into Rhode Island, Allyson knew we were going to Quanticut Beach. The untouched roads along the marshes were covered with snow. Allyson put in a tape and blasted Belinda Carlisle’s “Heaven Is a Place on Earth.” Driving through the snow reminded me of the *Millennium Falcon* going to light speed at the Stardust Drive-In all those years ago, but the uncertainty of my childhood was so far away. Allyson parked next to a streetlight in the vacant lot. Before we got out of the car, I reached in the back seat to get my sleeping bag and backpack. Distant waves crashed against the shore, and I could smell the salt of the sea.

“My god,” Allyson said, looking around. “This is…beautiful.”

“Happy Valentine’s Day,” I said. She smiled. Handing her a single red rose, I pulled her close. The snow was falling. When Allyson looked up at me and smiled, we kissed. I lifted her with my free arm, but the backpack fell off my shoulder. Getting the wood and sleeping bag, we headed up the dune and down to the beach. Once we found a spot, I unrolled the sleeping bag and set up the wood. I had just got a fire started when Allyson said that she was cold. Adding some kindling wood, I said, “We…are about to have a roaring fire.”

We took off our boots and got inside the sleeping bags. I’d brought two and zipped them together. Allyson sat between my legs, and I rubbed her shoulders and arms to keep her warm. We talked about prom and decided to get an apartment together after graduation. Allyson was going to go to UCONN and work part-time while I could get a job down at the Boat.

“Are you sure you don’t want to go to college?” Allyson asked.

“I just don’t see the point,” I told her. “Besides, if I work full-time, we can start saving for a house.”

“I’d love a house,” she said. When we kissed, I could feel her body was still tense. That told me she didn’t want to go any further. She just wanted to enjoy the evening, which made my work worth the effort. "This would be perfect if we had s'mores."

"Well, now that you mention it…" Reaching over, I took a small brown bag out of the backpack and handed it to her.

She looked inside, saw what it was, and said, "You did not!"

"Yeah, I did," I told her, smiling. I pulled two sticks out of the sack of wood.

She started toasting her marshmallow. I leaned in beside her and held mine over the fire.

"Making s'mores on the beach in the middle of the night by a roaring fire during a fucking blizzard has just got to be about the best thing ever."

"You can't go wrong with chocolate," I said. I was about to make my first s'mores when Allyson snatched my piece of chocolate and immediately ate it. "Hey!"

"You can if you share," she said. I thought she was done eating when she leaned in to kiss me, but instead she shoved a gob of chocolate in my mouth. We ended up with chocolate dripping down our chins and took turns licking it off of each other, laughing the whole time.

It was so cold her nose had turned red. She was beautiful. I loved her so much—at least I wanted to.

The snow fell mysteriously from the darkness, drifting around us in the light from the fire. With the ocean before us and the land behind us, the whole world was at our fingertips.

God, we were young.

Allyson had me drive back to Poquanicut. When she leaned over and set her head on my shoulder, I placed my arm around her and remembered Mom and Dad doing that on the way home from the drive-in theater all those years ago. By the time we got back to Connecticut, the snow had changed to a pouring rain. It was falling hard, like liquid bullets. Lightning flashed beyond the shadows of dead trees. I could feel the thunder over the engine.

We spent so much time at the beach I knew Kristine had already locked up and gone home. My father would lecture me if he found out I was late, but everything seemed to be in order at the station. I parked at the far end of the lot and shut off the headlights. Allyson and I just had to take the deposit to Rose City Savings Society, and nobody would never know we were there. Dad and Dorothy had plans to go out that night, but when I got inside the station, I found Dorothy in the office. She must have parked at the other end.

She was wearing a tan skirt with a patterned sweater that had shoulder pads. The rain had ruined her makeup, and her big hair was drenched. There was a cardboard box on the desk. She was holding a small, framed photograph of her and Dad that had been on the desk. She glanced at it a moment, as if lost, until she realized I was there.

"I wasn't expecting you," she said, setting the photograph in the box.

"I thought you and Dad were going out tonight."

"So did I."

"Dorothy, are you…You're not leaving, are you?"

"Back to Carolina."

"What do you mean? Why?"

"Ten years," she said, wiping the corner of her eye. "Ten years, and I still sleep more in a single night than he does in a whole week. He put his life into this place, you know. And I just wanted one night…"

"One night? Like, one night out? You go out once a week."

"It's Valentine's Day," she said. "I wanted tonight. I deserve tonight."

"I don't understand," I said. "I mean, what…what happened?"

"I don't know," she said, packing the box. "One minute he was fine, and the next he just crawled under the dining-room table and started trembling. At first, I thought he was having some kind of seizure, but…"

"Is he drinking again?"

She shook her head. "I was with him all day. He was just…Jesus, he was afraid. It was like he was scared to death. Of what, I don't know. He just put his hands over his ears and kept going on about the thunder."

"Thunder?" I realized that the storm must have brought back his traumatic memories of the war. "Where is he now?"

"Hiding under the table, like a baby," she said. "I told him if he didn't man up, I was going to leave."

"That's it? Just like that?"

She said something, but I didn't hear it.

"What?" I said. But she repeated herself in the same tone, and she wasn't facing me when she spoke that time either. Again, I asked, "What?"

"Never mind."

"No, tell me what you—"

"I said, I deserve better!" she shouted as a flash of rage filled her eyes. I was shocked. It was so sudden and intense that I felt bruised and humiliated—all because I didn't hear what she'd said. It was like getting slapped across the face for a mistake you didn't make. As the emotional sting lingered, she threw the last few items into the box, battering me with her movements as I waited anxiously, wondering if she would snap again. Instead, she let out a sigh. A moment later, like nothing happened, she said, "I'll miss you. I know this is hard, and I'm sorry it's come to—"

"So am I."

"I was really hoping we could have a sensible goodbye, Roger."

"Is that why you weren't expecting me?" I said. "By the way, don't ever talk to me like that again."

"What? Like what?"

"Like you did a moment ago. I didn't hear what you said, but you raised your voice in a condescending tone."

"I wasn't mad at you. I was mad at the situation."

"Maybe," I said. "But you have no business taking that out on me. And besides, my grandfather never put up with that, and I don't—"

"What are you talking about?"

"Communication," I said. "My god, you still don't get it."

"Don't get what? What happened to you? You used to be so sensitive, so understanding."

"I understand you want us to understand, but you don't want to understand us."

"I don't know what you're talking about."

"A night out or a traumatic flashback? There's no contest here."

"What contest?" she said. "Tell me, what?"

As much as I knew what I wanted to say, I knew now that I couldn't say it. Not to her. If Dorothy couldn't understand the enduring trauma of my father's experience in Vietnam, there was no sense trying to explain it to her now. She couldn't see the man my father was, who he had become because of the war, much less why he needed her support tonight. It was then I realized that she was the one Dad had told me about at the diner, and he'd been right about her all along—she never listened. She had wanted a relationship, but only on her terms. Once his trauma, his most profound emotion, had reared its ugly head she abandoned ship. She couldn't see past what she wanted; and when she didn't get what she wanted, the consequences, the punishment, were severe. So, like my father, I never said a word.

Dad was right: it was easier just to keep quiet.

"Fine," Dorothy said, marching past me. She stopped and turned around. "Let me give you some advice: if you're not careful, you're going to end up being as emotionally unavailable as your father."

"If you say so."

"What's that supposed to mean?"

"How can you hear so well and yet listen so badly?"

"For the last time, what in the hell are you talking about?"

"Dorothy, he is not emotionally unavailable," I said. "He is just emotionally unavailable to you. I mean, did it just not occur to you that we have our reasons? He needed you tonight, and you—"

"You have no right to blame this on me! No right!"

I shrugged. "You're the one who's leaving."

"I have been nothing but nice to you!" she said. Her face turned red as tears welled up in her eyes, like a crocodile. "I even took you to Mystic Aquarium when you were a kid. Does it all mean nothing to you now?"

"That's what you never understood," I told her, stepping forward. It was the first time in ten years that I realized what she was doing. "I never wanted to go the aquarium. I wanted to see my father."

"Why are you acting this way? What have I ever done to you?"

"Centering."

"What?" she said as her nose crinkled. It was her tell.

I cracked my neck. "Never mind."

A fierce wind caught the door as she stormed outside. I got the deposit from the safe and, as I was locking up, I saw Dorothy drive away, disappearing into the darkness.

And like that, she was gone.

"It's about time," Allyson said when I got back in the car. "What the fuck took you so long?"

I was going to tell her the truth but decided against it.

"Nothing," I said. "Just had to lock up. Sorry."

After dropping off the deposit in Rose City, I drove back to Poquanicut and stopped at the condo. When Allyson asked me what I was doing, I told her that Kristine had called Jake when I didn't show up on time and that he wanted to see me. The cold rain drenched me the moment I got out of the car. Since I didn't know how long I was going to be, I suggested that Allyson head home. She wasn't happy about having to drive in the rain so late at night, but I had so much on my mind I didn't want to deal with it.

"I can drive you back," I said. She sighed in disgust. "Well, what do you want to do? Hurry up. I'm freezing."

"Go on," she said. "Go! I'll wait."

"Just give me a few minutes."

When I got inside, I set my keys down on the counter and found my father asleep beneath the table. Getting a blanket, I carefully covered him up and set a pillow beside his head; I didn't want to risk moving him or waking him up. I checked the heat and saw that there was no beer in the fridge. The closet was mostly empty. Dorothy had even taken her shampoo and conditioner. It was hard to believe she could throw away ten years so easily. I wanted to stay with Dad, but I knew Allyson was already mad about having to wait.

When I got back outside, she was gone.

And that was when I realized I'd left my fucking keys on the counter.

The door to the condo was always locked. If I banged hard enough, I would have been able to wake my father up, but I was worried the noise would set off his trauma again.

I ran home in that ice-cold rain, cursing the whole goddamned world.

Over the next few weeks, as I worked alongside my father, he seemed to be a million miles away. Dad had found my keys and warned me not to misplace them again. He told me that Dorothy had gone home to North Carolina so he had to do the books from now on, and he needed me to pick up the slack at the station until he could hire an accountant. I never mentioned running into Dorothy or finding him under the table that night. Instead, I'd listen as he spent every spare moment teaching me the books. Dad even showed me how to plan a personal budget and monitor my credit report. Using a credit card responsibly was crucial to getting a low-interest loan, which Dad said would save me tens of thousands of dollars when I applied for a car loan or a mortgage. Otherwise, he said, I was just throwing my money away.

Behind it all, as Dad went over mindless numbers and endless details, I realized that he was burying his pain in his work. I could see in his eyes that he had changed, and I soon came to understand my father's pain without him ever having to talk about it. It was always there, always with him, and it wasn't hard to see once I knew what to look for; a man's pain, once you truly see it, cannot be unseen. After witnessing Dorothy's reaction that night, and in the days that followed, I came to understand why my father was the way he was, why he never talked about his trauma or his memories of the war. When the one person who is supposed to support you just doesn't get it, you have no choice but to suffer in silence. After all, what's the point of opening up when people just shut you down? Demons lurk in darkness but feast on silence.

It's a secret every man keeps to himself.

The first Saturday in March, after another long night working the rush at the station, I woke up to the sound of pounding hammers. Going downstairs, I found Mom in the basement talking to a few construction workers. The furniture had been moved up against the wall and the den was a massive mess of boards and sawdust and whatever they were building.

"Good morning," Mom said. She had a playful touch of sarcasm in her voice. "I was wondering if you'd ever get up. Do you want something to eat?"

"Maybe in a moment," I said. "What…what in the world is going on?"

"We're getting a hot tub," Mom said. "It should only take about a week. That's why they're building a separate room. They had to move your bike. It's outside with a few other things so they could bring stuff in through the garage."

One of the construction workers called for my mother. They started talking, going over details or something, but they were facing away from me and for some reason I couldn't hear them. I really had to give my mother credit: she had pulled herself out of the financial ruin she faced after the divorce. Mom had sold Grandpa's house last year to a young couple with three kids. After graduation, she had got a job working second shift at the Southeast Hospital, finally making good money. Mom had bought a VCR but decided against getting cable television. She had even got a loan for a used Honda Prelude. Not only had she managed to pay off the house, but she now went grocery shopping every week. It had taken her years, but my mother had actually gone from being flat broke back to middle class.

For the first time since Grandpa was alive, I felt like everything was going to be all right.

"What time will your father be here?" Mom asked.

"This afternoon," I told her. "One, maybe two. He wants to go over the books with me again. I'm going to grab a shower."

She scratched my chin. "You need a good, clean shave, young man."

"Tomorrow," I told her. "I need a new razor."

After I got out of the shower, I went to my bedroom and started looking through the box Grandpa had left me while waiting for Dad. There were so many of our old notes, and each one brought back memories that had become sacred to me now. I stared for what felt like hours at the old photographs, so carefully set in the albums. I smiled when I saw that Mom and Dad had taken me to Walt Disney World on opening day. Near the bottom of the box, I found a stack of letters addressed to Grandpa from Aunt Carol, tied together with a string. Turning it over, I saw the back of an old Polaroid and immediately recognized Grandpa's handwriting:

Roger Andrew Evans
23 January 1970

Untying the string, I carefully removed the photograph. The envelope had turned yellow with age; there was a white square outlined where the Polaroid had been. Once I saw Dad's truck pull into the driveway, the Polaroid fell to the ground as I set the stack of letters down on the couch. When I picked up the photograph, my whole world turned upside down.

Grandpa, Mom, and Dad were all standing at the bedside of a woman who was holding a newborn baby, her stomach still swollen from the pregnancy. My mother, as thin as she had always been, was smiling at them. As I looked closely at the new mother in the hospital bed, who was holding me, I saw that the resemblance was unmistakable.

Carol.

A flood of memories washed over me as I finally put it together.

> "I wanted so much to protect you from these horrors… Your mother is so very proud of you…I'm happy being your aunt...Carol remembers better than I do…My son, at last… Sometimes, things aren't always what they seem…It's better this way…Hopefully, you never will find out…The best kept secrets are best kept secret."

After all these years, I had finally learned the truth: my whole life had been a lie. Enraged and in shock, I stormed into the kitchen, where I found Jake and Mary sitting at the table. She saw that something was wrong. "What?"

I tossed the photograph down on the table. "You were never pregnant!"

"Oh, dear," Jake said.

"Who the hell are you?"

"We're your family," Mary said.

"Why did you do this?" I asked. "How did you do this?"

"Pennsylvania licenses didn't have photographs in 1970," Jake said. "So, when we finally got you to a hospital—"

"—I filled out the paperwork while they were taking care of you and Carol."

"After that, we got an apartment in Hartford until you was weaned and Carol moved back to Pennsylvania so we could raise you as our own."

"And that's when we moved to Poquanicut."

"With no one the wiser," Jake said.

"Until now."

"Well, what the…you…you're not even my mother. Who are you people? And who the hell is my father?"

There was a moment of silence, so loud it made my ears ring, before Mary finally whispered, "My brother."

"What? Why? None of that explains why everybody in this room is a goddamned liar!"

"We are trying to explain," Mary said. "But first, you need to calm down."

"Calm down?"

"Calm down!"

"Oh. Yeah. Sure. I never thought of that! My whole life has been a lie and…how stupid of me! I'll just calm down!"

"Listen," Jake said. "You was so close to your grandfather that we decided he was going to be the one to—"

"Shut your mouth," I snapped. Mary called my name. "Both of you, just shut up. I don't want to hear another word out of either one of you. You ain't never had no business telling me what to do in the first place. Got it?"

"We all agreed that it would be Carol's decision," Jake said. "After what she'd been through, it was…We just wanted to do the right thing."

"Fuck you!" I told him. "Fuck this shit!"

I ran down the stairs and flew out the door. When I saw my bike leaning against the house, I jumped on and started pedaling as fast as I could.

And I didn't stop until South Brockton.

CHAPTER THIRTEEN

GALLAUDET UNIVERSITY

THE MUSTANG ROARED DOWN the dark highway as I glanced up at the stars, freezing as the winter wind whipped my hair and cut my skin. Once I had got to South Brockton, I'd stopped at Miss Maggie's Grinders to get something to eat. My legs were so sore, and I was starving; I devoured a large turkey grinder with all the fixings and the best bowl of tomato soup I'd ever had in my life. After that, as the sun was setting, I rode to the arcade and locked my bike up. I was walking in just as James was walking out. He was happy to see me, but he said that a lot of shit had gone down since the last time we saw each other. "Like what?" I asked.

"For one thing, I got married."

"You got married? Jesus! When? Who?"

"October," he said. "Remember Melissa Reynolds?"

"Missy? Wasn't she a senior when we were both sophomores?"

"Yeah," James said. "We're getting a divorce now. Worst six months of my life, man."

We sat down on the bench outside. James took a pack of cigarettes out of his long black trench coat and handed one to me. He said that he had been working three jobs just to pay the bills, but Missy was making him so fucking miserable he couldn't take it anymore. When she wanted a waterbed, he got her a waterbed; when she wanted a new TV, he got her a new TV. But she would sleep all day while he was at work, and when he got home—exhausted, starving, and sore as hell—she would be up all night watching cable television with the sound blaring. Other times, she'd have friends over, and they'd be up all night talking up a fucking storm while he was trying to sleep. "Christ, I couldn't even eat without her staring at me like she was going to bite my fucking head off."

"That's why you dropped out of school," I realized.

He nodded. "We live in South Brockton. One time, I missed the bus to work so I asked her for a ride. That's it. Just a ride. Just a fucking ride to work. I mean, shit, you can't pay the bills if you can't get to work, right?"

"Right."

"Well, she got pissed because she wanted to go to bed. So, I got on her case about her never letting me sleep. After that, she made me sleep in the garage on some old-ass couch the last tenants left behind. Fucking bed bugs had a feast. Oh, my fucking god! But I knew if I fucking said anything to her about it, I'd just get in trouble again. And, you know, I wasn't asking for the whole world. I just wanted to be able to eat and sleep. Simple shit, you know? She made me crazy. My god, she made me so fucking crazy! That woman tortured and tormented me all day, every day, fucking nagging me to death. So, I fucking left. Fuck that."

"Tough to blame you," I said. "Does she work?"

"She used to," James said. "But the doctor told her to take it easy for a while. I don't care no more. She can figure it out. Fuck that. And then my father got stone fucking drunk the other night and tried to beat up a cop. He wanted me to bail him out, but I ain't doing that. He's the one who fucked up. Not me."

"When it rains, it sure as hell pours."

"Yeah, no shit."

"How's your mother doing?" I said, taking a drag from my cigarette. "Any news?"

He shrugged. "I ain't heard nothing. What have you been up to, Roger?"

"I quit the station," I told him. "And I ain't going back."

"Why?"

I shrugged. "It's a long story, man."

"You can always get a job around here," James said. "Or up in Brockton Heights. I know Waldbaum's is hiring. It's better up there anyway. You can get an efficiency pretty cheap. I saw it in the newspaper. One room, all you need—bathroom, shower, even a kitchen. It's small, but that's what I was thinking about doing."

"Maybe we could be roommates."

"That'd be cool," he said. We sat and smoked in solidarity. After we put our cigarettes out, James lit another and said, "You know, it's funny. All this reminds me of a riddle."

"Yeah? I love a good riddle."

"Let's see if you can solve this one," James said, taking a drag. "It's a test of character. There's a young man, a middle-aged man, and an old man sitting on a park bench. The young man says, 'I just broke up with my girlfriend. She never listens.' The middle-aged man says, 'I'm going through a nasty divorce. My wife never wants to hear what I have to say.' Finally, the old man tells them, 'I've been married for fifty years, and I don't say anything. Otherwise, I get in trouble.' Which man is the strongest?"

"The young one."

"Why?"

"Because he got out before he became the other two."

He smiled and patted me on the back.

"There is hope for you yet, Roger," James said. He gave me a cigarette; I lit it and listened. "I swear, every time I tell that riddle to a woman, they choose the old man. They never realize that the men are all talking about personal stuff, you know? Shit women never want to hear. And then they wonder why we make such a fucking spectacle at work or a meeting or whatever, standing up and giving a goddamned speech like Mr. Richards always fucking did. It's okay for us to talk about work. We're expected to work. I get that. I didn't work three jobs for shits and giggles, but it'll be a cold day in hell before we're allowed to talk about something important, you know? I mean, shit. Anytime I start talking, Missy just turns the whole conversation back to herself. They treat us like crap and then wonder why we don't show our emotions. It's that nature versus nurture bullshit when not one cell exists independent of its environment. So, we bottle it up until it all just fucking comes out sideways. And, man, that ain't no way to live. That ain't no way to live at all. Fuck that shit."

It was hard to believe James had changed so much, and yet so much about him hadn't changed at all: he had left a fucked-up life at home only to find himself in a fucked-up marriage. I wanted to help him, but I didn't know how —or if anyone could help him. "Have you thought about what you're going to do?"

"I ain't going back to Missy, that's for damn sure," he said. "And I sure as hell ain't going back home. Only good news is my father gave me the Mustang."

"He gave you the Mustang?"

"Hell, yeah."

"Jim, your father loves that car."

"Well, it's mine now," he told me. "I got it registered and insured. Title is in my name and everything. In fact, hold on a second…" He took a small envelope out of his trench coat, sorted through the papers, and started writing. A moment later, he handed me a bill of sale for the Mustang—which I'd apparently just bought for a dollar. "There you go. It's yours now, Roger."

"What! Jim, what the hell are you doing?"

"I don't want Missy to get it," he said, putting the papers back in his pocket.

"But it's in your name. She can't take it. Not legally."

"You fucking think that's gonna stop her?" he said, taking a long drag. "Let me explain something to you, Roger. There are women in the world who will stop at nothing to get what they want. Doesn't matter what it is or how much it costs or who paid for it or who fucking owns it. When a woman like Missy wants something, she will scorch the fucking earth to get it. And when seduction fails, like it always does, watch out! Because she will torture and torment you every minute of every day until you finally give up just to get a goddamned decent night's sleep. You will fucking sell your soul to the devil just to have a moment of peace. But I will fucking die before I let that woman steal my fucking car. I swear to fucking god! That's why you're my insurance policy."

He was so angry I hardly recognized him. "You sure you want to do this?"

"When a woman says no, she means no," James said. "When a man says no, it means nothing. She'll just fucking nag you to death until you fucking give up."

"Okay."

"I gave her everything she ever wanted, but it wasn't enough. It was never fucking enough. Three jobs? Not enough. Working eighty hours a week? Not enough. Nothing is ever good enough for that woman. The Mustang is all I have left. Well, that and I finally got the money my parents put aside for me to go to college. I ain't fucking going to college. Fuck that."

"I can't even imagine going to back to school right now," I said. "Honestly, I just want to get the hell out of here."

"I got a wad of cash and the greatest car ever created."

"Jim..."

"Come on, Roger. I'll take you anywhere you want to go. I mean, shit. We didn't start out this way, you know? There was a time we were young and innocent and all that crap, but people just treated us like shit, so we became somebody we never wanted to be. It's our time now, man. Besides, don't we deserve something good for a change? Something fun? I mean, hasn't it all been hard enough? For both of us? Come on, man. I'll take you anywhere you want to go. Anywhere."

The more I thought about it, the more I realized he had a point. And, honestly, I didn't care anymore. I was so angry I just didn't give a shit. We sat there for a moment, so long I realized I couldn't hear the passing cars on the street across the parking lot.

"Fuck it," I said. "Let's go to Disney World."

James had insisted on driving with the top down because he wanted me to feel the freedom of driving under the stars, but it was so cold I was fucking freezing. We stopped at the mall, and he bought me a leather jacket. I refused, but he insisted. After what Melissa had put him through, I agreed to let him get it for me only if he allowed me to pay him back. The jacket was thick and heavy, with snap-down lapels, a whole bunch of pockets, and a half-belt. Once I finally had it zipped and buckled, the icy wind became bearable. We stopped for gas at the last service plaza in Connecticut; James wanted to fill up before we went through New York. I had him pop the hood so I could check the oil. The engine was a 289 V8, a custom rebuild set up so that even the spark plug wires would be easy to change. The chrome shined like a mirror, and the air filter was so clean it looked like it had just come off the assembly line. After checking the oil—and taking the time to admire it a little more—I closed the hood and told James, "Damn, man, you made out like a bandit."

"That's why I ride it like I stole it," he said. "We don't need no heat."

Inside the store, I bought a six-pack of Coca-Cola Classic and a road atlas. By the time James returned with a carton of Marlboro, I had our route planned.

"Here you go," I said, handing him a soda as he got inside the Mustang. "We got about a twelve hundred miles to go. It's a straight shot down 95."

"That's not bad," James said, sipping his Coke.

"You sure you want to do this?"

With his index finger, he pulled his lower eyelid down. "You see an ounce of care in his eye?"

"Can't say that I do, no."

"How 'bout any give-a-fuck?"

"All right, well, I guess that answers that. We got twenty hours."

"What about New York?"

"It's two o'clock in the morning," I said. "We got nothing to worry about unless you want to stay here for the next four hours..."

"Fuck that," James said as the Mustang roared to life. Riding in that car was like going back in time. The interior was decked out in chrome and the seats had been redone in a rich red leather. There wasn't so much as a speck of dust on the dash. The engine felt like an old friend by the time we got to the Bronx. Manhattan looked completely different at night. The city glowed like electric stars, as if the constellations themselves had come down from heaven. Even with so many buildings and tractor trailers blocking our view, I was still awestruck by the magnificence. Once we got on the George Washington Bridge, I turned and saw the World Trade Center Towers proudly standing above the rest of the city.

"Can you imagine living here?" James asked.

"I was born here," I said, sipping my soda.

"You were born in New York?"

"I was born here," I told him. "Right here on the George Washington Bridge. A place between worlds. A part of both, belonging to neither. Feel like a fucking nomad."

"What do you mean?"

"It's a long story," I told him. "I basically found out that my mother and father are actually my aunt and uncle, which means my aunt and uncle are actually my parents."

"What the fuck are you talking about, Roger?"

"I guess it's like finding out you're adopted without actually being adopted. When I was born, my biological mother didn't want me. So, she let my aunt and uncle put their names on my birth certificate. I just grew up thinking they were my parents."

"So that means the woman you thought was your aunt..."

"...is actually my biological mother."

"And your mother..."

"...is my biological aunt."

"Wow," James said. "How did you even find out about all this?"

"I found an old photograph that was taken the day I was born. My grandfather kept it."

"That's fucked up, dude."

"No shit," I told him, tossing my empty can out onto the interstate. "That's why I fucking left. They lied. All of them. My whole life has just been one big fucking lie. So, I'm just a fucking nomad. No home, no family, no roots. Nothing. I got nothing."

"You got me," James said. He slowed down to pay the toll in Jersey. Once the operator handed him the change, he gunned the Mustang. "And we're going to the happiest fucking place on earth! We're going to Disney World, motherfucker!"

We drove into the darkness, screaming at the top of our lungs.

We hit rush-hour traffic that morning between Baltimore and Washington, DC. When I told James that I had been awake for over twenty-four hours, we decided to stop for the day. It was James's idea to tell the clerk at the Mayflower Hotel that we were college students on spring break. (I was surprised he had a credit card, but the clerk had said we needed one to get a room.) Checking out the room, I found six small rubber ducks in the bathtub. I felt totally different after taking a shower. Once James was done, we realized neither one of us had packed a suitcase; he decided to get us some clothes. I offered to pay him back, but he told me not to worry about it. Afterwards, we went to a restaurant close to the hotel to eat. The prices on the menu were astronomical.

"I think I'll just have a salad or something," I said as we sat down.

"How about a drink?" James asked. He waved for the waiter, a bald, middle-aged man who was wearing a green vest and a plaid bow tie. I could tell James was really enjoying himself when he ordered a round of lager. The waiter never asked for ID so I figured, What the hell. Allyson had once said that alcoholism was a disease, but, as the waiter served the lager, the idea that enjoying an ice-cold beer was supposed to be some sort of plague seemed ridiculous. Besides, how could a few drinks possibly make me an alcoholic? I did not know, of course, that Jim's journey to hell was a thousand miles long and that it had all begun with his first drink. The lager was rich and went down smooth. We had a few more rounds before the waiter finally brought our food. Later, he asked how everything was.

"This food is wicked," James said. The waiter took his plate. "What are you doing?"

"If you don't like the filet mignon, you can certainly order something else."

"I never said I didn't like it! I said it was wicked, as in wicked good! That's the best damned steak I ever had. And if you don't mind, I'd really like to finish."

The waiter smiled politely and set the plate back down.

"What's wrong with that guy?" I asked. The lager had made me feel pretty good. "I hate fancy restaurants. I'll take a grinder over caviar any day."

"Nobody knows what a grinder is down here," James said.

"I don't doubt it," I said. "It's a grinder, hero, hoagie, sub, torpedo…"

"They'd probably think it's just a fucking sandwich," James said. I laughed out loud. "When you were trying on jeans, I asked this one guy if he could tell me where there was a package store. Turns out he thought I wanted to go to the post office. What a fucking moron!"

I laughed so hard I dropped my cigarette on my lap. The sharp burn sobered me up for a moment. "Why…why were you looking for a package store?"

"Why do you think?"

"You get any?"

"Let's do a shot first." After we were done eating, we went over to the bar. James ordered a round of tequila. Once I downed the shot, straight back, I started coughing like my throat was on fire. James burst out laughing before he showed me how to do it with salt and lemon. "It's better that way."

"No, it's not," I said, coughing again. My lemon fell to the floor.

When we were ready to go, the waiter was pleased to bring us the check. I fought through the buzz and the exhaustion as it occurred to me that we'd probably run out of money before we ever got to Disney World, but James pulled out a wad of cash and started counting the bills. As I lit a cigarette, I saw a beautiful woman take a seat beside James. She smiled and rubbed his arm, but she spoke in such a low voice I didn't hear what she said.

"I'm a feminist," James told her. "Buy your own drink."

She threw a glass of water in his face. "Fuck you!"

"That went well," I said, laughing as she stormed off. My stomach suddenly felt like I was doing somersaults on the space shuttle.

"No shit," James said, wiping his face. "She never paid any attention to us until she saw how much money I had. And when I called her out on it, she got pissed. They're a feminist when it suits them, but as soon as they want something—"

"Jim?" The room was spinning.

"What? Whoa!" He caught me as I stumbled.

"I may have…I mean, I might have had a little…"

"All right," he said. "Let's get you back before you pass out."

I don't remember going back to the hotel.

James woke me long before I wanted to get up. Somehow, he had picked up a bottle of Captain Morgan that afternoon. After a few shots, I had spent the rest of the day throwing up in the bathroom. My whole stomach twisted itself into a knot as I kept convulsing through my dry heaves. I thought it would never end, and I vaguely remember James making sure I got into bed. I rolled over when he shook me.

"Come on!" James said. "Roger, you got to see this!"

My head weighed a ton. "What?"

"Get up!" James demanded. He lifted the mattress several times and let it fall. It was so annoying that I woke right up. "I'm serious! You got to see this!"

"All right," I said, pulling my hair back into a ponytail. "But this better be good. Rode thirty miles, barely slept a wink, and I have got a monster headache."

"It's a hangover," James said. "But never mind that. Look outside!"

The silence was loud. There were hundreds of deaf people on the sidewalk and the street, blocking the entrance to the hotel. I was so struck by the sight of so many of them signing at once that it took me a moment to process. Then, the whole crowd shook their hands above their heads to applaud, just like Grandpa and Lisa had done at my baseball games years ago.

"Oh…my…god!"

"What?" James asked. "What's going on?"

"They…they're college students," I said. "From Gallaudet University."

"Gallaudet University?"

"Gallaudet University is the only liberal arts college in the world for the deaf and hard-of-hearing. Lisa told me about it years ago. That's where George and Julie first met."

"Lisa was your grandfather's girlfriend, right?" James asked. But I was still trying to absorb the amazing scene before me. Some of the students had climbed up on traffic lights. "Wasn't she your sign language teacher too?"

"Yeah."

"Can you understand them at all?"

"It'd be easier if there wasn't so many," I said. But just then, the students started signing again and again: *Deaf President Now! Deaf President Now! Deaf President Now!*

"What does that mean?" James asked. "They're all doing it."

"They…they want to lead themselves," I said, mesmerized. "They want a deaf president for Gallaudet! And they want it now! I have got to get down there!"

"I'm going with you," James said. "I want to know!"

I threw on the leather jacket and raced out the door. In the hallway, there was a guy and a girl signing to a middle-aged man in a suit and tie. The interpreter had her work cut out.

We have waited too long, the guy signed. James and I stopped to listen. It was difficult for me to understand because the young man was so fluent, and I had not signed since Grandpa passed away. The interpreter made things easier though, and as I listened, I could tell that some of the Sign I had known was already coming back to me. *Catholic, women, Jewish, and black colleges all have like presidents! Now it is time for Gallaudet to have a Deaf president!*

"Wait," the man said. "She is qualified. Wait for her to get here and—"

We have waited too long!

The ancient Greeks banished us! the girl signed, her hands screaming. *The Nazis sterilized us when we were children, put us to death! But we are not babies anymore! We will not lay down and die tonight! We want a Deaf president now!*

I could barely follow the conversation, but I came to understand what was going on because the interpreter was translating. Earlier, a woman on Gallaudet University's board of trustees had said that deaf people couldn't make it in the hearing world. The middle-aged man seemed frustrated, but he defended the woman and the board of trustees. "I don't know if she did say that or if she didn't, but we're all confident the university is in capable hands."

Not without a Deaf president, the young man signed.

"I know you're upset that the new president is not deaf, but—"

But it's not just about the presidency, the girl signed. I listened to her hands while hearing the interpreter speak. *Her words prove she is incapable! She never should have been on the board of trustees to begin with!*

"*She's right*," I said and signed.

"Who are you?" the man asked, turning to me. As the interpreter was translating, she pointed to me and everybody turned my way. "Are you a student?"

"*My grandfather was deaf. I…care.*"

I lost track of the conversation when I saw the girl. Her full, rich dark hair fell across her shoulders, shining even in the dim lights aside the halls, and her hazel eyes glowed like an autumn sunset. I saw her—and then, I *really* saw her. God, she was beautiful. When James waved his hand in front of my face, the girl smiled.

"Anybody home?" James asked.

"I think," the man said as the interpreter signed. "I think she probably said that deaf people couldn't not make it in the hearing world."

The young man told the girl that he was going outside to tell the crowd. He was angry.

"It doesn't matter," I said, watching the interpreter. "English ain't math. Double negatives were used for emphasis. Didn't you ever read Chaucer?"

The man raised his eyebrows. "'Ain't'?"

"My brother always told me 'ain't' ain't a word," James said.

The man scoffed at James. "And on what authority did your brother come to that brilliant conclusion? Does he have a PhD in administration or adolescence?"

James launched at the man, and I could barely hold him back. The man just folded his arms and grinned as the interpreter and the girl stepped back. Once James had finally calmed down, I told the man that he had a lot to learn.

"I don't have to put up with this," the man said, opening the door to his hotel room. The interpreter was still translating. "Most of the trustees have made a career out of working for deaf people, myself included. If there is anything else I have to learn, who is going to teach me?"

Have you looked outside? the girl asked. *Who do you think?*

The man stepped inside his room and closed the door as the interpreter left.

"He don't know nothing!" James shouted, pounding on the door. "Nothing at all!"

His…brother died years ago, I explained to the girl. She could tell I didn't know much Sign but listened patiently.

Will he be okay? she asked. *He is so angry.*

I don't know, I signed with a shrug, taking a deep breath. James and I went with the girl to try to get outside, but the manager wasn't letting anyone in or out of the hotel. After we sat in the lobby, James went back up to the room when the girl and I started signing. I explained that I had learned sign language with my grandfather, adding that I had not used it in a few years. She was as patient with me as George and Julie had been; she didn't seem to mind finger-spelling and signing at a pace I was comfortable with either.

Kalin told me that Gallaudet University had been founded in 1864 when President Lincoln signed the charter, but it had never had a deaf president. The board of trustees had recently selected yet another hearing president, but the students believed one of their own should lead the university and the other two candidates were deaf. The new president, who was a woman, had no background in deafness. She didn't even know sign language, like the man in the hallway.

And he is on the board of trustees! the girl signed. *We were lucky that we saw him. He had just met with some of the student leaders, but he never listens to what we have to say. I hope he goes outside.*

"*What's your name?*" I asked.

Kalin, she signed with her index finger out, circling her hand toward herself and placing a *K* upon her shoulder. *K-a-l-i-n. My best friend, Shae/S-h-a-e, gave me that name my first day at a Deaf school because I didn't know Sign, but I loved it.*

R-o-g-e-r, I finger-spelled. I put an *R* to my chin and circled away like I was making the sign for *hearing. My grandfather gave me that name because I can hear.*

Is your grandfather in Washington?

No, I answered, shaking my head. *He...died three years ago.*

Sorry. Was he Deaf?

What do you mean?

If you have to ask, Kalin signed. *You'll never know.*

That's not fair, I signed. *I'm here because...I'm here with you because I want to know.*

Kalin sat up in her chair. *Deaf is our identity. We don't see our deafness as a handicap or a disability. We have our own culture and our own language. Hearing people want us to behave. They push us aside, treat us like children. When the board of trustees chose a hearing president, we refused to accept it. Now, we are doing things our way. We want a Deaf president now!*

I had never seen anyone sign with so much grace and passion. The movement of Kalin's hands was fluid and precise, like a symphony. I could see my reflection in her eyes. She smiled.

I think I understand, I signed. *deaf is...deaf, but Deaf is identity bound to language and culture. Right?*

Kalin nodded. *Was your grandfather born-deaf?*

Late-deafened, I signed. *Before I was born. We learned Sign together, but my mother...his daughter wouldn't. Not at first. I am still mad about that, I guess.*

As it turned out, Kalin's own parents were hearing. Originally, they had sent her to a hearing school for a few years, but they changed their minds after realizing how isolated she had become. They also insisted she learn lip-reading. As a child, she hated it. For the past few years, when Kalin was away at college, her parents had not signed unless she was home. They had learned so little in the first place that their skills had significantly digressed.

Are you sick? Kalin asked. *Your eyes are red, and you look pale. Have you been eating?*

I haven't slept. We drove all night from Connecticut. Where are you from?

Delaware. I was going home for spring break next week, but I'm staying here until this is over. I major in accounting and education. I want to teach at the

American School for the Deaf in Hartford. I will be a senior next year. Are you in college?

I'm on vacation, I told her. It was the first thing that came to mind.

Where do you work?

My father owns a gas station in Poquanicut, I signed.

Does he have an accountant? she asked.

She quit last month, I signed, shaking my head. *Are you engaged?*

Yeah, Kalin nodded. She looked at the diamond ring on her finger, twisting it around with her thumb. The young man from the hall came inside with a few other students. When he tapped Kalin on the shoulder, she turned around and smiled. Jessie, Kalin's fiancé, explained that the manager was now letting people leave the hotel. A woman on the board of trustees, who had made that degrading comment earlier, was going to address the crowd. A bunch of students were going to march to the White House afterwards. Kalin asked me if I wanted to go with them.

"Sure," I said, nodding. When I got up from my chair, a wave of fatigue hit me.

Jessie stepped between us. *We will do this ourselves!*

Kalin was trying to tell me something when Jessie, walking away, yanked her arm. The rest of the lobby emptied quickly, but a young woman had stayed behind.

Jessie is just jealous, she explained. *I'm Shae.*

I know. Kalin told me.

You can come with us if you want, Shae signed. *We appreciate your support.*

Thank you, I signed. *But I'm really tired. We are leaving tomorrow for Florida. And I don't want to start any...problems.*

Okay, Shae signed. *It was nice to meet you. Have a nice trip.*

Good luck.

Thank you, Shae signed. She started to walk away, but turned and signed, *We will finish. We must. Deaf president now!*

Deaf president forever, I signed as she left, smiling.

I sat in my chair for a while and just thought about things.

The hotel was going to charge us for an extra day anyway because I had slept so late, eighteen hours to be exact. I woke up starving, in a cold sweat, and showered for an hour. James and I devoured our room service before packing the Mustang. I could feel the cool twilight as he put the roof down.

"We need jobs," I said. "You think Disney World is hiring?"

"Disney World is always hiring," James said. "I mean, we might be cleaning toilets after the park closes, but we can get jobs down there somewhere."

"That'd be cool," I said. "And then we can get apartment. It shouldn't take too long if we're both working. I just don't know where we're going to stay in the meantime…"

"Don't sweat it," James said. "We'll figure it out. We always do, right?"

"Yeah," I said. "We always do."

"No problem," James said. He lit a cigarette and started the Mustang. As we made our way around the city, James soon realized that he had no idea how to get on the highway. We followed the signs to Interstate 95 but had to take several detours because of the construction. It seemed like every time we found our way, we had to take another detour. After a while, as the night had fallen, I realized we were just going in circles. Finally, I saw an open on-ramp to the interstate and yelled for James to take it, but it was too late—he floored the Mustang straight through a construction zone, and we almost flew out of the car when he ran into a ditch, somehow bouncing out of it. "What the fuck!"

"Should have told you sooner."

"You all right, Roger?"

"Yeah," I said. There was smoke coming from under the hood. "But I think the car might be another story…"

"Fuck! Fuck! Fuck!"

"Relax," I told him. "Whatever it is, we'll figure it out. Kill the engine and pop the hood. We'll take a look."

I could smell the engine burning as I walked around the car. Once I opened the hood, a blinding cloud of smoke escaped. Turning away, I waited for it to subside and asked if James had a flashlight. He reached into the glove compartment and handed me a small Mag-Lite.

"Do you know what's wrong with it?"

"I will," I told him. Getting down in the dirt, I turned on the flashlight and looked underneath the car. "We have an oil leak."

"Fuck!" he shouted. "Can you fix it? You can fix it, right? Tell me you can fix it."

"Of course I can fix it," I told him. "But we need the parts and we need tools, which means we need money. And that means Disney World is going to have to wait."

"No, it's not," James said. He walked to the back of the Mustang. Looking around, James opened the trunk and took out a small green duffel bag. He unzipped it and showed me a bundle of cash. "Will this be enough?"

"Where the hell did you get that?"

"Told you," he said, zipping the bag back up. "That's my college tuition. And since I ain't going to college, we got enough to get the car fixed and make it to Disney World."

"How much is there?"

"My parents had fourteen thousand, seven hundred, and sixty-three dollars saved," he said. "Minus what we spent so far. Half of it was supposed to be for Craig, but—"

"Jesus fucking Christ! You could buy a brand-new car for that much!"

"I ain't leaving Sally. Not now. Not ever."

"All right," I said. "We're still going to have to order the parts. And I won't know exactly what we need until I can get a look at it tomorrow."

James lit a cigarette. "Think we can drive it back to the hotel?"

"If you want a pile of molten steel," I said. "You're also leaking oil, which means we're going to leave a trail. And trails get attention…"

"Let's just drain it."

"Drain it? Here?"

"Yeah, here," he said. "What the fuck else are we going to do? By the time you find a jug and get back here, it'll all be drained anyway. We're in the dirt. Won't be hard to cover up. Then we can just have it towed back to the hotel. Can't be more than a couple blocks…"

"Man," I said. "Greenpeace is going to be pissed."

"You got a better idea?" James asked.

We found a payphone on a corner and flipped through the phone book to get the numbers for a towing company and an auto parts store that specialized in classic cars. After that, we waited half the night for the tow truck to arrive. The driver was a big, fat guy who smelled like old cigarettes and stale coffee. Once we got inside the truck, I thought I was going to die because of all the pine-tree air fresheners hanging from the CB radio bolted to the roof. After James paid the tow truck driver, we put the top up and set some newspapers under the Mustang in case it was still leaking.

After getting breakfast, we walked to the auto parts store and placed an order for the oil pan. The clerk told us that it wouldn't be in until Saturday.

James and I were stuck in Washington for the rest of the week.

CHAPTER FOURTEEN

DEAF PRESIDENT NOW

WHEN I SAW THE news on Monday night it was clear to me, if not the world, that the students at Gallaudet University were not going to give up. They had locked and barricaded the whole campus, placing cars before the gates and forming human walls on the sidewalks; nobody was going to get on that campus without their permission. Besides a Deaf president, the students demanded a majority of Deaf members of the board of trustees and the resignation of the chairwoman. Apparently, her comment last night had spread like a forest fire throughout the Deaf community, igniting thousands of years of oppression.

As I watched the news, I remembered what Kalin had told me about the ancient Greeks banishing deaf children and the Nazis sterilizing the deaf and disabled. Why hadn't I learned about that in school? Slavery, the Holocaust, and the civil rights movement I'd had to study again and again but hearing people honestly had pushed deaf people aside. And if mainstream schools ever did teach the truth about deaf people, would they get it right? When I was in elementary school, I had been taught that Columbus wanted to prove that the world wasn't flat, but my history teacher this year had told me that he wanted slaves and gold. He had even killed the natives. So why did the United States have a holiday for a greedy murderer? As I watched the news that night, I knew that the Deaf President Now protest at Gallaudet University would be a defining moment for me—my coming of age. But the more I thought about my life back home, the less sense I could make of it. At least the events unfolding in Washington, DC, made sense.

"I don't get it," I said when a commercial came on. "Why has Gallaudet never had a Deaf president? Why do hearing people treat the deaf like children? It doesn't make sense."

"Beats me," James said. He set down his cigarette and guzzled the Captain Morgan. I'd had some, but I wasn't drinking as much as yesterday.

The news anchor also mentioned that the Gallaudet students wanted no reprisals, but I knew they would never be that lucky. I had written a term paper last year on the protests during the Vietnam War. In Washington, DC, alone fourteen thousand people went to jail in the most massive arrest in the history of the United States. Would the Deaf students be thrown in jail? What would happen if the board of trustees closed the college? I couldn't begin to imagine what would happen if the police were to betray their duty like they had done to Grandpa. As soon as the thought came to me though, I pushed it out of my mind. Restless, I sat up in my chair.

"By the way," I said. "Lisa was right. Gallaudet University is the only liberal arts college for Deaf students in the entire world."

James was balancing the half-empty bottle of Captain Morgan upside down on his palm. It was annoying.

"How did you get that anyway?" I asked.

"Stole it," James answered. "How do you think?"

I snatched the bottle. "Isn't there anything else you can do? Don't you want to find out what's going on?"

"It don't make no difference to me," James said. "So they want the principal to resign. So what? What's the big deal?"

"President," I said. "And it's a very big deal. You wanted to know last night."

"Whatever," James said. "I got enough to deal with. Besides, if I thought I could get Mr. Willis to resign just by skipping class then he would have a long time ago. They're wasting their time."

James reached for the bottle, but I stepped back.

"But you skipped class because—"

"They were gonna fail me anyway. That's why I dropped out. Now, give me that."

I held the bottle away from James, but he started reaching for it like a selfish child who wanted his favorite toy. He grabbed my T-shirt and turned as I fell across his leg and onto the floor. He snatched the bottle.

"What the hell has gotten into you?" I asked, getting up.

"Nothing," James said, unscrewing the cap. He guzzled what was left of the rum. "I just wanted a drink."

"This is ridiculous," I said. "I'm going for a walk."

I grabbed my jacket and left the hotel.

Washington, DC, was a different place after midnight. With only a few passing cars, the city was quiet and calm. I wandered along the sidewalks, staring at the cracks, wondering why James had given up. But had he really? He still wanted to go to Disney World, and we had talked about getting jobs once we got down there. Maybe James wasn't willing to give up yet. I just didn't understand why he hated his father for drinking so much and still drank so much himself. Was that James's way of relating to his father? Maybe because his father drank so much James thought it was okay for him to drink. I felt as if my best friend was on the edge of an abyss, and I had to pull him back.

I had to save him. Somehow.

Taking a deep breath, I stopped walking and looked around. The White House stood before me like a giant castle coming out of the darkness. Seeing it on television was nothing compared to being so close. I stepped up to the gate and grabbed the bars. Looking through them made me feel distant, like I was in prison. Ron and Nancy were probably sound asleep. The last time I had been in the same place as the First Lady was the day Grandpa had been murdered, but she had no idea what had happened. I wondered how a president could possibly serve the people he represents without knowing the struggles they faced.

Walking along the fence, I realized that the Deaf students had a point: the hearing world would only listen when Deaf people made them listen. As I approached an entrance, I saw two policemen. Fear and rage rose inside me like a smoldering volcano about to erupt, but I stopped, closed my eyes, and took a deep breath to keep my composure. I was fucking scared to death. Getting closer, I saw that one of the policemen was much younger than the other one. They were talking like guys who would never be men.

"...wearing this low-cut dress, right? Then she leans over—"

"Oh, my god," the older officer said.

"—and I get this incredible view of both of them!" The cop held out his hand like the woman's breasts were right in front of him. They laughed.

I kept walking.

I saw a lot of historical buildings, but I was drawn to the Lincoln Memorial. The Reflecting Pool, surrounded years ago by supporters of the civil rights movement, looked like a swamp. It lay in the darkness like a banner of apathy. There was almost no light, and I kept my distance because I was afraid I would fall into that pool of paralysis. If Gallaudet University had never had a Deaf president, then civil rights certainly had a long way to go.

The Washington Monument glowed in the distance. It seemed pure, but as I got closer I could see the sections of brick that told the history of its construction. The surrounding lights left the overflowing garbage cans invisible in the darkness. I sat on a bench, cloaked in the night, as a single police car drove down the street. Did anybody ever see this side of America?

I was trying to find my way back to the hotel when I saw an old man sleeping on the street. He had a long, scraggly beard and had lost most of his gray hair. His clothes were filthy and worn. I couldn't help but stare—until I noticed the family sleeping in the shadows next to him. The child couldn't have been older than five or six. He slept peacefully between his parents, who were his only angels. Getting my wallet, I took out all the cash I had and carefully tucked it under the father's hand. I was shocked to see a family sleeping on the street, and a profound fear seized me as I thought of my own family. My whole life had been a lie. The same people who had indicated and introduced and named the whole world for me had betrayed me, including Grandpa. Like the garbage of history hidden in the night, it was a lie—all of it.

For so long, I had loved America with a naive innocence, but I had never really been outside of Poquanicut. It was a small town hidden deep in the Connecticut woods, sparsely populated by people who lived simple lives. Part of me wished that I had never found that photograph, that I had never learned the truth about my family. I wanted to be back at the station with Jake, gazing up at the neon sign before the lot, filled with a sense of pride from a job well done. It was so much easier to live a lie. When you don't know the truth, you don't know any better. You don't know that anything is different. Once you do learn the truth, you have to accept reality. Denial is the measure of the lies you believe before the realities you are unwilling to accept. I had been brought up to believe that the United States was the land of the free, but now the Deaf community was fighting for their rights against thousands of years of oppression.

And I had to do something.

I got to Gallaudet University before the sun was up. The students were already parking cars before the gates and flattening tires to make towing difficult. They were so well organized that I didn't know what to do except watch. As another car pulled up to the gate, the students knelt and started to let the air out of the tires. When I noticed one student was having a hard time, I tapped him on his shoulder.

Watch, I signed, letting the air out.

It was stuck! the student signed. I could tell that he was frustrated. *What if we get in trouble? What if they…*

I lost track of what he was trying to tell me. Looking around, I found a man on the other side of the car, letting the air out. I waited until he was done, then tapped him on the shoulder, and pointed out the other student. *He is worried about trouble*, I signed.

He walked around the car and asked the student, *What's going on?*

Yesterday, the student signed. I followed their hands as well as I could. *That guy punched John when—*

John just wanted to know where his car was being towed. He tugged the driver's arm to ask, but the driver was surprised. We promised there would be no violence.

The student stood up. *This isn't going to work.*

If we don't do this, the man signed. *Nobody will. We will do this together. Okay?*

The student, now calm, nodded. Soon, enough cars were in place to keep the tow trucks busy all day, if they got past the students. Someone tapped my arm. I turned around.

What's up? a man signed. *Have you signed the list?*

What list? I asked. As he started signing, I motioned for him to wait and explained that I was not a native signer. Following his hands was difficult, but I understood that the students were passing around a list announcing their withdrawal from Gallaudet if the board of trustees didn't reverse their decision. *No Deaf president, no students. No students, no university. No university, no research. No research, no money.*

"*I go to Brockton High School in Connecticut*," I said and signed. *My grandfather was deaf. I learned to sign with him, but it was years ago.*

Really! the man replied. *I'm glad you're here. Thank you for your support!*

You're welcome, I signed. It took every ounce of willpower not to break down thinking about Grandpa again. After John introduced himself, I asked if he could help me learn more sign language. *I haven't signed since my grandfather…died. Three years ago.*

John motioned for me to follow him. After we made our way through the crowd, he climbed up on a brick wall and told me, *We can practice here.*

I scaled the wall. John started by gauging how much I knew and taught me as we went along. At lunch, he invited me to join everybody for a barbecue. Afterwards, we agreed to meet in the same place tomorrow. The conversations I saw throughout the day proved Kalin correct, and I felt as though

I had finally crossed the bridge and stepped into another world. I came to understand that Sign really was a unique language. The Deaf students used their whole body to communicate. Their eyes would ask questions while hunched shoulders could show disappointment, exhaustion, or frustration. The fluidity and pace of their hands would reveal their excitement—and their fierce determination. I practiced so much with John, learning as much as I could about the protest, I thought my brain would overload. But the more we signed, the less I had to actually translate what he was signing into English. And there were no words for much of what I did see.

The Deaf made the most of the warm day. They had a cookout and sold hamburgers and hot dogs to support the protest. Behind the gates, some of the students were playing hacky sack or just tossing a frisbee. A few girls were lying out on the grass getting a tan while other students played with their pets. I saw one student signing commands to his dog. After the dog rolled over and played dead, I noticed the sign on his back: I UNDERSTAND SIGN BETTER THAN HEARING PRESIDENT. I made a sign for myself out of a cardboard soda case that read POQ. CT FOR DEAF PREZ, and John gave me a string so that I could tie it around my neck. My sign was small compared to some of the others.

—SPILMAN CAN'T MAKE IT IN A DEAF WORLD

—LISTENING IMPAIRED PREZ NOT ALLOWED

—SOUTH AFRICA HAD APARTHEID. WE HAVE DEAFTHEID

—HONK FOR A DEAF PRESIDENT

The horns blared all day, but, in the silence and majesty of Sign, I had absorbed the unity of their determination. It was like a reel of film running inside my head as I made my way back to the hotel at dusk. A couple of empty liquor bottles lay on the floor next to James's bed; he had already passed out. I had to talk to him tomorrow, when he was sober. Even when I went to sleep, I saw signs in moving in my mind.

That was the first time I dreamed in sign language.

James was gone by the time I woke up the next afternoon. I waited for him while watching the afternoon news. Elizabeth Zinser had assumed the presidency at Gallaudet University, announcing that she wanted to "take charge" because "crises demanded leadership." The students once again assured the university that there would be no violence, but they refused to stand down. By the time I met John on the wall, journalists were everywhere. The television reporters had learned to keep the camera on the Deaf while they held the microphone on the interpreter. One journalist got upset because he couldn't find an interpreter.

"*Now you know how they feel*," I said and signed. "*Frustrating, isn't it?*"

"You know sign language," the reporter said. "Can you interpret?"

"*I'm not certified*," I told her. "*And I don't know a lot of Sign*."

You could if you knew more, John told me. He explained that interpreters were wearing armbands made of masking tape with INTERPRETER written on them. Pointing to the reporter, John signed, *Can you explain the armbands to her?*

I did. As the reporter set off to find an interpreter, John and I discussed Zinser assuming the presidency. Apparently, she was going to use a helicopter to get on campus, but the students had made plans to swarm the athletic field to stop it from landing. I was watching the skies when the reporter came back with an interpreter and asked to interview John.

Once the cameraman got set up, the reporter asked John to introduce himself and if he thought Zinser could lead Gallaudet University if she learned sign language.

I'm a senior, John began. I watched him while listening to the interpreter. *My name is John. We need a president who understand the obstacles we face in the hearing world, someone who is proud of their deafness and shares our struggles, our history, and our culture. It's not just about knowing our language.*

"What obstacles, if any, have you faced at Gallaudet University?" the reporter asked as John watched the interpreter.

The hearing faculty and staff have tried to keep us on a leash, like pets. I went to career services last month, and they set up everything for me, including the taxi I needed to get to the interview. They didn't understand why I got so angry. Hearing people just don't see us as human beings, who we are or what we are capable of doing.

"If the protest is successful, if a deaf president is appointed, what happens afterwards? Do you think the protest will change people's attitudes toward deaf people?"

We had to change our attitudes about ourselves first, John signed. *We know most people in the world are hearing people. That is why Deaf people work so hard because we know the obstacles hearing people put in our way. We work ten times as hard just to compete with the mediocrity of hearing people. I think the only way hearing people's attitudes toward us will change is when we prove to them what we can do through the lives we live, the paths we chose, the work we do. The Deaf President Now protest here at Gallaudet University will be the foundation of that change.*

The reporter thanked John and the interpreter. When I noticed the camera was on me, I held up my sign. John and a lot of other students gathered around and started signing, *Deaf president now!* Once the camera was off, most of the students returned to block the gate. After climbing back up on the wall, John patted my shoulder.

Now you are famous, I told him.

But John just shook his head. *Let's sign.*

The student president of Gallaudet, Gregg Hlibok, was on *Nightline* that evening with the new hearing president, Elisabeth Zinser, and Oscar-winning actress Marlee Matlin. As Ted Koppel summarized the roots of the protest, James burst into the hotel. He slammed the door but fidgeted with the lock. I finally got up and locked it for him. "What's going on, Jim?"

He pulled two liters of Southern Comfort out of his jacket.

"Almost didn't get away," he said. Setting the bottles on the table, he opened one with shaking hands and guzzled almost half of it.

"How the hell did you get that at this time of night?"

"I waited for the bartender to go in back," he said, wiping his mouth. "Then, I hopped the bar, snatched the bottles, and ran like hell. Want some?"

"No," I said. "I don't want some. In fact, I don't want any. But I'll tell you one thing, I can't believe I never realized it before."

Looking at me, James raised the bottle and took a sip. "Like father, like son."

"Like hell," I shot back. "Do you really want to end up like your father? To waste your life and lose your family?"

The look in his eyes changed as his anger rose.

"Fuck you, lose my family. What do you know about my family? Besides, you've been at the same job for three years—"

"Four."

"—four years. There are opportunities passing you by every day. Everybody knows you're smart enough to go to college. Hell, you could ace that shit! You're just too damned scared to do it! You're too damned scared, man!"

"You know what, Jim? Just shut up! My future ain't none of your business, okay? I get enough of that from my parents."

"My family ain't none of your business," James said. "Besides, my father never cared about me. He only fucking gave me the Mustang because he was trying to make up for ruining my life. He ain't never cared about my mother neither."

"That's exactly my point!"

"There is no point," James said. He pointed to the television. Zinser had just said that Gallaudet would have a deaf president someday, but Hlibok and Matlin weren't having it. "I mean, look at that. You think they're changing anything? It's always 'someday,' isn't it? Not today, not tomorrow. Always someday. It's fucking bullshit. The whole world is full of lies. Lies and empty promises. And besides that, Craig is still fucking dead. I mean, so is your grandfather, right? Right?"

"Don't!"

"All right, all right," he said. "That was out of line. And I'm sorry. But seriously, what difference are they making? I mean, you think my father giving me that fucking Mustang made me feel better after all that shit he put me through when Craig died? I got this fucking hole in my life where my brother used to be, and all I want to do is forget. I just want to forget. Just wash it away."

During the commercial, he slid the other bottle across the table.

Maybe I could forget too. "We still going to Disney World?"

"Yeah," he said. Opening the bottle, he placed it in front of me. "Yeah, we're going. We'll go. We'll leave soon as the Mustang is fixed. But, for now? Tonight? Fuck it."

I took a swig. Before I had even set the bottle down, I felt light-headed and dizzy. We shared the Southern Comfort while watching the rest of *Nightline*. I had wanted so badly for Gallaudet University to have a Deaf president, but as I watched the news that night, reeling from the alcohol, I realized it was never going to happen. Grandpa had stormed the beach at Normandy, but, in a single moment, his life had meant absolutely nothing to the people who were paid to serve and protect him—the very ones he had enlisted to serve and protect during World War II. How could I balance the promise of America with the truth of the United States? The more I thought about it, the more I realized it was all so hopeless—and the more I drank.

After the news, James started flipping through the channels until he found *The Breakfast Club* on one of those dumb cable television networks that only showed the same movies every month. People had to be pretty stupid to pay for reruns when they could just watch new shows on regular television for free. When Bender caught his spit, James asked me which character I thought I was.

"Allison," I said. "The basket case. I'm a fucking misfit, a nomad."

"You're also Andy," James said. "Strong as an ox, but you're always trying to live up to your father's expectations. And Brian. Definitely smart as Brian. Shit, his parents damn near got him killed. You're discovering your inner Bender now too."

"You should be a psychologist," I told him.

"I want to be a photographer," James said.

"A photographer?"

"It's something I've always wanted to do," he said. "You know, when you...when you take a picture of a person, or just that one personality, you can save that moment, that truth, forever. It never changes. A photograph never changes, even if the person in the picture is always changing. There's a consistency to it, a stability. Security."

"That...was truly profound," I said, laughing and taking another swig. He told me to fuck off and lit a cigarette. "What about you? Which character are you?"

"Bender," James said. "Nobody understands that guy. Nobody fucking sees him. They all think he's a criminal or a bad boy or a troublemaker or a fucking bully. Watch when Vernon locks him in the closet. He's fucking scared to death. That kid gets his ass kicked at home every day of the week and twice on Sunday, but nobody cares about that. Nobody sees that he's just a frightened kid who became an angry teenager because nobody helped him. Nobody fucking helped him. Nobody listened. Nobody gives a shit about that guy."

Taking another drink, I finished the bottle as James opened the other one. I had quite a buzz, but I took another drink anyway. I realized that this must be what drunk felt like, and it felt good because I felt nothing. "Ain't no wonder he's angry."

"That's just it," James said. "That's the problem. That's the only way people see him. It's acceptable for him to be angry because it's easier for people to just fucking dismiss him as angry. It's convenient—for them. Nobody has the courage or the fucking wisdom to consider what made him so goddamned angry in the first place. Even when I was a kid, my parents, my teachers, everybody always told me, 'Don't be angry' or 'You need to control your temper.' But how the fuck am I supposed to control my anger when nobody cares why I'm angry? Nobody ever asked me 'What's wrong?' or 'What's the matter?' or 'Do you want to talk about it?' Nobody listens. Nobody cares."

"You ever go stomping off to your room?"

"Shit, yeah," he said. "That's how it starts. It's a fucking rite of passage these days, man. But by the time we go stomping off to our room, it's already too late. It's too fucking late. We leave because we've already learned that nobody cares how we feel."

"Do people always talk this much when they're drunk?"

"Some do," James said. "But it's all bullshit anyway. The fucking answer is always 'Don't be angry'—as if that solves the problem. And every time they'd say that? I'd just get even angrier because all they were telling me was that they didn't fucking care. People who think anger is the problem forget that it's actually a symptom of the problem. It's a fucking symptom. Nobody ever wants to hear that, though. Nobody listens. I wasn't born this way, you know? But nobody listens because they're too drunk or too fucking stupid. Fuck it."

I raised the bottle, as if giving a toast. "Fuck it."

The rest of that night is a blur. All I remember is throwing up until my stomach was in a knot—and I fell asleep wishing that I wouldn't wake up. It was all so fucking hopeless.

Zinser resigned within twenty-four hours.

CHAPTER FIFTEEN

A MORE PERFECT UNION

WHEN I GOT TO the campus gates late Thursday afternoon, still recovering from a monster hangover, John told me that Dr. Irving King Jordan, the dean of arts and sciences at Gallaudet University, had decided to support the protest. Dr. Jordan had announced that the demands were justified at a press conference earlier that day. I knew that Dr. Jordan had been one of the Deaf finalists for the presidency, and that he had originally supported the board's selection of a hearing president, but, like John told me, *He changed his mind.*

Some of the students, John explained, thought that Dr. Jordan had risked his future to support the protest while others believed it was a great victory for Gallaudet. With the support of Dr. Jordan, I realized now that the Deaf community was that much closer to a resolution—and the possibility that they might succeed began to materialize in my mind. I was still afraid that the university would be shut down permanently because of what the students were doing, but everybody was ecstatic. After John told me that everybody planned to march to the Capitol tomorrow, I agreed to meet him at our usual spot up on the wall, but I had to get back to the hotel to get some sleep.

I don't feel good right now, I signed. I hated hangovers.

Okay, John signed. *See you tomorrow!*

Back at the hotel, I called the auto store to make sure the parts would be in on Saturday. The clerk confirmed that the delivery was on schedule. After that, James went out to get more cigarettes while I decided to remove the old oil pan. I blocked the rear tires and raised the Mustang to set up the jack stands that James had bought. (It's so much easier to work when you have the room.) The bolts on the pan were stubborn, but I only skimmed my knuckles twice. By the time I was done, my hands were coated with oil. When I got back to the hotel room, I saw that James was sitting at the table, holding his head in his hands with his back toward me. He must not have heard me come inside.

I went to the bathroom to wash my hands, which took several minutes. When I came out, James was sitting on the bed, smoking a cigarette and staring at the television. I was drying my hands when he put a cigarette out on his forearm.

I could smell his burning flesh, but he didn't move or make a sound.

When it was over, he tossed the filter into the ashtray. "My mother always did that to me afterwards to keep me quiet."

"Afterwards? After what? Jim, what the hell…?"

"You know why my father sent her away that last time?"

"Sent her away?"

"To the mental hospital," he said. "The fucking nuthouse. It was because she forgot to pay the electric bill. No shit. Once the power got shut off, and she realized why, she bawled her fucking eyes out. Wailing. Just wailing. She knew, you know. She knew what he was going to do. And I…I can still hear her screaming. All that endless wailing. I've never in my life heard anybody cry like that…"

"Jim, what…what's going on?"

"It wasn't just because she forgot," he said. "And it wasn't because she knew what my father was going to do to her again. She hated that place. With the fury of a thousand suns, she fucking hated that nuthouse. But that day? It was like…like she knew she forgot, you know? Like she remembered when she could remember. She actually remembered when she was able to do simple things like that, like paying an electric bill. That's what made it all so hard for her, those moments. Even after everything she did to me, all those terrible things, all those fucking nightmares I have because of her…that's how I knew she was still my mother. And that's what my father never understood."

"What do you mean?"

"She wanted to get better," he told me as his tears fell. "And my father never understood that. Those moments? When she realized she was sick? That's what made me realize that she was sick. Her mind was just…she was sick. She couldn't help it. Even when I hit puberty and the real sex started, she'd have a moment where she'd realize what she had done and she…she'd just break down, wailing, promising she'd get better…"

Holy Christ. What the hell was he talking about? "Real sex?"

"I was four years old when it started," he said, lighting another cigarette. "That's also when she gave me my first drink. Other times, when it was over, she'd switch to a different personality. She'd become a completely different person, and there were times she'd beat me…beat me so bad I couldn't walk. It'd hurt just to lay down. If it wasn't her, it was my father. And it went on for years. Years and years. My father never cared. He never listened. Every time she went into the hospital, I thought she'd get better, but…man, they couldn't fix her. Nobody can. Bad as it was, there were still times I swear I could see my mother through that whole mess. Who she was. Who she wanted to be. Who she would have been if her mind hadn't been so goddamned sick. She'd promise she'd get better. She'd say we'd all be a family again. Go out for pizza. Take a trip to Disneyland…"

"Jim, we can still—"

"My father made bail," he said. "Just got off the phone with him. He found us."

"What do you mean?" I asked. "What does that have to do with—"

"You still don't get it, do you?" James said. "He is on his way, and he is gonna fucking kill me because I stole his credit cards, his pension, and his fucking car!"

"What? His…What!"

"His name is James Richard Croft," he said. "I'm James Robert Croft. Credit cards don't bother with middle names, only the initial. It was easy enough when the hotel asked for my ID, but that's how he found us."

"And the money?"

"He took a loan out on his pension to pay for my mother's time in the hospital, but the fucking joke's on him because she fucking killed herself the day the goddamned check cleared!"

"Jesus fucking Christ! Why…what is…What?"

"He deposited the check, the check from the loan he took out on his pension, he deposited that check into his savings account at Rose City Credit Union and withdrew the money once it cleared. But he didn't fucking make it to Brockton Bank & Trust in time to put the money into his checking account there. The bank had already closed. So, like a fucking moron, he hid the money under his mattress and went out and got drunk and got fucking busted. I went back home after I left Melissa. Once I found the money, I stole it and split."

"Wait. Why does he have two banks?"

"He always used two banks," Jim said. "Wouldn't you if your wife had multiple personalities? My parents never saved a goddamned dime for me to go to college. I swear to god, Roger, I had to get the fuck away from him. From her. From everything."

"And the Mustang?"

He laughed. "Christ, I just waited 'til he was seven sheets to the wind one night and had him sign a blank fucking piece of paper. Made it out as a bill of sale after he called and asked me to bail him out. I got it registered and insured the day we met at the arcade in South Brockton. Real stealing is done on paper. Legally, that car is mine."

"How the hell did you ever get him to sign a blank piece of paper?"

"I told him it was my report card."

"Are you fucking serious?"

"I'm dead serious."

"Jim, you're not even in school."

"He didn't know. Don't matter now anyway. He's coming. He's on his way, and he's gonna fucking kill me…"

I couldn't believe it. "You mean, all this…"

"Come on, Roger. I mean, what would you have said if I told you the truth?"

"There has to be a way we can—"

"What?" he asked. "What can we do? You tell me what the hell I'm supposed to do! Shit, even my own wife don't want fucking nothing to do with me!"

"What do you care what she thinks?" I said. "I thought you'd be glad to—"

"That's right, I forgot," James said, his voice rising in rage. "Because you were there in our most intimate moments and you heard every word she said!"

"Okay, Jesus. So, I wasn't there, and I don't get it. That still doesn't explain why you—?"

"She's pregnant."

"Jesus, are you done jacking up the mind-fuck quotient?"

"Yeah," he said. "But she is. She's pregnant. I just wanted to do the right thing, you know? I thought maybe I got a chance to have the family I never had. But, that last fight? You know what she told me?"

My mind was reeling. "What?"

"I said to her, 'Why do I have to be Prince Charming? Why do I have to be The One? Why do I have to be a knight in shining armor? Or fucking sent by god? Why can't you just love me for who I am?' You know what she told me?"

"What?" I asked. "What did she tell you?"

"She said she deserved better. Better than me…" He took a long drag from his cigarette. "And then she told me I was never going to see my kid. She said she wasn't even going to put my name on the fucking birth certificate. All I ever wanted was a family…"

"Jim," I said. "We can figure this out, you know? We'll figure it out. I mean, we—"

"It's too late for that," he said as his tears fell. "Far, far too late. I lost it all. Everything. All of it. My brother, my mother, my wife, my son...and now my father is going to kill me."

"Jim, we…we can figure this out. Somehow, we'll figure it out! We always do."

"You don't understand," he said, wiping his eyes. "There comes a time you can't go home again, a time you've used up all your chances. And the life you thought you had, at least the one you wanted, it's gone. Gone. It's just… gone. And you can't ever get it back. It doesn't matter how hard you work to make amends or to make things right. It doesn't matter how much apologizing or atoning you do. Some sins just can't be forgiven."

"There has to be a way," I said. I realized my hands were shaking when I picked up the pack of cigarettes. "There is always a way. Always."

"You're right," James said, getting up. I was lighting a cigarette when he shoved my head against the wall and kicked me several times while I was on the ground. "I'm sorry, Roger. It's the only way. I'm so sorry..."

Before I could get up, he ran out the door and disappeared.

I was supposed to meet John at eleven o'clock for the march to the Capitol, but I overslept because I had stayed up all night watching cable television and staring at the city outside my window, waiting for James to come back. Waking up, I checked the time, grabbed my jacket, and headed out. I was already late.

Until yesterday, I had no idea just how bad things had been for James or how much he'd messed things up himself. He was so scared of his father, so angry about his brother's death, and so tormented by his mother's multiple personalities. She must have been seriously sick to rape her own son. The thought of it was as disgusting as it was repulsive, and I couldn't help but wonder if James was sick as well. Even if his mother had not passed her illness on to him, what she had done to him was enough to send any child over the edge. There was no telling what James would do, and I realized that I needed help if I was going to find him. All the years I'd known James, I never knew that his family had secrets too. I didn't understand it, not at all, and I had no idea what to do. I felt so hopeless. Worse, the weight of what happened to him, and what he had done, was like an anchor pulling me down to the depths of despair.

When I turned the corner, I saw the massive crowd marching toward me, carrying a big blue-and-white sign that read WE STILL HAVE A DREAM. I recognized the banner because it had been used a few years ago to get the Rev. Dr. Martin Luther King, Jr.'s birthday declared a national holiday; it was all over the news. As the crowd encompassed me, I saw that there were thousands of Deaf people from across the country and around the world who had joined the Deaf students to support Gallaudet. There were signs from Maine, New York, California, Alabama, and Bolivia. I walked with the Deaf. Everywhere I turned, I saw hundreds of people signing. As I tried to absorb the profound complexities of their language, I longed for something that I couldn't explain and, as a hearing person, would never have. The Deaf, I realized, had a great identity. I saw everything that the hearing world had shoved aside, the wholeness of a people whole by themselves. Looking behind me, I saw a sign that read ONLY THE SICK NEED A DOCTOR. I bumped into someone.

It was Kalin.

Sorry, I signed. *I was just looking around.*

She smiled. *I thought you were going back to Connecticut.*

We have to get the car fixed first, but I think I would have stayed. This is amazing!

Is your friend here?

No, I told her. *I don't know where he is. He ran off yesterday and...* A wave of fatigue suddenly hit me as I realized that I had not eaten anything in over twenty-four hours. James still had his father's credit card and all that cash. If he really wanted to get away from his father, he certainly had the means to do it. Exhausted, I sat on a bench and ran my fingers through my hair.

Are you all right? Kalin asked. *What's wrong?*

Knowing she could read my lips, I looked right at her. "I think I fucked up."

After I had explained that James was missing and probably in danger, Kalin suggested that I file a missing person's report with the DC police department. I insisted that she come with me because, honestly, I was still too scared of who I might find behind the badge. Once we got to the police station, I only told the cops what they needed to know to find James. The officer was so patient and understanding that she soon put my fears to rest. The only thing I could do now was wait. When Kalin and I got back to the Capitol, Shae told her that Jessie was looking everywhere for her.

Where is he? Kalin asked.

I don't know, Shae answered. *Maybe at Gallaudet.*

I saw Gregg Hlibok signing to the crowd. I couldn't see everything he was signing from so far away, but his determination was clear. A wave of silent applause went through the crowd. As the refrain grew, Kalin and Shae motioned for me to join.

Deaf President Now! Deaf President Now! Deaf President Now!

As I stood with the Deaf that day, before the steps of the Capitol, I had a profound sense of joy in the midst of my immense despair. It was a defining moment for me as I finally learned to reconcile the promise of America with the truth of the United States. I came to understand that it is more than a place, more than a country. America is an idea, a dream rooted in a directed vision that boldly declares life is not simply meant to be endured but enjoyed through our pursuit of happiness; that liberty and justice are not granted by a privileged few but earned by the oppressed through the duty of their devotion toward a more perfect union; and that the progress of inching ever closer toward the sanctity of what America must be takes a multigenerational marathon of endurance, vigilance, and, above all, responsibility. And I knew, right then and there, that the Deaf would never stop, nor would they ever accept anything less than the fulfillment of the promise enshrined in the foundation of the United States of America.

As Kalin and I walked back to Gallaudet, she told me that Deaf culture had survived oralism behind closed doors. There was a time, she said, when deaf students were forbidden to use sign language to communicate at school, but Sign had thrived in the privacy of the dormitories. She still remembered signing with her old classmates the moment her teacher left the room or turned around, which was better than being tormented at a hearing school. *They thought I was stupid.*

Really?

Kalin nodded. *Now, I always feel like I have to prove myself.*

I think my grandfather felt like that sometimes, I signed. *I really wish he had lived to see this afternoon. I've never seen so many Deaf people signing so many different things before. I couldn't understand everything. I just looked around and saw how amazing it was to see everybody.*

It isn't something hearing people see very often, Kalin signed. *Sign is our language, and our culture has thrived because of it.*

I hope I'll survive when I get home, I signed. *If I get home.*

I wish I could help.

I don't think anyone can help now, I signed. *I guess I just wait.*

She grabbed my arm. I stopped walking.

Life is hard, she told me. Her eyes were fierce but filled with compassion. *But as hard as it is, there are always people trying to make the world a better place. Remember the light, okay?*

Smiling, I nodded. She had a point—and I'd seen proof today.

When Kalin and I got to Gallaudet, we said goodbye at the gates. It was then I realized I didn't want her to leave. As I watched her walk away, she turned, smiled, and waved one last time before disappearing into the crowd.

The next day, I took a taxi to the auto parts store to pick up the oil pan. When I traded in the old, cracked oil pan, I talked the clerk into taking the gasket out of the core charge. Usually, they couldn't do it without the credit card, but he was pretty cool about it; he knew what it was like to have a breakdown—and he knew the Mustang was a classic. The good news is he had ordered the gasket.

"I knew you forgot when you placed your order," the clerk said. He was about thirty and going bald. "I got you covered, though."

Low on cash, I walked back to the hotel. I missed Allyson. And I missed home. I wanted to call Mom—my aunt—but I had no idea what to say. I wondered why Carol had abandoned me. I was torn between my guilt for the way I had acted and my anger at my family for not telling me the truth in the first place. My whole life had been a lie, and the people I was supposed to trust the most were the ones responsible for it. Sitting on the floor, I lit a cigarette and watched television until I fell asleep.

When I woke up late Sunday afternoon, I knew Mary had already left for work. Knowing Jake had to be at the station, I finally decided to call Allyson. Rachel answered; I hung up. In the lobby of the hotel, I got a Coca-Cola Classic and went outside to fix the Mustang. Somehow, the work calmed me down. It made sense to me because the results were tangible; there are no questions when you turn a wrench. After filling the engine with oil, I got in, took a deep breath, and started it up.

The Mustang roared to life. James, I knew, would be happy. We could go to Disney World after all—if he ever got back.

Throwing on my leather jacket, I put the roof down and took the Mustang out for a spin. The air of the city cleared my head as I kept an eye out for James. I felt like a king in that car, and it was running pretty well. At dusk, I headed back to the hotel. When I got to the room, I saw that Jim's coat was sitting on the chair.

"Jim? Hey, Jim? Hey, I got Sally up and running. Jim?"

There was a wad of cash on the table, sitting next to the title for the Mustang and the bill of sale James had made out to me. I realized that was the only way his father couldn't get it back and his wife couldn't steal it. Knowing we'd need the money for Disney World, I folded up the cash with the bill of sale and put them in my pocket. I checked the bathroom, but there was still no sign of James.

It was then I saw it: a cloth tied around the doorknob, running up into the closet.

No.

Slowly, I walked over to the door. My ears were ringing as my trembling hand turned the knob and pulled.

"Holy mother of god!" I screamed when I saw his body. It swayed against the door as the shock roared through me. The chair had been turned on its side. His eyes had rolled back into his head. I staggered backward, but my knees gave way and I fell down. Rolling over, I crawled toward the phone. "Sweet Jesus! You son of a bitch!" My hand was shaking so much that the receiver was punching my chin. "Oh, no. Oh god, no! Please, no!" Leaning against the wall, I dialed.

"Nine-one-one," the operator said. My eyes were burning from the tears. I tried to speak but couldn't. "Hello? Can I help you?"

"He's already dead." I threw the phone across the room and wailed as my tears fell like rain. "Oh, god! Why? Why why why why? Why did you do this to me, Jim? Why did…you…? They'll be here soon, you know. Why don't… why don't we just find out what's going on, Jim? You wanted to know…"

Crawling over to the television, I heard the news anchor's voice before the picture came up. "…Dr. Irving King Jordan, the dean of the college of arts and sciences, has just been announced as the new, Deaf president of Gallaudet University. We go live now—"

My heart jumped when I heard a knock on the door. Paralyzed, I couldn't take my eyes off the TV. Dr. Jordan was announcing his acceptance of the presidency. *We will no longer accept limits on what we can achieve.*

"Hey, Jim? You're not going to believe this, but…they did it. Jim? They did it, man! They fucking did it! You got to see this…" Out of the corner of my eye, I saw the door open. A moment later, a police officer took off her hat and knelt beside me. Her hands were rough but warm and comforting. When I looked up, I realized I was crying. "Jesus, this really is the end…"

PART TWO

THE END OF THE BEGINNING

CHAPTER SIXTEEN

THE HEIGHTS

IN THE THREE YEARS following my high school graduation, the world changed as much as I did. As I came to understand the relationships between events, the calendar of my memories, I could also see their connections to my own life—and to my hometown. Mostly, everything was out of my control, but I still blamed myself for what happened to James. Everything I had done, with the best intentions, had led him to hang himself in that closet.

I had finally learned what my parents could not teach me, and it was the hardest lesson I'd ever had to learn: power is power, and the only difference between saving someone and destroying him lies within the smallest details of a few key decisions. It is what you do, and don't do, that counts. After all, decades of nuclear proliferation had put the end of the world at human fingertips with the touch of a button, but no one ever pushed that button. Like Grandpa's murder, James's suicide would be among the crucial threads in the tapestry that tangled me as history unraveled.

The United States had spent decades competing with the Soviet Union, the threat of nuclear annihilation looming constantly on the horizon as millions of Americans went to work, paid mortgages, and raised families. The United States Submarine Building Company was going to be my contribution to the war effort while college was my ticket to the American dream. When I had first met James at the arcade, I had no intention of ever going back to school, much less graduating and certainly not going to college, but witnessing the Deaf President Now protest at Gallaudet University had made me realize just how important my education really was. And I had seen firsthand that it was worth fighting for.

Once I'd finally made it back to Connecticut, I got the Mustang insured and registered in my name with the bill of sale James had made out to me. Neither the insurance agent nor the DMV clerk had questions. Legally, the car was mine, but I decided to put it in storage for safekeeping in case James's father ever came around. (Keeping the car was, in many ways, my revenge against the man who had betrayed his son by ignoring the horrors James had endured for years.) After that, I took the bus to Rose City Community College to get information about the fall semester. I glanced over the course catalog and student handbook while devouring a cheeseburger in the cafeteria. My tuition was going to cost three hundred and ninety-eight dollars for a full semester, plus about sixty dollars in books (according to the clerk at the campus bookstore). I wasn't about to go back to work at the station, so I took a newspaper that somebody had left on the table, searching the classified ads for a job and an apartment on the return bus to Brockton.

It turned out that I needed a high school diploma to get a job down at the Boat, so I ended up applying at Waldbaum's Foodmart. The manager, Mr. Gibbs, was a short, stocky guy who wore a blue suit and a purple tie. He had gold-rimmed glasses, but his wild gray hair made him look like a mad scientist out of some old black-and-white movie. When he asked if I wanted to work in grocery, produce, or seafood, I told him that I would take anything as long as I could get forty hours a week. It took some doing, but I was able to convince him that I could work full-time and finish high school.

I ended up getting an efficiency apartment for two hundred and thirty-five dollars a month in Brockton Heights. The old brick building, set high among the hills above the Poquanicut River, had once been a school. The wallpaper in the hallways was so filthy I thought dirt was the original color, but the apartment itself was crisp and clean. I could smell the fresh paint. It was on the second floor, furnished with a worn sofa that folded out into a full-size bed, a couple of broken-down chairs, and one wobbly-ass table that I'd had to fix. It also had a small fridge and a smaller stove. Heat, hot water, and electricity were included with the rent.

It wasn't great, but it was enough for me. Besides, I had no place else to go.

The life I had known was over. And the family I thought I knew was no more.

I was on my own now.

It was a cold, gray morning when I finally faced the horrors of going back to high school. My stomach was in knots. I had no idea where the bus was supposed to stop; I just figured I'd see other kids waiting for it somewhere.

Once it started drizzling, I felt like a fool standing alone on the street, waiting for a bus that may never come. After several minutes, I began to wonder if I had missed it. Returning to school scared the shit out of me, especially after everything that happened. I could spend the weekend making up the work I had missed, but I knew everybody would have questions about where I had been—especially Allyson. After her reaction to Grandpa's death, I dreaded her centering. Eventually, I decided to tell her that I had met Jim at the arcade, and we went on a road trip. It was less than the truth, but more than a lie. I'd just settled on my plan when I heard a voice behind me.

"Hey, you're the new guy across the hall," she said. Turning around, I saw her long tweed coat flowing as she came down the steps. She was wearing a baggy black sweatshirt and a pair of blue jeans that had faded so much that white strings lined the holes running down her legs. Her black winter boots were so old and worn that one of them was held together with duct tape. "What are you doing out at this hour?"

"Just waiting for the bus."

"The buses don't start running 'til later."

"The school bus," I said. She started walking around me.

"The school bus?" she said, laughing. "Aren't you a little old to be going to school?"

"I'm eighteen," I told her. "Three months left. Is there a reason you're doing that?"

"Doing what?"

"You keep walking around me, like you're looking for something."

"I'm a survivor," she said, still circling. "I never knew my father. My mother overdosed when I was five. So, I stayed with my grandmother for a few months until she passed away. After that, I went through seventeen foster homes, three group homes, and two reform schools in the next ten years."

"Do you always tell your life story to a stranger?"

"Saves time," she said with a shrug. She stopped pacing and stood before me. When she ran her fingers through her long jet-black hair, I saw that the sides of her head had been shaved just above her ears. "Besides, it's the only chance I have to get to know someone. Nobody stays once they get to know me. I've been on my own since I was sixteen."

"And how old are you now?"

"I'll be twenty-one next month," she said. "You're not from around here, are you?"

"What makes you say that?"

"People don't come here because they want to be here," she said. "They come because the lows got 'em. The lows bring you to The Heights."

"Yeah? Well, I ain't staying."

"Maybe not," she said. "But the lows don't leave just because you do. You got lows. I can see it. You didn't grow that beard because you wanted to. You stopped shaving when you got hit. You haven't even trimmed it yet."

"Who the fuck are you, Sherlock Holmes? What do you care?"

"Hey, I care," she said, taking a step toward me. We were the same height, but she was so close it made me uncomfortable. She was pale as a ghost, probably malnourished, and her deep, dark-blue eyes had a hint of yellow around her pupils, like an eclipse. "People always think I don't care, but you know what? I do. I may be a felon, but I give a fuck. Besides, I got a gift."

"Yeah? What's that?"

"I'm an artist," she said. "People are like books to me. And I do a lot of reading."

"Congratulations," I said, lighting a cigarette. "You want an award or something?"

"I'll take a cigarette," she said. As I handed her one, she grabbed the whole pack and put it in her pocket. "Got a light?"

She closed her eyes and took a deep drag.

"Can I have my cigarettes back?"

She shook her head. "With a jacket like that, you can afford more."

"It was a gift," I told her. "And you can get your own too."

"I need glue," she said. Taking another drag, she pointed to the intersection down the hill. A group of kids had gathered on the corner. "Your precious school bus stops down there."

When I saw that the bus had stopped at a traffic light a few blocks away, I started heading toward the group of kids. She walked backwards, still facing me as we crossed the street. I asked her, "You got a name?"

"Memphis."

"Memphis?"

"Memphis Skye Rhode," she said, smiling. She stepped up on the curb without so much as turning around or taking her eyes off me. "Like a bridge."

"I was born on a bridge," I told her.

"See that? It's like we know each other already."

"I wouldn't go that far."

"Don't forget, we need more cigarettes."

"So do you," I said. "Are you going to keep reading or you want to know my name?"

"Tell me tonight," she said. I got in the line for the bus as she kept walking. "I live across the hall. You're in The Heights now. We got to stick together."

"I got a girlfriend," I said. But she was too far away to hear me—or she didn't care. The only empty seat on the bus was across from two girls who both had red hair and freckles, the Piccoli twins. Their glasses were so thick they looked like the bottoms of a glass Coca-Cola bottle. They were both wearing matching flannel overalls: one red, one green. When they smiled, I saw their silver braces. "What?" I asked.

"Aren't you the one who was going out with Allyson Danes?" the one in red asked.

"Yeah, I am," I said. A moment later, I realized what she had said. "What do you mean 'was'?"

"She's going out with Blaine now," the one in green said.

"They met at a party at his house."

"He lives at The Point."

"In a mansion."

"I get the picture," I said as the bus lurched forward.

"With a pool."

"And he drives a Mercedes."

"Jesus, I get it, okay? I get it."

High school is a train that never stops until the ride is over. As my first day back dragged on, it soon became clear that the train had kept running without me, like nothing had ever happened. Kids would talk about sports and music, what was going on at home, or how much they hated their teachers. Listening to them now, they acted like they had all the problems in the world, but nothing they said seemed important after losing Jim. I'd ask my teachers about making up the assignments I'd missed while on vacation. It turned out I had a term paper due next week, a test to take, and a whole lot of reading to do. Focusing on the work got my mind off of Jim. I was going to talk to Allyson during lunch, but I made up my history test instead. We passed each other a few times in the hallway between classes, but I looked away as soon as I saw her. I thought I could avoid her after what I'd heard that morning—until she met me at my locker at the end of the day.

"Where were you?" Allyson asked as I shut my locker.

"Vacation," I said, zipping my backpack. I started walking.

She kept up. "Everything okay?"

"Why wouldn't it be?"

"I called your house," she said. "Your mother said she didn't know where you were."

"I moved out."

"Why?" she asked. "I mean, you were always so close to your family."

"People change."

"You could at least call her. She's really worried about you, Roger."

"She say anything else?" I asked. I felt a great sense of relief when Allyson shook her head. The last thing I wanted to explain to her now was the truth about my family, which I hadn't even digested yet. Hell, I hadn't processed anything. It was all just hanging over my head like a fucking cloud. The crowd of students poured out of the school, heading for their cars or to the buses. Blaine, dressed like Sonny Crocket in a white suit with a baby-blue T-shirt, was standing by his Mercedes. He called for Allyson.

"Is it true?" I asked her, nodding toward Blaine. "You and him?"

She shrugged, but her eyes seemed sad. "You disappeared."

"I went to Disney World with Jim. That's all. I mean, it's no big deal. It was fun. Real blast. Time of my life."

"I know you better than that, Roger," Allyson said. "I know when something is bothering you. Now, I know something happened."

"Why didn't you wait for me?" I asked.

"I told you. You disappeared."

"I meant on Valentine's Day. You left."

"I thought you were staying with your father that night."

"If I was, I wouldn't have asked you to wait," I told her. "As luck would have it, I left my keys on the counter and ended up running home. It was pouring, you know. Fucking pouring."

"I would have waited if I'd known."

"Allyson, you did know. You said you'd wait, but when I got outside you were gone."

"You still didn't answer my question," she said. "What happened? What's wrong?"

"If you must know," I said, lighting a cigarette. My hands were trembling. "Jim killed himself."

"Oh, my god."

"Hey," Blaine called. He waded over to us, leading his gang of yuppie scum. They looked like they had just stepped out of a Sears catalogue. "What's going on here? What the hell do you think you're doing? She's not your girl anymore."

"She was asking me a question," I said. "Do you mind?"

"Cool it, Captain Caveman," one of the yuppies said as the others chuckled. "We got places to go and people to do."

"Yeah, I mind," Blaine said, poking my shoulder. "She doesn't speak Wookie!"

There is a fragile point between the height of anger and the depth of pain. My grief was so overwhelming that I was on the verge of diving into that abyss. Instead, hoping to hold it back, I took a deep breath as a crowd gathered around us.

"Can you imagine—mating with a Sasquatch?" one of the girls said.

"So, answer the question already," Blaine said. "It can't be that important."

"Blaine, stop," Allyson said. "His best friend just killed himself."

"Coward," Blaine said. I felt like he had just poured napalm down my fucking spine. I heard him say the word "permanent" but as he was speaking, he turned his head to the side, and I couldn't hear the rest of what he said. One of the yuppies laughed.

I cracked my neck. "What…did you just say?"

"What are you, deaf?" Blaine snapped. I heard someone behind me say, "Oh shit," just before Blaine started poking my chest while shouting out the syllables, "PER-MA-NENT SO-LU-TION TO A TEM-PO-RARY PROB—"

I dropped my backpack and punched him in the face as hard as I could. As he stumbled backward, his nose bleeding, I said, "You see a solution now, asshole?"

In a fit of rage, Blaine charged and swung. I leaned back to avoid his fist, then punched him in the stomach and across the face so hard he fell to the ground. After that, I got on top of him and slammed his head against the concrete. Setting my knee on his back, I held his hand in the air and put my cigarette out of his forearm, just like James had done the last time—the very last time—I had seen him alive. Blaine screamed like a wild, wounded animal, but I was furious. "Hurts doesn't it, motherfucker? You think you know pain? Imagine a pain so great dying is easy, you stupid fuck!"

My long hair was hanging down, covering my face, but I could hear the crowd cheering me on between their shouts of horror. Somebody grabbed my arms and pulled me off of him. A moment later, I realized that somebody was both Tim and Junior.

"Come on, Roger," Junior said as they held me back. "Come on, come on! Be cool, man!"

"Yeah," Tim said. "Just relax, man!"

"I am cool!" I said, catching my breath. They let me go. "I'm cool, all right?"

When Blaine got up, I saw the blood on his shirt, still pouring from his nose. Mr. Richards burst through the crowd between the Piccoli twins. "What is going on here?"

"He broke my fucking nose!"

"He broke his fucking nose!"

"You broke his fucking nose!"

"Yeah, he said that already," Mr. Richards told the twins. Pointing toward the doors, he turned to me and said, "Evans, inside! Now!"

I grabbed my backpack. As I made my way through the crowd, Junior said that he could give me a ride home. At the threshold, I turned and saw Allyson walking away with Blaine.

And that was that.

CHAPTER SEVENTEEN

CRICKETS

I GOT SUSPENDED A week for beating up Blaine. I spent most of the time working, reading, and trying to sleep. I'd take the bus to Waldbaum's in the afternoon and walk back in the dead of night, usually with whatever groceries I'd need over the next few days. I even got into the habit of buying a pack of cigarettes for Memphis, which I'd slide under her door when I got home. After that first night, I discovered a package of Ramen noodles outside my apartment when I got home from work. The next time, I found a box of macaroni and cheese. On the third night, as I was walking up the steps, I could have sworn I saw her silhouette in the window. The lights in her apartment were dim, but when I looked again, she was gone—or it was just my imagination.

Inside, I carefully slid the pack of cigarettes under her door. After putting away my groceries, I made some noodles and read until I thought my eyeballs were going to fall out. Reading and doing my homework kept my mind occupied, which meant I didn't have to think about all the burdens I couldn't bear, including James.

My guilt consumed me through countless nights. The images of nightmares were seldom clear, but I always woke up in a cold sweat. In the one dream I did remember, I was watching James fall with a rope around his neck. As I was pulling him back up, I was horrified to see my own hands forcing the noose to go tight around his neck. I heard him banging on the closet door, like he was trying to get help, until I woke up and realized that somebody was knocking on my door. I stumbled out of bed and checked the time; it was three-thirty in the morning. When I opened the door, I saw that it was Memphis. Her hair had been set back, loosely covering the shaved sides above her ears. She was wearing a black sweat suit with the sleeves and legs pulled up to her elbows and knees.

"I'm sorry to bother you," she said. "I saw your light on."

"I dozed off while I was reading."

"Oh, okay," she said. "I was just going to make some macaroni and cheese, and I was wondering if you had any milk."

"Yeah," I said, rubbing my eyes. My whole body ached. Running my fingers through my hair, I realized I was soaked in sweat. After grabbing the carton of milk, I turned and saw that Memphis had stepped inside. She was barefoot and her toenails had been painted red. Around her left ankle was a string of pearls. "How much you need?"

"Enough for a box," she said. "Not exactly moved in yet, are you?"

"I think I'm about as moved in as I'm going to get for now," I said, handing her the carton. "I don't know how much you…It's been a long day."

"You hungry?" she asked. "I mean, I can never eat a whole box. So, if you want some…"

"Memphis?"

"…or maybe you could just heat it up tomorrow."

"It is tomorrow." And that was how our late-night dinners got started. We'd take turns making what meals we could afford. I'd toast some tuna and cheese or scramble some eggs; she'd make noodles or grilled cheese. Other times, we'd just have chips and salsa or walk to Rosie's Diner for a couple of milkshakes. On Fridays, we'd split a pizza from Angie's. That first night, it was macaroni and cheese with hot dogs.

Her apartment was filled with artwork. The walls were covered with paintings of autumn mountain meadows, the colors as intricate as fine leaves. A single black-and-white photograph of Memphis and an older man was set among the paintings; they were facing each other and smiling. On the floor was a giant white dollhouse with sky-blue shutters, complete with a white picket fence. A desk lamp sat on the table, which had a partially built replica of a 1970 Camaro sitting among piles of Popsicle sticks, razor blades, pliers, wire cutters, and tubes of paints and rubber cement. From the dashboard to the distributor cap, that model car was incredibly detailed. "Did you build this?"

"I did it all," Memphis said, chopping the hot dogs. She told me that she sold her work at a consignment shop downtown, usually making two to three pieces a week. Her paintings never sold as well as her Popsicle-stick creations, though. She would sometimes take special requests, the most memorable being a collection of the Peanuts gang, including Charlie Brown's pathetic Christmas tree. When I asked why she hadn't signed her paintings, Memphis said that she only signed the ones that sold. She also split and stacked firewood in the fall, shoveled snow in the winter, and would do landscaping in the spring and summer. That, she said, was how she managed to pay her rent. The shop owner, Ginny, had known her grandmother and agreed to sell her work for a percentage of the sales. Memphis had even got an offer on the dollhouse, but she didn't want to sell it. "It was the first thing I made when I got out of prison."

"You built that house?" I asked, amazed. She nodded. Taking a closer look, I could see the intricate layers of Popsicle sticks she had cut and carved. The shingles on the roof, even the bricks of the chimney, had been cut and set from individual pieces carefully glued into place. The siding had a random, realistic pattern and even the doors and shutters had been intimately crafted. It must have taken her forever. "You built all this from Popsicle sticks?"

"I'd walk the yard picking them up," Memphis said. "When I got out, it helped me stay clean and sober. And since nobody wants to hire a criminal… that's pretty much how I got started on selling my arts."

After learning the truth about James, her life somehow seemed normal—or at least more common than I had once thought. "I guess we all got our stories."

She drained the macaroni. "So, what's your story?"

"There really isn't much to tell," I said, avoiding her gaze. "Do you work from models? Or photos?"

"Sometimes," she said, adding the milk. "You ever see the movie *Six Pack* with Kenny Rogers? That's his car. When I was a kid, I used to pretend he was my dad. Of course, he never found me so I just kept walking. Want some coffee? It's kind of old, but"—she smelled what was left in the pot—"still works."

"Yeah, that'd be good," I said. I took another look at the Camaro. "How in the world did you get the tires so round?"

"Watch," Memphis said. She grabbed a pair of pliers and with lightning speed cracked a Popsicle stick about every quarter of an inch; it was bent, but not broken, which gave her the flexibility to shape the stick into anything she wanted it to be, including a tire. "Want to try?"

I shook my head. "Pretty sure I'll just break it."

"That's a first," she said, smiling. She set the pliers back on the table. "Everybody thinks they can do it until they try."

"I'm sure it takes a lot of practice."

"It does," Memphis said. "We have to eat on the couch. I don't want to move my work."

She handed me a paper plate filled with macaroni and cheese and chopped hot dogs. It felt awkward, mostly because I'd had to do so much for myself after Grandpa was murdered and Mom had spent so much time working and going to school. I couldn't remember the last time somebody had cooked for me. "Thanks."

We sat down. "So, how's school?"

"Couldn't tell you," I said. "I kind of…I got suspended."

"That's not like you," Memphis said. She must have seen my confusion because she answered my question before I had the chance to ask. "It's not that hard to figure out that a man who gets up at an ungodly hour to wait for the school bus would have a decent attendance record, especially one who is on his own for the first time."

It made sense once she had explained it. "I forgot you read people."

"You'll get used to it," she said. "Why'd you get suspended?"

I shrugged. "Fighting."

"Over a girl?"

"Not exactly." As I was eating, I could feel her staring at me.

"Who's Jim?" she asked. The mere mention of his name brought back a flood of memories. Once again, I could see her read my reaction. "You talk in your sleep."

"I do?"

"Well, more like screaming. I knocked on your door, but it took you a while to answer."

"You did?"

"I was going to bitch you out, but then I realized you were having a nightmare."

"Didn't mean to wake you."

"I wasn't sleeping," she said. "Want to talk about it?"

"I'm fine," I said. But my hands were shaking so badly my food fell to the floor. As that fucking tsunami came roaring back, I fought it with every fiber of my being. The pain was as constant as it was unbearable, and I wanted to run as hard and as fast and as far away as I could. That was the first time I realized that the memory of a traumatic experience can be just as powerful as the experience itself. Taking a deep breath, I got up to leave. "This is…I'm not…and he…"

"What?" Memphis asked.

"He killed himself," I managed to say.

She froze.

"Well, you asked."

Memphis set her plate down, got up, and gave me a hug. After a moment, I tried to move away but felt her arms tighten as she pulled me closer; the muscles in her back were as hard as rock. The strength of her compassion somehow calmed the raging waters roaring inside me. She was sensual but not seductive; intimate but not sexual. Unlike all those lectures I'd got when Grandpa had been killed, Memphis didn't say a word; she just let me be. She listened—and that's the best advice I ever got about grief.

"Why are you doing this?" I whispered.

"Because nobody did it for me," Memphis said quietly. Leaning back, she moved my hair away from my eyes. "No one ever cared enough about me to just care about me. And I know what it's like to lose somebody."

"Your grandmother?"

"Conrad," Memphis said. She threw away the paper plates and tossed the spoons into the sink. "That's him on the wall."

"What happened?"

"He overdosed," she said. "Three years ago."

"You miss him?"

She looked at me. "Every day."

"Sorry," I said. "That was a stupid question."

"Everybody's sorry," she said. "Least, they are at first. It gets to them after a while, though. The grief. They expect you to let go, but you can't move on. And even when you want to move on, you can't let go. Anyways, after he passed away, I went on a binge and…Ginny took me in when I got out. Sometimes, we all need a little help."

It took me a moment. "You knew?"

"You know 'em when you see 'em," Memphis said. "It's what we do with what we see, once we see it, that matters."

I thought of the crowd at school after I had beat up Blaine—not just for what he said, but for the way he had said it: shouting and talking down to me, drawing out those fucking syllables, treating me like I was a goddamned moron. The stigma of the stares I got that day, and the whispering I would see in the halls when I went back to school again, would follow me throughout the rest of the year; even my teachers treated me differently. Once word of James's suicide got around, as it inevitably did (probably because of Allyson), I became a marked man, a plague to be avoided by every means necessary because nobody could bear to see so much as the shadow of my grief. I had always been an outcast in high school, but now I felt like a castaway lost at sea in a nasty nor'easter. And nobody could see past the storm—except Memphis, who'd had a few of her own.

As the weeks dragged on, I kept having trouble sleeping. Memphis was the only one awake when I got up, soaked in sweat and reeling from yet another nightmare. I'd shower and then head across the hall. She would let me in and usually go right back to work while I'd make something for us to eat. If she was stuck on a project or waiting for a painting to dry, we'd cook together. She didn't mind the company, she'd said, because most of the time she was so focused on her artwork she'd forget to eat.

There were nights neither of us had a whole lot to say, but other times she'd share a random memory from her childhood, like picking apples in the backyard for her grandmother's pies or that time she took Memphis to Disneyland. I told her about Grandpa's famous root beer floats and learning sign language with him. She said that the only sign she knew was *I love you.* When she asked, I told her how he died. Once again, she never said a word; she just set her arms around my waist and leaned her head against my back as I was making French toast. In a way, we shared an unspoken understanding about the burdens of our griefs. I also learned that Memphis went to meetings five nights a week for Narcotics Anonymous, which helped her stay clean. More than once she'd mentioned that she was sick to death of guys asking her out at meetings; most of them were new to the program, which meant it was too much of a risk.

"My recovery comes first," Memphis told me. She was always fierce, but often fragile. "Besides, they just want to get laid. You can get that anywhere. I don't want any part of that. Sex is easy."

"Love is hard."

"I prefer a challenge."

"So, what do you want?" I asked. I glanced at the photograph of Memphis and Conrad as I handed her a plate of French toast. They looked happy.

"Thanks," Memphis said, setting down her paintbrush. She always folded her French toast and ate it with her hands, masterfully pouring syrup over each bite. "I want what I had. Well, I mean, I'll never have what I had, but…I don't know. When I was a kid, I believed in fairy tales. My grandmother always used to say that I was a princess, like Cinderella or Sleeping Beauty. I guess relationships are just too much these days. But, a best friend? They don't judge or use you or put you down. You never doubt their loyalty or devotion or commitment. You just know, you know? And that's what I want, a best friend. What about you?"

"What about me?"

"What do you want?"

"Haven't really thought about it," I said. "I know my last girlfriend couldn't possibly relate to my life now. Prom is coming up next month, but most of the girls at school look at me like I'm a freak. Suicide is such a fucking taboo. It's ridiculous."

"You should go," Memphis said. "Make 'em wonder why you're still smiling."

"I'd settle for a decent night's sleep."

"Roger, I'm serious," she said. "You only live once. Get it right the first time. Enjoy it."

She had a point. "You want to go?"

"Me? To a prom? Are you kidding?" Memphis said, laughing. This time, it took her a moment. "My god, you're serious."

"Is it really such a terrible idea?"

"What? No! It's just…I can't go to a prom. I can't. I don't even have a dress."

"If half of what you've told me about Ginny is true—"

"Life is not a fairy tale, Roger."

"Who says it has to be?"

"I can't."

"Why not?"

"Because I can't, okay? I just can't."

"Well, I guess it's easier to give advice than it is to follow it," I said. I didn't think she would say yes, but I certainly wasn't expecting her to laugh. Getting up, I headed for the threshold and opened the door.

"Just prom, right? Nothing else?"

"Just prom."

"Okay, I'll go," Memphis said. "As long as Ginny can help me find something decent to wear. And I want to get my nails done. Again, I mean. And my hair."

It had been a long time since I felt this good about anything. "We'll figure it out."

"And I suppose we're taking a limo?"

"I got something better."

"Better than a limo?"

The Mustang growled as we drove up to the front entrance of the school. Getting out, I walked around the car and opened the door for Memphis.

"Damn, man. Where'd you get the car?" Tim asked.

I took Memphis's hand as she got out. "Stole it."

"Forget the car," Junior said. "Where'd you meet the girl?"

"Next door," Memphis said. "You're the ones who give him a ride to school, aren't you?"

"That's us," Junior said. After introductions, Memphis said that she could wait with Tim and Junior while I parked the car. Once I'd got the Mustang out of storage yesterday afternoon, I washed and waxed it before picking up my tuxedo and getting my hair and beard trimmed. My tux was white tie. When Aunt Carol had taken me to get a suit for Grandpa's funeral, she'd said that formal occasions require discretion, adding that a simple look for a man puts the spotlight on the woman, which was how it should be. As I got dressed that afternoon, I couldn't help but wonder about my family. Mary and Carol—even Jake, in some ways—had always made such a big deal out of special events, but it wasn't until my family wasn't around anymore that I began to understand why.

It hit me once I'd started on the bowtie. No matter how many times I tried, I couldn't get that damned thing right. Finally, in a fit of grief, I broke down crying again as I realized that Grandpa would have done it for me. Mary would have told me how handsome I looked, Carol how proud she was of the man I'd become, and Jake would take pictures. Maybe he'd even do my tie, since Grandpa wasn't around. Prom was among my last passages before heading out into the world, but as I saw that stranger staring back at me in the mirror, I realized he had grown up far, far too soon. For years, I couldn't wait to be on my own, but now that I was, I needed help I didn't have—and I hated it. I hated leaving my family behind in the pursuit of my own life, a life I'd never wanted in the first place. But was my family even my family?

"What the hell happened to you?" I asked the man in the mirror. I had a prom date with a gorgeous woman who treated me like a human being; I was working full-time, supporting myself, and I was about to finish high school; I'd even had a job lined up down at the Boat and had planned my budget to start college in the fall. By any measure, I had a lot going for me at such a young age—and yet, my grief pressed upon me mercilessly. Wiping my eyes, I remembered what Memphis had told me: "Make 'em wonder why you're still smiling."

It was then I decided that I was going to live my life, in spite of the mess it had become.

Memphis had told me to pick her up at Ginny's house in Rose City. I'd met her at the shop a few months ago. She was a sweet, little old lady who had made me feel welcome (so much like Grandpa). Ginny was thrilled that Memphis was going to a prom. The moment I walked through the door, Ginny saw that I needed help with my tie. Without a second thought, she had it done in less than a minute. I had no idea what Memphis's dress looked like, but, hoping for the best, I'd bought a white corsage. When I saw her coming down the stairs, I froze.

Her immaculate white heels had to be four inches high. She wore that same string of pearls around her left ankle. She looked luminous in her sky-blue satin dress, cut at a curved angle from her knee to her calf. Ginny had made a fitted, sleeveless dress with a white off-the-shoulder neckline that came to a point above Memphis's heart. The color brought out her eyes in mesmerizing ways. Her smooth dark hair had a tint of red, caressed in the rays of the setting sun seeping through the window, with a long, flowing natural look trimmed and tied back at the base of her neck. A few stray strands lingered over her cheeks, whispering as she came down the stairs. I took her hand as she descended the last few steps; her nails were red as rubies.

"Jesus Christ, you look great," I whispered.

"Thank you," Memphis said, smiling. She took a deep breath. "You look pretty sharp there yourself."

"Well, Ginny had to help me with the tie," I said. "This is for you."

I handed her the corsage, but I was so nervous, and trembling so badly, Ginny had to put it on her wrist.

"And there we go," Ginny said as she finished. "Now, just wait one second. I'll be back."

"I forgot she wants a picture," Memphis said. "I kind of haven't had a date in two years…or three years or something. So, kind of a big deal."

A moment later, Ginny returned with a small wooden box. When Memphis saw the string of pearls inside, she gasped and brought her hand to her mouth as tears welled up in her eyes.

"She would want you to wear them tonight," Ginny said. After putting on the necklace, she gave Memphis a hug and took our picture. "Your granny would be so proud of you. Tonight, and every night. And don't let anyone tell you different, child. I always knew you was a princess, and tonight you get to be one for real, okay? You deserve this night, this prom."

Smiling, Memphis nodded as she wiped the corner of eyes.

"So does he," I heard her say quietly. "God, Ginny, if you only knew…"

We had dinner at The Up River Café, a five-star restaurant built out over the Pawcatuck River on the Rhode Island side. At the entrance, I glanced over the reviews and saw that they had won several awards from *Wine Spectator* for having one of the best wine lists in the world. (I wasn't old enough to drink, but it was still pretty impressive.) The hostess, Sienna, confirmed our reservation and led us to the lower dining room. A small fire glowed as I guided Memphis into her seat. Behind the sliding glass windows and brass rails, the river rushed from recent rains. The linen napkins matched the immaculate tablecloth as a single candle lingered in the center. The atmosphere was excellent.

Memphis couldn't decide what she wanted so she just got what I ordered—a grilled flat-iron steak over bleu cheese and a purple potato cake topped with pepper-cress salad and red wine jus. The food and the service were great. Even the owners, Dan and Jen, stopped by to wish us the best. Memphis told them that she was having a wonderful time, but added they needed to do a better job dusting; she had meant it as a joke, but they promised to discuss it with the cleaning contractor. (There is no second place, Dan had said, when it comes to excellence.) We ended up staying longer than I had expected. I didn't want Memphis to feel rushed, but I was worried we were going to be late. Once we got to the school, though, I realized we were early. We both had another cigarette after Tim and Junior went inside. As always, Memphis stole mine the moment I had it lit. I was about to light another when I saw Blaine's Mercedes racing around the parking lot, squealing around the flagpole lawn before us as the kids inside threw their empty liquor bottles out onto the ground.

"What a jerk," Memphis said. As the Mercedes slowed, Allyson looked directly at us before turning her head toward Blaine. A moment later, they took off like a bat out of hell.

"That's Blaine," I said. "The guy I beat up a few months ago."

"At least he's not staying," she said as the car squealed out of the lot. "You okay?"

"Yeah," I said. The cool, quiet night reminded me of the times Dad had to work late at the station so Mom and I would bring him dinner. "You know, when I was a kid, I could hear crickets on a night like tonight. I guess it's too early for that, though."

"There are crickets," Memphis said. "Can't you hear them?"

I listened for them in the silence, but silence was all I heard. As far as I knew, there were no crickets. And yet, in my mind, I could remember crickets. I knew they were supposed to be chirping, even Memphis had said so, but still I couldn't hear them. After a moment, the silence grew so loud my ears started buzzing so I just told her, "My ears ring when I get nervous."

"Don't feel bad," Memphis said. "I kind of…I haven't had a date in a while."

"You said that earlier."

"I mean, I don't know what the rules are," she said. "So maybe I'm breaking them, but you know this necklace? It belonged to my grandmother. The bracelet I got from Conrad. He gave it to me a few…well, a few weeks before it happened. It's probably not fair to you, but I wanted to wear it tonight. People keep telling me to move on—and, god, I hate that—because I honestly don't know if I can let go. Jesus, you must think I'm crazy for bringing all this up now. It's just…I just wanted you to know, if that's all right."

"Memphis, it's okay," I told her. "I mean, you know I still have nightmares about Jim. Haunts me every damned day. And I lost it earlier thinking about my grandpa. Letting go does not mean you've moved on. Moving on does not mean you must let go. They're both with you tonight. Always will be. And I get that. I do."

"I..." she started to speak, but a cool breeze came in off the coast. "I'm freezing."

"Here," I said, carefully setting my jacket over her shoulders.

"Thank you," Memphis said. She set her hand on my cheek, gently brushing my beard. The way she smiled in the lingering twilight, with her eyes shining in the streetlights, it was in that moment I knew she had me. She took my arm as I led us inside.

The lights in the gym faded to different colors, like we were dancing in a rainbow. We started at a distance but, as the night went on, got closer and closer until it felt like we were the only ones in the world dancing at prom. She wore my jacket all night. At eleven, we were about to leave, but Memphis wanted one more dance. Once I heard "Fairytale Lover" by UTFO start playing, I stood before her and started signing the lyrics.

Memphis, smiling, crossed her arms and pulled my jacket in around her shoulders as the crowd gathered behind her. Everybody started singing along as I repeated the chorus, but I just kept signing to Memphis like they weren't even there. When it was over, the crowd cheered as we embraced. Leaning in my ear, Memphis said, "Just a prom, my ass!"

"Nobody's perfect," I told her. She laughed. "Want a milkshake?"

She smiled. "I would love a milkshake."

"Let me just get our glasses," I said. "I also have to use the restroom."

"Go ahead," she said. "I can get the glasses."

I was finishing up when I heard a few guys come inside the bathroom. I couldn't hear what they were saying, but, by their tone, I could tell that they were drunk and being obnoxious. Looking beneath the stall, I saw two sets of black shoes walking toward white heels that were backing away. The string of pearls around her ankle was unmistakable. Just as I stepped out of the stall, Memphis scratched the eyes of the two boys beside her and kicked Blaine between the legs. When he keeled over, I grabbed Blaine and shoved his face down the toilet. He fell to the floor soaking wet, cowering in pain. Memphis had the other boys on the ground and was taking turns beating them to a pulp with her bloody white heels. When she saw me, we ran like hell.

The pouring rain pounded across the parking lot. We were halfway to the Mustang when Memphis stopped by the flagpole, fell to her knees, and started crying. I held her, hovering over her to shield her from the rain.

"It's okay," I said. "It's okay now. It's—"

"It's not okay!" she snapped, pushing me away. "Goddamnit, don't you get it?"

"What?" I asked. "What am I missing? What's—"

"I don't know how to fucking read!" she screamed, burying her face in her hands. I held her a moment then picked her up and carried her through the rain. "What are you doing?"

"Sometimes, we all need a little help."

"You're not ashamed of me?"

"Of course not," I told her. She ran her fingers through my hair, setting it back so that I could see, and brushed her hand against my beard.

She signed, *I love you* and said, "You and me?"

"Yeah, you and me," I told her. "You and me against the world."

"You and me against the whole goddamned world."

"Besides," I said. "There's something I think you should know…"

"Oh, god. What is it now?"

"Well, it's just…you know how I shoved his face down the toilet?"

"What about it?"

"I forgot to flush."

She burst out laughing, tilting her head back as the pouring rain washed away her tears.

"I need a milkshake," Memphis said, catching her breath as we got to the Mustang.

"We can do that," I said. Leaning over, she opened the door and I set her inside.

"You and me," I told her, signing, *I love you.*

After getting our milkshakes and stocking up on chocolate, we drove to the beach at Brockton Long Point. Once the storm had cleared, Memphis had me put the top down so we could watch the stars. We climbed into the back of the Mustang and spent the whole night talking and eating chocolate, sometimes playfully feeding each other. Memphis, tough as nails, admitted that she hated being vulnerable. She said that when I'd carried her to the Mustang, she had felt safe for the first time in a long time. She was grateful I hadn't judged her just because she didn't know how to read or write. Even when we had first met, and I found out that she was a convicted felon, Memphis knew I was different because I hadn't judged her that time either.

"That's why I kept testing you," she said. "You never even asked me why I was in prison."

"Well, I guess I just figured you'd tell me when you were ready."

She sat up. "That's why you haven't kissed me yet…"

"Well, yeah," I said. "I didn't want you to feel—"

She kissed me, madly, as if her soul had been starving for affection. We made love at dawn, and I watched the golden rays of the rising sun caress her smooth skin while she was on top of me, precious as a string of pearls, well into the morning.

CHAPTER EIGHTEEN

THE LITERACY OF COMPASSION

"YOU GOT TO BE fucking kidding!" Memphis said as we approached the clinic, looking for a place to park. Hundreds of people had chained themselves together, blocking the entrance so nobody could get in or out. At the back of the crowd, dozens more were standing with their arms locked in front of the clinic doors while others held signs with Bible verses and pictures of dead, mutilated babies. A television news van was parked in a traffic lane that had been closed down to make room for the firetrucks and police cars. A cop motioned for us to wait as oncoming cars crossed the lane of travel. "Can you believe this shit?"

"And today of all days," I said. With shaking hands, I lit a cigarette. Seeing the police officer and the chaos had brought back memories of the night Grandpa had been killed, and I suddenly had flashbacks to finding Jim. It's a hell of a thing to endure the horrors of losing the people you love to murder and suicide, to spend every goddamned day trying to make sense of the sheer torment of your grief, the nagging questions that haunt you so badly there are times you can't eat or sleep or breathe, but to see so many self-righteous fingers stuck in my face alongside countless gruesome pictures compounded my fucking agony. School and work had kept me busy, but there were times that fighting the anxiety and the panic, the tsunami of my grief, felt like a full-time job. Today, I was working overtime.

Three weeks after prom, Memphis had told me that she was late. Once she was certain, she made it clear that she didn't want a child to go through what she did growing up in foster care, shuffling from one family to the next, getting beaten and being molested, starving and neglected. As a kid, Memphis had only caused enough trouble to make the foster care system send her to another family; she kept hoping to find a family that would be her family, but never did. That, she said, is what drove her addiction—because drugs cry for those who cannot weep and mourn for those who cannot grieve. Memphis had suffered so much, for so long, in such a broken system that for years it was all she could do to forget the pain. It wasn't until Conrad had overdosed, and she had gone on a binge that had landed her in jail, that she'd finally hit rock bottom; after that, she knew she had to get clean and sober. Waiting in traffic as the scalding morning sun beat down on us pushed my patience to the limit. I ran my fingers through my long, sweat-soaked hair, wishing I had remembered to tie it back. With traffic still not moving, I put up the top and the windows and blasted the air conditioning.

"They can't stay here forever," I said. "We could come back."

"Fuck this shit!" Memphis got out of the car and plowed through the crowd blocking the clinic. The police officers and firefighters just stood and watched while the news crew kept filming. I couldn't believe it. When somebody grabbed her T-shirt, Memphis fell into the crowd and started screaming for them to let go of her. I put the Mustang in gear and jumped the curb between the van and the firetruck, parking at the far end of the clinic. As I tried to make my way to her, the mob started spewing vitriol. When I said I was an atheist, they told me that I was going to hell for not believing in god. When I said I was raised Catholic, they told me that I was going to hell for worshiping Mary (which, as a Catholic, I didn't even know I did). Finally, I told them that I was born a Jew—and they said I was going to burn in hell for killing Christ.

"What the fuck ever," I said, climbing over them. The closer I got to the clinic, the more their rage intensified. They started calling me names like "baby-killer," "demon," "murderer," even "spawn of Satan." The thought of being equated with Grandpa's killer filled me with such a burning rage that my heart could have scorched the throne of heaven itself. After that, I stopped stepping over them and started stomping on them. A police officer got a megaphone and told me to get off the crowd before I hurt somebody, but it was then I saw Memphis.

Several men and women were holding her arms and legs while she squirmed in a physical fury, trying to get free. I couldn't even see her head, but they had somehow ripped her old T-shirt apart; her bra was visible. A bald middle-aged man, who had his head bowed, held his hands on her belly. His eyes were closed, and I could see his lips moving. Without thinking, I set my foot on somebody and jumped. My head hit something hard when I landed, and the pounding pain echoed through my skull as I got up and started shoving people away from Memphis. Once her legs were free, she began kicking like a World Cup champion until they finally let her go. I took off my T-shirt and tapped her shoulder. In a fury, she quickly threw it on—and then she fought back.

"Keep your fucking hands off me!" Memphis screamed, pushing the middle-aged man away. She slapped that son of a bitch so hard she left a red handprint on his pale face. "Where the fuck were you people when I needed a home? Did you adopt? Did you? What the hell makes you think you can tell me what to do with my body when you motherfuckers refuse to help a million kids condemned to foster care? You're all a bunch of fucking hypocrites!"

The whole crowd became stone silent. When Memphis turned around, I saw the despair in her eyes. She stepped toward me and collapsed in my arms. I carried her through the back of the crowd, which had miraculously parted like the Red Sea. Memphis buried her face in her hands as we passed between the atrocious pictures.

"You and me," I told her, trying to catch my breath. I had never been so exhausted. "You and me against the—" The gunshot exploded as the bullet splattered blood and shattered the glass door in front of us. My left arm dropped, and my knees buckled as Memphis's feet hit the ground. A nurse, hunched over in her scrubs, appeared in the doorway and directed us inside the clinic, quickly leading us to a room that had no windows. After locking the door, she picked up the phone on the wall and said something about medical attention.

"My god, you're bleeding," Memphis said.

"I'm fine," I said. But I felt dizzy. "It's just...I just hit my head..."

"It's not your head," Memphis told me. She was in shock, frightened and trembling; I felt cold and numb. "Roger, you got fucking shot!"

"What...?" It was then I saw blood pouring down my chest.

A group of nurses quickly came in through another door. One of them led Memphis out of the room while another put a bandage on my shoulder, holding it there as she guided me to lay down on the exam table.

I felt the whole world fading away as I blacked out, bruised and bleeding to death.

That was the day I graduated high school.

In the state of Connecticut, attempted murder is a felony punishable by up to sixty years in prison. Since the police already had officers on the scene, they were easily able to piece together what happened and press charges. The shooter, who had parked across the street from the clinic, admitted to lying in wait to see if Memphis and I were going to get inside. Once he saw that the crowd had cleared a path, he got his rifle out of the trunk of his car and fired. After the shot, he dropped his gun, surrendered, and was taken into custody. He actually confessed to aiming for my head, but the bullet struck my left shoulder just above the collarbone; I ended up with thirty-four stitches, half of them holding my muscles together under the skin.

When I woke up untold hours later, exhausted from the pain and lingering shock, Detective Denniston relayed the details with icy precision after I had asked about Memphis. He said that he had just spoken with her and that she hadn't been injured in the shooting. He had spent the whole day investigating and interviewing witnesses but wanted me to confirm what happened. I answered his questions in monosyllabic grunts, secretly stewing over Grandpa's death; I considered asking him about it, but the truth is I just didn't have it in me. I just wanted to go home.

Once the detective left, the doctor came by and gave me prescriptions for an antibiotic and pain medication. He told me to get some rest and said that I'd have to get the stitches out in eight to ten weeks while the ones inside would eventually dissolve. The nurse brought me a scrub top that I could wear home. She helped me put it on and explained that the medical staff had wanted to transfer me to a hospital, but it was too dangerous with the panicked crowd still chained together outside. Several of them had been injured, trying to scatter after the gunshot. Whoever had the keys was long gone; it took the firefighters several hours to cut the locks once the area had been secured. "Of course, they're all gone now."

"Where's Memphis?"

"Aside from losing her glasses in the fight with the crowd, she's fine," the nurse said. Memphis didn't wear glasses, but that must have been how she got the staff to fill out the paperwork for her while I was giving my pound of flesh. "She's a brave woman. Those people were never going to stop her. We had to monitor her for a few hours after the procedure. She's doing well and ready to be released, as are you. Soon as I get your sling on..."

That nurse talked so damned much I thought she'd never stop.

The front door had been boarded up, but it was still operable. The empty streets were cloaked in the shadows of the setting sun. I could see the Mustang on the other side of yellow caution tape surrounding the lot. Memphis was sitting on the same steps where we had almost been killed that morning. Holding on to the railing, I carefully sat down beside her. I felt dizzy and groggy.

"They say you never truly live until you face your fear," Memphis said. She wouldn't look at me. "I spent the whole damned day wondering if you were going to make it."

"Little rough around the edges," I said. It was a massive understatement. "But still here. How you doing?"

"Sore," she said. "God, I'm so sore. I really didn't think I'd be able to go through with it, but then they made that whole mess out here this morning—grabbing me, holding me down. Violating me. Christ, they almost killed us. They spent all that time trying to stop me, and all they did was convince me that I had to do it. I can't bring a child into this world. I can't do it. Not this world. I can't."

"Honestly, I…Memphis, I don't recognize this world anymore. I don't even recognize me."

"But I do," she said. "Was I worth it?"

"That much I'm sure."

"Why?"

"Because Superman said so."

She looked at me. "You're not Superman."

"I'm not bulletproof," I said, "but I was brought up to believe we can be better. We can be more than who we are. And that…that's our gift, Memphis. We have the ability to learn, the capacity to change. We grow. That's how we become better. We evolve with each new lesson we learn, if we're willing to accept those lessons. Those people out here today? That's what happens when people reject their gift. The only people who won't change are the ones who want everybody else to change. You said it yourself: how can they help the kids who aren't here if they won't help the kids who are here?"

Tears welled up in her eyes. "I love you."

"I love you too," I said. She reached over and gave me a hug.

"Does it hurt?"

"Do you?"

"I want a milkshake," she said. I knew what that meant.

"Let's go to Rosie's," I said. Getting up, we headed to the Mustang. A man got out of the jet-black Buick parked near Sally and approached us. He was wearing a baby-blue Oxford with a scarlet tie and tan Levi's Dockers. He tried giving me his business card, but I wouldn't take it. "Who are you?"

"My name is John McCoy," he said. "I'm an elder at Sterling Bible Chapel. We—"

"You were the fuckheads blocking the clinic," Memphis said.

"We were saving lives."

"Could have fooled me, motherfucker."

"Are you here to kill me, John McCoy?" I asked.

"We don't do that," he said, laughing nervously as his face turned red. "In fact, I've been authorized to inform you that the church council has agreed to pay your medical expenses—"

"What about my medical expenses?" Memphis asked.

"—and I want to assure you that we were in no way involved with such a despicable act. The shooter admitted to acting alone. SBC does not condone violence of any—"

"The hell you don't!" Memphis snapped. "You bible-thumping fucks ripped my T-shirt to shreds and held me down! You fucking crucified me! Fuck you! Fuck you! You just don't want to get sued! You are an asshole!"

Memphis started walking aggressively toward him as he slowly backed away. Honestly, I wanted to beat John McCoy to pulp, but I was too weak—too tired, too hungry, too dizzy, and too goddamned sore. Instead, I took a deep breath and said, "Did it just not occur to you people that if you hadn't been here this morning, we wouldn't even be having this conversation? She could have walked in, got it done, and walked out. Instead, we damn near got killed—because of you. Get the fuck out of my face, man."

McCoy, ashamed, quietly said something to Memphis, but I couldn't hear what it was; I did hear what Memphis said back to him though, her voice rising as she spoke. "It's your fault he got fucking shot, asshole! Maybe you didn't pull the trigger, but your being here caused this! Are you going to bomb this place next week, motherfucker? Fuck you! Get the fuck away from me! Leave my body alone! And his too, you fuck-head!"

With my good arm, I made half an effort to hold Memphis back as McCoy walked away. Opening the door to his car, he turned to me and said, "The church council needs an answer as to whether or not you're going to accept our offer."

"You fucking people will say anything to make yourselves feel better," I said. "You'll do anything to justify your own self-righteousness. You want to pay the bill? Fine. Just get the hell away from us. Just go. I'm too old for this shit, so just…just go. Just go."

I watched his car disappear down the street.

"That was fun," Memphis said.

"He never even answered your question," I said. "He would have ignored you if you weren't..."

"What?"

"Well, if you weren't you."

"It's like you said," Memphis told me. "Hearing isn't listening."

"I am so goddamned tired," I said. As we got to Sally, I unlocked the door.

Memphis chuckled. "Jesus, you're something else."

"What?"

"Opening the door after taking a bullet for me," she said. "You're my hero."

"Don't call me that," I told her. "Please don't call me that."

"Why not?"

"Because by the time you do what it takes to be a hero, you don't want to be a hero," I told her. I was surprised at how much I sounded like my father, but I knew exactly what he had meant now. "Besides, I…let's go home, okay? I just want to go home. I'm so fucking tired. All that bullshit is more exhausting than losing all that blood."

I could see that she was in pain.

"I'm really glad you're all right, Roger," Memphis said. "I mean, I already lost Conrad, and I don't…I don't know what I'd do if…"

"Hey, it's all right," I told her, wiping a tear from her cheek. She came in close and started crying. Beneath her tough exterior, Memphis still allowed herself to be vulnerable in our private moments. I felt her body tremble as I held her with my good arm. "We're okay. It just takes time. It's all going to be okay…"

Sometimes, the only way to make things better is to believe that they will be.

I wouldn't recommend trying to teach your girlfriend how to drive on the same day you both fought a fucking mob of religious fanatics who tried to kill you. Memphis wasn't supposed to drive so soon after the procedure, but I was in no shape to get behind the wheel. So, we compromised and took turns driving from Hartford back to The Heights. She had never drove before so as I got us out of the city I gave her a few lessons on watching traffic, making turns, and keeping the car steady. I hadn't even used my arm, but the pain in my shoulder was excruciating. We stopped for a couple of Cokes and switched in Glastonbury.

With the Mustang bucking like a Bronco, I felt pain in places I didn't know it was possible to feel pain. Memphis drifted in and out of her lane more times than I could count, with so many panicked stops I almost had a heart attack. It was a miracle we didn't have an accident. My anxiety skyrocketed as it hit me that she wasn't insured and didn't even have a license. More than that, Sally was all that I had left of Jim; he had given the Mustang to me, trusting me to take care of it, but now I was scared to death that I would lose that too. It took every ounce of willpower to keep my cool. By the time we switched again in Colchester, the smallest bump or slightest shift in my seat was excruciating. I was relieved when we got to Rosie's Diner.

"We made it," I said, shutting off the car. "We actually fucking made it."

"It's about fucking time," Memphis said. "You want me to drive back to the apartment?"

"I can manage."

"How'd I do?"

"Not bad for your first lesson."

She chuckled. "You're a bad liar."

"We're alive," I said. "That's all I care about."

"You okay?"

"I'm fine. I just want to sit here. Just for a few minutes. Can you...Would you mind getting our milkshakes?"

"I'm starving," she said. "You want something to eat?"

"French toast with bananas—"

"And extra syrup," she said, opening the door. "Your comfort food. I know."

She got out of the car and went inside the diner. I lit a cigarette and felt the buzz. The humidity in the night air was cool. A moment later, somebody called my name. I looked up and saw two girls I'd seen in school, Jennifer and Michelle, dressed in hula skirts and bikini tops. It was then I remembered that our all-night graduation party had a Hawaiian theme. "Is this your car?" Michelle asked.

"I didn't see you at the ceremony," Jennifer said.

"I was...busy."

"But it's graduation," she said. Scott and Eric walked up and stood behind them. "It's our moment. We earned this. You earned this."

"Is this really your car?" Michelle asked. I told her it was. "Where'd you get it?"

"Stole it."

"Yeah, right," Scott said.

"What happened to your shoulder?" Jennifer asked.

"I got shot this morning."

"You are so full of shit," Eric said. Even from a distance, I could smell the vodka on his breath. "He probably pulled a muscle getting out of the shower. You expect us to believe you got shot stealing a '67 Mustang? What, are you trying to protect your image? Like you even got an image. 'Look at me! I'm a tough guy! I'm so cool I lie about everything!'"

I took a drag from my cigarette. "Sixty-four and a half."

"Come on," Scott said. "Let's get out of here. What a loser."

He walked away with the others, but Jennifer stayed behind. "Are you at least going to the party?"

"I have other plans," I said. Memphis came outside with our packaged dinner. She got in the car as Jennifer left.

"Who was that?" Memphis asked.

I waited for the hooting and hollering to fade as they squealed out of the parking lot and raced down the street.

"A couple of spoiled rich kids from school," I said. "Forget 'em."

"Let's just forget this whole day," she said. "All of it. Forever."

"Really?"

"Ten years in foster care? Hello? I detach at the drop of a fucking hat. Trust me. It's better to just forget the pain and get on with your life. Thinking about shit don't make it stink less. What?"

"Can I have my shake?"

Memphis wanted to stop at Waldbaum's to stock up on groceries while we were out. She hauled the paper bags inside while I did what I could to put things away. She got the rest of it as I settled into the recliner; it hurt too much to lay down. I dozed off while she was in the shower. When I woke up, I saw that Memphis was sleeping on the couch. I had intended to look after her once she'd had the abortion, but instead she was the one who had to look after me.

Memphis seemed so peaceful, so beautiful. I watched her sleep for a few minutes until I shifted in my seat and felt the pain in my shoulder. Getting up, I took another dose of medication and decided to put the Mustang back in storage. It was after three-thirty in the morning by the time I had it locked up.

The humid summer heat hit me while I was walking back. I stopped at a Nutmeg Farms gas station to use the bathroom. After washing my hands and face, I saw that stranger in the mirror staring back at me. As I tried to digest what had happened, I couldn't help but think of what my mother—Mary, that is—had warned me about years ago, how my life would one day become everything I never wanted it to be. Poquanicut was so far away to me now that even my memories felt like distant strangers. I had even missed my high school graduation. It would have been a lot of fun to go to the party.

As my new, horrifying reality began to sink in, the tsunami came roaring back in grunts and growls until I collapsed on the floor. I missed my parents, my job at the station, and my home back in Poquanicut. This time of year, I could smell the morning dew on the fresh-cut grass through my open window. Now, a man who knew nothing about me had made a deliberate decision to try to kill me. My immense grief became a maddening rage. That fucking cult at the clinic was nothing like the Deaf President Now protest at Gallaudet University. It had only taken the Deaf seven days to achieve every single one of their demands, but those pathetic religious fanatics had accomplished absolutely nothing except humiliating Memphis—and fucking shooting me. Whatever god those people worshiped, I'd rather burn in hell than be a part of it.

Grandpa had raised me as a Catholic, but my biological mother, Carol, was Jewish. I knew very little about Catholicism and even less about Judaism. When I wondered what it meant to be a Jew, all I could think of was light—bright, brilliant light dispelling darkness, like the candles Carol had lit so long ago. As I reached back even further, I remembered that Father Sullivan had once said that Satan means "accuser," but Lucifer was an angel of light—and that, I realized, is the Devil: the one who accuses you under the guise of it being for your own good.

It was a story as old as America itself, from Hester Prynne to John Proctor. Tribalism is a prison of perception. We just kept neglecting the gift of our own humanity, our ability to learn and to change, to evolve and embrace our capacity for compassion. Instead, we shoot our wounded, knocking each other down during our darkest hours. Getting up off the floor, I took off the sling and threw it in the trash. Memphis was half-right: those people weren't just a bunch of hypocrites—they were fucking Satanists.

My grief and guilt over Grandpa and James still haunted me, like a demon lurking in the shadows of my mind. The wound in my shoulder was a welcome relief from my emotional torment; whenever I felt the tsunami beginning to rise, I'd stretch the muscles in my shoulder just to feel the physical pain. It fucking hurt like a bitch, but, after Jim, I deserved it. Honestly, I felt like I was living somebody else's life. Drifting through the darkness that night was really no different than any other day. I just kept going; there was nothing else for me to do—and nothing else I could do. Besides, staying busy kept my mind off everything.

Welding down at the Boat made my muscles ache something fierce. I had already learned to favor my right hand, and I'd slowly test the strength of my left more and more as the wound healed. I could get lost working inside that submarine. It was like the horrors of the whole world would just fade away while I hid behind that heavy shield, breathing the stench of smoke and sweat. Once I started college, I'd shower down at the Boat and take the bus to campus, usually doing my homework just before class. My professors mumbled so much, and people kept talking over each other during discussions, that I never really got much out of my time in class. Instead, I'd just focus on my homework, writing essays and papers on weekends.

Memphis got me a battered old Underwood typewriter for Christmas, which saved me the trouble of having to go to the library every time I had to write a paper. I'd got her more art supplies, which she loved. We moved in together in January, getting a bigger apartment on the third floor, after Ginny had closed the shop and retired. Memphis kept trying to sell her artwork, but she couldn't find a place that would accept it. She had spent a lot of time chopping wood last fall, but her income dropped in late winter. When I told her that I could afford the bills, Memphis said that she wanted her independence. As it got more and more difficult for her to make a decent income, Memphis asked if I could teach her how to read and write. Between work and school, I really didn't have the time.

"What made you change your mind?" I asked.

"It's our gift," Memphis said. "We learn. We can be more than who we are. We change, evolving with each new lesson—"

"If we are willing."

"Roger, I want to be more than who I am," she said. When I saw the look in her eyes, I realized just how hard it had been for her to ask. "Will you please teach me how to read, please?"

I smiled. "Hell, yeah."

Somehow, I made the time. We started with the alphabet. I wrote the letters on index cards—upper- and lower-case in both print and cursive—and we would go through them while making our late-night dinners. After that, I'd shuffle the cards and we'd go through them again and again until she could recognize any letter at any time. When it came to writing, I decided to watch her paint to see how she might hold a pen. From what I could see, she really didn't have far to go when it came to penmanship. Her work was so detailed that I just told her to paint the letters from the index cards onto a piece of paper. As Memphis learned to make the letters smaller, using the lines as a guide, I could see that she was quickly getting more comfortable. After that, we started working on simple words.

It wasn't long before Memphis made me realize just how difficult the English language can be. The word "power" looked like "lower" but sounded like "sour"; while the word "pour" looked like "sour," and yet sounded like "lure." It would have been so much easier if she were deaf; that way, I could just make the signs, finger-spell the words, and she could write out the letters. Instead, speech had become a barrier to her education. Tonight was no exception.

"This doesn't make any fucking sense," Memphis snapped in a moment of frustration. "Why does 'their' sound like 'hair,' but not 'lair'? Who the hell thought of this shit?"

"I have no idea," I said, rubbing my eyes. "It is what it is. Why don't we take a break and start again after dinner? We need cigarettes anyway."

"I really wish you'd get the car out of storage," Memphis said. "It can't be easy taking the bus and walking everywhere. You need to rest, Roger."

"I don't mind taking the bus," I told her. "Walking helps clear my head, and Hans doesn't mind giving me a ride after class."

I had met Hans in class last year. He had a thin salt-and-pepper mustache and mullet. Hans used to work down at the Boat, but he had messed up his hands so bad he needed surgery to fix them. He still worked weekends as a medic but spent most of time taking care of his four kids while his wife worked; in the evenings, he went to class. Hans had admitted to seeing me on the news, carrying Memphis into the clinic. He hadn't told anybody except his wife; I let him know I appreciated his discretion.

"Most people burn the candle at both ends," Memphis said, "but you're using a flamethrower. I still can't believe you went back to work so soon after getting shot."

"I'm fine," I told her. But everything hurt all the time. "Want to get a pizza for dinner?"

"Let's get something different," Memphis said. "How does moussaka sound?"

I shook my head. "For the life of me, I'll never understand how anybody can eat a pizza with eggs and hamburg."

"Eggs and hamburg?" Memphis said. She was confused at first but then started laughing. "It's eggplant and hamburg!"

"It is?"

"Of course. Where in the world did you ever get 'eggs and hamburg'?"

Hearing her laugh made me feel stupid. The first time I'd heard the term "moussaka" was when Dad and Grandpa had ordered at Mrs. Pizza after my

Little League game. I could have sworn Dad had said "eggs and hamburg," which sounded like "eggplant and hamburg" or "eggplant, hamburg." Maybe I hadn't heard him or maybe Dad had just not used the conjunction. Whether it was him or me, it was a simple enough mistake to make—especially since I'd had no idea what eggplant even was when I was a kid.

"I don't mean to laugh," Memphis said. "I just thought it was funny."

"Get what you want," I told her. "I'm going out for cigarettes."

It was a crisp autumn afternoon. As I was walking, I saw dead leaves dancing in the winds, but the crinkle was gone. I remembered the sound but couldn't hear it anymore. Mary had said Grandpa had lost his hearing because of mastoid problems, but there was also the war to consider. That had to have an impact. But Uncle William, my biological father, had worn a hearing aid on his wedding day. Had he inherited it from Grandpa? And if he had, would I inherit it as well?

As I considered the possibility of going deaf, I remembered all the times people had demeaned me because I couldn't hear them at the time. My high school English teacher, Mr. Wright, had literally said that I would never amount to anything; Dorothy had viciously snapped at me; my college professors and peers just ignored me; and now Memphis had belittled me with her laughter. As my rage simmered, I thought of Grandpa's confrontation with Mary. I had never seen him so angry before in all my life. He had unloaded decades of being treated like shit in a single afternoon. As a pile of leaves blew quietly across my path, I knew one thing: I was never going to let anybody treat me like that. It was time to get my hearing checked.

It didn't take long for me to realize that while the science was conclusive, the scientists themselves were far from objective. The first audiologist I saw dressed like a boy-band reject. His dark hair had been combed in a wave up the side of his head, and his black shirt had a wide collar unbuttoned at the top, showing off his fake tan and gold chains. I had to wait over an hour in the lobby and another forty-five minutes in the exam room until he finally came to see me—two hours after my scheduled appointment time. My ears were buzzing so badly in the silence that my patience was razor thin. He wheeled up a small stool and sat down.

"Well, what can I do for you...Mr. Evans, is it?"

"I'd like to have my hearing tested."

"What makes you think you need to have your hearing tested?"

"What?"

"I said, 'What makes you think you need to have your hearing tested?'"

"You get paid for this?" I said. He didn't get that joke either.

"Very well," he said. Taking an otoscope out of his shirt pocket, he looked into my ears. "No excessive wax, and...I don't see any damage. Looks fine to me."

"You haven't tested it yet."

"Well, you're young," he said. Wheeling over to the counter, he made a note in my file. "With a few exceptions, hearing loss usually doesn't occur until we get older. In your case, much older. I really don't think there is anything to be concerned about. Just stay away from the bars and clubs. Concerts, that sort of thing."

"I've never been to a bar," I told him. "Or a concert. Never mind a club."

"Your speech is obviously very good," he said, closing my file. "A hearing test would be a waste of time."

"I just spent two hours waiting to get my hearing tested," I said. I could see from his expression that I had hit a nerve. "And you think I'm the one wasting time? For an audiologist, you sure don't listen very well."

"Have a nice day, Mr. Evans," he said, getting up. He muttered something under his breath as he left the room, but I couldn't hear what it was—and I'd bet that son of a bitch knew it too.

When I got to the front desk, I saw my file sitting on the counter. The receptionist said that she had forgot to get my insurance information. When the phone rang, and she turned to answer it, I quickly swiped my file and set it inside my jacket.

"I left my wallet in the car," I told her. She was still on the phone. "I'll be right back."

I walked straight to the bus stop and went home.

As the weeks and months went by, every day started to feel the same. I'd go to work in the morning and do my homework before class in the evening. The only time Memphis and I had together during the week was our late-night dinners. On weekends, I'd sleep in and teach her how to read and write between working on essays and term papers. I was so relieved when she asked to type my assignments; it gave me more time to read. After my first year of college, I still hadn't decided on a major. My adviser, Professor Henderson, said that I still had time. She suggested that I take a variety of classes to see what I enjoyed, but I was always so stressed out it was hard to enjoy anything.

In the fall, I had to give an oral presentation for my Literature & Composition class. I was supposed to write a poem, read it in front of the whole class like an idiot, and then facilitate a discussion. Professor Matthews had insisted that writers need to read their work out loud in order to understand their own words, but that didn't make no fucking sense because the words were always right in front of me. Who the hell needs to hear what they can see? Besides that, I read all the time—and I never knew anybody who had to read a book out loud to understand it. As I started writing, I began thinking of James again, about how he never really had a chance, and I tried to convey that in my poem.

Literature was never my best subject, but this was the one course I absolutely dreaded. The class had somehow got divided into factions, with Cindy and John being the respective frontrunners, who would argue every chance they could get. It was bullshit. I sat in the middle of the room next to Hans and Leona. She was a sweet little old lady, recently widowed, who had gone back to school. Hans had said that she was the one saving grace he'd found in that whole class, and I agreed; Leona was always up for a good laugh. The three of us all made it a point to stay out of the arguments. John wrote a poem about the true meaning of Christmas: how it was about more than shopping and that the world would be a better place if everybody realized how much Jesus loved them. I felt my heart pounding as memories of getting shot at the clinic last year came back to haunt me. The discussion was so intense that by the time it was over my shoulder was killing me. I'd had to fight the impulse to crawl under my desk and hide.

"Good discussion," Professor Matthews said, rolling her eyes. The arguments had clearly been getting on her nerves too. "And now, Roger, I believe you're the last one…"

I took my poem and headed for the podium. I had never spoke in front of people before, and I was nervous as hell. It didn't help when I saw everybody staring at me. I gripped the sides of the podium so hard my fingers hurt.

"This is called '*Autumnus Vox*,'" I said. "Which…well, I think that means 'Voice of Autumn.' At least, that's what I hope it means…"

"Passable," Professor Matthews said, smiling. "Go on, Roger."

Running my fingers through my long hair, I took a deep breath and started reading.

> I never saw the dawn of day,
>   but was born in time to die.
> I never had the chance to play,
>   but lived in time to cry.

I never left my solitary place,
  but stayed until my death.
I never saw my mother's face,
  but she seized my last breath.

I never knew, nor loved, my dad,
  but only as I was conceived.
I never will say that I am glad,
  but Mom had him so deceived.

I never knew his doubts, nor pains,
  but in darkness confusion reigns.
I never could have guessed her gains,
  but in darkness confusion reigns.

When I looked up, the whole class was still staring at me. For a moment, I thought I could just hand in my assignment and sit down until Hans said, "Wow."

Professor Matthews said something, but I didn't hear what it was.

"What's what?" I asked, facing her.

"I said the meter is excellent," she repeated. "Good rhyme scheme as well."

"Thank you," I replied. I couldn't help but smile. After all these years, I had finally beat my old high school English teacher, Mr. Wright, who had said I'd never amount to anything if I couldn't hear. The funny thing is, I still had no idea what the hell meter even was; I just wrote it.

"When did you start writing?" Leona asked.

"I learned the alphabet in kindergarten and just worked my way up from there," I said. It was a joy to make her laugh. "Seriously, though, I wrote it over the weekend."

"Why did you write it?" Cindy asked. I could tell she was angry about something, but I didn't think much of it because she was always angry about something.

I shrugged. "That was our assignment."

"I know that," Cindy snapped. "I mean, what gives you the right?"

"The right? What are you talking about? The right to—"

"He can write about abortion if he wants to!" John said. I was fucking shocked. "Men have just as many rights as women."

"My body, my choice!" Cindy shot back.

"We have a responsibility to stop infanticide!" Brian shouted.

Leona rolled her eyes, shaking her head slightly.

"Here we go again," I muttered. But they were already arguing so ferociously nobody had even heard me. Before long, Professor Matthews got up and tried to mediate, but it was clearly a lost cause. They were so loud, talking over and interrupting each other, that I couldn't hear anything anybody was saying; it was all just a bunch of goddamned noise. Hans tapped his shoulder and gave me a questioning look; I quietly shook my head. When Cindy and John got up and started screaming, pointing fingers at each other, I held my paper up before the class and ripped my poem to shreds.

"Settle down!" Professor Matthews said to the class as I finished. Finally, they all shut up. "Roger, what's going on?"

"Why did you do that?" John asked as I took my seat. "I was going to read it at my church."

"Motherfucker, it will be a cold day in hell before I allow you, or anyone, to read my poem at your church. You're just going to exploit my work for your own political agenda under the guise of your goddamned self-righteous religion. You want to save a child? Fine. You can start by taking care of the kids in foster care. Any fool can sit on a moral high horse when he isn't challenged by the reality of the race."

"Busted!" Cindy said. She raised her hand, as if to give me a high five. I ignored it.

"You're no better than he is."

"Excuse me?"

"I said, my best friend killed himself last year."

"Oh my god!"

"That's what it's about, genius. I mean, shit. Five minutes ago, I had no right. Now, I'm a member of the fucking club? I don't think so. A protest without a practical objective is meaningless. You can't join the movement for the thrill of the cause."

"You knew this class was like this," Brian said. "So why did you write about abortion knowing we were going to—"

"It's not about abortion, shit-head. I just told you that. I literally just told you that! You just assumed that's what it was about. All of you did. The second fucking line says, 'I was born.' Christ, I can't make it any more obvious than that. The problem is never what you believe, but that you demand everybody else believes it too. My writing tells you about the characters, but your interpretation tells me about your character. For someone who can hear, you sure don't listen very well. How in the hell can you hearing people not understand something I literally just…fucking …said!"

The silence in the room was so thick you could cut it with a knife.

"What's a hearing person?" Cindy asked.

"Oh my fuck—Never mind."

"Roger is talking about the literacy of interpretation," Professor Matthews said, "which is to say, you'll never understand somebody else's point of view if you're always assigning your own perspective to a work of art or literature. You will never learn anything if you're only looking to reinforce what you already know. Learning is not reinforcing. The challenge isn't to find the ways in which we agree or disagree with a work of art or literature, but to learn a different perspective from an author, a narrator, a character."

"What about Barthes?" Hans asked.

"Barthes is dead," Professor Matthews said. Leona chuckled, but I didn't get the joke. "We don't have time left for a detailed discussion tonight, so let me just say that there is a significant difference between the fluidity of interpretation and the rigidity of reinforcement. People who insist upon maintaining their own cognitive dissonance never learn anything when their perspective is challenged. A challenge to your perspective is less a threat than an opportunity to re-examine your convictions. It's also worth noting that, one day, you may read a story about a character with whom you are entirely unfamiliar."

I thought of Grandpa.

"So," Leona said, "whether you call it heads or tails, a quarter is still just twenty-five cents."

"Quite correct," Professor Matthews agreed, smiling.

I kept waiting for somebody to say they were sorry about what happened to Jim.

Someone, anyone. Something.

Instead, nothing.

I hated that class with a passion. I hated the arguments, the shouting. For all their talk, all their righteous rage, those people knew nothing of compassion; worse, most of them acted like they didn't know the difference between anger and kindness. They just spent their lives pointing fingers, as if accusation and condemnation were some sort of solution. If they couldn't shout from a soapbox, they had nothing to say.

After class, as we were walking to his car, Hans said, "What a night."

"No kidding," I said.

"Everything is a McApocalypse to those people," he said. "They think the sky is falling, but the universe is just laughing at them."

"I thought it would never end," I said. Hans asked me why I didn't show them my shoulder. I told him, "I ain't no fucking prop."

That was the last time I ever shared my writing.

In November, I got a loan for a brand-new black Nissan Sentra. It was expensive, but it would spare the Mustang my commute to UCONN next year. (And I didn't have to worry about Jim's father, wherever he was, finding me driving his old car; my anxiety about that always hung over me.) I'd also made an appointment to see another audiologist. He wore brown slacks and a tan V-neck sweater over a white turtleneck. His gray hair had a crew cut, and his bifocals made it look like he was always staring. I didn't have to wait as long to see him, which I thought was a good sign until he started my audiogram. That dark, soundproof room felt like a dungeon. The audiologist sat on the other side of the small glass window. My ears were buzzing like never before, and I couldn't tell if the tone was beeping or if it was just my ears ringing.

When it came to the speech portion, the audiologist instructed me to repeat the words as he spoke. As soon as I said one word, he immediately shot out another word. That guy spoke so goddamned fast it sounded like he was just saying the same word over and over again. No matter how many times he repeated the word—if he even was repeating that same word—I still couldn't hear what the hell he was saying. When the test was over, I took off the headphones and tossed them onto the floor. A few minutes later, he led me into his office.

"You have a mild-to-moderate hearing loss," he said, showing me the audiogram. "Did you say that both your grandfather and your father were hearing impaired?"

"My grandfather was deaf," I said, correcting him. "My biological father was hard-of-hearing. I have a question about my audiogram. Well, audiograms in general."

"Okay."

"Why does the vertical line descend as the volume increases?"

He looked at the test he had just given me. "What do you mean?"

"Well, it's quite a connotation," I said. "I've never in my life turned a knob down to increase the volume. Or anything, for that matter. Televisions, radios, fans, ovens…even light switches go up if you want more visibility."

"So?"

Leaning over, I drew my finger down the numbers. "So why do the decibels descend as the volume goes up?"

"Oh!" he said as his eyes popped open. "We do that to compare it with normal hearing, which is at the top. So we have a reference."

"But shouldn't the lowest volume be at bottom?"

"That's…just the way it's done," he said. He either didn't understand or, more likely, didn't care. Worse, he probably knew exactly what I was talking about. "Now, I noticed on your form you put down that you suffer from depression. Are you taking any medication?"

"No."

"That might be worth looking into," he said. "It's been proven many times that hearing loss leads to depression."

"I'm depressed because the people I love are dead," I said. "I don't think my deafness has anything to do with that."

"Irregardless," he said. "For the type of hearing loss that you have I'd normally recommend hearing aids, but there are a number of inconsistencies in your test. For instance, in the audio portion, your hearing loss is slightly more significant in your right ear, but your speech discernment is better on that side than it is in your left ear."

"I'm right-handed."

"Well, what does that have to do with anything?"

"I use my right ear when I'm on the phone," I told him. "It's had more practice."

"Well, I've been doing this for a while now," he said, chuckling. "And we still don't think your hearing is as bad as this test indicates. Why don't you come back in a year, and we'll see if anything has changed?"

I wanted to slap that stupid smirk off his face.

CHAPTER NINETEEN

THE RULES OF NATURAL LAW

THE SOVIET UNION COLLAPSED after the Berlin Wall fell in November 1989. The apparent end of the Cold War had left a lot of people with the illusion that the world had become a safer place, but the greatest dangers lurk in the darkness of our own ignorance. As America adjusted to its new role as the only superpower in the world, government cutbacks escalated rumors down at the Boat.

The guys at work would talk about layoffs, even a plant shutdown, as the Navy canceled contracts. I never paid much attention to the rumors because I was so busy with school. In my last semester at Rose City Community College, I took a course on twentieth-century history. Professor Fenton had restructured the class to focus on the Cold War, but his teaching style always left me out.

Small groups were the worst. I'd always tell them that I was hard-of-hearing. One minute they'd say it didn't bother them, and the next they'd tell me to forget it. They spent more time talking over each other than they ever did listening to me. When I'd ask one of them to repeat a question or comment, another would interrupt before I ever got a response. After that, they went right back to talking among themselves, and I had no idea what they were discussing because I'd missed that one crucial part of the conversation. I'd hear pieces of it—a word here or a phrase there—but it wasn't enough to know the details of what they were planning, much less to contribute. Instead, they chose me to write out the assignment for the next class because they said I never did anything; I'd collect their notes, throw them away when

I got home, and just do it on my own. We always got an A, so they didn't care. But as they cast me aside during class discussions, I turned inward and began making mental notes of what they were doing and why.

Human beings have a bad habit of defining a diverse world based upon their own perspective. When you speak, people always assume you can hear. And because so many hearing people equate speech with language, there is an underlying assumption that the ability to hear is somehow tied to intelligence. Growing up with a deaf grandfather and having seen a sea of native signers at Gallaudet University, I knew better. I knew that communication was never merely a matter of speech because with Sign I'd learned to read visual inflections like facial expressions and body posture, all of which I found to be more telling than the deceptive subtleties of speech. With speech, there was often, if not always, a significant difference between what people said and what they meant. Even an audiologist will admit that, long before acknowledging that Sign is a much more effective and superior means of communication.

I had thought about getting an interpreter for class, but, aside from my time in Washington, I hadn't signed consistently since Grandpa was alive. Besides that, I knew there were still plenty of sounds I could hear. Most of the time, I could make my way through casual conversations at work ("How ya doin'?"/"Good, and you?"), but it wasn't so easy to hear what my professors were saying during lectures because they kept pacing, turning away from me, while the handful of students who spoke in class often sat too far away for me to hear them; I'd already got into the habit of sitting front and center because that gave me the best opportunity to hear my professors, minimizing the distance between us, but I was still left out in mainstream education too often and too much. I seriously considered applying to Gallaudet University, but I'd already been accepted to UCONN. After this semester, I only had two years left until I got my degree, and I wanted to get it over with as soon as possible so that I could get a better job. That meant I had to find a competent audiologist—if there was such a thing.

Each time I went to see Dr. Steldman, he always seemed to be discussing his divorce with somebody. From what I could gather, he was going to close his practice in a few months so his estranged wife would lose out in the settlement. And he was always wearing a head mirror. I never saw him use it, though; it was like he only wore it as an archaic symbol of his authority. Despite telling Dr. Steldman my family history, he had insisted on a slew of tests to determine the cause of my emerging deafness. I spent the next few months getting six vials of blood drawn, a CT scan, and even an MRI. I'd wait for the results of my most recent test only to be told that another possibility had simply been eliminated. As the weeks wore on, I began to wonder what the purpose was of all those tests. Finally, Dr. Steldman requested copies of the CT scans of my inner ears, which had been taken before he had ordered my MRI.

"You have a mild-to-moderate hearing loss," Dr. Steldman said.

"I told you that the first time I saw you."

He just ignored me and set up the film from my CT scan and turned on the light so we could see the images.

"It's in the high frequencies, which are obtained in the depths of the inner ear. Now, normally, the inner ear circles about two and a half times. Yours, not so much. Take a look."

With a pen, he pointed out the small spirals of my inner ears.

"Do you have an image of an average one for comparison?"

"You don't need that," he said dismissively. "It turns out that your inner ear never fully developed. See? They only circle one and a half times. That's why you're missing those high frequencies like birds and crickets. Consonants are up there as well. You may have noticed we scream in vowels. The only good news is your speech discernment is excellent. You average seventy-nine percent between your left and right. That makes you a good candidate for hearing aids."

"Well, at least I have good insurance."

"Blue Cross doesn't pay for hearing aids," Dr. Steldman said. "Now, you said that—"

"Wait a minute," I said. "You're telling me that Blue Cross paid for all these damn tests but won't cover my hearing aids?"

"You're welcome to check," Dr. Steldman said. "I've just never heard of an insurance company that covers them. Besides, I think we used it all up anyway. Now, you said that both your grandfather and your father are both hearing impaired. Any brothers or sisters?"

Shaking my head, I told him, "No. What I said was my grandfather was deaf. My father was hard-of-hearing."

"I asked about your brothers and sisters."

"I don't have any siblings," I said. Getting up, Dr. Steldman grabbed a big book off the shelf. After flipping through the pages, he showed me a genetic family tree and said that hearing loss runs in my family. "Doc, I told you that the first time I saw you. So, what the hell was the purpose of all these damned tests?"

"We had to be sure," he said, closing the book. "Can I be frank with you?"

"Sure."

"You want to be careful who you marry."

"No shit."

"You just want to make sure there is no history of hearing loss on your wife's side," Dr. Steldman said. He took down the images, placed them in my file, and shut off the lamp. "After all, you certainly don't want to pass this on to your children, do you?"

My pounding heart echoed in my skull. I was fucking pissed.

"Let me get this straight," I said. "You maxed out my insurance just to tell me what I already knew. Now, you're trying to tell me that my inner ears never fully developed, and that's why I can't hear birds and crickets. But if my inner ears never fully developed, then how come I fucking remember birds singing and crickets chirping? And if the images from my CT scan are so goddamned conclusive, why did you insist on the MRI after I had the fucking CT scan?"

"You can leave now," Dr. Steldman said. When he grabbed my arm and pushed me, I shoved him back against the wall, catching his head mirror as it fell. After frantically feeling his chest, he went over to the sink and took off a locket that had been hidden beneath his shirt. Quickly, he turned on the water and started wiping away the white powder on his shirt and tie.

"Thanks for the crown, doc," I said, glancing at his head mirror. "Not every day I usurp a throne. Do I fucking look like I'm 'impaired?'"

"Get out!" he demanded. "Get out of my office!"

"Just remember—you push us, we push back."

When I got back to the apartment, Memphis was typing up another résumé; her job search had begun in earnest once she'd grown confident of her literacy. She had changed a lot over the past two years, and it was impressive to see her ferocity evolve into authority. I got a can of Coca-Cola Classic from the fridge and sat beside her at the couch so I could hear her better. She had prints of her portfolio scattered across the coffee table. "How did it go?"

"Like shit," I said, taking a sip. "He tried pulling the eugenics card. Turns out the guy's just a fucking coke addict who maxed out my insurance to support his addiction."

"Eugenics?"

"Selective breeding," I said. "Eliminating characteristics considered to be undesirable through euthanasia and controlled reproduction, including sterilization. Fucking bullshit. Jesus, I've been to three doctors in the past eighteen months, and every time it's the same damned thing. None of them can separate the science from their own superiority complex. It shouldn't have to be this hard."

"That doesn't make any sense," Memphis said. "Are you going to see another doctor? I mean, what if they can fix it?"

"Memphis, I don't need to be fixed. It's hereditary—and it's progressive. My hard-of-hearing uncle would have been deaf if he had lived as long as my grandfather."

"Your uncle? You mean your father."

"I guess. Yeah, whatever."

"Maybe you should talk to your mother about it," Memphis suggested. "She might know something."

I took a deep breath. "How is your job hunt going?"

"Roger, I'm serious," she said. "I know you're angry about what your parents did, but they still gave you a home. You still have a family."

"Can we please not talk about this?"

"Do you know what I would give to have had a family? To have a home, and clean clothes? To take a bath every day and have dinner every—"

"Please, just stop!" I snapped. I buried my face in my hands as I fought back tears. Of all the matters I'd tried to sort out in the past two years, what my family had done was still the most difficult for me to accept. I rubbed my eyes and lit a cigarette. "A house isn't always a home, Memphis, no matter how much you cook and clean. My father was a raging alcoholic who got post-traumatic stress in Vietnam that drove him to a fucking suicide attempt. My grandfather was the greatest man I've ever known, and…and Jim cut my fucking life in half! I can't remember what my life was like before I found him. I can't remember who I want to be. Jesus, I even got fucking shot, Memphis! Isn't that enough? Haven't I been through enough?"

"All right already," she said. I could see that she meant it.

"Do you realize my professors think I'm a fucking idiot because I can't hear everything they say? The other students treat me like I'm a goddamned second-class citizen just because I can't hear a few key words. After that, I can't follow the fucking conversation. And when I speak up about it, they just tell me, 'Pay attention!' I want to shake them silly because I am paying attention; I just can't hear! Not like I used to. And then I go see an audiologist who has the fucking nerve to try to tell me that hearing loss leads to isolation and depression, but they never say, 'We're the ones who isolate you by demanding you be somebody you're not!' Because they refuse to educate their clients on their own goddamned hearing habits! There is more to communication than sound. And, you know, I'm not stupid. I made the fucking dean's list. This bullshit is just fucking exhausting."

"Feel better?"

"Yeah, I do," I said. "Memphis, I'm just trying to build a life. It's all I know to do because it's all I can do. And I'm trying to get what I need so I can do that, but I just can't find anybody who gives a fuck."

"Hey, I give a fuck," Memphis said. "Didn't I get frustrated when you were teaching me how to read?"

"Yeah, you did."

"So just do what you taught me to do. Just keep going until you get it."

She tossed the phone book onto the coffee table.

A few days later, I had an appointment to see Dr. Collins in South Brockton. All things considered, I was skeptical, but the receptionist had said that he had been in business for thirty-seven years. I had grilled her over the phone, explaining what I had been through with other audiologists and that I needed professional results instead of personal opinions. She assured me that Dr. Collins knew what he was doing, and that if my audiogram revealed that I was eligible for hearing aids we could work something out.

Dr. Collins was a short, elderly man with gray hair and glasses. He actually wore jeans with a suede crimson sport coat over his white shirt with a bright blue Mickey Mouse tie. When he called me in from the waiting room and led me into his office, I saw that he was wearing a small pair of in-the-ear hearing aids. Immediately, the burden I'd felt about seeing another audiologist dissipated. Besides, how could you not love a man who wears a Mickey Mouse tie?

After taking my audiogram, Dr. Collins reviewed the different types of hearing aids with me. The greater the hearing loss, he said, the bigger the hearing aids had to be. Because my emerging deafness was still mild-to-moderate, he said that I could choose between the four sizes he had available, which varied from completely-in-the-canal to behind-the-ear. The more I wanted to hide my hearing loss, he said, the more I'd have to pay for hearing aids. My hair was still so long and thick that size didn't matter; I ordered the behind-the-ear ones, which were the biggest and cheapest hearing aids available.

We worked out a payment plan once I'd confirmed that Blue Cross wouldn't cover my hearing aids. I ended up canceling my policy. If Blue Cross wasn't going to pay for what I needed, then I wasn't going to pay them at all. I was still young and healthy so I could get by without medical insurance and, hopefully, get a better policy after graduation. My hearing aids were the only thing I needed—not all those damned tests—but Blue Cross refused. Worst of all, the only explanation I got from them over the phone was, "We just don't. We never have."

Dr. Collins made molds of my ears to get a fitting for my hearing aids. He set a small piece of foam, attached to a string, inside my canal and squeezed a bright green goop into my ears. After that, he gave me a piece of gum and held up a handwritten note that read "chew." My residual hearing faded as the molds hardened; I had never in my life known such peace. For a few minutes, a whole new world had opened up for me, one without the burden of those damning expectations I had endured at school and work, and it was so relaxing I felt disappointed when Dr. Collins removed the molds.

Three weeks later, my hearing aids were ready. Dr. Collins fit the tubing and had me put them on. Immediately, a high-pitched squeal hit me like a sharp scratch. Once I'd adjusted them, Dr. Collins warned that my hearing aids would buzz like that if they weren't set properly or if something was pressed against my ears. A massive rush of sound poured into my ears. I could hear the fabric of his shirt as he moved, the air blowing through the vents, but his voice was loud and strange. "How do I sound?" he asked.

"Like you're right next to my ear," I told him. "It's almost like it's too loud."

"You'll get used to it," Dr. Collins said. He had likened my getting hearing aids to putting on a pair of prescription glasses for the first time. Just as the ground seemed to move closer because the image was sharper, I had to adjust to processing sounds that had become unfamiliar. As he turned a page in my file, the crinkle of the paper was so unexpected that my eyes were drawn to it as much as my ears, like my eyes had to tell my ears what I was hearing.

Picking up a sheet of paper, I watched as I slowly tore it in half. I had memories of the sound, but the experience of hearing it now seemed unnatural and artificial. When I washed my hands in the restroom, the water sounded staticky, like a television set after the networks had signed off for the night. Doors creaked in resistance, rugs scuffled as I felt them beneath my feet, and a pen scratched as I signed the check for my first payment. The more sounds I could hear, the more I realized just how many of them were unnecessary.

Memphis was waiting for me in the lobby. "Well?"

"It…it's loud," I told her as we left the office. "Everything is loud, but it's more than that."

"What do you mean?"

"It's like the difference between seeing a painting and a photograph," I said. "The sounds that I remember are just drastically different than what I'm hearing now. Say something."

"Something."

I smiled. "Say something else."

"Something else."

"Oh my god," I said, laughing. "Come on, Memphis."

"What?"

"That's my line."

"Not anymore."

"Let's hope so," I said as we stepped outside. Immediately, the wind blowing over the microphones hit me like a maddening itch. "Jesus!"

"What's wrong?"

"You ever hear wind blowing over a microphone?"

"Is it bad?"

"It's annoying as all hell," I told her. I turned my head so that the breeze wasn't directly hitting the microphones. No sooner had I done so than the wind shifted. "This is going to take a little getting used to…"

"You'll figure it out," Memphis said. "Just put that college brain to work."

There are more things that audiologists don't tell you about hearing aids than they do tell you. For me, the turning point came a few weeks later. It was a Saturday morning. Memphis had gone to make more prints for her portfolio, and I had to go to the library to work on my research paper. I stopped at McDonald's for breakfast. The restaurant was so crowded I couldn't hear what the hell anybody was saying because everybody was roaring and laughing and shouting all at the same time. It was excruciating, like torture.

A short young man stood behind the counter. His hat was pulled down to his eyebrows, and a sign on top of the register hid most of his face. All I could see was his eyes, but when he looked down at the register, I couldn't see him at all. I knew he was talking, but I couldn't understand him without seeing his face. Each time I asked him to repeat himself, he would just look back down at the register. I had been up all night studying for final exams, and I was so tired and so hungry I just kept getting more and more frustrated with that kid.

Finally, I thought of Grandpa. The rest was easy.

"The hell with this," I said. Snatching the sign off the top of the register, I set it on the counter. "Now, say what you just said."

His face was red. "I was just asking if you wanted a drink with your breakfast."

"Medium coffee," I told him. "Black."

When the kid told me what I owed, he looked back down at the register yet again as he spoke, his hat covering most of his face. Instead of telling him to repeat the total, I just handed him a twenty-dollar bill and put the sign back up on top of the register. He gave me my change and receipt. As the kid was getting my order, he went to the far side of the counter, turned toward me, and spoke just as the men behind me roared in a burst of laughter and blaring speech. Taking a deep breath, I motioned for the kid to come closer.

"What's that?" I asked. The kid repeated his question, but I still couldn't hear what he was saying over the noise from the crowd. "Say that again!"

He spoke up but wasn't condescending. "Salt and pepper?"

"Yes, thank you," I told him. I double-checked my order; he'd got it right.

I had already learned in class that if I simply said, "What?" then people just thought I wasn't paying attention, but if I said, "What's that?" in a deep, commanding voice I got a better result because it got their attention. If I didn't hear what people said the second time, I would give them a command, "Say that again!" in a much deeper, more authoritative voice. Every day, in every conversation, I had to take a stand. No hearing person in the world ever had the patience to make it past the second "What?" After that, I always got "Never mind" or "Forget it" and my professors would just ask another student, if one hadn't interrupted me first. Because hearing came so easily to them, they had no patience for me. I hated it so much my rage nourished my intellect.

As I was eating, I started writing notes about what had just happened. The more I thought about it, the more I realized that I had been in unfavorable situations like that thousands of times. Reaching way back, I could even remember the first time it happened: a customer had insulted Amos at the station, a memorable moment because Amos had knocked him out. I'd heard part of the conversation, but the customer had been pacing as he spoke, turning away from me, and I'd missed that one word which, as my father would explain, had an atrocious history behind it—and, like Dad had said, it was particularly disrespectful to a veteran like Amos.

But today was the first time I'd realized that if people talking to me turned their heads, covered their lips, spoke as they were walking away, or were just too far away then I couldn't hear what they were saying. The direction of sound always had an impact on the capabilities of my hearing aids. If a person was facing away from me, the clarity of their voice also traveled away from me. And while I knew I didn't read lips, seeing their face empowered my visual acuity, which had increased with my visual dependence on facial expressions. I worked best when I could use my hearing aids with my eyes.

I had been taught that humans have five separate senses. Now, I was learning just how much those individual senses worked together to empower our capacity to communicate. We hear sequentially but see simultaneously. Growing up as a hearing person, my ears had been trained to ascertain just one word at a time because that's exactly how people speak. Visually, I could see everything at once, all the time, and those clues had become crucial to communication.

Next, I considered the impact that noise had on my ability to aurally discern speech. If the crowd at the counter had not been roaring, I may very well have heard what the kid was saying, but too many voices, too much sound, meant too much competition. The kid's voice also hadn't changed yet; it was higher than the deep voices of the men laughing so obnoxiously and talking so loudly behind me, which had made it more difficult for me to hear what the kid was saying. In my notes, I defined noise as "every unpleasant, unwanted, and unnecessary sound or speech—including interruption." Maybe what the men were saying to each other was important to them, but it wasn't necessary for me while I was trying to hear what the kid was saying. Of course, by that definition, a pen scratching on paper in a quiet room was noise because it wasn't necessary; it just is. I found it fascinating that over millions of years of evolution, human ears had yet to develop the physical capacity to differentiate between important sounds and insignificant noise.

Finally, I realized that when the kid was standing at the far end of the counter, I couldn't hear what he was saying, even though I could hear what he was saying when he was right in front of me and I could see his face. As a matter of simple math, it was obvious that the level of speech and sound got reduced by half if the distance was twice as far. That also explained why I was having such a hard time hearing the students in class who sat so far away from me.

In my notebook, I wrote the words "Visibility Noise Distance" beside my notes and drew a square around them. Those tenets were the keys to my new kingdom. The rules of natural law. The more I thought about it, the more I realized that those rules didn't just apply to me but had to be used by hearing people as well. Listening means learning, understanding without dismissing, and that is only achieved accurately without distraction. Hearing people seldom, if ever, listened—truly listened—to each other. I knew this because I had been a hearing person. I had, in fact, lived most of my life as a hearing person, but I was different now. Not Deaf—at least, not yet—but hard-of-hearing. And I had to fight the massive misconceptions about my emerging deafness every day. I knew from experience just how much hearing people equated speech with intelligence. It's ridiculous. Even Professor Matthews had insisted that writers need to be able to hear their work by reading it out loud in order to understand their own writing—as if I couldn't fucking see what was right in front of me!

The idea that writing is somehow connected to hearing was among the most common misconceptions of language proficiency and linguistic mastery, one that had been used to demean and degrade deaf and hard-of-hearing people for centuries. Reading your writing out loud was just a habit hearing people had cultivated. I knew this because I had been a hearing person, but maybe hearing authors were just incapable of writing well without hearing their own work. Maybe they really do need to read their work out loud. Thinking about Professor Matthews now, I couldn't help but shake my head: of all the papers and essays I had written in college, the only time I'd ever read my work out loud was for her Literature & Composition class—and I had never been so drastically misinterpreted.

Read out loud, my ass, I thought. *God, what a fucking joke!*

I decided to do my research paper on deafness and Deaf culture. I learned that there were four degrees of deafness: mild, moderate, severe, and profound. Each level was based upon frequency and volume. For most people with deafness, the higher the frequency, the louder the volume had to be—which explained why I couldn't hear birds chirping (high frequencies), but I could hear the deep voices of the men I knew at work (low frequencies). Mild-to-moderate was generally considered hard-of-hearing, while severe-to-profound usually meant deaf. The levels often overlapped, though, which meant it wasn't so easy to classify a person based upon a standard test.

That overlapping also explained common misconceptions about the deaf and hard-of-hearing. A person born with a moderate-to-severe deafness may identify as Deaf, while a person who had acquired a severe-to-profound hearing loss late in life may think of themselves as hard-of-hearing or late-deafened. Hearing aids and cochlea implants worked for some people but not everyone. (I certainly knew that never worked for Grandpa, who, by his own example, had taught me that it was a mortal sin to judge people based upon our own misconceptions.) Family history, linguistic acquisition, and culture—the holy grail of deafness, capital-D Deaf—also had a profound impact on identity. The diversity of deafness, I realized, was easily among its most misunderstood characteristics, at least among hearing people.

Most deaf children were born to hearing parents, many of whom had no idea that sign was such a profound, beautiful language. Instead, they relied on the advice of doctors and audiologists who treated deafness like a medical defect, often convincing hearing parents to spend over tens of thousands of dollars to get a cochlea implant so their child could be "normal." But cochlea implants, like hearing aids, were a poor substitute: the computers inside those devices, no matter how advanced, still couldn't distinguish or isolate sounds, determine distance or direction, and had a limited range for speech discernment. The average human ear had a capacity to discern speech up to thirty feet away, but even the most advanced hearing aid had a limited range of just six to ten feet, depending upon pitch, tone, background noise, and visibility of the speaker. The sound of speech was seldom spoken at the same level: children have higher voices than women, who have higher voices than men.

With my hearing aids off, I spent the whole day studying. Without a single distraction, I began to see clearly, through the lens of my own experience, what I could gain. My emerging deafness was not an obstacle to be overcome, and it sure as hell wasn't some sort of genetic defect or a physical impairment. Instead, I saw my deafness as an identity to be embraced, an aspiration to be achieved that would lead me to become the man I was meant to be.

It was, for me, as natural as it was inevitable.

And I had the power, the capability, to learn. I would make myself a better man. I would become more than who I was, more than what the hearing world would have me be. More, even, than I ever thought I could be. Like a phoenix, I would rise from the ashes of the hearing world and soar into the sky.

Free, at last.

CHAPTER TWENTY

THE AMERICANS WITH DISABILITIES ACT

WITH SCHOOL OUT FOR the summer, I made the most of my weekends with Memphis. We'd go out to eat on Friday nights and rent a movie from Blockbuster, which allowed me to confirm that a film was captioned before I paid to see it. Other times, we'd just head to the beach after hitting Rosie's for our late-night milkshakes. I'd take my hearing aids out because of the wind. Memphis didn't mind getting close so I could hear what she was saying.

I had learned it was best to go places where people knew us because they were less likely to judge me. I'd also watch how people reacted when they saw my hearing aids. Most of them would avert their eyes to my ears while we were having a conversation. Reading facial expressions empowered me to anticipate the level of ignorance I was about to face. The first time we went out to eat after I'd got my hearing aids, I realized that Memphis was the first one I had to educate when she'd ordered for me.

It had been so hot I'd tied my hair back, which had made my hearing aids visible. Our waitress, an older woman who was about thirty, took one look at me and immediately turned to Memphis. As they were talking, I saw the waitress point to her ear and motion in my direction with her thumb. Their conversation lasted longer than I had expected. After the waitress was gone, Memphis said, "I got you a steak and baked potato."

I leaned back in my chair. "Did you now?"

"It comes with a salad," she said, "and I got you ranch dressing."

"Memphis, why did you do that?"

"You don't like bleu cheese."

"That's not what I mean," I told her. "Why did you order for me?"

"She saw you have a hearing problem. I was just trying to make things easier."

"Come on, Memphis. You don't know me better than that?"

"What?"

"My deafness only becomes a problem when hearing people make it a problem."

"I was only trying to help," Memphis said. "She didn't know."

"I'm pretty sure I can decide for myself what I want for dinner," I told her. "Besides, not only did you order for me, you never even asked me what I wanted. Don't speak for me, Memphis, and don't do something for me when you know damn well I can do it myself. When I need your help, I'll ask."

Her cheeks grew red. "Okay."

"Besides, how is she supposed to learn when you're the one doing everything for me? You're only reinforcing her misconceptions."

"I'm learning as we go," Memphis said. "She didn't know what to expect."

"So, think it through," I told her. "What if I came here by myself? Or what if I was deaf instead of hard-of-hearing?"

After a moment, Memphis said, "She had a pen. If you were deaf, she could just write it down. You could write your responses."

"Exactly."

"Well, two years ago, I didn't know how to read or write," she said. "If I can do that, I can sure as hell learn this shit. So, how does it work? What do you need?"

"Hearing aids are not human ears," I said. I put my research and experience to work. "They cannot distinguish or isolate sounds, determine distance or direction, and have a limited range when it comes to speech discernment. Just face me when you speak, be mindful of the noise, and aware of distance. The closer you are, the more likely my hearing aids will pick up what you say. It all comes down to visibility, noise, and distance. They may be separate concepts, but they all work together."

"Visibility, noise, distance," Memphis repeated. "I can do that. That's easy. Just remind me when I forget."

"Oh, I will," I said. When our waitress brought our drinks, I told her, "I'd like to order."

"You're all set," she said. "She took care of you."

"Let me rephrase that," I said. "I would like to change my order."

"Okay," she said, taking out her pen and pad. But she was clearly agitated. "No salad?"

"No. No steak and baked potato. I want to order something else."

"Well, I already put it in," the waitress said. "And the chef's gonna be pissed at me again if I have to change it."

"You should have thought of that before you ignored me."

"Sir, I wasn't ignoring you. I only asked her what you wanted because I saw your…" She stopped herself once she realized what she was about to say. In that moment, I knew I had her—but it was still going to take tact.

"May I suggest that next time you not make such an assumption?" I said. "After all, speech may be the dominant mode of communication in our present epoch, but it was, in fact, the last mode of communication to evolve. We needed our hands to cultivate our food long before we had the convenience of vocal cords to order it. So, would you like to take my order now?"

I could tell my lecture had settled her by the way she asked, "What would you like?"

"I will have the stuffed chicken breast with lemon-butter asparagus and a side of mashed potatoes with cheese, bacon, and extra butter. Ranch dressing for my salad."

"Excellent choice, sir."

After she left, Memphis chuckled. "You enjoyed that way too much."

"Damn right." To one extent or another, I would encounter such ignorance thousands of times through thousands of meals. Worst of all, hearing people were surprised by my intelligence once I'd explain how hearing aids worked. They were surprised to see a person instead of a disability. Memphis, to her credit, had been willing to learn. She soon accepted our new reality—and the sex with alacrity, once I'd learned to line my lips up with hers after her thighs had crushed my head, making my hearing aids buzz in that agonizing, high-pitched squeal while she was consumed by her orgasm. She didn't even know what had happened until I'd told her about it later.

She apologized profusely, of course, and was pretty embarrassed.

I thought it was hilarious.

A cool breeze came in off the Poquanicut River as I sat on the dock, eating my lunch beneath the bright blue sky. My coworkers were still talking about layoffs. Once our overtime got cut, I started making breakfast at home and packing a lunch instead of buying meals at the cafeteria.

I'd had my hearing aids for three months now. Most of the people who knew me had gotten used to my being hard-of-hearing. They already knew to tap my shoulder to get my attention when I was welding, but I'd learned to repeat instructions back to them so that we were certain of what I needed to do. Whenever they violated the pillars of visibility, noise, and distance (usually out of a lifetime of hearing habits), I'd remind them to face me when they speak, point out the noise as I stepped forward, or motion for them to come closer.

Most of my coworkers were pretty cool about it. Some of them had worked so hard over the years they'd had to take medical leave for surgeries and rehabilitation, or they knew people who had been injured on the job and couldn't work at all anymore. In some ways, it's easier for people to accept a disability when they're intimately familiar with their own potential to become disabled themselves, though there were exceptions.

Big Ben was the only one who gave me a hard time. He would constantly snap at me, raising his voice in a condescending, mocking tone after I didn't hear what he had said, either because his head was turned, people were talking over him, or he was walking away while speaking. The first time I told him to face me when he speaks, Big Ben asked if I could read lips. I started to explain that everybody reads lips to a certain extent and that I needed visual clues like facial expressions, but Big Ben just didn't want to hear it. He lost his cool.

"Motherfucker, I ain't got time for that shit! Just pay attention, dumb-ass!"

"Looks who's talking, genius," I shot back. "I just told you—"

"I can fucking hear you!"

"So, can I," I told him. "I just have to do a few things differently. It's not my fault you're too stupid to figure it out."

"Fuck you, Shakespeare!" he shouted. "CAN YOU HEAR ME NOW! Jesus fucking Christ, one minute you can hear, the next you're just fucking ignoring me! What the fuck? You and your goddamned selective hearing! Fucking pay attention already! Jesus!"

As he walked away, a raging fire burned in the pit of my stomach. I knew then that I was going to get him. It was only a matter of time. Living with my emerging deafness, I'd quickly learned that explaining it once was never enough. Communication permeates culture, impacting everything, so I'd drill visibility, noise, and distance into the minds of the people around me. There were those who got it, and there were those who needed to be reminded time and time again, but Big Ben deliberately made things more difficult than they needed to be—for both of us.

After our confrontation, he started blasting country and western music from his boom box while he was working. It would echo through the hull and into my welding shield. For me, it was excruciating—and I hated country and western music with a passion. Worst of all, Big Ben would always try to talk over the distorted, screeching twangs, and he'd get mad when nobody—and I mean, nobody—could hear him. When he bitched about my "selective hearing" again, I decided I'd had enough.

The next day, I waited in the break room for Big Ben to leave. Once he was gone, I poured the coffee out of his Thermos and replaced it with a fresh pot, but instead of sugar I used salt—a whole lot of salt. During our first break, Big Ben took one sip, spit it out, and started screaming bloody murder while our coworkers burst out laughing. Raising my can of Coke, I smiled at my coworkers from my seat on the dock. When we all went back to work, Big Ben asked if I was the one who had done it. I'd heard him but just deadpanned, "What."

"I said, 'Did you put fucking salt in my coffee?'"

His radio wasn't even playing, but I said, "I can't hear you over the music."

"Fuck you, Shakespeare! You fucking rat's snot puke! Want to get your head beat off?"

"Enjoy your lunch."

He pushed me up against the hull. "What the hell did you do to my lunch?"

I chuckled. "I didn't do anything to your lunch."

"I don't believe you."

"That's the point," I told him. "After the coffee, I didn't have to do anything. I just wanted you to believe I did. Got you twice. Only had to get you once. Not bad for Shakespeare, huh?"

"You want to mess with me? I'll fucking shove that torch straight up your ass!"

"I'll shit it out and take you with me."

"Fuck you!"

Pushing him away, it took all my strength to hold him against the hull. He was huge.

"You are a fucking idiot, you know that? That 'selective hearing' bullshit is exactly what you fucking people think when you ignore the rules of natural law."

"What rules? What law? What the fuck are you talking about?"

"Visibility, noise, distance," I said. My muscles started to knot up as I kept him pinned. I spoke calmly but firmly. "Face me when you speak, be mindful of the noise, and aware of the distance. Get it straight already. It ain't fucking rocket science. That's how it's done because that's the only way I do it. Now, you can stop being such an asshole or we can do this shit every goddamned day until you retire."

He could see that I meant it. "Just stay away from my coffee."

"Fine," I said, letting him go. My muscles were exhausted. "I have to admit, this was a lot more fun than I thought it would be."

I cracked my neck. He cringed.

"You're crazy, Shakespeare," he said before walking away.

"Oh, yeah," I said, igniting my torch. "Definitely more fun than I thought it would be."

After that, he left me alone.

Two weeks later, I had to trade my badge in for a pink slip. The hopelessness of getting laid off hit my stomach like a neutron bomb. Most of my coworkers had different reactions. A few guys patted me on the back or wished me luck. One woman thought I should be grateful because I didn't have to worry about the next round of layoffs. Leaving the yard for the last time, I remembered all the other times I had gone home to Memphis. She had always given me something to look forward to, but now we faced an uncertain future. As I passed the gate, Big Ben tapped my shoulder with his newspaper, handed it to me, and kept walking. I didn't think much of it until I saw the headline about President Bush signing the Americans with Disabilities Act.

My heart raced as I read the article while walking home. The new law was designed to ensure equality for people with disabilities in employment, public services, private business, and telecommunications through accessibility and accommodations. In his public remarks, some of which the newspaper had reprinted, President Bush had proudly proclaimed that the Americans with Disabilities Act "brings us closer to that day when no Americans will ever again be deprived of their basic guarantee of life, liberty, and the pursuit of happiness…we will not accept, we will not excuse, we will not tolerate discrimination in America [because] with the precious privilege of being an American comes a sacred duty to ensure that every other American's rights are also guaranteed."

With the signing of the act, the United States had come that much closer to fulfilling the promise of America. It was an historically significant step, one that I knew had been accelerated by the Deaf President Now protest at Gallaudet University two years ago.

By the time I got home, I was crying tears of joy.

"What's going on?" Memphis asked. She was still dressed up from her job interview that afternoon and was putting together another portfolio. "Is everything okay?"

"Yeah," I said. I could feel myself smiling. "Yeah, it's okay. At least, it's going to be. It will be. I got laid off today, but…it's all finally going to be okay!"

"Why are you so happy about losing your job?"

"Because the world has changed!" I said, showing her the article. "President Bush signed the Americans with Disabilities Act! Don't you see? I have rights now. This is the world my grandfather fought for, but it's one he could only dream of. God, I wish he could see this."

I lit a cigarette, pacing while Memphis read the article. "Holy fucking shit!"

"See what I mean?"

"Yeah, I do," she said. "But, Jesus, it's 1990. We're just now getting to this?"

"But I lived to see it!" I said, sitting down beside her. "And I'm alive to live it! How did your job interview go?"

"They said they'd get back to me."

"So, you're waiting on the follow-up interview?"

"This was the follow-up interview," Memphis said. "At least I have some landscaping I can do next week. We should be okay for a while."

"I'm going to get another job," I told her. "That won't be a problem now!"

If I only knew.

On Monday, I got up bright and early to mail out a dozen copies of my résumé. After filing for unemployment benefits, I headed downtown to fill out as many applications as I could. I visited fifteen businesses that first day, but only eight of them gave me an application. Five had said they would keep my résumé on file in case a position became available. Kenyon Technologies, Kingston Power Conversion, and Dell County Insurance all promised to review my résumé. After six weeks of endless submissions and applications, I was still getting the runaround from countless companies through legions of follow-ups. By the last week of August, I was down to convenience stores and gas stations.

"We're not hiring right now," the manager at 7-Eleven said. "But we'll keep your application on file in case something opens up."

"Thank you," I said. Stepping outside, I lit a cigarette and looked around. The tourists were making a last-ditch effort to enjoy the summer. A father carried his little girl on his shoulders, a mother held her children's hands while they watched their balloons bobbing in the breeze, and two teenagers were thrilled with their haul of chips and soda. I was about to leave when I saw Junior heading into the store, wearing a bright red 7-Eleven shirt. "You work here, Junior?"

"I'm the assistant manager," he said. "How have you been, Roger?"

"Not bad," I told him. "Still living in The Heights with Memphis. What about you?"

"Brockton," he said. He lit a Newport and looked at his watch. "Rochelle and I are getting married next year."

"Congratulations." I was surprised, but I knew if anyone could handle the responsibility at such a young age, it was Junior. Even now, he was so calm, cool, and collected, like he had it all together, compared to me, at least.

"You should have your invitation next month," Junior said. "Tim is going to be my best man. I was hoping you'd be an usher."

"Of course."

"Thanks," Junior said. "Still at the Boat?"

"I got laid off. In fact, I just put in an application. How is it here?"

"Could be better," Junior said with a shrug. "The day always comes up short for some reason. This week alone, it was twenty-seven dollars one day, twenty-three the next, thirty-two, then eighteen. Plus change, which is to be expected."

"A hundred dollars in four days at the end of the month? That's meticulous. Somebody is having a tough time keeping up the bills and wants it to appear random."

"That's exactly what I was thinking," Junior said. "But I went over everything three times yesterday and still couldn't find it. The manager thinks one of the employees is skimming, but we don't have any idea who it is. I don't even know who to watch."

"That's easy," I said. "Just set up a mandatory meeting for your employees at the most inconvenient time you can imagine. The first one to show up is the one you want to watch."

"How do you figure that?"

"Because to everybody else it's just a waste of time, but the first one to show up has something to prove."

"Never thought of it like that," Junior said. "You ever think about going back to the station?"

I took a deep breath. "I didn't exactly leave on the best of terms."

"Well, family is family," Junior said. "You can always go home again. I'll see you around, Roger."

He put out his cigarette and went inside.

The distant streetlights lingered in the darkness as the summer humidity sent a chill down my spine. Ahead of us, Cumbies stood at the fork in the road. There were two cars parked at opposite sides of the convenience store, each facing in different directions. As we got closer, I noticed a woman was sitting in one of the cars, looking around between the puffs of cigarette smoke that she sent out the window. Awake and aware, she wanted to be seen; it was her first defense.

In the other car, the driver's window was all the way down, but the passenger's side was only cracked. It allowed for a slight breeze while still being a deterrent. The old man's eyes were glued to his side mirror, which had been set up to watch the entrance of the store. Memphis waited outside to finish her cigarette. The clerk behind the counter had her long blond hair back in a purple banana clip. When she got up, I saw that she was pregnant—very pregnant, in fact. "Can I help you?" she asked.

"Pack of Marlboro," I said. She rang up my cigarettes. Her name tag read "Amelia E." I saw that Memphis was watching us through the window. "Hey, we're headed to Rosie's. Just up the street. You want anything?"

"I'm fine, thank you," she said. "I do appreciate the offer, though."

"It's no problem," I told her. "Number's in the book, if you change your mind. Just ask for Roger or Memphis. We'll be headed back this way."

"I'll think about it."

When I got outside, Memphis asked, "What was that about?"

"She's having problems with her boyfriend," I said. "Serious problems."

"How do you know that?"

"There are two people watching the store like hawks, looking out for her," I said as we started walking. "No ring, no husband. So, it's a boyfriend. A deadbeat with a violent history who recently threatened her again."

"Who are you, Sherlock Holmes?"

"Hey, people are like books to me," I said. "I had a great teacher."

"So did I," Memphis said. "But I read books now, not just people."

"You've come a long way."

"I want to go further."

"You will."

"I got another job offer," she said. "It's for an advertising agency in Providence. They even said they'd pay me to relocate."

I stopped walking. "Another one?"

"They usually hire out of Rhode Island School of Design, but I guess they were impressed with my portfolio. They offered me a good salary with medical insurance and a 401k. I've even been looking into organizing a gallery for my art."

"Memphis, I…how many offers have you had?"

"I've had few," she said, "but, I wasn't…Roger, it's a big step. I'm scared."

"You're a survivor."

"I've been in survival mode since my grandmother died. I never thought I could be more until I learned to read."

"I could come with you," I said. "There must be jobs in Providence."

"You start school next week," Memphis said. "There is no way we can afford a five-day commute from Providence to Storrs, and the long-distance telephone bills would bankrupt us. Plus, I already looked into it. You'd have to wait at least a year to establish residency in Rhode Island because the cost of out-of-state tuition is so high. And once you're declared an out-of-state resident, you're always considered an out-of-state resident. At least as far as tuition is concerned."

"Wow," I said. "You've really done your homework."

"I had a great teacher," she said, laughing as tears welled up in her eyes. "I was trying to find a way, some way, any way that this could work for us. I thought maybe we could have weekends, but then you got laid off. You don't even know if you'll be available on weekends."

"And I can't give up on school any more than you can give up your career."

"It's been my dream since I first picked up a crayon."

I sighed. "Well, we tried."

"We did."

"When do you start?"

"They want me to start on Monday," she said. "We can still try to make it work. I mean, we'll have time at Thanksgiving and Christmas. Maybe some other holidays too."

"Memphis, I know you. Your attention to detail takes everything. You're going to give this all you've got. And you should. We both know I'd just get in the way."

"Roger…"

"Don't make this harder by trying to let me down easy," I said. "That's insulting."

"I wouldn't have made it if it weren't for you," Memphis said. But I shook my head. "Roger, you made my life possible. I know how to drive. I got my license. I have a credit card, a savings account, and I can sign my own name on my checks. I'm somebody. I'm somebody now. And you're the one who taught me that I could be more, that I can change. I can learn. I have that gift, just like everybody else. I know you don't believe that, but what you've done for me—"

"Anybody would have done."

"If that were true, I would have learned to read a long time ago," she told me. "You're the only one who cared enough about me to just care about me."

"I just did for you what you did for me."

"You get me," she said. "And I get you. I know you. You taught me how to read because you want to make amends for Jim."

"You think so?" I asked.

She nodded. "Forgive him."

"Some sins can't be forgiven."

"That's Jim talking," Memphis said. "Roger, don't you see? You have a chance. A chance to make a choice. To do something. Do the one thing Jim never could—forgive yourself."

"Grief is a door that cannot be closed until you know precisely what is in the room."

"You once told me that you can't remember who you want to be," Memphis said. She came in close, like the day we had first met. "There are always moments in life when we lose ourselves, but we're never lost. Not really. Sometimes we just can't see who are, or who we have been, to the people around us—the ones we love, those who love us. Sometimes, you just have to remember that you made it this far. You can go a little longer."

"It's too late," I said. The tsunami was coming. "Some sins just can't be forgiven. Don't you see? I could have done more, and I didn't. I could have saved him."

"I know," she said softly. The waves rolled back; it was a relief not to be judged by advice. "But, honestly? It's too late for that now. Jim may be gone, but you're not. You get to see everything he missed."

"You're the best friend I ever had."

"You never did do shortcuts," she said, chuckling. We kissed. *I love you.*

I love you too, I told her.

"I need a milkshake," Memphis said, taking my arm. "And chocolate. Lots of chocolate. Just run me a hot bath again and feed me chocolate all night."

Holding her close, I kissed her cheek. "We can do that."

"And the beach," she said. "I want to make love on the beach at sunrise before I leave."

"Like last month?"

"But don't forget the baby oil this time. Or the blindfold."

"Think it'll rain again?"

"I hope so!" she said. Our laughter echoed into the hot summer night.

I knew that it was time for her to move on without me, but I had no idea how I was going to move on without her.

The fierce wind cut like a knife as I made my way through the falling snow. Grounders was a small, smoke-filled bar and grill just a few blocks from my apartment. It had been built across the street from the eight-foot fences surrounding the Boat. The spiraled barbed wire had long since rusted, and a handful of security guards at the gates watched as thousands of men and women with backpacks and lunchpails entered the yard. The third shifters were complaining about security when I showed up. "…want to blow up the base it'd be easier than taking a piss with the seat down."

"Or cheating at poker."

They roared with laughter as I took a seat at the bar. Two days ago, I'd turned twenty-one. Since it was Friday night, I figured I'd have a drink to celebrate. I hadn't seen Memphis since she moved to Rhode Island. We spoke a few times, but she was always busy with work or getting her art gallery together. I did make Grandpa's meatloaf for Thanksgiving, but Christmas ended up being just another day. As a child, I'd had to divide the holidays between my parents after the divorce, but there was never enough time; now, all I had was time—and I still couldn't get a job to save my life.

A few weeks ago, I'd stopped at a supermarket in Rose City and saw a hand-written sign that read HELP WANTED: PART-TIME BAKERY on the front door. After filling out an application, I asked the clerk at the front desk when a good time would be for me to check back. She told me that the bakery manager would be available for interviews tomorrow at two o'clock. I did my grocery shopping, headed home, and returned the next day at one-thirty. It turned out that the manager had already left for the day. When I asked when she would be available, the baker, a middle-aged woman with thick glasses, said that the manager could do my interview tomorrow at noon. This time, I arrived at eleven-thirty, but the same baker said that the manager had gone home early.

Again, I asked when I could come for an interview. Again, the baker told me that the manager would be available tomorrow at ten o'clock. Again, I arrived early—this time, at nine o'clock in the morning—only to have that same baker tell me that the manager took the day off. The next day, I was the first one through the door once the store had opened. A young man, who was about my age, was behind the counter. When he had said that I was his very first customer, I asked when he applied. He said, "Yesterday."

"You know, I actually need to get a cake for my girlfriend," I told him. "No offense, but it needs to be perfect. Could I see the manager?"

"Of course," the kid said. He went into the back. A moment later, the same woman who had kept telling me to come back tomorrow appeared. Needless to say, I got the message. If it hadn't happened to me, I never would have believed it.

The greatest myth about the Americans with Disabilities Act was that companies would hire people with disabilities if they were legally required to provide access and accommodations, but nobody could see past my hearing aids. At best, people saw me as an inconvenience to be ignored; at worst, companies treated me like an expense to be avoided. At the station and the Boat, I'd worked like a racehorse, but now my work ethic was never seen an asset. Nobody realized that people with disabilities wanted to work. We were hungry and ambitious. We were the ones who had to prove ourselves. We were the ones who had to work ten times as hard just to compete with mediocrity. If all those fucking "normal" people ever had the sense to see that, the law would have never been necessary in the first place. Instead, the myth of hearing superiority was bound to an assumption of competence; when any society clings to a preconceived model, such prejudice mandates a pretense of proficiency.

In the past five months, I'd seen so many companies get around the law, disguising their efforts in such ways as to make their discrimination legally invisible—and it was all so subtle I couldn't even see it until I realized that baker bitch had flat-out lied to my fucking face.

All things considered, it was time for a drink.

"Got ID?" the barmaid asked. I showed her my driver's license. "What'll it be?"

"Kamikaze."

"On the rocks?"

"Straight."

"You driving?" she asked after I downed the shot. My stomach rumbled as I shook my head. The few shots of Captain Morgan that I'd had at home were beginning to hit me. "Want a bite to eat?"

"Plate of fries, some bar burgers, and…make it a Coors Light," I said. On television, the eleven o'clock news was reporting on the Gulf War while I finished eating and ordered another shot. It wasn't so long ago that I would have cared about what was happening halfway across the world. Now, I didn't have that luxury; I spent most of my time just trying to get out of bed. There were days I would be lying there, telling myself to get up over and over again, but the weight of my depression was so paralyzing I just couldn't fucking move. Days went by without my so much as taking a shower. Empty soda cans and pizza boxes were scattered all over my apartment. Only school kept me going, but I felt so out of place at UCONN.

Rose City Community College had been filled with adults who wanted to make their lives better. Most of them had been pursuing a new career after an injury or layoff; others had just wanted to stay busy in retirement or, like Leona, were trying to survive the loss of a spouse. UCONN felt like I'd gone back in time to the spoiled brats I'd known in high school. On my first day of class, I saw a kid in the cafeteria try to flip a burger. He pushed the patty all the way across the grill until it fell on the floor. Never in my life had I laughed so hard. Who the fuck doesn't know how to flip a goddamned hamburger?

That was the first time I began to realize the advantages of being a child of divorce. With Jake and Mary working so much after Grandpa was killed, I'd had to learn to take care of myself. Doing laundry, packing a lunch, washing the dishes, making dinners with Memphis, and cleaning up had all become second nature. But what was normal to me was all new to those kids. They were on their own for the first time, and some of them had been so pampered they'd never bothered to learn how to cook.

The kids would talk about concerts, parties, and clubs. Sometimes they'd discuss how hard their professors were or which ones to avoid. Once in a while, usually when waiting in the hall for my history class to start, I'd hear part of a conversation. Two rich kids would be talking about Churchill wanting to stage a second front in Eastern Europe or the futility of the Vietnam War. To them, it was just a paper to write or a test to take. They didn't know the difference between reading a map and living the journey, much less the enduring trauma of war that lingered for years. Vietnam had haunted my father so much he had lost his family in that jungle. Now, I was the one who got lost.

My mind kept racing as I passed the legal limit. If I couldn't get a job without a degree, how could I hope to get one with a degree? The only option I had was to contact the National Association of the Deaf to see if I could get legal representation. My unemployment was up next month. I considered applying for disability benefits, but people would just think I was lazy. And that's when it hit me: the same fuckers who hated freeloaders were the same ones who had refused to hire me. They'd force me to apply for disability benefits and then bitch about my being on welfare. It was as absurd as it was systemic. People will pay millions of dollars in taxes, legal fees, and lawsuits just to enforce their own prejudice through discrimination, just to look at another human being and believe that they're better than somebody else—somebody black, somebody gay, somebody disabled. Prejudice is the most expensive bullshit in history.

Downing the shot, I ordered another beer. Johnny Carson was doing his opening monologue on *The Tonight Show* when someone patted my back. "Charlie! Hey! How ya doin'?"

"Not bad," he said. "Not too bad, anyway. Buried my sister last month. Wasn't exactly up for another one so soon."

"My condolences."

"It is what it is, kid," Charlie said. "You know, my father always used to say there's three stages to life: birthday parties, weddings, and funerals."

"I'm celebrating my birthday," I told him. "The big two-one. Feels more like...I don't know. Mine is an old soul trapped in the body of a young man."

"Well, happy birthday, kid," he said. "What have you been up to?"

"UCONN."

"UCONN? No shit. What's your major?"

"I haven't decided," I told him. "I did take a course in Shakespeare when I was at Rose City. I was honestly surprised at how much I enjoyed it, but Critical Theory at UCONN fucking killed my love of literature. It's all Freud. Everything's a phallus to those people. Everything."

"A phallus?" Charlie said. "What the hell's that got to do with anything?"

"Beats me," I said. "I mean, I've had a penis all my life. I usually use it to pee. Once in a while I've used it for something else, but I've never in my life taken a leak and thought, 'Well now, that sure looks like a gun!'"

"No shit," Charlie said, laughing. "You know, my nephew once said that academia is its own little world."

"The funny thing is, everybody in Critical Theory is thinking the same damned thing," I said. "They hate it. They're just too damned scared to say it. They want a good grade. So, they play along. They're all drinking the same Kool-Aid, man. I couldn't do it. That's why I'm undecided, flying in the wind. Free as a bird. Maybe a phoenix."

"I'll have the usual, Jean," Charlie said to the barmaid. He set a ten on the counter. She gave him an egg salad sandwich, a cup of coffee, and his change. "How about that? A half dollar. Hey, kid, did I ever tell you what I did with my first fifty-cent piece?"

"You married her?" Jean said. I laughed so hard I spit up my beer.

"You're hitting the sauce hard tonight, kid," Charlie said. "Can't say as I blame you, though. You still with Allyson?"

"No! Oh god, no! I haven't seen her in years. I knew that wasn't going to work. I mean, there's always signs, right? You always know, you know? Even when you don't know, you know. You know?"

I laughed at my own joke and chugged my beer.

"What signs?" Charlie asked. "How bad was it?"

"Well," I said, "the minute I found out she didn't know what a fluffernutter was, I should have bailed."

"That's bad," Charlie said. "Hey, Jean, bring another round for fluffy boy here!"

"I was seeing someone," I said. "She was quite a character, to be honest. Yeah, she was special...is special."

"So, what happened?"

"She got a job up in Providence," I told him. Jean gave me another beer. "You'd like her, Charlie. She could split wood and change a tire. Kind of ironic that her job came through just after I lost mine."

"Happens to the best of us, kid," Charlie said.

I took a sip. "What are you talking about?"

"Seen it a million times," he said. "They love us to death until the money runs out."

"She would never do that to me."

"Then why did she?" Charlie asked. I suddenly remembered Memphis telling me that she had got several job offers but only accepted one after I'd got laid off. Was everybody I cared about just a fucking liar? I chugged my beer and told Jean I wanted another shot.

She set it up and said, "Last call."

Charlie raised his cup of coffee, as if to give a toast. "To Jake."

My stomach rumbled as the kamikaze hit. "My father?"

"Your father."

"What about him?"

"Oh, shit."

"Charlie, what—?"

"Christ, I'm sorry, kid. I thought you knew."

The moment I stood up, the room started spinning. "Knew what? What are you talking about? What happened to my father?"

"He's dead."

"What?"

"He's dead. Died on Tuesday. Damn aneurysm burst. That or the shrapnel got him. I swear to god, kid, I thought you knew."

I started screaming, flailing, and grabbing his coat. "What? What! WHAT!"

The rest of the night is a blur. Did I fall down or did someone push me? Or had I bumped into somebody at the bar? I can vaguely recall Charlie getting me up off the floor and taking me outside. He must have put me in the taxi because the next thing I knew I was throwing up in the back seat. After that, I just remember the driver grabbing me and tossing me to the ground—but dreaming, somehow, that I was a phoenix falling into searing flames.

Most of all, I remember what my mother would never forget.

In the distance, a small light flickered through the storm as she flew out of the house. And that was how she found me—stone drunk and soaked in my own vomit, swimming in the snow and freezing to death in the polar vortex.

After three years, I had come home.

CHAPTER TWENTY-ONE

REDWOODS

"YOU ARE MY SON," Carol said, sipping her steaming cocoa. She cleared a small patch of snow off the porch railing and set down her mug. "Today, I have become your mother."

She slapped me across the face so hard my neck snapped to the side. The sting lingered in the brutal cold as the shock rolled through me. After this morning, it was not how I expected the rest of the day to go.

The house had been warm and cozy when I'd woke up back in my old bed, stark naked and soaked in sweat, with a hangover that would have leveled Frankenstein. Slowly sitting up, my head had felt like it had been encased in concrete. My bedroom seemed smaller, but everything was exactly the way I'd left it. The pile of clean clothes I'd meant to put away were still sitting on Grandpa's couch, and the box he had left me lay open on the floor beside the stack of Carol's letters. My clock radio was collecting dust on top of my dresser next to the small black-and-white television set that Dad had got me one Christmas. Even my baseball glove was still on the nightstand. For a moment, I wondered if the past three years had been a nightmare that I was just now waking up from—until I remembered why I'd got the couch in the first place.

My memories of the night before had gaps. I knew that I had seen Charlie and that he had put me in the cab. He'd probably called Mary as well, but he had no idea that Poquanicut was the last place I wanted to be. Either Charlie didn't know I lived just a few blocks from the bar, or I'd been too drunk to tell him. Or maybe my mother had insisted that he send me home.

Getting out of bed, I put on my black sweatpants and a T-shirt, neither of which fit very well now. Peering through the curtain, I saw Mary bundled up and shoveling snow in the driveway. I grabbed some of my clothes and set them in the bathroom. As I reached the threshold of the kitchen, I realized that the living room had been remodeled. That ugly faux wood-paneling was finally gone and with so much snow reflected from outside, the crisp white paint lit up the whole room. She had replaced the furniture with a chartreuse set that had a white floral pattern. There were so many pillows, placed so meticulously, it looked like nobody had ever used the couch. A copy of *Lady Boss* by Jackie Collins was sitting on the coffee table.

The new emerald rug felt fresh on my bare feet as I approached the big storm window, staying back so Mary wouldn't see me. She was about halfway done with the driveway, moving side to side and packing the snow with a couple of kicks against the shovel. I'd had no idea we were going to get such a heavy storm, but I seldom watched the news or read the paper. It was fitting, in a way, since I felt like a stranger in my childhood home. After checking the time, I got a glass of orange juice and drank it straight down as my stomach rumbled. There was a plate of oatmeal raisin cookies on the counter. When I poked the plastic wrap, the cookie felt hard. I was putting the jug back when I saw a newspaper clipping on the refrigerator.

It was my father's obituary.

That's what Charlie told me last night, I realized. That's why I was screaming.

The front door opened just as I headed back to the bathroom. I couldn't lock that door fast enough. A few moments later, beneath the scalding-hot water in the bathtub, I collapsed in a fit of tears over my father's death.

Worst of all, over what I had done.

My anger at Mom and Dad for not telling me the truth had blinded me to the consequences of cutting them out of my life. My foolishness had robbed me of my father as much as his death had taken him from me. He had tried to explain it all that day I'd discovered the truth; I could hear him, but I wasn't listening. It was ironic that I was now hard-of-hearing and wanted to listen. Drowning in anguish, seething with agony as I bawled my eyes out, I remembered being a kid and my father giving me a bath in this very tub. When it was over, he would lift me up, and I'd run on air to try to get the water off. He'd even play peek-a-boo while drying my hair with a towel.

One summer evening, as I was waiting for him to get me out of the tub, Dad came and asked if I was done yet. I held my arms out, hopeful, reaching for him, but he just said, "One of these days, you'll have to pick yourself up. Might as well get started because I can't do it forever."

My trembling hand reached for the bar of soap.

It was time to get started.

When I got out of the shower, I found my mother—Mary, that is—in the kitchen making French toast. She had already cut the bananas and set the table. Her nose was red from working outside. She now had a blend of light-gray and blond hair, with faint wrinkles lingering, somehow hiding her age even as she made no effort to conceal it. She worked methodically but seemed guarded. When she spoke, I told her, *I'm hard-of-hearing now. I need my hearing aids.*

She pointed to my jacket, which was sitting on the back of the chair. Searching, I found my hearing aids inside the lapel pocket. As I put them on, I saw that Dad's obituary had been taken off the fridge. I couldn't help but wonder why she was acting like last night, or even the past three years, had never happened.

"Good morning," she said, setting the French toast on a plate. "How are you feeling?"

"Hungover."

"Let that be a lesson to you."

"Think I've learned a few."

"So I heard," she said. She handed me a mug of steaming hot cocoa, turned off the stove, and gave me the plate. "French toast with bananas. Happy birthday."

"Thanks," I said, sitting down.

"Remember Granny and Papa used to make it for you?"

"You mean Dad's parents?" I asked.

She nodded. "Every Christmas when you were a kid."

"I remember," I said. "Never thought I'd see this place again."

"You were always welcome," she said. The burden of being back somehow faded once I heard her say that. "You slept so long I wasn't sure if I should make breakfast or lunch."

"Thank you," I said, taking a bite. She sat down. Once she started cutting her slice, I could see that she was nervous but trying her best to hide it. I had seen her eat a million times, but I was just now noticing that her stiff posture and tense hands revealed her emotions.

"You know, your grandfather started to lose his hearing when he was about the same age you are now."

"I don't see the world through his eyes," I said. "I just hear it through his ears."

"William was also your age when his started," she said. "Is it a mastoid infection? That's what they said it was with Grandpa and William."

"They were wrong," I said. When Mom asked me how I knew, I told her it was unlikely the same infection would occur in both ears over three successive generations. Like Grandpa, I had no swelling or other symptoms of infection. "The doctor ruled that out pretty quick."

"So, what caused it?"

"Mom, come on."

"What?"

"Exactly," I said. "When you live with something every day, you don't want to discuss it all the time."

"I haven't seen you in three years," she said. "Of course, I'm going to have questions."

"According to the doctor's interpretation of my CT scan, I have a bilateral sensorineural progression. It's hereditary, as you know, but seemingly conducive to the male members of the family. Simply stated, our inner ears never fully developed."

"But if that's true, how could you hear so well at birth?"

"That was my question as well," I told her. "Unfortunately, the doctor I saw couldn't answer it. I can only surmise that the progression is an exponential termination of the lining of the labyrinth in perpetuity."

Her eyebrows went up as her head jolted back. "You sound like a professor."

"Just medical jargon," I said, shaking my head. "Doesn't have anything to do with me. I had good insurance, so they used it all up just to tell me what I already knew."

"Looks like you've done pretty well for yourself," she said. "We saw your name in the paper when you made the dean's list."

"School got a lot easier once I got laid off at the Boat," I told her. "Finding a job during a recession, not so much. Being disabled doesn't exactly help matters either. I managed to pay my tuition at Rose City but had to get a loan for UCONN."

"You got a loan?" Mom said. "Roger, why didn't you just ask your father? He had all that money saved from when you were working for him. He even set aside some of his own so you could go to college. We all did. All of us, even Carol."

"Just didn't seem right," I said, "asking him for help after what I did."

"We're your family," Mom said. "Don't you see? We all want our children to surpass us. That's why we set up your college fund. We wanted to give you the opportunities that we never had, and that so many of us lost. You shouldn't be paying tuition anyway. That was part of my settlement."

"What settlement?"

"After your grandfather was killed, I filed a wrongful death lawsuit against the state. That's what the attorney general wanted to discuss when you told him to go to hell."

"Actually, I told him to fuck off."

"Not a step up."

"And the horse he rode in on."

"Well, after that they offered me a settlement, but I told my lawyer I wouldn't budge unless they agreed to let you attend any state college or university free of tuition."

"You got a settlement?"

"You think I got your grandfather back home to Elliott on tips?" she said. "That settlement paid for the loan I needed to get him there. My parents and my brother are together. That's all I care about. That, and your tuition. The rest of what you see here I did myself. Never spoiled you, buddy, 'cause my father never spoiled me."

"What did you mean when you said you heard about the lessons I learned?"

"Memphis called."

"Memphis?"

"We spoke for about an hour," she said. "Your cab took it slow in the storm. You actually called her from the bar last night. She thought you'd be too far gone to remember. Looks like she was right. Charlie told her that he was sending you home, so she asked for my number. She's quite a character. I called her a hot shit, and she took it as compliment."

"That's Memphis, all right."

"Did you really teach her how to read?"

I leaned back in my chair. "What else did she say?"

"Enough," Mom said. She took a deep breath. "Honey, I'm so sorry about Jim. If I'd have known…"

"He always said shit happens."

"You can't blame yourself for—"

"I don't want to talk about it," I said. "Every time I try, nobody listens. Every time, Mom. Every goddamned time."

"I'm listening."

I shook my head. "My last three months of high school, people treated me like a leper. And I once made the mistake of writing about Jim for my composition class. It was a poem. My stupid professor thinks writers need to be able to hear in order to understand their work. Well, guess what? I read it out loud, and those people were off by light years. They just started arguing, getting in each other's face, acting like they knew more about my experience than I did. Worst of all, I became an inspiration."

"What's so bad about that?"

"Mom, come on," I said. "Do you have any idea how it feels when a complete stranger ambushes you after class one night and says, 'You're my inspiration'? I thought maybe I wrote a paper or aced a test, but it turned out somebody she hasn't even seen since second grade passed away. I don't know what the hell that girl was thinking, and I don't care. And then, after I got my hearing aids and I was at UCONN, one girl starts going on about how I'm overcoming obstacles, and all that other bullshit, because of my deafness."

"What did you tell her?"

"'Don't applaud just because I overcame the obstacles you put in my path in the first place,'" I said. "Besides, what the hell is so inspiring about losing somebody to suicide?"

She sipped her cocoa, calm as could be. "People always make the mistake of thinking that because you helped them that you must not need help. If you made them feel good, they assume you feel good. If you inspired them to keep going, they think you can keep going."

"It doesn't work that way."

"No, it doesn't," Mom said. "But, unfortunately, that's how a lot of people think. They forget that the people who help the most are often the ones who need the most help. Our greatest pain teaches us compassion. It's just not very useful without wisdom."

"Is that why you became a nurse?"

"I became a nurse so you could eat," she said, "and I didn't want to lose the house."

"I like what you've done with the place."

"Thank you." Getting up, she set her plate in the sink and asked if I wanted more.

"I'm good, thanks," I told her. She started doing the dishes while I cleared the table. "What else did Memphis have to say?"

"She offered to pick Carol up at the airport in Providence," Mom said. "Carol had already made arrangements to get a rental car. She'll be here this afternoon, unless her flight gets delayed again because of the blizzard."

"It's your turn. Why did you and Dad—"

"She also told me about the riot at the clinic," Mom said. She started washing dishes with a rising ferocity. "Christ, Roger, you almost got killed..."

"Mom."

"...I really didn't want to believe it, but then I saw the scar on your shoulder when I had to get your clothes off because, of course, you were covered in vomit."

"Mom..."

"They're in the dryer, by the way. Don't be embarrassed. I changed your diaper."

"Mom!"

"All right!" she finally said. The plate broke when she slammed it into the rack. I was about to pick up the pieces when she told me to just leave it. Some things, I guess, just can't be fixed. Taking a deep breath, Mom dried her hands and wiped her eyes. "It's just...Roger, we had no idea where you were or who you were with or what you were even doing. And then to find out...we lost you three years ago. I don't want to lose you again."

"Is that why you took his obituary down off the fridge?"

"We were only trying to protect you."

"So, you spent all this time trying to protect me from the truth when you should have told me the truth to prepare me."

"Roger, we...we had our reasons. There are just too many things you don't understand."

"Then I think it's time for me understand them," I told her. "I think it's time for you to the explain why the best kept secrets are best kept secret."

"Very well," she said. "My twin brother, William, is your biological father, but he didn't die in a car accident. We all agreed that if you ever got curious or asked—"

"Shouldn't Carol be the one to tell me this?"

"I told you a long time ago she doesn't like talking about it. Maybe when you learn what happened, you'll begin to understand why."

"So, if William didn't die in a car accident, then—"

"He was murdered."

"You got to be fucking kidding!"

"Do you want the truth or not?"

"I'm too old for this shit."

"You're just getting started, kiddo," Mom said. "It was my job to get you there."

"All right," I said. We sat down. "What happened?"

"He was beaten and stabbed to death," Mom said. She told me that Carol was six months pregnant with me at the time—and that she had seen the whole thing. Someone had followed them after they came out of the theater. The attack happened a few blocks away. After dropping the gun in the struggle, the man drew a knife and started stabbing William while shouting obscenities about Jews. He had claimed to be a superior race, Mom said, but he was nothing more than a savage. People like that have no identity outside of their own hatred. It was a life without love, without compassion, without beauty, dignity, or grace—and that was no life at all. Hate had devoured that man. "It was that same savage hatred that led the Nazis to murder six million Jews during the Holocaust, including your grandparents, your aunts, and uncles…your cousins."

"And Carol survived," I said, "only to lose her husband twenty-five years later."

"It was too much," Mom said. She told me that Carol had been the youngest of seven children. She had spent her childhood, including the war, moving from place to place with other families, living in cellars, barns, sheds. Sometimes a forest. A closet, if she was lucky. A Catholic family had taken her in for several months. They gave Carol a rosary to help hide her identity—the same one she carried to this very day. They had told her that she only needed to pretend to be Catholic in order to stay alive because she was a Jew—and Jews were being hunted, enslaved, and killed. Toward the end of the war, the Nazis had found Carol and sent her to Dachau. A few months later, she met Grandpa when his unit liberated the concentration camp.

"Grandpa once told me that he could never forget seeing all those bodies," Mom said. "So many dying, dead, decomposing—but there she was: this adorable little girl, so troubled and yet so innocent, standing among them. He figured if he could help her, then maybe he could do something good. Maybe he could show her that there was still hope in the world."

"So, she hid me," I realized. "Just as she was hidden."

"That's it exactly," Mom said. When Carol lost William, it had brought back all those traumatic memories. After that, Carol couldn't bear to raise me by herself, but she didn't want to give me up for adoption. So, Jake and

Mary took me in and raised me as their own son. Once I was weaned, Carol went back to Pennsylvania, and they moved to Poquanicut. "A Catholic with a name like Evans, raised in a small town hidden deep in the Connecticut woods, really was the best we could hope for. In a place like this, everybody thinks they know everything—especially when they don't."

"But you didn't want me to be Catholic," I said. "Grandpa stopped taking me to church after—"

"After you learned the story of Moses, whose own mother had to hide him as well."

"That was the first thing Carol told me when I met her."

"Not the first time," Mom said, sipping her cocoa. "So, now you know. And now that you know, you must never forget. Anti-Semitism can be just as dangerous today as it was during the Holocaust. There is nothing superior about supremacy. It's just savagery, plain and simple."

I thought of what my father had told me after Amos had punched that customer, about the atrocious history behind that word, and how Dad had said he'd never fire a man for defending his own dignity. It didn't take much to see the connection.

"That's what Carol knew," I realized. "She knew that America has its own history. That's why she was so afraid."

"And she knows that better than anyone," Mom said. "That's why we never questioned her decision. Her experience, all that she endured…it's beyond our judgment. She hasn't practiced Judaism since William was alive. So, your father and I decided to let you choose your own path, if you wanted one."

A wave of fatigue had washed over me. Taking a deep breath, I leaned back and rubbed my eyes, trying to process what she had told me. Everything I had learned in school and college about the Holocaust had always been more than just a matter of history, but what was once Carol's story had become mine now as well. The more I tried to understand the depths of what my family had endured, the more I realized why Carol had chosen to hide me. "I think…I think maybe I get it now."

"And I think I overloaded your mind," Mom said. "You should go lie down."

"You know I was never mad at Carol, don't you? I mean, she knows that, right? Please tell me she knows, please? Because I don't think I could—"

"She knows," Mom said. "She knows."

"Mom, I swear I didn't know about Dad," I said. "I would have been there! I swear I would have been there!"

"It's all right," she said, holding my hand. "It's all right. He knew you had to find your own way. He knew, Roger. We tried to get ahold of you. We knew you were in Brockton Heights. We just didn't know where. Your number wasn't listed."

"That was Memphis's idea," I said, wiping my eyes. "She didn't want anybody harassing her anymore."

"I can understand that," Mom said. "You know, it was never that Carol didn't want you. She just wanted to protect you. We all did, even Grandpa. He was going to tell you, but—"

The tsunami came roaring back with a vengeance. I broke down and bawled my eyes out in the agony of grief and the shame of my own foolishness. By the time it was over, I was spent from the shock and the horror. My whole life had been defined by violence, a tragic trajectory that had shaped me before I was even born. Wiping my eyes, I asked, "Anything else you want to tell me, Mom?"

"Why don't you go lie down?"

I felt my heartbeat echo through my body as I settled into bed, slowly drifting off to sleep. The joy of sleeping in silence, without my hearing aids, always helped me relax. Despite everything, it felt good to be home again. My mother had been far, far more gracious than I deserved. Being older, I'd learned to appreciate our conversations more—but, god, I missed Dad. My mind played memories of him like movies. I saw him ice skating, quickly and gracefully, down at Ledge Lake; the smile on his face as he let me ride the snow shovel while he dragged it behind him, clearing a path so we could go sledding; that first fresh tomato he always gave me from the garden; and that fateful night, the one night, I knew I'd made him proud.

Now, the emptiness of losing the only father I'd ever known hung over me like a cloud, growing darker and more dreadful as I considered the family I'd lost to the greatest horror in history. As I was lying there, I felt my body begin to move, rolling over hundreds of skin-and-bone bodies being plowed into a pit while men in uniform watched us fall. The gray sky passed above me as we kept rolling, the faces of the dead still staring back at me as they all began shouting, "Remember! Remember! Remember!"

Their screaming echoed as I fell into the pit, buried beneath the dead. In the darkness, paralyzed under the weight of history, I could feel them all reaching for me. It wasn't until the light returned, faint at first, that I realized I could find my way out. As it grew brighter and brighter, I begged and prayed and pleaded for them to hold on to me so we could all get out together.

We reached the light just as I woke up.

When I got to the living room, Mom told me that Carol was outside. I made some cocoa for the both of us. The blinding snow hit me the moment I stepped out onto the porch. A few flurries danced in the stillness as I handed a mug to Carol. She sipped her steaming cocoa, holding it close to stay warm. I wanted so badly to hug her, to tell her how sorry I was, and that I knew now just how foolish I'd been. She cleared a spot of snow off the railing, set her mug down, and then slapped me silly. We stood in silence as the shock and the sting slowly faded.

"Was that for last night?" I asked. "Or the past three years?"

"That was for last night," Carol said. She slapped me across the face again. "That was for the past three years."

"Mom!"

"You were of age."

"I didn't know."

"You knew I had my reasons," she said fiercely. "I don't believe in god because I have met the devil! Those demons took my family away from me! And from you! All of them! Everybody! Until I—"

"We have to remember them."

"Do you think I forgot?"

"You've been hiding so long that you hid me," I said. "Every time we remember those who have gone before, we honor them. We liberate them. We deliver them from the grave. Don't you see? We preserve our future by remembering our past. And that…that's the light. Demons that lurk in darkness feast on silence."

I was so afraid that I had crossed a line, but, as tears welled up in her anguished eyes, I could see her heart melting. "When did you get so smart?"

"It's been a long three years," I said. "When you can't hear, you learn to listen."

She sipped her cocoa and looked out across the yard. The forest was covered in snow and the wind was still. We stood there, in the silence of our solidarity, for several moments.

"Have you ever seen a Redwood tree?" Carol asked. I shook my head. "When I first came to America, my great-grandparents, Gershon and Miriam, took me to California. It was my first time on a plane."

"Were you scared?"

"Very," she said. "Looking back now, I'm honestly surprised they could make the trip at their age. It wasn't until we got there that I understood why they had taken me."

"To see the Redwoods."

"It was the most magnificent sight I'd ever seen," she said. "Gershon taught me about them. Did you know that a single Redwood can grow up to three hundred and seventy-five feet tall? They can reach twenty-four feet across. Some of them have been around for over two thousand years. They're the oldest living things on Earth. Perhaps the most resilient too.

"When the ground level rises or shifts because of a flood, a Redwood will grow a new root system to survive. After hundreds of years, a single Redwood can endure a half-dozen serious floods, and it will grow a new root system each time. And if, by some chance, a Redwood is knocked over, the branches still continue to grow. Eventually, those branches become trees. So, even when it falls over after hundreds of years, sometimes thousands of years, it is just beginning the cycle of life. And I still remember what Gershon told me that day. God, seeing you now is like going back in time. You look just like him."

"What did he say?"

"He said that when we face times of turbulence, the floods of tragedy that disrupt our lives…well, it's not the end. It may feel like it, but it's not. It's just time to grow a new root. When the ones we love fall over, it's simply our turn to grow. We learn by doing. And just as the fallen Redwood nourishes the new trees, the hearts and the memories and the gifts of those who have gone before must nourish us. When we remember, we become just as magnificent in our humanity as the Redwoods are in their enduring beauty. That, he said, is why we must never forget the *Shoah*. That's why they took me. That's what they wanted me to know, that the lessons of our past, no matter how horrifying, must be remembered if we are to preserve our future. Civilization thrives in vigilance—not complacency."

"He was a smart man."

"You have his eyes," she said, looking at me. "And his vision."

"You're just now remembering all this?"

"Memories are like waves," Carol said. "They come and go. Sometimes, I recognize them; sometimes, I want to forget. After your father was murdered, I just put it all away. I lost sight of the wisdom Gershon shared with me that day, many days. He'd be happy to know you were the one to remind me."

The cocoa was so hot I felt it all the way down.

"I miss my dad," I told her. "Both of them. And Grandpa and Jim."

"The price of love is grief," Carol said, "and the cost of our laughter will be our tears. Every path, in this life, will soon lead us to a pain as dreadful as our love has been wonderful. It's inevitable. And it is most unfortunate that so many people miss that about this life. But, giving yourself permission to grieve, even to cry, is to accept precisely how much you have loved those you have lost. Deny your pain and you deny your ability to love. Took me a long time to learn that. A long time."

"Loving somebody just means you're going to lose them?"

"Only from your sight," Carol said. "When we ask questions, we want answers. But the explanations we get are often far beyond the answers we so passionately demand, especially in our grief."

"So, what's the explanation?"

"Perhaps it is better to have loved and to have lost than to never have loved at all, but to love after having lost takes courage because to love in innocence is to love with ignorance."

"Tennyson?"

"Congreve."

"I didn't know that."

"I love your father," Carol said. She was trembling, either from the cold or our conversation—or both. "Nothing will ever change that. Nothing. Not ever. He was the one who taught me that love after death is possible. You're proof of that. He was a good man, a great man. If he could see you today, and all that you've accomplished, he'd be so proud of you—just like Jacob was proud of you."

"Can I ask you something?"

She took a deep breath. "Yes."

"Did...did they at least catch the guy who took William from us?"

"He was shot that night," Carol said, looking away. "Didn't make it."

"So William got him?"

A cutting wind rose from the north. "Not exactly."

"Suicide?"

"Not quite," Carol said as we went inside. "Not quite."

CHAPTER TWENTY-TWO

THE ONE YOU WERE GIVEN

DRIVING THROUGH THE DARK roads of a dying town, I realized just how hard the recession had hit Poquanicut. James's old house was up for sale again, along with several others. The convenience store at Lucy's had gone out of business, and the Sunoco gas station on the other side of town had been shuttered. The only good news, for me, was that I finally got a part-time job at Angelo's Sub Shop in Rose City. That, and Dad had left his house in order. He had willed both the station and the condo to me, but I couldn't decide what to do about the station; I only knew that I didn't deserve a damned thing.

A few weeks after my father's funeral, I met with my father's lawyer about the will. The first thing Dad had wanted me to have was a set of keys. I knew immediately which ones were for what. Finalizing ownership of the station would take several months to be approved by the court. At the time, I'd had an offer from Standard Gas. As tempting as it was to sell, I just told them that it was too soon for me to make a decision. Since I could live at the condo while it was in probate, there wasn't much point to staying in the apartment. Charlie, Tim, and Junior had to help me move.

Inside the condo, I felt my father's presence in the place. An empty can of ginger ale sat on the coffee table next to a bowl of popcorn, the dead kernels sitting at the bottom. He still had that lumpy old couch—and the television set on which we'd watched that infamous Game 6. His bed had been made with military precision, a stark contrast to how it had looked after my parents first separated. I had asked Mary and Carol to help me go through his clothes, slowly placing them into paper bags for donation. They were taking a load down to the car when I opened the top dresser drawer.

The cigar boxes were full of surprises. Besides his class ring and graduation tassel, there were some foreign currencies and old newspaper clippings, mostly obituaries of veterans. The original certificate of marriage was behind the divorce decree. Dad had won a blue ribbon in the Elliott Elementary School Art Show. Rows of baby teeth had been glued to an index card, and there was a date scribbled beneath each one in my father's handwriting. I also found a condom in the drawer, the same brand that mysteriously appeared once I'd started seeing Allyson.

"Son of a gun," I said, sitting down on the bed. "So, you were the tooth fairy..."

It took me a while to get settled that semester. I'd read or type my essays between working on the condo. I started with minor changes—curtains, the bathroom mats, and hamper. By the time mid-terms came, I decided to paint the place over spring break. After the paint was dry, I moved into the master bedroom. With the changes I'd made, the condo didn't feel as haunting. Grandpa's couch fit perfectly in the living room; I had set it up on the opposite side and moved the television to the center of the room.

Once I'd got all the utilities connected, I called Dr. Collins to order fire alarms with strobe lights and an adapter for my amplified telephone so that a lamp would flash when I had a call. Rewiring the doorbell was another story. Since I had no experience with electrical work, and I didn't want to burn down the building, I hired a licensed electrician who could safely connect the strobe lights and set up the alert for prolonged flashes. I could never forget my father but upgrading the place he had called home made it mine as much as it had been his.

God, I missed him.

As the months dragged on, my guilt and arrogance haunted me. Most nights, I couldn't sleep. It wasn't just Dad, but James and Grandpa—and William too. No sooner had I begun to process one loss than I'd had to endure another. My grief had made me a shadow of the man I'd wanted to be. Worst of all, my last words to Dad had been spoken in a fit of rage. I was so angry at the one thing I thought my father did wrong I couldn't see everything he had done right.

My parents had honored Carol's wish to protect me from the horrors she had endured, the savagery that had taken her own family—and her husband.

Dad had given me a home and raised me as his own son. He chose to be my father, after my father had been taken from me, and that said more about his character than it ever did about mine.

Worst of all, I never got to say goodbye, nor did I want to—not when I'd watched the SEALs pound their Tridents onto his casket, not when his gun salute shook me to my core, not when I was handed that folded American flag. After the funeral, I'd had it framed; it was the first thing I hung on the wall at the condo, right above his couch.

I hadn't slept in days when Carol called to tell me that the life insurance payment had been approved. Dad had bought his policy through her company, and Carol had personally delivered the check after my final exams were done. That was my first shower in a week. We met Mom at Mystic Pizza, which had been recently renovated after the movie came out a few years ago. It was something having lunch with Julia Roberts. She really was a pretty woman. The waitress brought our pizza. She had said a grand total of two words to me when we ordered our drinks, "And you?" It was ridiculous. I wondered if the character Julia Roberts had played in the movie would be more considerate to a customer who was hard-of-hearing.

"Have you decided what you're going to do with the station?" Carol asked.

"It's still in probate," I said. "Honestly, I haven't even been down there. I did get an offer from Standard Gas, but they haven't contacted me in months."

"You'll be done with school next year," Mom said. "After that, you can do anything."

"I told them I'd think about it," I said. Once I'd got the money that my family had saved for me to go to college, and Mom helped me clear up the situation with my gratis tuition, I paid off the Sentra and my student loan. Of course, the money meant jack shit after losing Dad and Grandpa and Jim. I'd reviewed the books for the station. The grocery sales had dropped slightly, but Dad had sold less gas in his last six months than I'd ever seen. Checking the dates confirmed a correlation to the first round of layoffs at the Boat, and it was all downhill from there. "The numbers don't look good."

"The Poquanicut tribe got federal recognition last year," Mom said. "They've already broke ground on a new casino. It's expected to be up and running early next year."

"They only expect to hire a couple hundred people," I said. "That won't come close to replacing the business Dad lost in the layoffs."

"Even so," Carol said, "the casino will bring in business with all the entertainment."

"To Poquanicut?" I said. "All the movie stars in this state live west of the Connecticut River, closer to New York. They got it all over there: the privacy of living in the country, the beauty of the coast, and the glamour of the city right at their fingertips. They never come east."

"Julia Roberts did," Mom said.

"That's true."

"Well, what do you want to do?" Carol asked.

"I just realized I don't know what to call you," I said. "It seems kind of strange to keep referring to you as my aunt."

"You can call me Carol," she said. "Better yet, how about Ma?"

"That's what we used to call your grandmother," Mom said. "She'd like that."

"Oh, she was a sweetheart."

"So, Mom and Ma," I said. "That'll work. As for what I want to do, I don't even have a major. My degree will just be in general studies. Not the best way to build a life."

"Sometimes," Ma said, "the best way to build the life you want is to remember the one you were given."

I knew exactly what she meant.

After lunch, Ma said that she wanted me to come and visit her in Pennsylvania as soon as I could. Since school was out, and the station was still in probate, I decided to drive out the next day after taking her to the airport that morning. She offered to buy me a plane ticket, but I wanted to drive. After getting the Mustang out of storage, I put the top down, took my hearing aids out, and hit the road. It was so good to feel the freedom of the open road again, with the wind in my hair and the world at my fingertips.

I stopped at The Way to Go, that old diner where I'd had my first, and last, heart-to-heart conversation with my father. I even sat in the same seat and ordered the same meal, as if recreating my memories could somehow bring him back. Of course, he never came. Memories were all that I had left of him, and even those would die with me. Maybe, I thought, if I can make the station work, I could pass it on to my own kids one day. Maybe I could share with them the lessons Dad had worked so hard to teach me. Maybe, in that way, his memory would endure. It was a simple life, but it was the one he had given me. When I got to the register, I laughed once I realized I'd left the receipt on the table again.

The mountains and valleys along Interstate 80 in Pennsylvania stretched across the horizon. The gray clouds kissed the peaks while distant shadows danced across the farms and fields. I was so taken by the beauty and majesty of the landscape that I stopped near mile marker 180 to take several photographs with my 35mm camera. At least this was a moment I could preserve, a memory I could protect. When Ma took me to get the film developed, she chose her favorite photograph of the landscape; I got it enlarged and gave it to her as a gift. The only frame left at Sadie's Department Store was black. It was fitting, in a way, to see the joy of summer surrounded by a solstice of mourning, a reminder of all that we had endured and all that we had gained.

After so many years in hiding, Ma and I spent that week reviewing the stack of letters I'd found in the box Grandpa had left for me. Although Ma had sent them to Grandpa, she'd addressed them to me. Ma started writing when she'd first gone back to Pennsylvania, after I was weaned. She had hoped that those letters would provide some kind of record of her decision in case something happened to her before I'd come of age. Some of what she wrote I already knew, either from Mom or what Ma herself had told me. The last letter had been written just before she'd come to visit for my tenth birthday. She was so afraid to see me again, so scared of how she might feel, but the weight of her curiosity and longing to see me again had become too much to bear. As we sat outside on the porch one evening, with the distant mountains glowing in the setting sun, my mother finally released the burden she'd buried for so long, filling in the details she had deliberately left out of her letters.

She had been born in Berlin, 1933. Five years later, during *Kristallnacht*—the "Night of Broken Glass"—she would escape the savage Nazi mob looting and burning hospitals, schools, businesses, and homes. My grandparents had been tailors for years, running a small shop on the first floor of their house, but they lost everything when the Nazis attacked that night. My grandmother, who had got my mother out, begged a German nurse to watch her while she ran back into burning house to get the rest of her children. They were trapped on the second floor, screaming through the rising smoke and flames. That was the last time my mother saw her family. My grandfather and oldest uncles had already been taken by that time. It wasn't until after the war, while Ma was staying at an orphanage for displaced children, that she learned they had been killed at Auschwitz. When I asked how they had been found, she told me that their names had been discovered in the records.

"They started by searching for my surname," she said. "My father made us write it over and over again when we were kids. All their names, my aunts and uncles and cousins and brothers and sisters, so we'd remember. He knew what was going on, what might happen. Memory was our insurance policy."

"What was his name?" I asked. "I mean, your maiden name?"

"Frimer."

"What happened after they burned the house?"

"The nurse took me." As it turned out, the nurse was a devout Catholic who gave Ma the same rosary she still wore to this very day. It would protect her, the nurse had said, because people would think she was Catholic instead of Jewish. Ma had never believed in the divine; she only knew, at the time, that Jews were being taken away. The nurse looked after my mother and a handful of other children for over three years. They'd hide under the floorboards beneath the bed, which rested on a rug. That space kept getting smaller as the children grew. One day, the nurse had gone out to get rations and never came back. Walter, their cranky old neighbor, had told Ma and the other kids that the Nazis had taken her. Somebody, who probably just wanted her rations, had tipped them off that she had been hiding the children. "I never did find out what happened to her."

"What was her name?"

"Erika," Ma said. "That's all I know. Honestly, I resented her for the longest time. To me, to the child I was, she was a constant reminder to me of what had happened to my mother. I remember there were so many people just standing there, some throwing bricks and bottles, shouting, watching that house burn…burning as she ran inside. That house was my home, and that woman was my mother. That family…was my family. Our family."

I didn't know what to say. The moment a thought crossed my mind, I realized just how foolish my words would be. Mom had warned me years ago that some experiences are beyond judgment, and I was just beginning to understand the depths of what she had meant. I waited for Ma to speak. Then, I listened.

"After they took Erika, those of us who were left escaped the city that night," Ma said. She told me that Walter had led her and the other two kids as far away as he could. He knew it was only a matter of time before they would be found so they ended up going into the mountains. Walter knew how to survive because he had grown up in those mountains; he would build shelters and hunt or fish, but it wasn't long before food was scarce.

Often starving and always scared, Ma spent the next few years moving from place to place, town to town, avoiding the war and the camps by hiding where she could, running when she couldn't. They had hoped to make it far enough to book passage to the United States. As the war raged on, though, the despair of such brutal conditions—frostbite, malnutrition, and infection—took a toll until only Walter and Ma were left. One night, while hiding in a barn, Walter had built a fire to keep them from freezing to death. They were captured by the Nazis the next morning and taken to Dachau. "Three months later, an eternity if ever there was one, your grandfather found me."

"What happened to Walter?"

Ma shook her head. "There are times I look out at these mountains just to remember him. What he did for us. What they all did for me, especially your grandpa. Walter and Erika, I've never spoken of them until now. I just want you to understand why I did what I did. Of course, when I married your father, I thought I could put all this shit behind me…"

Reaching, I held her hand.

"Roger, you're a miracle," Ma said, tears in her eyes. "I've wanted so long to tell you. Your father and I tried for ten years to have children. We'd long since given up hope by the time you came along. But, you're here. You're here. You are my son, and you are a miracle. Don't ever forget that."

We held each other and cried in excruciating joy.

As I absorbed her words that night, I thought that learning the truth about my family would add to the burden of my grief, but, somehow, I'd found an enduring light in our survival.

A light that would never be extinguished.

"So much history wrapped up in a single life," I said. "What was yours has become mine. All that, and we're still here."

She took off her rosary and gave it to me.

"I want you to have this," she said, holding it in my hands. "I want you to keep it as a reminder that there is still good in the world. I've seen it, lived it. And I want you to remember the people who proved it, including your grandpa."

"He was a good man."

"The best."

"You know, he told me something a long time ago," I said. "Something I don't think I ever understood until tonight."

"What's that?"

"He said, 'When a boy becomes a man, he must choose between the life he was given and who he wants to be. Remember who you want to be.'"

"Quite a pearl."

"Took me long enough."

"Every heart has got a story," Ma said. "Listen for the ones nobody wants to hear."

"But I can't hear."

"That's how you learned to listen."

"I think I get it now," I said, kissing her hand. She smiled, tears in her eyes. "I remember who I want to be."

When I got back to Poquanicut, I was still wide awake after twelve hours on the road. I spent half the night tossing and turning, thinking of my family and trying to decide what to do. No matter how many times I did the math, the numbers for the station just didn't add up. It was hopeless without the rush of traffic from the Boat. Finally, at two-thirty in the morning, I got up and made a pot of coffee. That's when it hit me: I'd got an offer from a major corporation that had built hundreds of gas stations throughout the northeast. A single station in a small town like Poquanicut was certainly no threat to them. So why would Standard Gas make an offer if the station wasn't economically viable? If they knew it would fold, why would they want to buy it? Since sleep was a lost cause, I decided to go for a drive. After touring Poquanicut, I ended up at the station.

Even with the sun coming up, I hardly recognized the place. The grass was overgrown. Trash strewn from one end of the parking lot to the other. The pumps were wrapped in yellow caution tape, and the handles had been chained and locked. Dust and dirt covered what was left of the windows, one of which had been boarded up with a sheet of plywood and several signs warning trespassers to keep out. Reaching for my keys, I remembered the last night I'd worked with my father. "How come you gave the Hostess guy such a hard time today?"

"I just argue with the vendors to keep them on their toes," Dad said, flicking the ash off his cigarette. "Besides, we ran out of donuts yesterday. And if we don't have anything to sell—"

"We're not going to make any money."

"That's right," Dad said. "On the other hand, we don't have a lot of room inside the store, so we've got to make sure we don't waste space."

"If it doesn't sell, we don't want it."

"Right again. But we really don't make a lot of money from groceries. It's meant to draw in our customers. We sell more gas than anything."

"That's why the markup is so small."

"We're a small business. Our prices have always been competitive, but—"

"Our service makes the difference," I said. "That's why we're the only full-service gas station east of the Connecticut River, if not the state. We check the fluids, change the wipers, and wash their windows. And if a regular makes a request, we make it a point to get it."

He smiled. "You're going to do just fine, son. It'll all work out."

The next day, I left with James.

Looking back now, I wondered if Dad had wanted me to run the place someday. He knew my family history, all that we had lost. Was that the real reason he'd worked so hard for so long? So that I would have the opportunities my family had stolen from them? He had said that everything was going to be all right. Was that his way of telling me that I could do it? Did he have that much confidence in me? In who I was becoming? A chill went down my spine as I unlocked the front door.

With the power shut off, the store was hot inside and smelled stale, the air heavy. In the early morning light, I could see that the boarded-up window had been smashed. Pieces of broken glass lay among the cigarettes, candy bars, and snacks all scattered on the floor. Everything my father had worked for had been reduced to a pile of garbage in a decrepit building.

I was devastated—and angry at myself for letting it come to such a mess.

Going to the backroom, I got a broom and pushed all the merchandise and glass on the floor into a pile. Propping open the door, I went outside and started sweeping the lot. The trash cans were soon full, and there was so much gunk on the bottom I'd have to hose them down. That was when I realized the water had been shut off as well. I was taking an inventory of the snacks I'd have to write off when a tall old man appeared in the doorway. He was holding a lead pipe. It took me a moment to recognize him. "Oh, my god! Mac?"

"About time you showed up," he said. Mac, the original owner, had built the station in the Fifties, when the automobile industry had inadvertently created the suburbs. When the USS *Nautilus* crossed the Northwest Passage, Mac had a stable, growing business that would endure for decades—until the end of the Cold War. I hadn't seen Mac since he'd retired and Dad bought the station. We went outside. He sat on the tailgate of his truck. "Where you been, kid?"

"UCONN," I said. "What happened to the window?"

Mac adjusted his hat. "Couple o' kids broke in late last winter. I chased them off, but not before they had their fun. After that, I boarded the place up and locked it down. Figured you'd be along eventually. He didn't have anybody else."

"I appreciate that, Mac," I said. "I just came by to clean up a bit."

He chuckled. "You'll need a lot more than a little cleaning before you open up again."

"I'm thinking about it," I told him. "I haven't decided yet. Besides, I have a job."

"You have a job? What job do you have?"

"I make sandwiches for a living."

"You make sandwiches?"

"They're…steak sandwiches?"

"Let me guess," Mac said, scratching his head. "Part-time at four dollars and eighty-five cents an hour leaves you with less than eighty dollars a week. Have I got that right?"

"Just about, yeah."

"So, what the hell is there for you to decide? You can earn a decent living right here, kid."

"Mac, I went over the numbers," I said. "In his last six months, Dad had a razor-thin profit margin."

"Floods test bridges," Mac said. "Fortify under clear skies. A smart businessman always prepares for the worst when he is doing his best. In thirty years, I had more ups and downs than your father ever had. As long as people are driving, they'll need fuel. Trust me, kid. You'll bounce back."

"Place doesn't even have power."

"I can fix that," Mac said, getting up. "You just hang tight. I'll be back."

Later that morning, Mac brought me lunch and a small generator. The halogen lamp was hotter than hell, so I set the fan up in the doorway to air the place out. Mac cut the grass while I worked all day and into the night, writing off old groceries as I cleared the shelves. After months of sitting in the dead air of the cooler, the milk had evolved into a new life form. I took an inventory of the cooler shelf by shelf, draining the contents down the floor sink, then hauling the bottles and cans to the dumpster out back. By the time I was done, it was filled with expired inventory. I'd been awake for over forty-eight hours, and my whole body ached. When I got back to the condo, I slept all night.

I spent the next afternoon on the phone, going through Dad's numbers. He had labeled his contacts not by name but based on what they did. I made arrangements to get the water and electricity turned on, the window replaced, and to rent a power washer for next week. The number for Connecticut Relay was next to the listing for his accountant, which meant Dad had hired a new one after all. I called on my TTY.

HELLO GA

GOOD AFTERNOON I AM CALLING ON BEHALF OF EVANS FOOD AND FUEL LOOKING FOR ACCOUNTANT QQ GA

MR EVANS PASSED AWAY SIX MONTHS AGO WHO ARE YOU QQ GA

MY NAME IS ROGER EVANS I AM THE SON OF JACOB EVANS WONDERING IF YOUR SERVICES ARE STILL AVAILABLE QQ GA

I AM SORRY FOR YOUR LOSS MY CONDOLENCES STATION OPEN QQ GA

STILL IN PROBATE IVE BEEN OVER THE NUMBERS FOR HIS LAST SIX MONTHS THEY DON T ADD UP WOULD APPRECIATE ANY INSIGHT YOU MAY HAVE ALSO NEED ACCOUNTANT TOO GA

KNOW ASL QQ GA

SOME BUT NOT FLUENT NOT USED ASL SINCE DPN THREE YEARS AGO GRANDPA WAS LDA HE KNEW SIGN BUT PASSED AWAY I WAS BORN HEARING NOW HH WILLING TO LEARN GA

YOU KNOW DPN QQ GA

WAS THERE YOU QQ GA

CLASS OF 1990 DID YOU MEET A WOMAN NAMED KALIN THE NIGHT DPN BEGAN QQ GA

YES WHY QQ GA

WHERE DID YOU MEET HER QQ GA

LOBBY MAYFLOWER HOTEL AGAIN DURING MARCH GA

HAHA I THOUGHT IT WAS YOU SAW YOUR PICTURE ON DESK THIS IS KALIN GA

SMALL WORLD DAD MENTIONED HIRING AN ACCOUNTANT BUT NEVER WOULD HAVE GUESSED YOU RE THE ONE GA

FUNNY DO YOU STILL HAVE YOUR BEARD QQ AND THAT JACKET QQ DO YOU STILL HAVE THAT JACKET QQ GA

YES TO BOTH YOU STILL HAVE CONTACTS QQ GA

CONTACTS QQ GA

I COULD SEE MY REFLECTION IN YOUR CONTACTS GA

NEVER HAD CONTACTS GA

EMBARRASSED ARE YOU TEACHING AT AMERICAN SCHOOL FOR THE DEAF NOW AS WELL AS ACCOUNTING QQ GA

APPLIED BUT MY ROOMMATE SHAE GOT THE POSITION YOU MET HER NIGHT DPN BEGAN REMEMBER QQ I WORK IN INSURANCE AND DO ACCOUNTING WHAT ABOUT YOU QQ GA

I REMEMBER SHAE YES I GO TO UCONN USE NOTETAKER IN CLASS COURTESY OF ADA MILES TO GO ON THAT EMPLOYERS DANCE AROUND COMPLIANCE BULLSHIT YOU ASK ME GA

DEAF DO IT BETTER WORK HARDER THAN HEARING PEOPLE WE HAVE TO JUST TO GET A JOB MAKE YOURSELF INVALUABLE YOUR WORK EXCEPTIONAL GIVE THEM NO CHOICE BUT TO HIRE YOU ALSO LOVE BEING SELF EMPLOYED HOPE TO DO ACCOUNTING FULL TIME ONE DAY GA

CAN WE SET UP A TIME TO MEET GO OVER DETAILS QQ GA

NEED TO CONFIRM INTERPRETER AVAILABLE WHEN QQ GA

SCHEDULE OPEN DAYS GOOD TTY HERE AT HOME BUT NOT AT STATION YET GA

JAKE USED RELAY NICE MAN SORRY MISSED FUNERAL STORM GA

BLIZZARD DELAYED FUNERAL SERVICE WAS RESCHEDULED NOT IN PAPER HAVE INVENTORY OF WRITE OFFS FOR TAXES NEED UTILITIES ON SOON GA

HAVE YOU SET UP LLC QQ GA

LLC QQ GA

LIMITED LIABILITY COMPANY PROTECTS PERSONAL ASSETS IF LEGAL PROBLEMS ARISE BETTER FOR TAXES AS WELL NEEDS TO BE DONE THROUGH STATE OF CT FEE PAID ONCE PER YEAR CHOOSE NAME GET TAX ID FOR PAYROLL ETC SUGGEST SETTING UP UTILITIES ACCOUNTS PAYABLE ETC THROUGH LLC CAN OBTAIN AND SUBMIT PAPERWORK IF YOU RE HIRING ME GA

IT SAYS A LOT THAT MY FATHER HIRED YOU BUT WOULD LIKE TO CHECK YOUR REFERENCES FIRST GA

CHECK BROCKTON LIQUORS BRYANT MOBIL JORDANS BAR AND GRILL MISS MAGGIES GRINDERS ROSE CITY CAFE UNDER THE HOOD CAR SPECIALISTS AND UNICORN COMICS HAVE MORE IF NEEDED GA

I was expecting three references, but Kalin never even hesitated. Once I had them all written down, I realized that she had given them in alphabetical order. If she had that many accounts and a full-time job, she sure knew her shit. I gave her my home number.

SEVEN REFERENCES WILL BE FINE THANKS CAN WE MEET AT STATION NEXT THURSDAY AT 0900 QQ NEED TO EAT GA

WILL CONFIRM INTERPRETER AVAILABLE AND LET YOU KNOW GA OR SK

HOPE TO SEE YOU THEN KALIN SK

SEE YOU LATER SK

Learning that my father had hired a Deaf accountant surpassed the amazement of connecting with Kalin again. It was like finding a pearl of joy in the swamp of my grief; I knew, now, that Dad had accepted Grandpa—and that he would have accepted me as well. I was really looking forward to seeing Kalin again. Having lived so long as a hearing person, and attending a mainstream school, I didn't have any Deaf friends. It would be a relief not having to explain the rules of natural law when I had my hearing aids in or my emerging deafness when I wasn't wearing them.

So many times, too many times, I'd be walking to class in the rain and a hearing person would approach and just start talking. I seldom wore my hearing aids when I was outside because of the wind and never when it was raining. At first, I'd speak, telling them that I was hard-of-hearing, but they just kept talking as if I could hear. Worse, they treated me like I was the one who couldn't understand what they were saying!

I got so sick of it that I'd just sign *I'm deaf* while shaking my head, sometimes defiantly but often in disgust. Even then, they still spoke as though I could hear. Nobody ever thought to use a pen and paper, nor would they bother to write when I took out a notepad for them. It was so bad that every time I saw a hearing person approaching, I immediately felt the weight of their ignorance. In the past year, it had become such a burden that I'd mastered the art of avoidance.

I'd known many audiologists who had said that hearing loss leads to isolation, but they never realized that it was because of the way hearing people treated us—or they just didn't care. I couldn't change my deafness, but all it took for hearing people to communicate adequately was simple courtesy. The ignorance of expectation defines misconceptions about people with disabilities far, far more than our physical capacities.

"The world is a pretty big place," Ma had told me once. "And it is a fool's errand to presume people must think and act or believe as you do. The only people who won't change are the ones who want everybody else to change."

If I had learned anything in the past three years, it was that the world was full of fools.

As I was making dinner, my mind drifted to the success of the Deaf President Now protest. In some way, the Deaf had saved me. They had become a beacon of hope in my own hopeless world. Throughout history, hearing people had banished, euthanized, constrained, and sterilized the deaf and hard-of-hearing. Like books, we are judged by our covers—and so few people have the courage to see what's inside, much less the wisdom to learn;

instead, they search for ways to reinforce what they already know. But, as much as Grandpa had enabled me to accept the changes my body was going through, the Deaf had empowered me to embrace them. Remembering what the Deaf community had proved to the world that week in Washington was like Grandpa finding me in the woods as a child—somebody knew where I was and how I could get home again.

And I was.

I spent the whole summer down at the station. My initial decision not to run the place while it was in probate turned out to be a mistake, but I used the time to clean up. Once I'd got the window replaced, I covered the glass with old newspapers to keep the thieves away—out of sight, out of mind. In the cooler, which I kept off because it was empty, I took the shelves down off the racks and started scrubbing. So many bottles and cans had burst in the heat that the floor under the shelves was covered in caked-on caramel syrup. I let it soak with steaming-hot soap and water while I washed and sanitized the walls. It wasn't long before the heat had me soaked in sweat. Taking off my T-shirt, I tossed it onto the office chair and started scrubbing the floor. I kept thinking of all the times Dad and I had stocked the cooler. Experiences that were once so annoying to me had now become precious memories, and all of them ran through my head as I was getting the water up with the Shop-Vac. I had just finished putting the racks back up when Kalin arrived.

Hi, she signed, smiling, from the threshold. Her dark hair was longer, loosely held in a ponytail at the base of her neck, flowing down over her right shoulder. She was wearing a white, short-sleeved blouse and a pleated turquoise midi-skirt with white flowers. Lilies, I think. I couldn't tell if she had any makeup on. Around her neck was a small silver locket, and she was carrying a leather notebook. She looked professional but comfortable. Confident and secure, Kalin had become a beautiful woman. *You're Roger, right?*

I nodded. Like a scene from a bad movie, I was covered in sweat and shirtless, wearing faded jeans and an old beat-up pair of boots. Looking at my watch, I realized that she was thirty minutes early. Dad would have been impressed. *Wait a minute. I need to wash my hands.*

When I was done, I put on my T-shirt. Kalin was waving her hand in front of her face.

It is really hot in here, she signed. *I'm waiting for my interpreter. She will be here soon.*

The humidity from the damp floor was lurking. *Let's go outside.*

I put the ledger and adding machine into a milk crate and carried it outside with a couple of folding chairs. We sat in the shade on the west side. When Kalin handed me her résumé—a single page, direct and to the point—I saw that she no longer had her engagement ring. After graduating from Gallaudet, Kalin had taken an accounting job with an insurance firm while building her clientele. She had recently moved to Rose City after acquiring several local accounts but still kept her job in Hartford. When her interpreter, Jackie, arrived Kalin introduced us. I gave her the other folding chair and sat on the milk crate. After putting in my hearing aids, we started the interview.

"Okay," I said, after the rush of sound settled. Jackie translated. "Your references certainly checked out. High praise all around. How long were you working for Jake?"

About a year. He had a simple system, easy to manage and track expenses.

"And you run over a dozen local accounts and commute five days a week to a full-time job in Hartford?"

Yes. I have also applied for several more local accounts. I hope to get enough business in the next few years to leave my job in Hartford and do accounting full-time.

"Let's see what you got." I handed Kalin the ledger and adding machine. Before I had even sat back down, she was scribbling away. She never even touched the adding machine but did it all in her head. Within minutes, Kalin gave the ledger back to me. I started looking it over.

"Is this right?" I asked.

Yes, she nodded. *Once the mortgage on the condo was paid, he focused on the loan for the station, often paying toward it every week to cut down on interest. He wanted to pay it off quickly. He owned it outright eighteen months ago. I calculated your base payment for insurance with the average of payroll, utilities, and expenses.*

"What about estimated taxes?"

Check line seventeen, she told me. And there it was.

"Sales dropped significantly in his last six months."

I know.

"It's worse now with all the layoffs," I said. "So, I need to know—do you think this is a viable business?"

She smiled. *You're just like your father. He was cautious about everything. He always said he earned his money twice: working like he needed it and spending like he didn't have it.*

I chuckled. "Yeah, he would say that. All right. You're hired."

She gave me the paperwork to create an LLC. *If you have any questions, use TTY.*

"I will," I said, getting my checkbook. "Thank you."

Can I have a tour? Kalin asked. *I want to know everything.*

"Now really isn't the best time," I told her. I gave Jackie her check and thanked her for coming. "I have a lot to do around here before we open, as you can see."

I understand, Kalin signed. *See you soon.*

After they left, I found myself wishing I'd given her that tour.

Kalin transferred the utilities after setting up my LLC. She also detailed my anticipated profit margin for the gasoline and groceries, submitted a pay scale with raises and bonuses, and worked out a buying plan for what I'd need before opening. Listening to Kalin while hearing her interpreter was exhausting after working all night. I was processing two languages at once, which soon drove me to learn as much Sign as I could so we wouldn't need an interpreter.

Kalin would sometimes stop by on her way home from work to see how things were going. The more I saw her, the more Sign I started to remember. She was surprisingly patient as I learned, much more patient than the hearing people I'd known. She would ask about the probate or when I'd be ready to start placing orders. It was her idea that I landscape the median on the other side of the gas island and plant some flowers. *This place needs more color.*

Good idea, I signed. *But I don't know anything about flowers.*

Why not?

I shrugged. *I just never learned.*

I meant, why not add flowers? she signed, laughing. *Maybe a flagpole? You could set up picnic tables and expand the parking lot for a farmers market. It will draw in business and be good for the town. Maybe a small fenced-in area for dogs. Family friendly, family first.*

Dogs and a farmers market? I like that idea. Always wanted a dog. I need a survey of the land and an estimate for the parking lot.

Maybe some more lights to brighten everything up, she suggested.

Yeah, I agreed. *I can build the fence and picnic tables, easy. I have so much to do before opening.*

A few days later, a nasty nor'easter came through and left a leak in the roof that destroyed the floor of the station. So much water had gone under the cracks beneath the shelves that I could feel it just by stepping on the tiles. Once I found out how much it would cost to repair the roof and redo the floor, I went over my budget with Kalin and decided to do the work myself. That was the first time I began to wonder if the place was even worth it.

Washing away the dirt on the outside brought out the white trim and gave the forest-green paint a fresh look. I built a farmhouse fence around the dumpster and painted it to match the store. It was better than looking at that rusty old thing. Locking it up would also stop people from dumping their garbage, which meant I'd pay less for collection. I set up two lights, each with three bulbs, on the front corners of the store and a couple more in the back. It'd come in handy during those long winter nights in New England. After the parking lot expansion was done, I sealed the lot to give it a uniform look. Painting the curbs and spaces again made it look brand new. Seeing it so crisp and clean reminded me of when Dad had first bought the place.

The week before school started, I landscaped the median on the other side of the pumps and put up a flagpole. Kalin chose the flowers, planting them over the weekend. It was amazing how much brighter and more colorful everything looked. Flowers, like Kalin, did that. By that time, we weren't using an interpreter at all, and I only put my hearing aids in when I had to deal with contractors. We reviewed the orders I'd have to place before opening. She made suggestions based on sales while I considered security and delivery schedules. The new wooden shelves I'd built were the exact dimensions of the old ones, but I'd set them up on rubber stoppers and had left enough room to clean underneath. We placed notes where everything would go. All I had to do now was wait for the probate court.

Locking up, I took a long last look before we left. The station was no longer a dingy, mangy, decrepit old building; it had come alive with the renovations. I still felt empty, though. All that I had accomplished meant nothing without Dad. I'd got my start scraping gum, but the way it looked now I was actually beginning to believe I could run the place. Maybe, I thought, Dad would be proud. Maybe I could honor my father after all. I just wished he had lived to see it. Kalin caught my reverie, waving her fingers to get my attention. *What are you thinking?*

I miss my dad, I told her.

He was a good man, Kalin signed. *He was the first to hire me after graduation, when I moved to Rose City with Shae. He gave me a great reference every time I wanted another client.*

I wish I hadn't wasted so much time.

I can tell you more about him, she signed. *Are you hungry?*

Pizza? I asked. She nodded.

We signed for hours at the Pizza Galley. Kalin had learned about my family's history of progressive deafness the day Dad had hired her. He told her that he'd used a Vietnamese translator during the war so communicating through an ASL interpreter was no problem for him. Like me, Dad had been amazed that Kalin could just look at a set of numbers and immediately calculate the answer. (It actually took her longer to write the answer than it did for her to figure it out.) While Dad had picked up a few signs here and there, they would usually use the TTY or write notes to each other when Jackie wasn't available, like we had done with Grandpa. After seeing my photograph in his office, Kalin had told Dad about meeting me in Washington, DC.

What did he say? I asked.

He asked if I knew where you were now, Kalin signed. *I told him I didn't know. He hoped you'd be back someday. I can see why he always said you were his best worker. He went through a lot of employees when I was there.*

He taught me to do my best, I signed. *And he made sure I did.*

The best parents always want their children to have a better life than they did, to succeed where they failed, to do better than they did. If he could see everything you accomplished this summer, I know he'd be proud of you.

Did your hearing parents ever learn sign language?

No, Kalin told me. *That's why I chose Connecticut with Shae.*

What happened with Jessie?

I wanted a husband, not a parent, Kalin signed. When I asked her what she meant, Kalin said that Jessie had wanted her to move to Rochester with him after graduation, but she'd already got a job in Hartford. He was also very controlling, always wanting to know where she was, who she was with, when she would be back. She could also read lips better than him, but every time they went out to eat, he'd always order for her. Having been raised in a hearing family, Kalin was fierce about her independence. *What about you? Do you have a girlfriend?*

I shook my head. *My life is work work work. Soon, school and work. No time.*

Do you have time for me?

Do you have the time, the patience, for me to learn American Sign Language? I've learned a lot signing with you, but I know there is so much more to learn.

My hearing parents never learned sign language, remember? When she was a child, Kalin's parents had kept trying to make her a hearing person, sending her to a speech pathologist in the hopes that she would learn to speak. Kalin hated it with a passion. It got so bad that once Kalin finally started going to a Deaf school, she would beg her teachers to let her stay during vacations. Everybody understood her at school, but nobody understood her at home. Later, Kalin had tried to teach them sign language, often stubbornly insisting, but they just never wanted to learn. *My hearing parents never understood their own limitations.*

I considered my own experience over the past few years.

I thought I understood deafness because I grew up with a deaf grandfather. Now that I'm hard-of-hearing, I'm just beginning to realize how much I never understood deafness. It's like the difference between reading a book and writing the story. Now, I guess I'm writing my own story. You must have enjoyed Gallaudet.

It was tough sometimes at Gallaudet, she admitted. *I knew Deaf people, born to Deaf families, educated in Deaf schools, who treated me different because my parents are hearing, because I spent time in mainstream school, because I'm the only Deaf person in my family.*

You were bullied?

Sometimes, yes. That's why I never really fit in at Gallaudet. I got so depressed that I almost transferred to the University of Delaware.

I shook my head. *Every school, community, group, whatever has people who think they're better than the rest of us. When I was in high school, the rich kids from Brockton Point thought they were better than the poor kids from the projects in South Brockton. In college, it was so much worse. The liberals thought they were better than the conservatives, but the conservatives thought they were better than the liberals.*

Religion is the same way, Kalin pointed out. *I've met Christians who think Catholics and Jews are going to hell. Not for me.*

My birth mother is Jewish, but my adoptive parents raised me as a Catholic.

She smiled. *And you're hard-of-hearing, like a bridge.*

I was born on a bridge, the George Washington Bridge, a place between worlds. Part of both but belonging to neither. I'm not hearing enough for the hearing world, but I'm not Deaf enough for the Deaf community.

You're Deaf enough for me, Kalin signed. *You're willing to learn.*

And you're Deaf enough for me! I told her. She laughed so hard her face turned red; she knew what I meant. *Even when I was a hearing person in the hearing world, I was an outcast, a misfit. So, not Deaf enough, not hearing enough, that's nothing new to me. I mean, I just did my own thing.*

You're an individual, she signed. *You chose your own path.*

The waiter gave us a note, telling us that they had to close. As I went to pay the bill, I thought about all the time I'd spent with Kalin. I didn't have the same burden with her that I did when I was around hearing people. I never had to explain anything or remind her that I was hard-of-hearing. She had even been patient with my lack of proficiency in Sign, teaching me as we went along. More than that, she knew what it was like to be an outcast.

You say you're writing your own story, Kalin signed after we stepped outside. *Never let anyone dictate your narrative.*

Exactly, I agreed.

It was years before I learned that myself. Most Deaf people, like Shae and Gregg, her boyfriend who is now in law school, accept me.

Will they accept me?

I accept you.

Want dessert? I asked, hopeful. She smiled.

We went back to my place.

Later that night, our first kiss consumed us by candlelight. It was then, in that moment, I knew she had me—and I realized, finally, that I had her too. That one true kiss had revealed more than any language ever could.

Our life was just beginning.

CHAPTER TWENTY-THREE

COLD WAR 2.0

THE MOVIE THEATER WAS packed for opening night of *Star Trek VI: The Undiscovered Country*. I had planned to see the ten o'clock show with Tim and Junior, but we had to catch the one at eleven-thirty instead. Even then, we stood shoulder to shoulder with the crowd, hoping to get good seats. We had all grown up with *Star Trek*; it had even inspired Jim's brother, Craig, to join the Air Force. After twenty-five years, the original crew of the *Enterprise* was about to take their final voyage. It was the end of an era.

"You know what's weird?" Tim said. Surprisingly, the crowd was quiet. "I can't believe it's been three years since we graduated high school."

"I can't believe it's only been three years."

"Yeah, right," Junior said. "Seems like it was only yesterday we were arguing about rap music and heavy metal."

"Rap was never the same after Run-DMC chopped off the devil's head."

"You were a headbanger by the time *Raising Hell* came out, Tim," Junior said.

"I can't believe you thought I was a Satanist," Tim chuckled. He had spent a few months staying with me at the condo after his parents, who were very religious, threw him out of the house after he'd told them that he was gay. They cut him off completely and had even stopped paying for his tuition. Last month, Tim got an apartment with his boyfriend, Alejandro. Having seen my non-existent social life, Tim was the one who dragged me out tonight. "I get enough of that from my parents."

"The Satanic panic was a farce," Junior said, laughing. "Hey, how come Alejandro couldn't make it tonight?"

"They got him working the graveyard shift at Rosie's," Tim said. "I told him we'd see it on Tuesday."

"Tell him to keep a job open for me."

"Not if I need one first," Tim said.

"Thanks, guys," I said. The grand opening of the station last week had been a bust. I'd hired Tim while he was staying at the condo and Junior once I'd found out that he had lost his job at 7-Eleven. He had discovered that his boss was the one who had been stealing. Before Junior could report it, though, he got fired for "too many complaints." I knew it was bullshit. Business was so bad at the station that the morning rush had been reduced to my picking up cigarette butts around the lot. At first, I'd hoped to break even, but now I'd be lucky if I didn't fold. "That's very encouraging."

"We didn't mean it like that, Roger," Junior said. The ushers finally started taking tickets. "But, man, I got a wife with a kid on the way. I have to think of them first."

"Believe me, I get it."

"We know you're doing all you can," Tim said. "Sometimes, it's possible to make no mistakes and yet still fail."

"That I learned a long time ago," I said, handing my ticket to the usher. We couldn't find three empty seats next to each other. It was almost two o'clock in the morning when we got out. I downshifted up the onramp to the highway. It was ice cold outside, but I could see the stars through the passing streetlights. When Tim said that it was great to be alive in a world finally free of the threat of nuclear war, I told him, "I don't know about that."

"What do you mean?" he asked.

"*The Undiscovered Country* is a cautionary tale, a warning for future generations."

"But the Federation made peace with the Klingon Empire. We know that from *Star Trek: The Next Generation*. The Khitomer Conference is how it began."

"I wasn't talking about *Star Trek*," I said. "I was talking about us. Our future. You think because Kirk and Gorkon changed, that every Cold Warrior is going to change?"

"Val'eris sure as hell didn't," Junior said. "And then there was that Romulan fuck."

I laughed. "Romulan fuck?"

"So, a few of them had a tough time," Tim said. "That doesn't mean—"

"It only takes a few," Junior said. "That's what led to Gorkon's assassination. Some people will do anything to preserve the old ways, especially their hatred."

"What are you guys saying?" Tim asked. "That the Cold War didn't end?"

"The Soviet Union collapsed," I said. "We won, but we didn't beat them. There's a difference. A big difference."

"What do you mean?" Tim asked.

"Some people fear change," Junior said. "Better the devil you know than the angel you don't."

"Not everybody wants to embrace a brave new world," I said. "And I certainly think it's worth remembering that Russia invaded and divided Poland with the Nazis in 1939. Stalin himself was there when the agreement was signed between the Soviet Union and Nazi Germany."

"The Molotov-Ribbentrop Pact," Junior said. "Look, Tim, it's like that word processing program you were talking about earlier, the one Alejandro gave you. It's the same program. It's just an updated version."

"So, the Cold War got an update? Like a computer upgrade?"

"Call it Cold War II," Junior said. "Or Cold War two-point-oh. Same animosity, different era. New weapons, old enemies. Archaic attitudes do not die with a whimper."

"If you ask me, it all depends on whether or not the new Russian government clings to the past like Chang or learns to embrace the future like Kirk. That's why I said *The Undiscovered Country* is a cautionary tale. I don't know about you guys, but I'm not holding my breath."

"So how will we know?" Tim asked.

"Heroes learn," I said. "Villains don't. Every weapon, each new technology just becomes another means of attack because they're too damned scared to let go of the past. Without an enemy, the old guard has nothing to live for, like General Chang and Admiral Cartwright."

"You'll know if Yeltsin steps down," Junior said. "Yeltsin and his successors, I should say. The one who clings to power cares more about power than he does his own people. Simple."

"Makes sense."

"Or if one of them tries to restore a fallen empire," I said.

"You know," Tim said. "I'll never forget the first time Dave and I saw *Terminator* on cable television. He was so scared he took the dining room chairs and put his bedspread over them, like a tent. I used to scare him by saying I saw robots coming."

"That's nothing," Junior said. "Aaron used to beat me up all the time just to impress the girls. We always got in trouble for it. One time, Ma asked us what happened, and Aaron was like, 'It all started when he hit me back!'"

Their laughter made me wish I had a brother.

"You want to know what's really funny? Any time Dave wanted something he used to tell our parents that I wanted to know."

"We did that too!"

"'Tim wants to know if I can have some ice cream!'"

"You know what my favorite one was?" Junior said. He was laughing so hard I wondered if he would be able to tell us at all. "When Aaron said I wanted to know if he could sleep over at Sam's, and I was in Virginia with our cousins! Ma was like, 'What are you talking about?'"

Junior had to catch his breath, but I thought Tim was hyperventilating. "Dave once took my spot…in front of the TV…and I mushed a whole handful…of grape jelly in his hair! He almost killed me!"

"All right, already," I said. "It's not that funny."

"Yes, it is," Tim said. He burst out laughing again but soon started crying. "Oh, shit! All those years growing up together, and now he doesn't want anything to do with me! Christ, I should have just kept my fucking mouth shut."

"No, man," Junior said. "If he can't accept you, that's on him. That ain't on you. Why should you be anything less than who you are, right? Right?"

"I guess."

"Kalin once told me, 'Never let anyone dictate your narrative.' Your story is your life, Tim. It's yours, and yours alone, to live. Live and let live. Simple."

"Smart woman," Junior said. "All right, Roger. It's your turn."

I flicked my cigarette out the window and watched the ash explode in the wind. "My turn? My turn for what?"

"Tell a story," Tim said. "A funny one. I need a good laugh."

"I'm an only child," I said. "I don't have any stories like that."

"There must be something," Junior said.

"Yeah," Tim said. "Something silly or strange or ridiculous. Anything."

I had to think about it for a moment. "When I left with Jim, we stopped at the mall so I could get a jacket. This jacket, in fact. We cut through Sears, and I noticed one of those telephone intercoms had been left on…" I started laughing, just thinking about it again. "…so, Jim picks it up, and he just randomly…he starts quoting the garbage men from *Star Trek IV*, going on about toaster ovens and shit!"

"For real?" Junior said.

"Swear to god," I told him. "And then this big old burly security guard starts marching toward us, like he's about to bring the wrath of Kahn down on us!"

"What did you guys do?" Tim asked.

"We split up and ran like hell," I said. "Jim got to the car first, but I was still inside trying to evade that security guard. He almost had me when I made a mad dash for the door and got outside just as Jim pulled up."

"Then what happened?" Junior asked.

"I jumped in the car and he took off like a bat out of hell! God, all that shit over toaster ovens!"

I was laughing so hard. We all were.

"Anybody see that kid in line behind us?" Tim said, catching his breath. "The one with the big shoes and bell-bottoms?"

"He looked like a clown who got lost on his way to the circus," I said. "I guess they're not called bell-bottoms anymore."

"Bootcut, slim-fit, hip-hugging, low-riders," Tim said. "Ripe for a rave. That's where I met Alex."

"We all go through that phase," Junior said. "Like Roger and his Toughskins."

"I never wore Toughskins," I said.

"Yeah, you did," Tim said. "I remember you did."

"I wore parachute pants in the Eighties, but I never wore Toughskins in the Seventies."

"You did too," Tim said.

"I did not."

"Did too."

"Did not!"

"Did too!"

"I DID NOT!"

In January, I was working seven days a week while going to school. I would check in vendors and run the store while Junior trained new employees on how to handle cars and run the pumps. He had hired a few people to work nights with Tim, but I was always back to lock the place up and set the alarm. When I wasn't at the station, I was either commuting to Storrs, doing homework, or going over the books with Kalin. Saturdays were the only time we had together because we were both working so much. Running the station and going to school full-time was maddening, but I was finally in my last semester at UCONN. I had dozed off at my desk one night when the flashing lamp for the phone woke me up.

"Hello? Is this Mr. Evans?"

"Yeah," I mumbled, rubbing my eyes. I kept the volume all the way up.

"Mr. Evans, this is Rick. It's my first night. You wanted me to call you so we could close the station tonight."

I could hear the register over the people talking. "Rick, it's ten-thirty. Why didn't you call me earlier?"

"I don't think we can close, sir."

I hated being called "sir." I was twenty-two years old, for heaven's sake. "Well, get the people out of there and—"

"That's what I've been trying to do!" Rick said, almost in a panic. I heard a customer ask for rolling papers. "We don't sell them."

"Not at all?" the customer asked.

"Nope," Rick said. "No rolling papers, no cigars, no lottery. The boss is kind of a straight arrow, if you know what I mean."

I'd rather be a straight arrow than a target, I thought. I heard the register open and waited for Rick to close it. "We went over this, Rick."

"You don't understand," he said. "I've been trying to get them out of here, but they just keep coming!"

"All right," I said. "Just take it easy. I'm leaving now."

The winter wind hit hard as I stepped outside. The stream of traffic led me straight to the station. The lot was filled with cars, the store with people. For the life of me, I couldn't figure out why until someone, who was obviously from out of state, asked me for directions to the casino.

I pointed. "Three miles that way."

"Three miles that way?"

"Yeah," I said. The door slammed into my back as three or four people came outside. "You can't see it from here, but it's just beyond those trees. Can't miss it."

"Thanks," the man said. "Is it on the right or the left?"

I wanted to scream. "You'll find it."

I was about to go inside when I saw a car take off with the hose still in the tank. By law, gas pumps now had to have a quick-release system to prevent spills. The hose whipped in the winter wind as I ran after the car like Mo Vaughn stretching out a double at Fenway.

"Hey!" I screamed. "Stop! You stupid—"

Finally, the car pulled over. A young couple got out and tried to get the hose out of the tank. My chest was burning. Mo would have made it to Portland by the time I caught that car.

"I'm sorry," the girl said. "I didn't realize it was still in the—"

"The thing," the guy said.

"—pump spot place."

I took the hose out of the tank and walked back to the station. All I wanted was to go home and get a good night's sleep. I reconnected the hose to the pump. When Rick saw me go back inside, he put on his coat and ran around the counter for the front door. He spun around as I caught his arm. "I know you're not leaving until your work is done."

"Mr. Evans, come on!" he whined. Getting to the register, I told Rick to put the rug up and mop the floor so nobody would slip. People had been tracking slush inside for half the night. After he put down the clean rug from the backroom, Rick could wipe the counters and empty the trash—like he was supposed to do. "But I wanted to be out of here by ten!"

I rang in someone's gas and coffee. "You're not done with your work yet. And you know how I am about keeping this place clean."

"That's the most important part," a customer said.

"You're not being fair!" Rick cried. "I told you, I was supposed to be out of here at ten! I was supposed to go out with my friends tonight! I stayed longer than I should have anyway!"

"If you leave now," I said, handing the customer his change, "don't bother coming back."

"I won't," Rick said. He threw open the door and left.

I ended up staying at the station all night. The Poquanicut tribe had finally opened their new casino, Sunwoods, and it had brought flocks of people to the reservation and the town. The faces had changed, but the steady stream of people was like a constant rush from the Boat. People just kept coming. As the night wore on, I finally had time to get ahead for the morning crowd. At dawn, Charlie came in to get his newspaper and coffee and cigarettes.

"Did you open early to get ready for the casino?" Charlie asked. "I heard they were supposed to close, but there was so many people they just couldn't fucking do it."

Suddenly, I couldn't stop laughing. My bones ached, and I was exhausted.

"You losing your marbles, kid?" Charlie asked.

"You wouldn't believe the night I had."

"Got to be better than last year," Charlie said, sipping his coffee. "Don't tell me you've been up all night too. Jesus, kid, go home and get some sleep."

"Just a few more hours until Junior comes in," I said. The milkman was also scheduled for a stop, and George couldn't run full-serve and the store by himself. I now needed to hire a few people to work the new third shift, but

Rick was just the beginning. Over the next few months, I would go through more people than I could remember. It seemed impossible to find someone who was willing to learn the job. If they had the register down, they had no idea how to check oil. Some people never showed up; others were constantly late or calling in sick. In March, I stopped by to check on the night crew, but the front door was locked. I just assumed they were stocking the cooler and went inside. When I opened the door to the backroom, I found them going at it. They rushed to cover themselves as I quickly closed the door.

"Be right out, Boss," the girl called.

"That's okay," I said. "Just…finish what you're doing and—"

"Give us about five more minutes," the guy said.

"Five minutes?" I whispered, shaking my head. After that night, I started working third shift full-time. My last semester of college turned out to be the hardest. I'd head home after class, shower, grab my books, and go in at about nine to get ahead on the cooler, working as fast as I possibly could so that I'd have more time to read. If I wasn't at work, I was either on my way to class or at the library doing research. The rest of the time, I'd be falling asleep while typing a paper or reading in the bathtub. The hot water soothed my aching, knotted muscles; I'd slowly drift off to sleep with my legs stretched out, keeping my head and chest well above the water, until the cold woke me up. After that, I'd drain half the tub, fill it right back up with scalding-hot water, and read until I fell sleep again.

The week I took my final exams, Los Angeles was on fire. The acquittal of the four police officers charged with beating Rodney King had ignited America's racial tensions yet again. Every day I heard students talking about it before class. Some of them were passionate; some were angry. Some spoke cautiously; others shouted foolishly. Very few people had the wisdom to listen. I kept my cool as the students argued, but I felt like I was fighting a volcano in my chest listening to some of them. I just wanted the whole goddamned thing to go away because it reminded of what had happened to Grandpa, but it was precisely because of what happened to Grandpa that I knew it would never go away.

Four years, I thought, and it's come to this. I had learned so much, studied so hard, only to discover that, in the end, I knew nothing at all. Honestly, I didn't even want to attend my own graduation, but my mothers had missed out on my high school ceremony. So, I went. When Mom asked me what I wanted, I told her that a decent meal would be nice; I'd been so busy that semester I had no time to cook. It felt good to be home again. My mothers were delighted to meet Kalin, and they had no trouble using an interpreter. I took the leftovers to work that night; they were gone by morning. By that time, I had everything down so well at the station that I'd get most of my work done by two o'clock. After that, I'd go over the paperwork for that day, review the inventory, or read until Charlie showed up.

"Good morning, Charlie," I said, snapping his pack of Luckies down on the counter. John Carpenter came inside and headed for the coffee like he always did.

"You see the presidential debate last night?" Charlie asked, tossing crumpled ones onto the counter. I told him I hadn't. "You didn't miss much."

"Speaking of presidents," John said. "I heard Bush went to a supermarket and didn't know what a UPC scanner was, but Clinton can tell you how much a carton of eggs and a gallon of milk cost. He's for the people."

"He also said he plans to cut the deficit in half in four years," Charlie said. "I'll believe that when I see it. We can't just keep spending."

"I think Clinton is going to win, though," I said.

"Casting your vote ain't about winning or losing, kid," Charlie said. "The most certain consequence of living in a democracy is that absolutely nobody ever gets everything they want. That's why I say voting is about making a decision and being able to live with it."

Looking around, I knew exactly what he meant.

A year after the casino opened, Kalin left her job in Hartford to do accounting full-time. Despite managing so many clients, she still wanted to learn everything about the station. She had asked about purchases and markups, sales and write-offs, even adjustments and transfers, going over the inventory with a militant efficiency to maximize profits and minimize losses. By that time, I had set up visual fire alarms and bought a new TTY so she could use the office. Junior had become the manager while Tim worked second shift as the assistant manager. Over the years, so many people would come and go, but the four of us would all stick it out together.

During those first few years, we met once a month to go over business at the condo. Tim was out picking up the pizza when Kalin and her interpreter arrived.

Providence Petroleum just raised their prices, Kalin told me. *Two more cents.*

"*Are you sure?*" I asked. Kalin showed me the report. "*Junior, have we had any complaints about the prices?*"

"A few people mentioned it," Junior said. "Nothing unusual. A few comments. Honestly, even if you go up five cents, you'll still be cheaper than 7-Eleven."

"*Five more cents it is*," I said and signed. "*Our prices have always been competitive, but we need to give people a reason to choose us over the competition.*"

"I think you should consider full-serve," Junior suggested.

We have full-serve, Kalin signed.

"Full service full-time," Junior said as Jackie translated. "You'd have a higher payroll, but you'd get more done at night with two people. Our customers could get their merchandise or use the restroom while their cars are being filled up. And it saves the trouble of explaining how to pump gas to all those people coming up from Jersey."

And less time parked at the pump means more time for more fill-ups, Kalin signed. *Especially with just four pumps. It will also help with security. Less drive-offs if they pay the attendant first. One trip inside. Convenient.*

"Exactly," Junior said. "Sunwoods is also expanding. They're adding a bigger venue for more entertainment. Word is they'll be drawing big names, top talent. All those stars in Fairfield County won't mind a forty-minute ride to make ten thousand dollars an hour, or whatever it is. And honestly, I think we need to be prepared this time."

"*All right, I'm sold*," I said and signed. "*Personnel is your responsibility, Junior. Let me know how it goes. I want them ready before you send them to me on third.*"

"What if we get a good one who wants to work overnight but can't train on first shift?"

"*Just send them to me*," I told him. "*Anything else?*"

The farmers market, Kalin pointed out. *We could expand it to include flowers in the spring, the autumn harvest with fresh apple cider and pumpkins, and trees and wreaths for the holiday season. With more business you can charge a lower percentage but still make more money.*

"Damn," Junior said. "Now I know why he hired you."

"*It's good for everybody*," I said and signed. "*I'll start making calls around town, see who is interested. It won't take long for word to get around. Kalin, can you work out a new percentage for leasing space on a seasonal basis?*"

She agreed. When Tim got back with the pizza, Junior introduced him to Kalin and Jackie.

"I heard about her," Tim said to Jackie. "I work second shift, so I haven't met her yet. It's not every day you see a deaf accountant."

Jackie had translated, but I was the one on the defensive. "Maybe that's because you don't know—"

"I don't even know how deaf people go to school," Tim interrupted. Jackie translated. "HOW DID YOU MEET ROGER?"

Kalin was about to sign when I slammed my bottle of beer down on the table.

"*You were there the night my grandfather was murdered*," I told Tim. *"Don't ever talk to us like that again. It's disrespect—"*

"Roger, I swear to god, I didn't mean to be."

"And don't ever, ever interrupt me again. Okay? Ever. When you interrupt me, then your voice is competing with mine, and that...is noise. And noise and I don't get along. Noise is the root of all evil. Now, once again, I'm going to make this simple. Repeat after me: 'It all comes down to visibility, noise, distance.'"

"It all comes down to visibility, noise, distance," Tim said.

"Thank you."

Be respectful, Kalin signed, facing Tim. *Not insulting.*

"It took me a little while to get used to an interpreter too," Junior said. "The secret is to just see them as an invisible conduit."

Kalin waved to get Tim's attention.

Roger and I met five years ago in Washington DC, Kalin said. She had their interest now. After explaining the roots of the Deaf President Now protest, Kalin told Tim and Junior what she knew about James—including the missing person report I filed. Taking a huge bite of my pizza, I leaned back in my chair.

"Roger don't talk much about Jim," Junior said. "It's kind of an unwritten rule."

I took a deep breath, pushing down the tsunami. "*That is not your story to tell*."

Beneath the table, Kalin set her hand on mine, like she was letting me know it was okay that I wasn't okay. My anxiety faded with her comforting gesture. Her taking a moment to acknowledge how difficult it was for me gave me a sense of relief. Maybe Tim and Junior thought I had finally learned to live with losing Grandpa and James and Dad. And maybe I had. After so many years of living with the pain, I couldn't remember a time when I didn't feel it. And all the work I had put into school, and now the station, forced me to move forward, at least in some way. We wrapped things up before Jackie had to leave. Kalin had to give her a ride home but said that she would be back soon. *Okay*, I told her.

I watched her turn toward the elevator, then closed the door.

"Does anyone want to see *Jurassic Park* this weekend?" Tim asked. "Alex and I really want to go, but our car died."

"I read the book," I said. "The book is always better than the movie."

"Well, it's been a shitty year," Tim said.

"How so?" Junior asked.

"For one thing, the World Trade Center was bombed."

"I remember that," I said. The room got quiet. The bombing of the World Trade Center last February had shaken the whole country, if not the world. It had shown us that America was vulnerable, and we could still feel the loss. "At least most of the people got out."

"And the towers are still standing," Junior said.

"Terrorism is political violence," Tim said. "Theater."

"We'll get them," Junior said. "We always do."

"Anyone up for the movie?"

"I can't go with you," Junior said. "I promised Rochelle that we would take her niece and nephews."

"Are you taking Malcolm?" I asked.

Junior shook his head. "He's finally sleeping through the night but way too fussy to be in a loud movie theater for two whole hours. My parents are happy to watch him."

"Can't Rochelle's sister take Malcolm?" Tim asked.

"We take turns," Junior told him. "They have Malcolm on Fridays while we get Danielle and Renée on Saturdays. Besides, for them it kind of defeats the purpose of date night. Sorry, Tim. You'll have to find another way to go see a bunch of scientists play god."

"God died a long time ago," Tim said. I shook my head. It was a wonder Tim and Junior were friends at all. They were still arguing when Kalin got back. I grabbed another beer from the fridge, gave one to her, and updated her on the conversation about the movie. She thanked me for the beer as we sat back down. "And can you honestly tell me that you wouldn't want to live forever? Cloning can do that—better than religion, anyway."

"*I don't like the idea of cloning people*," I said and signed.

"It's unethical," Junior said. "The Faustian bargain."

"Technology is neutral," Tim said.

I asked Kalin, *What do think about cloning?*

If god wanted us to fly, he would have given us the intelligence to build an airplane.

A moment passed between us. We both took a deep breath.

"I think we overstayed our welcome," Junior said, chuckling. He got up to leave.

Maybe the pilot does the flying, I signed. *But we choose our destination by getting on the plane. Or not.*

"Hey, what are you guys saying?" Tim said as Junior dragged him to the door. "Come on! That's not fair!"

I shut my hearing aids off.

CHAPTER TWENTY-FOUR

A CONNECTICUT MORNING

IF YOU TAKE INTERSTATE 95 north from Florida to exit 94 in Connecticut, make a left at the light, and drive north for ten miles, you can see Sunwoods Resort Casino towering above the forests of my hometown. The expansion of Sunwoods brought more traffic through town than Route 12 could handle. Poquanicut, Brockton, and Rose City were at odds with the state over who should pay to expand the road or build a bypass. The never-ending argument took place in the town halls and, of course, by the coffee machine at the station. Every morning the regulars had something to say about it. Junior and I would ring them in between giving directions to the gamblers. One guy, who took a wrong turn and got lost, gave us a dissertation.

"Hi," the man said. He reeked of credit card debt with his crisp white shirt, black tie and slacks, and shiny new sunglasses. "I recently experienced a lapse in judgment and as a result of which I am currently directionally challenged. If you are so knowledgeable, I would be greatly appreciative if you could provide some sort of viable guidance toward the newly constructed gaming facilities."

Exhausted, I could barely make sense of "gaming facilities."

Junior pointed. "That way."

The man smiled and waved and left.

Constantly giving directions to Sunwoods was just one of the many hassles of running the station. Besides the new vapor recovery system at the pumps, I now had to sell gas with the MTBE additive, but the Clean Air

Act didn't complicate things as much as a local media report led people to believe that the new gas caused their car problems. The television press always seemed to find the dumbest man on Earth and put him on camera. When MTBE had first come out, I'd had to explain countless times that it was harmless and required by federal law for cleaner air. It was remarkable how much people feared even the slightest change.

I hated cleaning the bathroom on third shift. Drunk tourists clogged the toilet and teenagers scribbled obscenities on the walls and mirror. People would also leave the water running and throw dirty diapers in the sink. It was disgusting! Finally, I spent a whole weekend changing the tiles on the walls, painting the ceiling, and putting down an oriental rug. I also set a glass case above the urinal with the Sunday funnies and got a fancy ashtray. Kalin bought an artificial tree and a landscape from Rochelle that one of her clients had painted. Making the bathroom immaculate made people think twice before making a mess, and the compliments were well worth the effort of keeping it up.

"That has to be the nicest restroom I have ever seen at a gas station," one woman said as she returned the key. "It's nicer than my bathroom at home."

"It'll be our secret," I told her, smiling. I turned to Junior. "Good to know some things are finally going right around here."

"Some things," Junior said, "but I had to fire George yesterday."

"Why?" I asked. "He was our first hire."

"I stopped in to check on him and he was filling his backpack. When I asked what he was doing, he said he was helping himself."

"Well, just because god helps those who helps themselves doesn't mean I have to. So many people come and go. All right. What's next?"

"Hey, kid," Charlie said. "You catch the Miss America Pageant last night? The woman who won is just like your girlfriend."

"I saw it," Isabel said. Junior had hired her for weekends. She'd brought her daughter to the interview last week, but once Rochelle had found her a good babysitter, she was able to work full-time. "That deaf woman won."

"Heather Whitestone," I said. "Miss Alabama. Hey, Charlie. Guess what?"

"What?"

"It's morning again in Connecticut."

"That slogan worked for Reagan," Charlie said. "You should run for president."

"I meant, business is good."

"Yeah? You got a hot date tonight or something?" Charlie often joked that any woman would want me because he thought I had money, but most of what I made I put back into the station. Besides the bathroom makeover, I'd also bought a new sign, added a couple more streetlights to the expanded parking lot, and got embroidered T-shirts and sweatshirts for my full-time employees. Raises were consistent but based on performance and duration of employment. With all the payments and bills—electric, phone, insurance, payroll, and bonuses—I doubt I could have kept up without Kalin. She had moved into the condo last month. It was amazing watching her work; what took Dorothy all day to do, Kalin could finish in forty-five minutes flat.

Outside, Tom and Dominic had the hoods open and the pumps going. There was a line of cars in both directions waiting their turn. People appreciated full service that included a thorough check on their cars. "Hey, Junior, since we got a line, why don't you give her the rundown on checking cars? I can handle the register."

"Is Junior a nickname?" Isabel asked.

"Nope," he said. "My father gave me that name. He said he wanted to acknowledge the past and represent the future."

"Smart man."

"I always thought so," Junior said, handing her a change bank. "What about you?"

"I was born in Cuba," she said, strapping on the belt. I listened carefully because I wasn't used to her accent. "My mother, my brothers and sisters all live here now. We escaped to Florida after my father was killed in prison."

My heart sank. "I'm sorry."

"Thank you."

"Prison?" Junior asked.

"He spoke out against the government," Isabel said. "He basically just wanted us to have clean water, electricity, food we could afford, that sort of thing. Communist governments don't like being criticized, but...he believed we could do better. He challenged the regime. They killed him."

"What brought you to Connecticut?" Junior asked, opening the door for her.

"Most of my family works at the casino," she said. "We wanted to stay together..."

A baby boomer came inside as they were going out. Her bangs hung down to the top of her big black glasses. She was wearing a tan trench coat and a red blouse. While she was getting her coffee, Charlie pointed out a car that had just pulled up to the pump. "You know, they say that a Ford Taurus has more computers than the Apollo missions to the moon."

"But a Ford Taurus can't take you to the moon," I said. "Just goes to show you how much we lost because of technology."

"You think so?" Charlie said. "They always said it'd make life easier."

"I'm serious," I told him. "The promise of a better life through everyday technology is an epic myth. We waste more time trying to figure out how to figure out that junk than we do doing what it's supposed to do. Give it a generation or so. Whoever reinvents the car is going to make a fortune. People want simplicity. There is nothing in the world like hitting the road and seeing the country with a full tank of gas and no distractions. Computers are so complicated they're more trouble than they're worth. Just the coffee today, ma'am?"

She had come to the counter but was looking down and going through her purse. I didn't hear what she said.

"What's that?" I asked in a deep voice. But she kept searching her purse and spoke again in the same tone. I lowered my voice more and, this time, gave her a command, "Say that again."

"Pack of Belair!" she snapped. "The cigarettes! Jesus!"

"That's not necessary," I said. Calmly, I pointed out my hearing aids as she finally looked up. "I just do a few things differently."

"Oh, I know how you feel," she said. "I had an ear infection when I was six months old. They said I've lost ninety percent of my hearing in my left ear, and fifty percent in my right."

I knew it was bullshit just by the sound of her voice, an imaginary tale I must have heard a million times. "Audiologists don't do percentages. It all comes down to—"

"They did in my day."

"Yeah, a baby would remember that," I said. She handed me a ten-dollar bill. "It all comes down to visibility, noise, distance. Those are the rules. Face me when you speak, be mindful of the noise, and aware of the distance."

She wasn't even listening.

"Now, my husband has selective hearing," she said as I gave her the change. "He hears what he wants to hear. God, it drives me up a fucking wall, you know? You know. You know what I mean. One minute we're in the kitchen and he can hear me just fine, but if I go into the other room, he pretends he can't hear me."

I let out a long sigh. "As I was saying."

"What? What were you saying?"

"I just told you. I literally just told you."

She scoffed. "Don't be rude. You know, you shouldn't treat your customers like that. I just wanted my coffee and cigarettes and now you're being rude. You're being rude to me for no reason. You are."

Taking a deep breath, I told her, "Selective hearing is exactly what you people think when you ignore the rules of natural law."

"What the fuck are you even talking about?"

"One more time," I said. "The rules are visibility, noise, dis—"

"Don't be such a smart-ass! God, all I wanted was a coffee and some cigarettes! It's not my fault you can't hear! Don't take it out on me!"

"You got your coffee. You got your cigarettes. You can leave now."

"Fuck you!"

"Have a nice day," I said as she left.

"What a piece of work that was," Charlie said. I saw the woman talking to Junior outside. "Christ, you could have told her you found Jimmy Hoffa playing cards with Puff the Magic Dragon on fucking Vulcan or some shit, and she still would have ignored you. People like that never listen."

"Yeah, no shit."

"Hey, kid. Did you know the tallest building in Poquanicut is the public library? It's got fifty thousand stories."

"That wasn't funny," I said. "Nothing you say is funny."

"Of course not," Charlie said, sipping his coffee. "That's what's so funny."

Junior came inside and asked, "What was that all about?"

"Same shit, different day," I said. When I went to the backroom, Junior followed and closed the door. "Look, it's over. She's gone. It's done."

"I know," Junior said. "Just wondering how you're doing."

"It'd be a lot easier if people would just accept me for who I am."

"That'll never happen," Junior said. "I've been black all my life. I know."

"There is no way this is what you wanted to talk to me about."

"Yeah, you're right about that," he said, chuckling. "You are getting a little rough around the edges, though. I mean, you deal with customers like that all the time, but I never saw it get to you like that before."

"What's your point?"

"When was the last time you took a vacation?"

"What difference does it make? Junior, I can't fail. All right? I can't. I can't fail. This place is all I have left, and...You know the last time I saw my father, I told him to fuck off? I did. I did that. And he did this, all this. Worked his ass off, then left it to me. And I was just a spoiled brat who couldn't think more than fifteen minutes in front of me."

"You don't see the world the same way now as you did when we were in high school," Junior said. "You're not the same person, so why would you treat yourself the same way?"

"Because I got a hole in my chest where my heart used to be," I said, "and I am so fucking sick of it, but it never goes away. No matter what I do, or how hard I work, it just never fucking goes away. I thought if I could just keep this place going—"

"So, take a break. Take Kalin someplace nice. Just the two of you. Have some fun. Live a little. What's the point in working so hard to build a life if you never take the time to enjoy it? Tim and I, we got this place down. Besides, Coltrane is finally sleeping through the night."

"What about Malcolm?"

"Malcolm decided to wear a whole jar of peanut butter yesterday."

"Peanut butter?"

"Kid was covered," Junior said, stretching.

"Covered? In peanut butter?"

"He's a kid, Roger. Kids do that. Honestly, it was the funniest thing I'd ever seen. Cleaning it up, not so much. Goes with the territory, though. Peanut butter and the joys of parenting."

"Maybe a weekend getaway would be nice."

"Trust me," Junior said. "We'll be fine."

"I never took a day off before," I told him. "You got this, right? You really got this?"

"Long as we don't start selling no damned peanut butter."

In October, Kalin and I spent a weekend at the Oceanside Bed & Breakfast in Maine. It was one of the few places in Kennebunkport to stay open during the off-season, but it had taken me several weeks to find the right bed and breakfast. I'd go to the library and search through stacks of travel magazines. All the B&Bs were nice, but I needed one that was capable of providing our accommodations.

Most of the hotels I'd contacted had no idea how to use relay; they kept speaking in third person, saying, "Ma'am, could you tell him…" or "See if he wants…" I'd hang up and move on to the next one. It wasn't long before I was back at the library, searching through another stack. Among the handful of hearing people who were actually smart enough to understand relay, most of them had no idea about the accommodations their hotels were legally required to provide. Others, for whatever reason, didn't know the difference between being deaf and handicapped. I'd lost my cool more than once.

> HOW AM I SUPPOSED TO ORDER ROOM SERVICE WITHOUT A TTY QQ FOR THE PRICE YOU RE CHARGING YOU COULD AT LEAST KNOW WHAT YOU RE DOING SK

> IM DEAF NOT HANDICAPPED SK

> LETS GET ONE THING STRAIGHT I AM NOT BURNING TO DEATH BECAUSE YOU RE NOT IN COMPLIANCE SK

Finally, I got in touch with a woman named Maureen at Oceanside. When I asked about their compliance kits for the deaf and hard-of-hearing, she told me that they included a TTY, an amplified telephone adapter, and a shaking alarm clock. She also said that all of their television sets had built-in captioning (which, of course, I knew was now required by law, but nevertheless found it impressive that she knew). Maureen went on to say that the inn had been remodeled recently and that the renovations included visual alerts instead of doorbells because it just made sense for their deaf and hard-of-hearing clients.

> AND OF COURSE ALL OF OUR ROOMS ALSO HAVE FIRE ALARMS WITH STROBE LIGHTS AND CLEARLY MARKED VISIBLE EXITS AS WELL GA

> IM IMPRESSED I MUST HAVE CALLED DOZENS HOTELS AND YOU RE THE FIRST PERSON IVE ENCOUNTERED WHO WAS SO EDUCATED AND THOROUGH ABOUT LEGAL COMPLIANCE GA

> WE CERTAINLY APPRECIATE THAT CAN I INTEREST YOU IN OUR LUXURIOUS LIGHTHOUSE SUITE FOR A MEMORABLE WEEKEND GET AWAY QQ IT HAS A PRIVATE BALCONY WITH AN OCEAN VIEW AND A FIREPLACE FOR COZYING UP ON THOSE BRISK AUTUMN NIGHTS OR IF YOU RE IN THE MOOD YOU CAN JUST RELAX IN THE JACUZZI AMENITIES

INCLUDE A COMPLIMENTARY BOTTLE OF CHAMPAGNE AND STRAWBERRIES READY UPON YOUR ARRIVAL GA

YOU HAD ME AT TTY GA

(LAUGHING) WELL WE APPRECIATE OUR GUESTS GA

It was a such a relief to finally deal with somebody who knew what they were doing. Too many times, I'd found customer service to be so formulaic, as if they were selling general admission instead of a custom experience. Not only had Maureen addressed my concerns before offering us the suite, she understood that our legal accommodations had to be the genesis of her sales pitch. In the past five years, my deafness had progressed from mild-to-moderate to moderate-to-severe. Since I was spending the weekend with Kalin, I left my hearing aids in Connecticut. The three-hour drive to Kennebunkport was worth it, knowing compliance was the one thing we didn't have to worry about, at least not this time.

Stretching as we got out of the car, I could smell the damp leaves dancing with the salt of the sea, lingering among the wood-burning stoves. We got our luggage and headed inside. A middle-aged woman with dark curly hair greeted us at the front desk. Kalin handed her a note that detailed our reservation and accommodations; it also directed her not to speak, but to write her questions and responses. I gave my driver's license and credit card to the clerk, then asked Kalin, *What do you think?*

Beautiful, she signed. *I could live here. How did you find out about this place?*

I did my homework, I told her. *I just thought we deserved someplace nice.*

And we're only staying the weekend?

We can make it longer, if you like.

I have too much work to do, Kalin signed. She had been as reluctant to take a day off as I was. After three years, I'd learned that her mind was always running an intellectual marathon; even when she wasn't working, she was. The clerk set our room keys and a small case on the counter. Smiling politely, she handed us a note.

—Welcome to Oceanside. We hope you enjoy your stay with us. My name is Maureen, and I'll be your concierge. If you need anything, just let me know. Your reservations for

> our Lighthouse Suite and Enchanted Spa day are confirmed. We usually require dining reservations as well, but October is our off-season so feel free to enjoy the fine food at The Salty Fork. I have your convenience kit as well.

Can we see the kit? Kalin asked, holding two fingers to her eye and then pointing to the case. Maureen opened the kit, showing us that it included a TTY, a portable telephone amplifier, and a shaking alarm clock—exactly what she had said it would have. I could tell by the way it was packed that it had been used before, which was usually a good sign that everything worked.

> —If you have no more questions, I'd be delighted to show you to your room.

Nodding, we told her that she could. Maureen called for a bellhop, who took our luggage, while she led us to the elevator. The inn was a classic, Federal-style mansion that had been built at the dawn of the eighteenth century. It had kept its character through several renovations, boasting an in-house spa and seaside dining atop a sloped green leading to the Atlantic. Kalin was stunned when she saw our room. The Lighthouse Suite had a king-size bed and French doors leading to a private balcony overlooking the ocean. There was already a roaring fire in the fireplace. *This is so beautiful, so romantic!*

You like it?

I love it! I've never seen anything so gorgeous!

I picked up the bottle. *Champagne?*

Maybe later, she signed. *I want to get settled and take a shower. And I'm hungry.*

We had a late dinner at The Salty Fork, a cozy, candlelit restaurant with a rustic wooden floor and tall windows that stretched to the ceiling. We chose a table overlooking the garden, with bright autumn leaves rising in the shadows of the lower lights, drifting in the winds as the ocean flowed across the distant horizon. Kalin wore a long white evening gown with a black shawl scarf draped over her shoulders; the scarf had two red roses stitched on the front, flowing down to her knees. As I pulled out her chair, Kalin carefully removed her shawl and sat down. I'd got a new suit, black, with a vest, and a red tie to match her roses. Sipping her wine, Kalin glowed in the candlelight as her eyes reflected the flames. For an appetizer, she ordered grilled hearts of romaine with Caesar and shaved parmesan; I chose lobster ravioli with sugar peas and cream, so smooth it melted in my mouth.

Looks good, Kalin signed.

Want to try? I asked, offering a spoonful. She playfully, yet seductively, took the ravioli in her mouth, like a model auditioning for a sexy commercial. She lost it at the same time I did, and accidentally spit out a small piece of ravioli before quickly covering her mouth as we laughed hysterically. Kalin ordered more wine when our waitress brought our entrées. We both got applewood smoked salmon with herbed rice and lemon-butter asparagus. Finishing my wine, I asked Kalin, *Want dessert?*

I wanted to try the blueberry soufflé, she told me. *But I think I'm full.*

We can always order room service later.

Let's get another bottle of wine, she signed, smiling. I knew that look. When we got back to our suite, I locked the door just as Kalin shut off the lights. In the glow from the fireplace, she slipped out of her gown—and got me out of that suit like it was on fire. The couch was first. After that, we moved to the bed for more room, then it was on to the jacuzzi until the heat and wine and sheer exhaustion finally caught up to us. She got off me and set her head on my shoulder. I was dizzy from the sweltering heat, feeling like I was about to pass out. Kalin reached for her glass of wine and took a sip. *That was wonderful.*

I did not know a woman could move like that, I told her. She laughed. I was no longer an awkward teenager or an inexperienced young man but had come full circle with Kalin. In our three years together, we had learned to read each other; I knew what she wanted before she did, just as she knew what I wanted before I did. And she was great.

You wore me out, I said. *I am so tired. I don't even know what time it is.*

She got my watch on the counter. *Two-thirty.*

I was shocked. *Two-thirty?!*

You kept going when we were on the bed.

You didn't want me to stop.

Leaning in, she smiled and gave me a kiss. *I didn't.*

I love you, Kay.

I love you too, she told me. I could see in her eyes that she meant it. *You were right—we really needed this time. I want to come back soon. And I want another glass of wine.*

She got out of the tub and put on her robe. I took a moment to relax. Shutting off the jacuzzi, I let it drain completely before getting out. Kalin was standing outside on the balcony. She had left the doors open, and the fire had dwindled to a bed of embers. I added a couple of logs, stoking the embers to keep it going.

I'd been waiting for the right moment, and my heart started racing as I realized this might be it. I quickly dug the small black case out of my luggage and stepped out onto the balcony. Across the sea, through the storm, a distant lighthouse cast her silhouette against the falling snow, mingling with the leaves in the brisk wind. Opening the case, I got down on one knee and tapped her leg.

She turned around, dropped her glass, and started crying tears of joy—pure joy. Wiping her eyes, Kalin gave me a long hug as I got up. I could feel her body trembling. Taking the ring, I slowly placed it on her finger. She smiled and stared at the glowing diamond as the lighthouse flashed. *It's so beautiful! I love you so much!*

I love you too, I told her. *Will you marry me?*

Kalin set her hand on my cheek. Coming close, I felt her breath on my ear.

She said, "Yes."

It was the only time I'd ever heard her speak, a moment she had reserved just for me—without fear or judgment or condemnation. In that moment, we became our own community: the best of friends, the greatest of lovers. I wrapped my arms around her in the storm and, as we kissed in the ice-cold wind, the one thing I knew, maybe the only thing I ever knew, was that she had led me to this moment. We kept no secrets, took no detours. We were just two people, standing against a storm. People who had never really belonged anywhere.

Except here, with each other.

Together.

CHAPTER TWENTY-FIVE

AS THE CROW FLIES

AS THE COLD WINTER nights drifted to warm spring days, I started spending my afternoons down at Green Field with the Little League team I'd sponsored. Watching the kids play, seeing the joy of a hit, sometimes a home run, made me feel like a kid again. I'd even got myself a candy bar and a Coke; it was nice not to have to ask my mother for the money. If my team won, I would take them and their parents to the Pizza Galley. Major League Baseball had just ended a strike a few weeks ago. There was no World Series last year, and the kids had been crushed.

"Mr. Evans?" Robbie asked, taking a bite of his cheese pizza. His voice was high in the crowded restaurant, but he was sitting right beside me. "How come they didn't want to play ball? Is money really more important to them than the game?"

"Sometimes," I said, "adults forget what they knew they were kids."

"Oh," Robbie said. He swung his legs beneath his chair and took another bite of his pizza. When he smiled, I saw his missing tooth. "I hope I don't forget."

"Well, I never did," I said, smiling. Kids are always so genuine. Looking outside, I saw that the rest of the parents were starting to arrive. "Before you go, I just want you all to know that you played a great game today. Coming from behind is never easy. You guys just make it look easy."

The kids cheered. I felt so alive just seeing them, as if could get back the best of my childhood that I'd lost so long ago. Watching those kids play made me realize that maybe the world wasn't such a bad place after all. The restaurant emptied as the parents took their children home. Coach Harris wanted to split the bill.

"That's all right," I said, snatching the receipt. "You've done enough, Coach. You really have. They may not win a championship this year, but at least they can play."

"This team wouldn't exist without you," Coach Harris said. He patted my back. "You're a good man, Roger."

After figuring out the tip, I saw Kalin's car pull into the lot. I had just come out the door when I saw her ask, *Did you remember the receipt?*

I laughed and went back inside to get it. This was one of the patterns that had emerged in our marriage. As thorough as I was with running the station, I left my job at work once I stepped out the door. Living with an accountant was another story, though, because Kalin insisted on tracking every expense, both personal and business, no matter how small or insignificant. She could do any math equation at any time, all in her head. Tim, who was back in college to finish his degree, had even made a bet with Kalin on whether or not she could do advanced algebra and trigonometry as easily as basic math. Within seconds, he had to pay up. Once I had the receipt, I got in the car and shut off my hearing aids.

Since we spent so much time together now, I was using my hearing aids less and less. On weekends, we would go for a walk down at the park or drive to Hartford for dinner and a movie. It was the closest theater that had captions because of its proximity to the American School for the Deaf. Afterwards, we would spend hours catching up with friends, often getting the latest news on legal cases being handled by the National Association of the Deaf, including the Individuals with Disabilities Education Act and the Americans with Disabilities Act. Since the hearing press never covered the stories that were so crucial to us, we kept up ourselves by keeping up with each other.

Recently, there had been a proposal by certain members of the Connecticut state legislature to stop providing captions for *The Jerry Springer Show*, but the Deaf community wouldn't stand for it. It wasn't that any of us cared about Springer—no one I knew even watched the show—but we did know that if the hearing world could legally censor one program nothing would stop them from deciding which programs we could, and could not, watch. Once that first domino falls, the rest follow.

The Deaf community accepted us, and we'd even invited some of them to our wedding last month. Kalin chose Shae to be her maid of honor; Junior was my best man. It was a small ceremony, like Kalin wanted, at Oceanside

Bed & Breakfast in Maine; we'd even booked the same suite for our honeymoon. We exchanged vows outside, barefoot in the middle of a snowstorm while the sea whispered a gentle, salty breeze. My mothers were proud. But, damn, I missed Dad.

Kalin's parents had also come, though she insisted that we walk down the aisle together. Seeing the way that they treated her at times—signing awkwardly, talking down to her, ignoring the interpreter, shouting out syllables—was infuriating; I'd decked Blaine for far less, but my mothers managed to keep them occupied whenever they'd step out of line. After that, I decided to get involved in the Deaf community more with Kalin. We were fiercely active in legal matters; we had to be because we knew that nobody else would ever fight for us. I'd known many hearing people, water-cooler warriors, who would bitch about the world's problems down at the station, but, unlike the Deaf community, none of them ever did a damned thing about it. We were constantly reviewing and lobbying for legislation, including captions for *Jerry Springer*.

When I would get home from work in the morning, I'd give Kalin the paperwork from the station. She had it done by the time I got out of the shower, complete with estimates of how much gas I needed to order and when I would need to order it. Once the town council authorized a new public library to be built across the street from the station that summer, I told Kalin that I wanted to make a donation. She immediately knew how much we could afford to give, which was more than I had expected.

Over the summer, I'd try to spend the extra time reading. The gamblers seldom, if ever, left me alone. I could tell the winners from the losers like night and day. Winners splurged; losers were depressed. Some of them would even try to sell their jewelry or have their tanks filled before paying. As a precaution, I set up security cameras and posted signs about the video surveillance. Sarah and Jean, who pumped gas on third shift, had said that they were grateful for the security. In the fall, some of the regulars were still giving me a hard time about it.

"This is ridiculous," John Carpenter said, slapping his wallet on the counter. He had been drinking; I could smell it. "If this keeps up, we'll all be living in a police state. We never even had an income tax in Connecticut until just before that casino went up. The state knew they were going to be getting millions of dollars every year. And where's the money? Where?"

When Tim came out of the cooler and heard John complaining, he went right back inside. I wanted to fire him.

"At the end of the rainbow?" I said. He didn't like my joke.

"I noticed your gas prices went up again. You're taking our money just like they are."

"My prices are based on the market," I told him. "People get what they pay for, based upon what I have to pay. Besides, if you think gas is expensive, you should try coffee."

It looked like John was about to say something, but he never did. A van pulled into the parking lot but stopped short of the gas island. Four men, dressed as the rock band KISS for Halloween, staggered out the side door, falling out of the van and over each other. They unzipped themselves and started urinating in the parking lot. I went outside, turned on the water hose, and shouted, "Hey, KISS!"

They turned my way just as I shot the water at them. They laughed and ran back to the van for ammunition. The first egg hit John Carpenter square in the head as he was coming outside. An onslaught of eggs followed as Sarah and Jean started laughing hysterically, sprinting across the street to the library parking lot. John ran behind the store. I locked myself inside the box. It wasn't long before the windows were covered in slimy eggs. I couldn't believe it.

"What a day," I said, shaking my head. It was so ridiculous I had to laugh.

The tire iron smashed the window. The Demon, as he was called, stuck his tongue out and reached for the cigarettes, but I grabbed his arm tightly and held him down against the wall. The others kept throwing eggs, though they couldn't hit me.

"Cool costume," I said, still holding his arm.

"Thanks," the Demon said. "I worked hard to—" An egg pegged him in the back of the head and the slime exploded. He got so angry when I started laughing it just made me laugh even harder. They kept throwing eggs as he was shouting, "You guys, quit it! Will you fucking quit it? He's got my fucking arm! Guys, he's got my fucking arm! You're only hitting me! I can't even reach the fucking cigarettes!"

"You're not stealing my cigarettes," I told him. They must have had a thousand eggs, and he had to be covered in hundreds of them. I was wondering if they would ever stop when I heard and felt a tremendous boom. It didn't sound like a gunshot, but I let go of his arm and ducked. He ran like hell. Peering through the window, I looked across the street and saw Sarah and Jean sitting on the steps of the library. I was about to go outside when I heard another boom. KISS dropped their eggs, ran to get in the van, and drove away as fast it would take them. Sarah and Jean started heading back.

I slumped down inside the box and stared at the mess around me. "What a fucking day."

An egg flew through the window, hitting the door on the other side. Staying down, I unlocked the latch and ran for the water hose. When I turned around, Kalin hit me with an egg square in my chest. Shooting the hose at her, but purposely missing, I chased her around the parking lot. She threw a handful of eggs at me, most of which fell to the ground. Tim and John came around from the back of the building.

"Get her!" Tim called.

"Well, this is one hell of a Halloween," Jean said.

"I know, right?" Sarah added.

"All right, that's enough," John said. "It's only funny until somebody gets hurt."

"Yeah," Tim said, picking up an egg. "Then it's really funny!"

I dodged it.

"That was *lame*, Tim," I said, shaking my head. "*Where did that explosion come from?*"

Tim showed me what was left of a two-liter bottle of soda. He had made bottle-bombs from some of the stuff inside the store and had gone out back to set them off in hopes of clearing the crowd. I didn't want to know how he made them.

"So," John said. "You had four jerks dressed up as The Beatles, fucking pissing in the parking lot, and chucking eggs all over the goddamned place. They even smashed your window. Do you still think Sunwoods is worth it?"

Sarah and Jean both looked at each other and said, "The Beatles?"

"This used to be a decent place to live," John snapped.

"It still is," Jean told him. She was sweeping up the shells that Sarah had hosed into a pile. "It's just different. We have to—"

"My wife teaches at Poquanicut Elementary School," John interrupted. "The other day she brought home essays the kids had written about what they want to be when they grow up. Forget cops and astronauts. Those kids want to be blackjack dealers!"

"So?" Sarah said. I noticed Kalin was reading their lips.

"So, they're taking everything we worked for!"

"*The Poquanicut tribe didn't even have clean water when I was a kid,*" I told him. "*You can't tell me they don't deserve everything they have now.*"

Things change, Kalin signed as I translated. *Even land and sea must change as the crow flies.*

"They took my car and my house!" John screamed.

No one forced you to sign over your car or your house, Kalin signed. *You obviously have a gambling problem. And you're an alcoholic who thinks the world owes him a favor.*

"What!" he snapped. Kalin was about to answer, but he grabbed her hands. "Speak, you dumb bitch!"

I punched him in the back of his neck as hard as I could, just like my father had done to Guy ten years ago. He, too, fell to the ground. He, too, did not move again. Kalin was so furious her hands flew like lightning as she cursed that man to the depths of Dante's *Inferno*.

"Holy shit!" Sarah said as Kalin went inside the store.

"Get him out of my sight," I told them.

"You don't need to be fluent in sign language to understand just how pissed she is," Jean said. She grabbed John's legs. "Oh, my god! This fucker's heavy!"

"Tim, give them a hand."

"What the hell are we supposed to do with him? Roger, you fucking knocked him out!"

"Just get him out of here," I told him. "I don't care what it takes. Get his keys. Take his car. Sarah and Jean can follow and bring you back."

"You want us to kidnap him?"

"It's not kidnapping if we take him home," Sarah said.

"Yeah, right," Jean agreed. "Don't fuck with a small town."

I went in the back to check on Kalin. She was sitting at the desk. *Is he gone?*

And never coming back, I told her. When she reached for me, I held her in my arms as she cried. Part of me wanted to tell her that I was sorry for what had happened, but that, I knew, would only make things worse. The past takes a different shape in the future, and any apology I might have offered would hardly resolve the abuse she had endured growing up. She needed me—not my advice.

After several minutes, Kalin leaned back. *I love you.*

I know, I told her. *I love you too.*

Are you hungry? she asked. I nodded. *I thought so. You woke up late and didn't eat before you left home. I brought you dinner.*

When she lifted the lid off the Crock-Pot, I could smell the meatballs.

A few weeks later, Junior went on vacation, so I split the days with Tim. It was exhausting having to wear my hearing aids for twelve hours straight, but I kept my patience with the customers when they lost their patience with me.

A woman with short, bleached-blond hair on the fritz came by one afternoon with a couple of kids. I couldn't place it, but there was something familiar about her oldest boy, who ran right to the candy. The woman set the baby by the register and started searching through her purse. She wiped the baby's nose and tossed the tissue onto the counter. I threw it away and sanitized my hands.

"Do you take food stamps?" the woman asked. She looked up from her purse and saw me. "Oh! It's you!"

"Do we know each other?"

"You went to Brockton High School, didn't you? Class of 1988, right?"

"And you are?"

"Missy Reynolds, class of 1985," she said. An atomic bomb exploded in my chest. "I believe you know, or knew, my ex-husband."

"Your husband?"

"Does the name James Robert Croft ring any bells?" she asked. "He's the fucking deadbeat who disappeared off the face of the Earth because he couldn't man up enough to raise his own son. That fucking asshole walked out on us and left me with exactly jack shit! Son of a bitch owes me eight years of child support! He's got to be working under the table somewhere. And I know you were his best friend back in high school so if you know where he is—"

"We don't take food stamps," I finally told her. I took a deep breath, trying to calm down, even as I realized the boy was the spitting image of Jim. A chill went down my spine.

"That's it, isn't it?" Melissa said. The baby started crying. I felt a sudden sense of relief as I saw Tim's car pulling into the lot. "You know where he is, but you won't tell me. And now you're giving me a hard time because I'm on food stamps? You don't give a fuck about anybody!"

"We're not a grocery store," I said. "That's pretty much why we can't accept food stamps. Also, I…I got to say, I'd really appreciate it if you could calm down."

She threw a box of candy onto the floor. "Fuck you!"

"And now you need to leave."

Picking up the baby, she released a slew of profanity as she snatched the boy's hand and dragged him out the door. They marched past Tim, who stopped and turned as he saw the boy. From the gas island, Dom looked at me. I shook my head, warning him not to provoke her any further.

"Roger, did you see that?" Tim said, coming inside. "I could swear that kid looks just like James."

I lit a cigarette. My hands were shaking.

"That's his son," I said, sitting down. "He married Melissa Reynolds after they found out that she was pregnant. That's why he dropped out of high school. It's also why, one of the reasons why, he killed himself."

"Are you serious?" he said. I nodded. "Well, I don't get it. Why the hell would he—"

"Because she made him that fucking miserable," I said. "She even threatened to keep his name off the birth certificate so he'd never see his own kid."

"Jesus. Are you okay?"

I shrugged. "Now you know why I never want talk about it."

The cigarette had given me a buzz. I was just starting to calm down when Missy came back and kicked the door so hard the glass shattered, like a spider web. Her face was red with a maddening rage as she started screaming and flipping me off. I picked up the telephone and made it look like I was dialing, mouthing words as she watched me. A second later, she ran like hell and her car roared out of the lot.

I hung up the phone and sat back down. As the horror began to sink in, I realized now, without a doubt, that James had told me the truth about his marriage. Melissa had just answered all my questions with a vengeance. That woman literally spent five minutes inside the store and…she really had made his life a living hell.

"What was that all about?" Dom asked, standing at the threshold.

"Nothing," Tim said. "It's not important."

"I got her license plate for the police," Dom said to me. "You did call them, didn't you?"

"Hell no, I didn't call them," I said. "I just made it look like I was calling them so she would leave. If I call them, that means I have to deal with her again. And I don't ever want to see that woman again. Ever. I'm too old for that shit."

"Why don't you go home, Boss?" Tim suggested.

"I can board that door up until you get it fixed," Dom said.

"Yeah, we got this," Tim said. "Go home and see your wife. Take it easy. Maybe get some rest. It's been a long week for the both of us."

I had just noticed that he'd got blue highlights. "Nice hair."

"You're not my type," Tim said. "You're straight."

I chuckled.

"I'll see you tomorrow," I said as I left. The tension and stress from my encounter with Melissa started to fade the moment I took out my hearing aids in the car. My deafness was soothing and peaceful—not chaotic and raging like the hearing world. The farther away I got from the station, and the closer I got to home, the more the madness dissipated. I didn't have to hold on to it. I didn't have to let her drag me down. I didn't have to allow her to destroy me like she had destroyed Jim. I knew better now. People who cannot master their emotions are always enslaved by their feelings. Having them doesn't mean you have to act on them. Like wearing my hearing aids or taking them out, I could choose between sound and fury or silence and serenity.

When I got to the condo, Kalin had just finished pouring the soda. *What's this?* I asked.

Tim called, she signed. *He said you had a bad day so I thought we could have root beer floats for dinner.*

Thank you so much.

You're cooking when Junior gets back from vacation, she signed playfully.

After today, I'll make you breakfast in bed! I told her, sitting down. *Tim used the TTY?*

You're silly, she signed, smiling. *Even a hearing person can learn. You know that.*

I laughed so hard I spit up my root beer. After five years together, we sure had our share of jokes.

But that was the thing about Kalin. She knew when I needed to laugh and when I wanted to be left alone. And I knew she'd hold me to breakfast in bed. She was my best friend, my partner, and my companion. She made everything better, including me. And it was never anything she did directly or deliberately. It was just who she was.

My true north.

That's what made her my wife.

CHAPTER TWENTY-SIX

MAY THE FOURTH

IN THE SPRING OF 1997, I closed the station. Things usually slowed down at about two o'clock on third shift. After taking down the outside displays, I brought in the cases of motor oil and bottles of windshield fluid. I shut off the outside lights and finished cleaning up. Tim had already done the cooler and stocked the groceries last night. A gambler stopped by, but I told him the station was closed. "You can try Bryant Mobil in Brockton. Fifteen miles north on 12. They're open twenty-four hours."

"You got a sign right here that says you're open twenty-four hours," he said through the glass. Reaching over, I clicked off the neon sign. "You're really closed? Forever?"

"Try Bryant Mobil."

"I've been driving all night," he said, rubbing his eyes. "Is it Saturday or Sunday?"

"The fourth," I told him. "Sunday."

Walking away, he shook his head and muttered something that I couldn't hear. Now that the station was officially closed, I took out my hearing aids and double-checked that I had locked the door. The silence was such a relief, like taking off a tight pair of shoes after running a marathon.

At sunrise, when I had everything squared away, I stepped outside and lit a cigarette. The morning dew sparkled on the sunbeams falling through the forest to the grass. I had transformed the surrounding land, which had been full of fallen leaves and brush, into a lawn, but it wasn't as smooth as the yard Dad had made for the house all those years ago. Looking up, I saw the neon green sign for EVANS FOOD & FUEL. I knew Dad wouldn't approve of what I was doing, but I figured I deserved a day.

An old truck drove by the station. Memory told me that its engine was growling, and the exhaust roaring, but I could only hear a dull hum. Kalin, who had taken me to work last night before she'd gone to Hartford, was supposed to pick me up at seven, which meant she'd be here any moment, since it was almost six-thirty. Taking a deep breath, I could smell the crisp spring air while I waited. Tossing my cigarette into the ash can, I was about to unlock the door just as Kalin's car pulled into the lot. I sat in the back because Shae, who was pregnant, was with her.

We are meeting Gregg at the casino, Kalin told me. After pulling out of the lot, she quickly glanced in the rearview mirror, meeting my eyes. *Breakfast.*

I'm starving, I told her.

You really did it? Kalin asked when we got to the casino.

I nodded. *Did you catch a late show?*

Yeah, Kalin signed. *We all went to Shae's house afterwards.*

You closed the station just to see a couple of movies? Shae asked as we were walking. The lights of the slot machines were blaring.

It's the twentieth anniversary of Star Wars, *but I never saw all three movies.*

You never saw the Star Wars *trilogy? Really?*

Look at him! Kalin signed. *He is grinning like a little kid!*

I feel like a little kid! I would usually go to the movies with Kalin in Hartford so we could see a captioned showing. Every couple of months, though, I'd catch a film with Tim and Junior. Getting away from the station had enabled us to remain good friends, and it had also helped me keep my sanity. When we found out that the *Star Wars* trilogy was being rereleased, Junior mentioned that he wanted to take Rochelle and the kids, Tim wanted to go with Alejandro, and Isabel had plans to take her daughter. Business was going well, and since everybody wanted to see it, I decided to take them. Closing the station for the day made things easier because nobody would be left out.

I wish I could have gone with you last night, I told Kalin. *I really do, but I promised everybody I would take them.*

It's okay, Kalin signed. *You're making it up to me in Maine next week, remember? Besides, we got to see it first. You won't believe what happens when—*

Looking away, I waved my hands, warning her not to tell me. Of course, I knew she was only teasing when she tapped my shoulder. Shae pointed out a restaurant. *This is the place.*

How is everybody in Hartford? I asked.

Doing good, Kalin signed. *We went to the club after* Return of the Jedi. *We were the last ones to leave.*

That's why I needed a nap, Shae told me. *I'm due in two weeks, and I can't wait to get this baby out of me!*

We are always the last ones to leave, I signed. *We have to catch up on news, families, friends, work…everything. How is Gregg?*

His firm still works with CAD on compliance and enforcement, Shae told me as we sat down. CAD was the Connecticut Association of the Deaf; as a lawyer, Gregg was crucial to our legal efforts and legislative involvement. *He should be here any minute.*

She smiled and stood when Gregg approached our table. He was built like a linebacker, but his smile had always made me feel like I was in good company—which, of course, I was. Shae and Gregg gave each other a hug and kiss, which lasted longer than I had expected.

Like I told you, Kalin signed, rolling her eyes.

You're just as bad with him, Shae told her, meaning me. *Just as bad.*

Worse, Kalin signed. *So much worse it's wonderful!*

Twice a year, Kalin and I would reserve the same suite for a weekend getaway at Oceanside. We were trying to get pregnant—and had made a pretty good effort again just yesterday—but, so far, we weren't having much luck.

This time, we decided to take a whole week.

"I still can't believe you did this for everybody, Boss," Alejandro said. He didn't work for me, but Tim had somehow got him into the habit of calling me "Boss" like everybody else. Rochelle, Junior, and Isabel had taken the kids to get snacks with Sarah and Jean. The rest of the crew was waiting in the lobby while the three of us got the tickets.

"I am so fucking psyched to see these movies!" Alejandro said. "I wish Kalin could be here, though."

"She caught the captioned version in Hartford last night," I said. "I promised to make it up to her next week."

"What do you have planned?" Tim asked. "Something special?"

"That's none of your business," I told him, smiling. When I got our tickets, I asked the clerk for an assistive listening device. She had to search through all the cabinets before she finally found a headset. "You don't have a neck loop for my telecoil?"

"A what?"

"Never mind," I told her. I checked to make sure it had batteries and turned it on so I knew it would work.

"They're programmed," the clerk said. She was a young girl, probably still in high school, who had a crooked name tag. "You'll have to get a separate one for each movie. You can't use the same one in a different theater."

"Thanks," I said. "This is my first time at the movies."

We went to meet the rest of the crew.

"Is it always so much fun?" Tim asked, facing me.

"Not always," I told him. "But often."

"I have a question," Alejandro said. "What is a telecoil?"

"The telecoil is a feature in my hearing aids designed to pick up electromagnetic energy, which is how hearing-aid compatible telephones transmit sound. It's beneficial because it isolates the background noise on the rare occasion that I actually use the phone. It also prevents my hearing aids from buzzing when I use the telephone, most of the time."

"So how does that work with a neck loop?" Tim asked.

"The neck loop is a cable that puts out electromagnetic energy," I said. "In a setting like this, a large movie theater, I can just turn on the t-switch to activate the telecoil, so I get a direct transmission of the dialogue and sound from neck loop. It also isolates the acoustics. Movie theaters never have neck loops, but it doesn't hurt to ask."

"That sucks," Tim said. "I thought they were required to be compliant with the Americans with Disabilities Act. Why don't they have captions?"

"Compliance is very different than access," I told him. "Besides, hearing people bitch about captions. Movie studios would rather lose millions in ticket sales than provide an accessible screening."

Junior was handing out popcorn tubs and soft drinks to the crew. When I asked if we were almost done, he said that we were last ones who needed to order. Somebody in a Darth Vader costume bumped into Tim as we were getting in line for snacks. "Watch it, Dad Vader!"

"Did you just say 'Dad Vader?'" I asked. He said he had. "I thought it was Darth Vader."

"Vader is Luke's father," Alejandro said. "You didn't know that?"

"For the last time, guys, I only saw the first film," I said. "But I remember Ben Kenobi telling Luke that Vader was the one who killed his father. How could he be his father if his dad is dead? He's not his father."

They looked at me funny.

"What planet are you from?" Junior said. He handed the last tubs of popcorn to Sarah and Jean.

"All right," Tim said. "When was the first appearance of Boba Fett?"

"*The Empire Strikes Back*," Alejandro answered.

"Not anymore," Tim told us. "Now, it's the first film."

"You're both wrong," I said. "The first appearance of Boba Fett was in a cartoon broadcast during *The Star Wars Holiday Special* in 1978. Han had to get Chewie home in time for Life Day."

"How in the world did you remember that?" Junior asked.

"I'll never forget that Christmas," I said. It was the first year I'd had to divide the holidays between my parents. I could still see my father, a giant to the child I was, screaming at me for opening my Christmas presents early. Shaking my head, I pushed away the memory as I realized that he had stopped drinking shortly after that. Dad had made his share of mistakes, but he did his best to beat his demons. A little forgiveness, I'd learned, goes a long way. "Anyway, Vader tried to kill Luke. He even blew R2-D2 to smithereens. Dads don't do that."

"Do you want to bet?" Tim asked. I paid for the snacks.

"As a matter of fact, I do. I'll bet you a hundred dollars that Darth Vader is not Luke Skywalker's father."

"You're on!"

"Oh, my word," Junior said. "You're gonna lose, Boss."

"If Darth Vader knew that Ben was on the Death Star, he certainly would have known if his son was flying in that ship."

"I never thought of that before," Alejandro said. "That is a major plot hole."

"We should take our seats," Junior said. "Got enough damned popcorn here to fill a Star Destroyer."

We got settled in the middle of the theater, letting the parents decide where they wanted the kids. I ended up sitting toward the back, with Sarah on one side and Tim on the other. When the opening theme started, the whole theater cheered as we all began our magical escape to that galaxy far, far away. After the first film, which was now called *A New Hope*, I exchanged my headset and demanded Tim pay me.

"It's not over yet," he said, lighting a cigarette. We had about a half an hour between films for bathroom and cigarette breaks. Junior, Rochelle, and the rest of the parents had their hands full with all the kids. I kept wondering what it would be like to be a father, hoping Kalin and I would have our chance soon. I also thought of my own fathers, wondering how William felt when Ma told him the news. Was he scared? Hopeful? Did Jake have his own hopes and dreams for me, even after losing William?

Until tonight, the only time I had seen *Star Wars* was at the drive-in theater with Mom and Dad. I still remembered sitting in the Fairlane, waiting in line, when some crazy old man started a sword fight with the staff, who ended up carrying him away. A lightsaber fight, I guess. I could still see that hippie sitting on top of that yellow Volkswagen bus, yelling, "Hey, man! Down with that Vader dude, man!" It made me smile now; not all childhood memories are bad ones. I just wished Jim had lived long enough to learn that.

"Hey, Roger," Tim called. I walked over to where he was sitting with Alejandro. "There is something I don't understand."

"What's that?" I asked.

"Ronald McDonald is a clown, right?"

"Yeah," Alejandro said. "And Birdie is the early bird. Hamburglar is a thief—"

"Mayor McCheese governs McDonaldland," I said. "What's your point, Tim?"

"Well, what's Grimace?"

We burst out laughing.

"He's always coming up with stuff like that," Alejandro said. "Guy could talk the devil out of his pitchfork."

"It's time, guys," Junior called, waving us over. "We need to get in line."

"Man," I said, going inside. "What the hell is Grimace anyway…?"

When my headset didn't work during the previews for *The Empire Strikes Back*, I went back to the ticket booth to get another one. The clerk told me to wait while she was taking care of the line.

"The previews are starting," I told her. "This doesn't work. I need another one."

"It sometimes doesn't work during the previews," she said, still handing out tickets.

"It did for the first film."

"Just wait for the movie to start," she said. "It should be fine."

I had learned a long time ago that "should" almost always meant "no." But, since she was still selling tickets, I went back inside the theater, waiting by the door with my headset on. When the opening sequence started, the signal was still dead. I went back to the ticket booth.

"The movie started, and it still doesn't work," I said. "I'm missing the movie. I really need one that works!"

Taking the headset, she started searching through the cabinets again. I watched her check two of them before she finally handed me another one.

"Try this one," she said. Again, I went back to the theater. Again, the fucking headset didn't work. And again, I was back at the ticket booth. "I think that was the last one we have."

"Well, why don't they work?" I asked. "Do they just need new batteries or what?"

"The batteries are rechargeable," the clerk said. "I think we wore them out."

"You wore them out? You?"

"We used to put them on and listen to the films while we were selling tickets."

"Let me get this straight," I said. "I waited twenty years to see this movie. Now, you're telling me that I can't because you thought it would be fun to play with the one fucking thing I need to watch the movie?"

"Um, I can offer you a refund. If you want."

"Yeah, you're damn right you can give me a refund," I told her, slapping my receipt on the counter. By that point, the other customers were staring.

"Who bought all these tickets?" she asked.

"I did."

"You bought all these tickets?"

"I just told you that."

"Well, what I mean is, is how did you buy so many?"

"I walked through the door, came to the counter, and I said, 'Hello. I would like to buy some tickets.' What the hell do you think I did?"

"Why so many?"

"Jesus, because we all wanted to see the rerelease *Star Wars*! Everybody else is watching the fucking movie! You want me to drag them all out of the theater and bring them up here so that every single one of them can explain to you what I have been telling you for the past ten fucking minutes?"

"Sir, you need to calm down. All right?"

"How many times do I have to explain the same thing?"

"We're just trying to figure this out."

"What the hell is there to figure out? You're the ones who drained the batteries on all the assistive listening devices that I need! I just want a fucking refund!"

"All I can do is give you a refund," she said. "Just you."

"And you figured this out all by yourself?" I said, rubbing my forehead. She started punching numbers on the register. "Do you realize what you've done? I mean, are you even remotely aware—"

"Hey, channel five," someone called. I turned and saw a middle-aged man holding his hands to his ears, his index fingers pointing up as he rotated, mimicking a radio antenna. "Channel five…channel five…come in, channel five!"

The woman beside him burst out laughing. He put his hands down and told me to step aside so that everybody else could get their tickets.

"If they did their job—"

"Take your pity party someplace else," the man said. "You don't do that on my time."

"Your time?"

"Yeah, my time," he said, stepping up to the counter. The clerk still hadn't given me a refund, but instead took his money. "I'm a paying customer. Didn't your father ever teach you any manners?"

"My father is dead," I said. "You want to meet him?"

The woman gasped in shock, but the man, who was standing right beside me, wasn't listening—though it was obvious that he could, in fact, hear me.

"You want to make it in this world, you got to work hard," the man said.

"Hey, Skippy, who the fuck are you to lecture me?"

"You're a goddamned fool for crying disability! Now, why don't you get the hell out of here and let the rest of us enjoy the show."

When he tried to leave, I stepped in front of him. My heart could have consumed the fires of hell. "I got a better idea."

"What?"

I cracked my neck. "Dare me, motherfucker!"

Reaching behind him, the man took his wife's hand—it was then I noticed their rings—and said, "Just let us go and watch our movie."

"And what makes you think you have the right?"

"You think I'm afraid of you?"

"Do you think I'm not afraid of you?"

"You're both holding up the line," the clerk said. "Please move along, please?"

"You know, you people always make the mistake," I said as Sarah came out of the movie theater. "You look at me, and you see just one person, one patron. One man. But you're forgetting about the thirty million *deaf* and *hard-of-hearing people standing beside me.*"

“I’ll gladly give you a refund,” she said, finally counting it out. “Please just go, please?”

“We’re done here,” I said, “but you’re finished.”

As I was walking away, Sarah caught me. “What’s going on?”

“I can’t watch the movie,” I said.

“What? Why not?”

“Because they thought it would be fun to use the fucking headsets while they were selling tickets. All the batteries are dead.”

“Are you fucking shitting me?”

“Enjoy the show,” I told her. “I’m going home.”

I heard her call my name as I flung open the door and left. The late-afternoon sun lingered beyond the dark-gray clouds. Heading west, I put on my aviator sunglasses. Driving through town, I stopped at a convenience store to get a pack of cigarettes and a Coke. While waiting in line, I saw a headline in the newspaper rack about Mary Kay Letourneau, the elementary school teacher who had raped one of her sixth-grade students. The story had been in the papers and tabloids for months, sensationalized for sales, with no consideration given to any of the underage male victims of sexual assault.

It had been nine years since Jim killed himself—and the world still didn’t give a shit.

When I got outside, it was sprinkling. By the time I got on the interstate, the pounding rain was falling like bullets. Turning on my hazard lights, I slowed to forty-five and took a deep breath to calm down as the tsunami of my grief swelled.

“Don’t,” I said out loud, wiping my eyes, trying to push the waves back down. Traffic was stopped in front of me. I pumped the brake gently to avoid hydroplaning. The downpour let up shortly after I had stopped. I lit a cigarette and rolled down my window.

The last thing I saw, in my side mirror, was a tractor trailer flying up behind me, jack-knifing as it sped into a skid.

CHAPTER TWENTY-SEVEN

THE REPENTANCE OF JUDAS

I WOKE UP IN the middle of a fire burning off my clothes, watching helplessly as the flames seared away the flesh on my hands. The charred bones of my fingers grew, spreading out until my arms became wings. Trapped in the wreckage, I screamed as the sheer agony consumed me in a demonic possession of pain.

Suddenly, I rose from the fire with a piercing screech, like I had finally scratched a lifelong itch. I was a phoenix reborn through a baptism of fire. My majestic wings flapped in the wind as the flames dissolved, the smoke drifting away behind me. Gliding beneath the great wide open, that heavenly blue sky, I felt as free as I'd ever been in my life. At last, I could see clearly.

My dream faded as the white pillars slowly came into focus. After a moment, I realized that they weren't pillars at all, but casts wrapped around my arms, tied to a frame above my bed. Both of my arms were broken, along with my left leg. I could see a bunch of tubes on my left, but I couldn't turn my head. Ma was reading a book at my bedside. She closed it when I called, "Ma?"

She laughed and cried, signing, *Good morning!*

"Kalin?"

Kalin was here this morning. She will be back this evening.

"The station?"

It's fine, Ma told me. *Don't worry about that now.*

"What...what happened?" I could feel my voice more than I could hear it, but speaking was a struggle through the pain and whatever drugs they had put in my system. I dozed off while Ma was digging through her purse. A few minutes later, or maybe it was hours, she showed me what she had written, explaining that I'd been in a serious accident. The words blurred; I could barely keep my eyes open, and it took every ounce of willpower just to keep reading.

My car had been hit at an angle, rolling over several times down the steep bank along the interstate, until finally landing deep in the woods. Mom was on duty when the ambulance brought me in; she immediately got in touch with Kalin and raised holy hell with the hospital about providing an interpreter. Along with my arms and leg, I had a broken neck and five broken ribs and a collapsed lung and one hundred and sixty-seven stitches.

I'd been out for five days.

A moment later, the world disappeared.

I woke up again, briefly, when the nurses moved me to a different room. The morning sun was rising through the window. Its warm, soothing light covered me like a blanket. It was the first true, good thing I had felt in a long, long time.

I saw Mom. She was crying.

That evening, or the next morning, I found my mothers sitting with Kalin, who was watching the interpreter while the nurse spoke. There were flowers by the window. When Ma pointed, Kalin turned and saw that I was awake. She came to my bedside, wiping the corner of her eye. She looked exhausted, but she was still so beautiful, like a priceless diamond on a ring of gold. All I wanted was to be as close to her as I possibly could. It hurt to smile, but I managed. "Hi."

Now that you're awake, I need to check something, the nurse said as the interpreter translated. I felt her touch my big toe on my right leg. *Can you feel that?*

"Yeah," I said. One by one, she wiggled my toes. "All good."

She made a note on her clipboard and left.

Hi, Kalin signed. She smiled. *How are you feeling?*

"Sorry we…missed…Maine," I said. It took a moment for me to remember that my arms were in casts. I'd speak while the interpreter translated for Kalin, who would then sign to me. My mothers, who were not yet fluent, would speak and the interpreter would translate them for me.

We'll have another chance, Kalin told me. *The doctor says that you're stable now.*

"I should have…gone with you…and Shae."

She shook her head. *I knew who you were, and who you could be, the moment we met. I fell in love with that man, the man who loves me for who I am because he has the courage to be who he is. Remember? We're just two people who never belonged anywhere, except with each other. Together.*

I smiled. "I love…you…so much."

I love you, Kalin signed as her eyes filled with tears. Slowly, she leaned down and kissed my cheek. *We know you're going to be okay now. You will. I love you. We'll go to Maine soon.*

But I could see that she was scared, and I knew that her mask of confidence was as much for her benefit as it was for mine.

That, I knew.

Over the next few days, Ma and Kalin would take turns feeding me the slop they served at the hospital while Mom would stop in throughout the day. Kalin told me that Gregg had investigated my accident. He discovered that the truck driver had violated hours-of-service regulations, falsifying his logbook to make it look like he had a co-driver when he was really driving over eighteen hours a day by himself. Federal law mandated that truckers could only drive for eleven hours before they were legally required to take a ten-hour break to rest. According to Gregg, it was likely that the company would settle out of court to avoid a protracted lawsuit; their insurance company was covering my medical bills.

"Well," I said, "at least that's one thing we don't have to worry about."

Do you want Gregg to represent you?

"Of course," I said. "I'd rather have him anyway. I don't want somebody who…I don't want a hearing person to represent me. I'm sick of explaining everything all the time."

I know. I'll let him know.

"How are you doing, Kalin?" I asked. She looked tired, yet glanced at Ma, who was getting ready to feed me another mystery sandwich; I could never tell if it was tuna fish or chicken salad or some fucking turkey-Spam surprise shit. "You okay?"

I'm fine, Kalin told me. It was then I knew that there was something she wasn't telling me, but I knew her well enough to know that, whatever it was, she had her reasons. *You need to eat, get your strength back.*

"The food is terrible in this place."

Why didn't you tell us? Kalin asked.

We would have brought you something from home, Ma said. She got a pad and pen from her purse. *What do you want? We'll bring anything you want.*

"Meatloaf," I said as she started writing, "with a baked potato and green beans. And pot roast. Pot roast with mashed potatoes and gravy and grilled vegetables—grilled to a char, like Grandpa used to do with his cast iron. And chicken with rice and asparagus and a meatball grinder. Or two. Make it three. I could eat three right now."

Ma gave me that look. I had definitely earned it.

Let's start with meatloaf, Ma said. *We can do the rest later.*

"Don't worry. I'll be here."

After she finished feeding me my dinner, Ma set the tray aside.

Get some rest, she told me. She kissed my cheek. *We'll be back tonight—with food.*

When she left, I tried not to think about how hard it was for her to see me like this. After everything she had been through, perhaps her only solace was that I'd simply been in the wrong place at the wrong time. That's what I kept telling myself, anyway.

What? Kalin asked.

"Who brought the flowers?"

Those are from the crew, she told me. *Rochelle picked them up. The bouquet is from Shae and Gregg. Your mothers brought the fern.*

"And the roses?"

Me.

I smiled. "Thank you. Nice to have some color."

Is there anything you want me to bring tomorrow?

"I'd ask for a book if I could hold it," I said. She asked about the television. "It's too old. Doesn't have captioning."

I'll see what I can do, Kalin told me. She gave me a kiss. *I love you.*

"Love you too," I said. I always closed my eyes when the interpreter and Kalin left because I couldn't bear to watch her leave. The hardest part about my recovery was the time between the end of visiting hours and when I'd finally fall asleep. The dead clock on the wall, forever stuck at six-twenty, gave me an eternal sense of tormenting time. At night, minutes felt like days. Hours, weeks. I would sleep as much as I could, trying to breathe through the pain in my broken ribs, but it wasn't long before I couldn't tell the difference between dusk and dawn. My mind became a candle, leading me down into the deepest, darkest caverns of my heart.

There really isn't much to do when you have to spend all day, every day, stuck in a hospital bed, waiting for your body to heal and wondering just how well it was going to heal. When the body endures a trauma so severe as to alter its own capacities, the mind must also adapt or the soul stays trapped in a purgatory of expectation, of who you were and what once you could do. And yet, like that asshole at the movie theater, the world is filled with fools whose expectations remain rooted in their own obscene assumptions. To those so far removed from the realities of deafness and disability, majority rules are the only rules, simply because such people are incapable of learning, of seeing the world beyond their own small point of view. I grew up thinking Grandpa was the rule, that people could embrace their greatest gift throughout their lives, the gift of learning, but the older I got, the more I realized that Grandpa was the exception.

Grandpa had taught me that the hearing world would always be ignorant of the deaf. In my experience, most hearing people never tried to understand. And yet, how could they? I had spent seventeen years getting a mainstream education, but not once had I read a deaf novelist, nor had I studied Deaf history or culture in school. Instead, I'd had to educate myself on how to be hard-of-hearing in a hearing world. Now, I was a late-deafened adult.

Having been a hearing person, I knew just how much they made the connection between speech and language, even intellect. That myth was so ingrained in them that they never gave it a second thought—and that, I'd learned, was what made my life so difficult. It wasn't my deafness, nor would it be my disability, but it was their ignorance about deafness and disability; in that way, my life was only hard because the majority constantly and deliberately chose to make it so difficult. Arrogance breeds ignorance.

Accepting a disability is the first step in learning to live with it. As I considered just how much my body had changed over the years, that soon became pretty easy to do. At birth, I'd been completely dependent upon my mothers and my father. Soon, I'd learned to sit up and to crawl, to stand, and to walk. As a teenager, my body had continued to develop as well. From growing up to growing old, our bodies are always changing, yet too often we avoid the truth of our own existence, as if our own ignorance alone can make us immortal. Now, my body had to heal—though how much I would recover remained to be seen.

There was still so much I wanted to do, and so much of it I could have done if I hadn't spent all that time working at the station. I had taken an average of six days off every year, escaping to Maine with Kalin twice a year—just six fucking days—and my devotion to work had only grown after Dad died. It was easier to bury myself in a job than it was to face my pain, though I'd had my moments when the tsunami hit. Still, I'd wanted to honor my father's memory, to live up to his expectations, and to make him proud by ensuring that the business he had built would survive, endure, and thrive.

Dad had put his life into that station, a life that had ended far, far too soon—so soon that I felt robbed. He had worked so hard for so long, often sleeping just a few hours each night. It was only now that I was beginning to understand the greatest lesson my father never taught me, a lesson I'd finally learned once my body had been broken to pieces: that a life built on absolutely nothing more than work was as far from living as a man could get. Now, as the nights creeped by so slowly, I wanted to remember the joy I'd once known.

Lifetimes ago, James and I had played "snowball" in the backyard and went on to win the town championship. I could still see Craig spinning him around after the game. It was the only time I had ever seen him so happy, laughing like he didn't have a care in the world. Craig had taught James to hit, and he had more home runs than anybody that year. They had stared at the stars together, dreaming the dreams of childhood, the endless possibilities of innocence and imagination, plotting a path through their own constellations with confidence.

There was even a time James and I had such dreams ourselves, of finishing the lives our parents had started, but the abuse he endured had become too much to bear. As I began to piece the warning signs together, I realized that James had started drinking after Craig died, probably because he could relate to his brother that way. Or maybe it was because James had just wanted to drown the pain. Maybe it was both. With Craig gone, there was nobody left to protect him from his mother, who had beaten, molested, and raped him from such a young age. An ice-cold chill went down my spine just thinking about it.

My life now was decades removed from Craig chasing me the day of the championship game: "If you're Jimmy's friend, that makes you family!" he'd said. He was right, of course—James was the closest I ever came to having a brother. If their mother had assaulted James, had she done the same to Craig? Was that why Craig had drank so much himself? My guilt and grief over James had haunted me for years, but I'd kept it hidden, never taking the time to sort it out. Now, all I had was time.

James had been so determined to build his own life that his desperation had left him vulnerable. He escaped an abusive family only to end up with an abusive wife, recreating the emotions and environment so familiar to him. In the five minutes I'd known Melissa, she had made my life a living hell. Even her imagination ran wild, fantasizing about child support a dead man couldn't possibly pay, as if the world owed her a favor. And there was nothing I could do for Jim's son—the last testament to his existence.

Worst of all, Melissa had used their child against him, threatening James by telling him that he would never see his son, that she would make certain of it by never putting his name on the birth certificate. Not only had I seen the boy's resemblance to James, but Melissa herself had said that he was the father. It was beyond my comprehension how a woman could be so cruel. No wonder Jim had shared the Riddle of the Three Men. No wonder he killed himself.

I'd seen my share of horror stories from men over the years, both down at the Boat and the station. Like Jim, we never discuss our daily tortures. At least not publicly. Instead, we hide. We suffer in silence, burying our pain until we learn to endure the misery, or it just boils over in a rage that will never be understood, only condemned. Because nobody cared enough about Jim to try to understand. Nobody who could actually help him, anyway. Now, I was left to carry the burden myself. Even if Jim had told the truth, who the hell would believe him?

That's when it hit me: if Jim's mother had multiple personalities lurking within her, was it possible that he did as well? And if he did, was it really James who took his life or had it been one of his alternate personalities? It was such a maddening equation that I began to understand why so many people chose religion over reason. Christianity itself had a way of reducing complex anatomies to archaic answers and simplistic clichés, but life—real life, the examined life—was far, far too profound to be so damned shallow.

I wondered if there was an afterlife for people who commit suicide. The most well-known suicide in scripture was Judas, who had betrayed Jesus. He hung himself once he realized that Jesus had been condemned to death. I knew that Jesus had spoken about hell, a spiritual punishment, but he had only a made a physical reference to the fate of his betrayer, saying that it would be better for Judas to be tied to a stone and thrown into the sea.

But the tree Judas had used to hang himself collapsed under his weight. The sea would have killed him quickly. Instead, he fell down the cliff, dying slowly and in agony, with his body as broken and battered as mine was now. It was disturbing to think that Jesus, of all people, thought it would be best for Judas to drown—especially once I remembered that Judas had confronted the religious leaders after his betrayal, confessing his sin and seeking redemption; he had even returned those thirty pieces of silver. He couldn't go to Jesus, who was in prison. That, like so much else, is what the Christians missed.

Christians don't understand their own stories.

Judas repented.

All he had to do was wait a few days until Jesus rose from the grave, reconciling humanity and the divine, just as all Jim had to do was wait a few hours and he would have seen that the Deaf President Now protest had been successful. A moment may be remembered for a lifetime, but a lifetime is always more than a moment. I didn't believe in god—I'd hardly bothered after the Christians tried to kill me—but at least I understood the lesson of the story: if you can hang on for just a little while longer, you will see that there is still hope in the world.

The sun always rises. Wait. Just wait.

Just a little while longer. And the dawn will come.

My eyes burned as tears rolled down my cheeks. I cried for Jim, so innocent and yet gone so soon. I cried for Grandpa, the greatest man I'd ever known. I cried for Dad, who had taught me the truth about forgiveness. I cried for Mom, her broken nose bleeding onto the kitchen floor. And I cried for Ma, who had endured untold horrors, escaping them by hiding—just as she had hidden me; nobody knew or cared that I was Jewish. Most of all, I cried for the father and the family I never knew, the ones I'd lost in the Holocaust.

Exhausted and overwhelmed, I closed my eyes and drifted off to sleep.

The candle kept burning.

The nurse gave me the last spoonful of scrambled eggs and wiped my mouth. After that, she checked my vitals and my breathing again. As the interpreter translated, the nurse said that she would be back to take more stitches out this afternoon. After the nurse took the tray and left, Kalin came into my room carrying a bag and holding two coffee mugs. Setting everything down, she smiled as I asked, "What are you up to?"

We have a surprise for you.

"What is it?" I asked. "And who's 'we'?"

Just wait, Kalin told me. She went to the door and waved for someone to come inside. A moment later, Sarah and Jean brought in a television set and a VCR. They set it down on my dinner tray as a technician began organizing the cords. Reaching into the bag, Kalin showed me that she'd brought VHS tapes of all three *Star Wars* films. *You never got to see the movies, so we brought the movies to you.*

"Really?" I asked. Nodding, Kalin set a straw in one of the mugs.

"You look pretty good for an old man," Jean said as the interpreter translated. She had ten years on me but would often joke about my age because I thought I was older when we'd first met. Jean and Sarah were both still wearing their uniforms. "I'm sorry you didn't get to see it."

"We didn't stay," Sarah said. "None of us did once we realized your device wasn't working. Instead, we all marched back to the box office and demanded refunds."

"You didn't have to do that."

"It was a rerelease anyway," Jean said. "We all saw it before—except you."

"We donated the money to the library," Sarah added. "We thought you'd appreciate that."

"Yeah, that's good."

This was Tim's idea, Kalin told me. *I guess he wanted to settle your bet once and for all.*

"And Kalin told us what size TV to get," Jean said. "Charlie picked it up yesterday. It has built-in captioning."

Once the technician was done setting up the cords, Jean turned on the television and VCR to make sure they were working. She raised her arms in triumph, then Sarah gave her a kiss.

I smiled; it was nice to see love and kindness in the world.

"I finally get to see the *Star Wars* trilogy," I said. "This is so fucking cool!"

"It's the least we could do," Sarah said.

"I wish we could stay and watch them with you, old man, but we have to get some sleep before work tonight."

"Might want to talk to your boss," I said. They laughed so hard their faces turned red. Once they left, I said to Kalin, "Thank you so much."

I have something else for you, Kalin told me. Reaching into the bag, she pulled out a copy of the *Kingdom Come* Limited Edition Book Set signed by Mark Waid and Alex Ross; it was a rare collector's item. I felt like a kid at Christmas. *This is for you.*

"You really went all out."

I know how much you love Superman.

"I just need my arms back so I can read it."

I can hold it, Kalin told me. *Unless you want to watch* Star Wars.

"I've waited over twenty years to see these movies so…*Star Wars*."

She sat down and put her hand on my arm, keeping it there while we were watching the movies. I couldn't feel it beneath the cast but just knowing her hand was there, that she was there, was both a comfort and a reminder that I was not alone. The first time I saw Yoda, who lived in a swamp, I thought he was just a giant frog with mutated ears. He turned out to be quite a character, though, and I was sad when he died. Or disappeared. Or whatever it was a mutant Jedi frog does after nine hundred years. It was Kalin's suggestion that

Tim and I call it even on the bet because, like Ben had told Luke, the truth was a matter of perspective.

In the evening, Ma brought us meatloaf for dinner. Kalin would eat while Ma fed me, patiently placing each forkful in my mouth. It took me an hour to finish, but at least I didn't have to worry about the hospital staff leaving before I was done. Most of them would lose their patience when I was about halfway through, asking if I'd had enough. It was always more of a statement than it was a question.

When she got a break, Mom would stop by for a few minutes or visit when she got off work. It seemed like every time her shift was done, the other nurses would always drop in to ask her a question or tell her something. It became so common that afterwards, Mom would update me on my progress, discuss my physical therapy, or shuffle my blankets around until I finally told her to stop. I said that I dealt with doctors and nurses all day, every day, and that I didn't want to be treated like another one of her patients, especially when she was off duty.

For a moment, I thought she'd get upset, but Mom just sat down, exasperated, and finally took a moment to relax.

Never knew it was so bad, I said. Kalin set her hand on my shoulder. After several months, I was finally out of those casts and had started physical therapy. We were home, back at the condo, and Kalin had just helped me out of the tub. Bracing myself on the walker, I stood before the long mirror on the door, seeing my battered body for the first time since the accident.

My muscles had grown soft from a lack of exercise. A few small scars were scattered across my cheeks and forehead. My left side had a massive gash of tender scar tissue on my ribcage and another on my leg where my bone had snapped through my flesh. Reaching up, I rubbed the old scar on my shoulder. The invincibility I had known in my youth had long since vanished; my shining armor was shattered.

I don't recognize that man anymore, I told Kalin.

But I know who he is, she said. Kalin guided me to the chair beside the bed to help me get dressed. While I was in the hospital, she had bought me a bunch of new clothes, including several colorful pairs of Disney pajamas. Tonight, she chose a matching set of Mickey and Minnie for the both of us. As I lifted my left leg, she set the bunched-up pajama pants around my ankle.

I don't know what to do now, I told her, lifting my other leg. *I can't work seven days a week now. I know that. And I've still got twelve to eighteen months of physical therapy.*

Maybe work five days, Kalin suggested. She pulled the pajamas up over my knees. *Maybe just six hours in the morning, to see how things are going with third and first shift. And maybe just stop by in the evenings after you're done with physical therapy. Ready to stand?*

I placed my hands around her shoulders to pull myself up while she set her forearms under me. After years of listening to each other, she knew exactly when to rise just by the pace of my breathing. I kept my hands on her back for balance as she quickly pulled up my pajamas. We followed the same routine as she guided me back to my seat.

I can do that, I said. *That's a good idea. No rush, I know that.*

Junior, Tim, Sarah, and Jean can handle the station, she told me. *They all did a great job over the past few months, everybody. And they all appreciate what you've done for them, especially their quarterly bonuses.*

We give bonuses?

She nodded. *Managers, assistant managers, and all employees who have worked for at least a year. Like your father explained to me once: 'Customers get what they pay for, but employees will give what you pay them for.'*

Sometimes, I think you know my father better than I did, I said. *After all the work I put into the place, I want to take it easy now. My father worked himself to death.*

He wanted you to learn from his mistakes.

How do you know that?

Because he regretted them so much, she said, *and he told me. He wanted you to be better. All parents want that for their children.*

I love my father, Kalin, but I don't want to end up like he did. Not like that.

You won't, she told me. *Like your new pajamas?*

I love them. I never knew Disney made pajamas for couples.

That's what I wanted to tell you, she said, smiling as her eyes sparkled. Sitting up, she gave me a kiss. *I wanted to wait for the right time. Now that you're home—*

For what? The right time for what? Tell me what?

It was a family set, Kalin said. Reaching beneath the pillow, she pulled out a tiny pair of matching pajamas. *I'm pregnant.*

CHAPTER TWENTY-EIGHT

DISNEYLAND

AS THE SUN SET on the twentieth century, a great darkness arose at the dawn of the new millennium. The impeachment of President Clinton, who was charged with perjury and obstruction of justice after his affair with an intern became public, had dominated the news for over a year. I had long since thought it was absurd, a political farce staged by the Republicans, but I stopped following the scandal after reading about Monica Lewinsky struggling with suicide. She had been branded with a scarlet letter, publicly shamed on a global scale, and humiliated day after day in the sensationalized programming of news networks desperate for ratings, regardless of the consequences. After Jim, I just couldn't be a part of that.

Two months after President Clinton was acquitted by the Senate, Kalin and I bought a plot of land across the street from my childhood home in Poquanicut and broke ground on our new house. Once the land was cleared, we stopped by to see the foundation. I had William strapped to my chest in his baby carrier. He was fidgeting, as he often did, when Mom came over to tell us that there had been a massive shooting at a high school in Colorado. Initial reports had said that several students and at least one teacher were dead but many more had been injured. As we walked across the street, back to the television to find out what was going on, I wrapped my arms around my son, kissing his head several times. The dawn of darkness had begun.

Kalin, like a lot of people, saw the shooting at Columbine High School as an exception, an anomaly, but I was in panic mode. My whole life had been marked by violence—from losing my family in the Holocaust to those careless hunters at Ledge Lake, from Grandpa's murder and Jim's suicide to my own deadly encounter on the front lines of that so-called "culture war" at the clinic. Like the Clinton impeachment, it was a war only the Christians wanted—and they had nearly killed me in the middle of it. Only now, in the dawn of darkness, could I see the ripples in the pond, the culture of violence that had spread across America. There were times it felt like I was using all my energy fighting my fear, anxiety, and panic. Or was that just part of being a parent?

William Isaac Evans was the greatest present I ever got. He was born on my twenty-eighth birthday, delivered by his grandmother, who had traded the stress of her nursing coworkers to become a midwife. Kalin had kept our pregnancy a secret while I was in the hospital; she believed it was bad luck to tell everybody during the first trimester. When she had showed me those adorable, miniature pajamas, filling out the family set, my whole life flashed before my eyes. I saw all the mistakes my parents had made—from scolding me at the dinner table to being so hard on me at work—and I knew I would never make those same mistakes with my children. (I laugh about that now, having learned just how much I didn't know about parenting.) As Kalin and I looked over the images of her first ultrasound, we figured out, based on his size, that William had been conceived about two weeks before my accident. I didn't even know he existed, and he almost lost me.

At first, I had been determined to finish physical therapy before he was born. I wanted to be healthy for my family. So, I'd get up in the middle of the night and push my body even as the pain warned me to stop, but no amount of willpower or wishful thinking can defy the laws of biological physics. I had tried so hard to recover so fast that I ended up impeding my progress. The fatigue soon meant afternoon naps that often left Kalin having to do the housework we had scheduled for me. She didn't like that, especially since she was working full-time. Once I realized what I had done, I decided to leave my illusions of invincibility in the past, where they belonged. In all, it took me sixteen months to regain my strength, my range of motion, my balance, and to learn to walk again.

By the time William was born, I could only hold him if I was sitting down.

He was so tiny, so fragile. So pure.

I'd stare at him as he slept in my arms, watching the soft spot on his head pulsate as he slept. Everything about him mesmerized us. He was a part of me, a new life that had developed and grown inside his mother, and he amazed us every day. During our Lamaze classes, I'd learned just how powerful a woman's body could be, that during birth the uterus becomes the strongest muscle a human body ever produced. I wanted so badly to be a good husband and a good father, for my son's life to be better than mine. But, as I saw my life through his eyes, I began to understand why Ma had chosen to hide me.

I, too, would do anything to protect my son.

Anything.

When we finally moved into the house later that summer, we invited Gregg and Shae over for a cookout. By that time, Kalin and I were at odds over William's future, especially his education. She insisted that he attend the American School for the Deaf in Hartford, but I wanted us to teach him at home, where he would be safe. Between the two of us, our college experience gave us an extensive background, and I had, after all, taught Memphis how to read. Gregg took over the grill while I sat down with William, trying to get the buns and condiments ready while he fidgeted in his carrier. He was growing fast and getting heavy. I took him out of the carrier and strapped him into his high chair.

How's the station? Gregg asked, flipping the burgers.

It's good, I said. *Business has been steady. The crew is happy.*

Once William had started sleeping through the night, I'd gone back to work but limited myself to Monday through Thursday. I'd get up at four, have breakfast, and be at the station from five until nine-thirty. When I got home, Kalin would work from ten to three at the condo. She got done quicker without distractions and appreciated the time alone. We had made the spare bedroom into an office for the both of us (and would often make use of the master bedroom on date night).

Mostly, I focused on doing the books, even taking on some of Kalin's accounts so she could have more time. She had bought one of those new iMac computers from Apple. It looked like a psychedelic television set from the Seventies, but it saved on paperwork, I guess. I kept using my big, leather-bound ledgers for the station though, thick as a Gutenberg bible, because I liked to stick with what works: one page per day, one book per year. I even had the same mechanical registers that Mac had bought in the Fifties. I'd clean and oil them once a year. Tim had suggested once that I buy computerized registers, but I could easily take the old ones apart and fix them any time there was a problem.

"*You can't do that with a computer*," I told Tim. The station was the only place I wore my hearing aids, but I signed all the time since getting out of the hospital. My most recent audiogram revealed that my deafness had progressed significantly; I was severe-to-profound now. "*You have to hire a technician. That's like going for an oil change and getting a new engine.*"

"What's the point to getting a new engine when you can just buy a new car?" Tim said.

"*Exactly,*" I said. "*If I can put my hands on it, I can fix it. If it's programmed, I have to learn everything I don't need to know just to do one thing.*"

"Those old registers work just fine," Junior said. "If there's one thing I learned from you over the years, Roger, it's that you're always open to ideas, but new isn't always better."

Junior and the crew had kept the station in shipshape while I was away. The crew had set up a "Welcome Back" banner and balloons for my first day back. Alejandro, who now had his own restaurant in Rose City, had even baked a cake. It was like coming home to an old friend. Junior and I had made communication etiquette part of the training, including both the rules of natural law (visibility, noise, and distance) and situational awareness for people with disabilities. I had sought Gregg's input due to his legal expertise.

How is Shondra? I asked Gregg.

Learning more every day, he said, beaming with pride. He told me that Shondra had already learned hundreds of signs, and she was only two years old. Language acquisition, Gregg had said, was crucial for a child's early years, and he didn't want his daughter to grow up isolated like he had. *We got her off to a good start, unlike me when I was her age.*

When did you first discover Sign? I asked. William's little hands had mimicked mine. Reaching over, I playfully rubbed his cheeks, smiling as I told him, *Wonderful! You are learning so much! You are so smart!*

He was delighted. *I'm smart!*

I was nine years old, Gregg told me. William followed our conversation, watching in wonder and listening intensely. I started slicing the tomatoes, pausing as I watched Gregg. *I saw a couple of deaf teenagers signing at a service plaza in New Jersey. It was amazing to see that for the first time, a language I could use without limits.*

When did you start attending a deaf school?

When I was twelve, he said. No sooner had I given William a tomato slice than he tossed it on the ground. After picking it up and setting it on a napkin, I gave him another one and told him to eat. He put it to his mouth and took a small bite. It was good to have a break from his fussiness. *I had a lot to learn because I missed so much.*

What do you mean? I asked.

My hearing parents did the best they could, he said, *and they did a shitty job.*

That's why Kalin and I told our parents, 'You can't see your grandson if you're going to talk to him. You will only sign to him'. My mothers were more understanding about it than her parents. Finally, we had to tell them, 'If you talk, you leave.'

Do you still use your hearing aids? Gregg asked.

Only at work, I said. *I told the crew that I wear them for their convenience, not mine.*

How do you want your burger?

Medium. Kalin likes hers well done.

He flipped the burgers and added seasoning. *Have you thought any more about school?*

We haven't decided yet, I told him. *There was a copycat about a week after Columbine.*

Gregg shook his head. *Copycats are just people who can't think for themselves.*

It keeps me up at night, knowing there will be more.

How do you know there will be more?

Look at what the politicians are saying about Columbine, I said. *They blame video games and movies for what happened. They blame the outcasts, the subculture. It's ridiculous, stupid. I played violent video games. I watched violent movies. I was an outcast in high school, which was so much worse after Jim. You never saw me shoot up a school. They're just avoiding the problem, postponing a definitive solution, like responsible gun laws.*

Postpone a decision long enough and you never have to make it, Gregg said. *Maybe if the Republicans weren't so obsessed with President Clinton's sex life, they would have accomplished something by now. Maybe it never would have happened if Congress had been paying attention, doing their job. There is a difference between civil service and politics.*

Politics is the nemesis of government, I said.

Effective government, Gregg clarified. He set the burgers on a plate and sat down. I told Kalin and Shae, who were sitting on the porch with Shondra, that we were ready to eat. Gregg asked if we had made a decision about William's education.

We have a few years before he starts school, I said.

We have time to decide what we want to do, Kalin agreed. *He is learning a lot at home with us.*

She had come to know my anxiety and panic attacks all too well. When Kalin asked William if he liked his tomato, he signed *Yes* as his face lit up. He took another bite and smiled. I never knew a tomato could bring so much joy.

We have to survive Y2K first! Shae said jokingly. Gregg rolled his eyes.

In 1999, the mythological computer programming flaw, known as Y2K, which would supposedly replace the two-digit abbreviation "99" with "100" instead of recognizing the year as 2000, had become a well-known joke, like all those religious nuts who were expecting the apocalypse or the rapture on New Year's Eve. Tim's parents had even bought several months of canned goods and had plans to hide in the basement. I hadn't had a conversation about religion with a Christian since I was in physical therapy. He was working through another knee replacement and seemed to be a decent fellow—they always do at first—and we'd sometimes get to talking during our sessions. When I tried to explain what I'd learned about suicide, that the sun always rises, he got so hung up on my quoting the wrong passage about the fate of Judas that he completely missed the significance of the lesson. Still, there were times I found myself wishing that the rapture actually would happen just so all the Christians would disappear and the rest of us could live our lives in peace.

But that, I knew, was as much a delusion as religion itself.

Kalin and I rang in the new millennium with a bottle of wine and a quiet evening at home by a roaring fire. When the ball dropped, we kissed. Nine months later, we had a daughter.

Faith Marie. My baby girl.

She was just so beautiful. Majestic.

When the election of 2000 came around, we were getting up every few hours to feed Faith, so we just decided to stay up and wait for the results. Ma had retired by that time, but it had taken her two years to sell the house in Elliott. Last summer, she had moved in with Mom to be closer to her grandchildren. Florida still hadn't been called when Kalin went to bed at two a.m. It was going to be a long night.

Bush lost the popular vote, Ma said, using one hand. She was holding Faith, who had just fallen asleep. *If he had any dignity, he should concede.*

I agree, Mom said. They had both learned a lot of sign as we taught William but were still far from fluent. Nevertheless, they respected the decision Kalin and I had made that they only sign around the kids. It was easy enough for them to remember, especially since I never wore my hearing aids at home.

Unfortunately, the electoral college complicates things a little bit, I said. I'd voted for Al Gore, hoping he would continue to be fiscally responsible because Clinton had balanced the budget. Bush, whom I had expected to win, wanted to raid the surplus for no economically viable reason. The moment a hurricane or an earthquake hit, America would need that money to rebuild. Only a fool spends a rainy-day fund under a blue sky.

I looked at Faith. Her tiny lips moved, like she was dreaming of being fed.

You can go to sleep, Roger, Mom said. *We'll wake Kalin when Faith needs to eat again.*

You know, William is growing up fast, I told her. *He poops on the potty now. Sometimes. But watching him sit up and crawl and stand and walk...it reminds me of how much time I lost those three years I was living in Brockton Heights.*

You can't blame yourself, Mom said. When Faith woke up for a moment and yawned, Ma handed her to Mom.

Think of the time I lost, Ma said. *There are so many things I missed. I never got to see your first day of school. I never went to your open house. I was never there when you were waiting for the school bus on a Saturday.*

I was pleasantly surprised she knew I'd done that. *How did you know about that?*

Grandpa wrote me all the time, she said. *But, I mean, I'm here now. I get to see my grandchildren doing all the things I missed with you.*

Look to the future, Mom said, using her free hand.

Right, Ma agreed. *Look to the future. Learn from the past, but don't let your fear dictate your decisions. Sooner or later, every parent must send their children out into the world. I just did that a lot sooner than I ever wanted to.*

Is that why you hid me? I asked. *Because you were afraid?*

That's part of it, she said.

But she was also grieving your father, Mom said. *Have you thought about therapy?*

Kalin told you about my panic attacks, didn't she? When I saw the revealing look on Mom's face, I got up and went out on the porch. It was snowing lightly but not cold. As the porch light faded out over the lawn, I saw that the grass I had planted last year had come in pretty good. A moment later, Mom came outside and handed me a note.

> —I kept my promise. I did what you wanted. William and Faith are both sleeping. Can you please put in your hearing aids? I'm sorry, but I don't know how to say what I want to say in ASL.

When Mom held out my hearing aids in her hand, I put them in as a blast of sound hit in my ears. A moment later, my mind adjusted as I began to process the sound of silence.

"Thank you for doing that," Mom said.

"*Thank you for acknowledging your limitations,*" I told her. "*What's on your mind?*"

"I just…we're worried about you. You've been through so much, more than most men twice your age."

"*Do you remember when I was a kid and you and Dad first bought the house? How it stood in the middle of that field of mud?*"

"Of course, I remember," Mom said. "That was the first thing I thought of when you had the land cleared here."

"*I was just thinking about Dad taking out all those rocks, how he'd pick them up and throw them deep into the woods.*"

"I remember you helping him."

"*But I couldn't throw them as far as he could. So, I'd pick them up one at a time, run to the edge of the forest, and then I'd throw them. Even then, I wanted him to be proud of me.*"

"He was," she said. "Roger, he was always so proud of you. We both are."

Wiping my eyes, I shook my head. "*Mom, I can't…I can't shake this feeling that…all I want to do is protect my kids, but I can't. I know I can't. Everything I know about my family and my life tells me that I can't. Not all the time. It's just…it's impossible. And I…I just have this constant panic, like there's a monster in my chest. It started when William was born, but after Columbine my anxiety skyrocketed. It was the summer of 1985 all over again, when we got the news about Grandpa. It was finding Jim's body in that closet. It was finally coming home after three years only to realize I was too late. And I don't…I don't know what to do. I thought I'd have all the answers by the time I became a dad, but I don't.*"

"No one does," Mom said. She fished her necklace out from underneath her sweater, took it off, and handed it to me. As the snow drifted down through the darkness, glowing in the porch light, I could see the diamond on a ring of gold. "You know what that is?"

"*Looks familiar.*"

"That's your grandmother's wedding ring," Mom said. "She gave it to your father when he proposed to me. Do you remember I said I was going to give it to you when the time came?"

"*Why didn't you?*"

"Because your father gave it to me again ten years ago," she said. "He proposed."

"*What?*"

"We got back together."

"*Are you serious?*"

"I am serious."

"*Why didn't you tell me?*"

She chuckled. "Honestly, Roger, since when is my love life any concern of yours?"

"*All right. You're right about that.*"

"I know he's your father, but that…I want to keep that. I deserve that."

"*So, I'm not the only one with regrets? Is that what you're telling me? How can people live their whole lives and, in the end, say they have no regrets?*"

"You'll get there."

"*I know it's none of my business, but can I ask what happened? I mean, what brought you together again?*"

"The house needed a new roof," Mom said. "So, I stopped by the station and asked if he would be willing to do the work if I bought the materials. It wasn't long before one thing led to another. We never set a date, mostly because we were waiting for you to come back."

"*Just like that?*"

"Not quite," Mom said. "You have to remember that he spent years getting his act together. He stopped drinking. He went to counseling. When we got divorced, I told him I didn't even recognize him anymore, but he slowly became the man I knew he could be. And I knew he had to do it on his own; I couldn't force him to do anything. It took years, but, little by little, I started to see the man I once knew."

"*So, in a way, I got back the family I lost.*"

"I suppose so," Mom said. "You know, he never asked for my forgiveness. Instead, he earned his redemption. He did the work, Roger. You know I love Kalin. She's a great woman, as brilliant as she is beautiful, and a wonderful mother. She's smarter and wiser than all of us. But you've got your own work to do. You may as well do it now or it'll just eat you up inside as the years go by, like it did with your father. And Kalin might not be as gracious with you as I was with him."

She held out her hand. I gave her back the ring.

"*Think we'll ever get a new president?*" I asked.

"I thought you'd have learned by now it'll all work out in the end," Mom said. "We did our part when we voted yesterday morning. The only question, for America and for you as well, is which path will you chose? Think about it."

I started therapy that week.

* * *

"*We're leaving Tuesday,*" I told Dr. Walsh. She was a bald, middle-aged woman who had insisted on working through her cancer treatments. My progress in therapy somehow seemed connected to her recovery, which had been going well. "*Kalin got us a good deal on a flight out of Boston.*"

"When was your last vacation?" Dr. Walsh asked.

"*A few months after the wedding,*" I said. "*We went to Maine for a week in the fall, maybe seven or eight months before my accident. After that I had physical therapy for about a year. Meanwhile, William came along. Then, Faith.*"

"I'd say you're overdue."

"*It was Kalin's idea,*" I said. "*I told her the kids wouldn't even remember a trip to Disneyland at their age. She said, 'We will.'*"

"I certainly think you've earned a vacation."

"*What about you?*" I asked. "*When was the last time you took a vacation?*"

"Before my mastectomy," she said. "Megan took me to Paris, just in case."

"*Paris? Wow.*"

She smiled. "Just in case."

"*And the doctor said you're in remission?*"

"I am. Of course, there is still a chance it could come back, but Megan and I made a deal in Paris that if we got through this, we would take another trip."

"*I'd say you're overdue.*"

"Well, we both had some work to do first," Dr. Walsh said. "You know, I am supposed to maintain my professional detachment, but I...I want to thank you for your support. Means a lot."

"*We're all in this together,*" I said. I had gotten to know Dr. Walsh during our sessions together almost as much as she knew me. It started with my asking how her treatment was going and slowly evolved to her sharing some of the struggles and challenges of living with the disease. I never said much when she spoke; it was better to listen, which was exactly what Dr. Walsh had done for me.

In the past ten months, we had worked our way from Dad's post-traumatic stress to mine, which I'd learned was the genesis of my anxiety and panic. It started with the night I had seen my father hit my mother and just kept piling on through the years. Dr. Walsh had guided me through the hunters at Ledge Lake to Grandpa getting killed and my getting shot by the Christians at the clinic to the day I'd learned about Columbine. She had told me that it was rare people had the courage and the wisdom to face their pain. Instead, they make it a point to avoid their anguish, letting their grief simmer until it boils over—which was often how and why and when victims become abusers.

I'd seen it happen with Jim, whose marriage had been a recreation of his own horrific trauma. The emotional, physical, psychological, and sexual abuse he'd endured as a child had manifested itself years later in his animosity toward women. I saw it with Dad, whose personal demons had plagued him after the war until his private hell scorched the family he had once held so dear. And I was guilty as well, having beaten Blaine to a pulp for being such an asshole after Jim killed himself.

The line between being a victim and becoming an abuser was a thin one, Dr. Walsh had said, but the secret was to acknowledge our pain, to allow ourselves to feel it, accept it, and embrace it because the alternative would only lead us into an emotional abyss, one so powerful we dragged our most intimate partners into our private hell. If we didn't learn to control our feelings, then our feelings would control us. She also pointed out that my father, Jake, had come of age during a time when so little was known about the psychological trauma of war and that such ignorance, coupled with the social expectations of masculinity, was a recipe for disaster.

"*Is that what he meant when he said, 'a lifetime of being ignored can have toxic side effects?'*" I asked.

"I think so, yes. But I also want to give credit where credit is due. Like your mother said, your father was wise enough to know that he needed help."

"*He still made mistakes.*"

"The path to redemption is seldom smooth," Dr. Walsh had said. "It's often quite a rocky road. Knowing where we need to go doesn't automatically get us there. It's just the first step."

"*It's the last step that bothers me.*"

"What's the last step?"

"*I never got to say goodbye,*" I told her. "*Not to my father, not to Jim, not to my grandfather. Not to...not to the family I lost in the Holocaust. Not to any of them. Thinking about it now reminds me of something Memphis once told me.*"

"What was that?"

"*She said that Jim is gone, but I'm not. I get to see everything he missed.*"

"Smart woman," Dr. Walsh had said. "You've come quite a long way since our first session."

"*I felt paralyzed that day,*" I told her. "*I honestly thought I'd leave after the first five minutes, but I knew you were different when I told you the Riddle of the Three Men.*"

"How so?"

"*You were the first one to realize that they all had the same problem.*"

"But it was obvious," Dr. Walsh said. "I just don't see why anyone would choose divorce or a lifetime of misery."

I loaded the luggage the night before we left. It was a challenge getting the kids up at four o'clock in the morning; I carried them to the car while Kalin strapped them into their seats. It was ninety miles to the airport. As the dark highway stretched out before us, I found myself wishing we had got a hotel in Boston instead of having to hit the road so early to beat rush-hour traffic. We stopped at a service plaza so Kalin could feed Faith. I took William with me to refill the Thermos and asked if he had to use the bathroom; he insisted that he didn't have to go.

When we got to Boston, we had enough time to grab a quick breakfast before checking in our luggage. Kalin ordered eggs Benedict while I had banana pancakes. We got scrambled eggs for William, who was now wide awake under the bright lights. Faith, full of wonder, kept looking around and taking in all the sights. Feeding her had been a good idea; she was calm and fell asleep in her carrier while we were checking in our luggage at Terminal C.

If you have to pee, go now, I told William.

I don't have to pee.

Are you sure? I asked.

Come on, Dad, he said, slouching his shoulders. *I don't have to pee!*

Once we got to Gate 19, I confirmed our flight number with the attendant, who wrote that it had been pushed out by fifteen minutes. When I told Kalin, she asked about the receipt from the restaurant.

They're boarding, I said, exasperated. *Do we really need it?*

You just said they pushed out our departure. You still have time. Now, go!

Reluctantly, I headed to the restaurant. When I looked back, I saw Kalin handing our tickets to the gate attendant. Once I found our waitress, I gave her a note requesting our receipt. She spoke but held up her index finger, indicating that I had to wait. I watched her take two orders and bring out for three meals before I wrote another note, telling her that my flight would be leaving any minute now and that she needed to hurry. When she spoke again, I shook my head and told her *I'm deaf*, then pointed to the pen and pad I'd set down on the counter. Annoyed, she took her sweet time writing on the pad, asking me what we had ordered.

I looked at my watch again. My plane was scheduled to depart in three minutes. By the time I got back to the gate, I was out of breath from running so fast.

Kalin and the kids were nowhere to be found.

The plane was gone.

I found a TTY and called my mothers to let them know that I had missed the plane. Ma offered to get in touch with our hotel in California and leave a message for Kalin to let her know that I was trying to get another flight. I told Ma that I would call back once I knew what I could find. I was waiting in line at the ticket counter when I saw a group of people gathering around a television set. There were watching a movie about a burning building. The captions were on, but I was too far away to see them.

It was then I noticed a few people running through the airport. A woman was trembling and crying. People were hugging.

I headed for the television and made my way through the crowd so that I could read the choppy captions.

> REPORTS OF A HIJACKING FROM BOSTON HEADED TO LOS ANGELES

It wasn't a movie.

The World Trade Center had been attacked.

A plane flew into the second building and exploded.

It can't be our flight, I thought. They just left. No plane in the world could make it from Boston to New York that fast. It can't possibly be our flight.

I watched the Towers burn. Waiting.

Helpless. Frozen. Hopeless.

The captions began to blur once I realized that it had been a terrorist attack. A suicide mission. The smoke coming from the Twin Towers became a haze as the dizziness hit me. I felt queasy. Another plane had hit the Pentagon. I was going into shock.

Boston. Headed to Los Angeles.

The South Tower collapsed in a cloud of dust.

In a daze, floating through the crowd, I sank to the floor, leaned against the wall, and fell to my side.

Boston to Los Angeles. New York.

I closed my eyes. Numb.

The great darkness had risen.

My leg. Who touched my leg?

Somebody touched my leg again. And again.

I woke up, still in shock and half asleep, but my heart soared when I saw William standing in front of me. Immediately, I gave him a hug and stood up as my little buddy wrapped his arms and legs around me. Kalin, still carrying Faith, had tears in her anguished eyes.

We waited at the restaurant for an hour, she said as her hands trembled. *The waitress told me what happened, so I called your mothers and my parents and Shae and Junior. Alejandro found out it was our flight. It was our flight!*

I held them, my wife and children, as we cried and cried and cried. We cried for those who had been lost. We wept for America. But our tears, that day, in that moment, were filled with an excruciating joy as well.

Because we missed our flight. The one the whole world had seen hit the South Tower. United 175.

When I started wiping away Kalin's tears, William got mine. I laughed and gave him a hug.

I never got the receipt, I told Kalin. She laughed and cried. *What happened? I saw you getting on the plane.*

William had to pee, Kalin said. *That's why we missed our flight! He had to pee!*

I never loved that kid so much in my life.

CHAPTER TWENTY-NINE

WHEN HOPE MAKES HISTORY

IT HAS BECOME MY nightly ritual to check the kids before bed. I can't sleep unless I know they're safe. It's as much for me as it is for them.

William has gotten so big. And yet, he is still so small. As I cover him up, I wonder who he will become, what kind of man he will be when he grows up. I think of my own father too, as I watch my son sleep. I remember waking up and seeing Dad jump for joy as Carlton Fisk waved the ball to stay fair so many years ago. The memory brings a smile to my face as I take a long last look at my son before closing the door.

My little angels, Faith and Joy, are in the next room. In the dim light from the hall, I see the small pink and blue elephants on Faith's pajamas rise and fall with each of her deep, short breaths—the breath of life. The other day, Mom commented on how stubborn Faith can be, but I don't see her that way at all.

She's passionate, I told Mom. *Determined and smart. That girl will do great things when she grows up.*

Leaning down, I gently kiss her cheek. Kalin's shadow moves across the wall as she comes into the room. She stands beside me as we watch our little bundle, Joy, sleeping so peacefully. We agreed to home-school the kids after September 11. As I look back now on that devastating morning, I still think of the thousands lost—including the passengers of United 93, whose courage has become a testament to America's resilience; despite the horror, it took just seventy-one minutes for us to start fighting back. It has now been over three years since the attacks. The healing, and the rebuilding, have begun.

Can't sleep? I ask.

I had to pee, Kalin tells me, rolling her eyes. *How was the Red Sox game?*

We got clobbered, 19-8, I tell her. Her jaw drops in shock and disappointment. She caught the fever last October, when the Red Sox came within four outs of ending the Curse of the Bambino—and blew it. She was smart to go bed early tonight. *Now, we're one game away from elimination.*

Maybe this one will bring us luck, Kalin says, rubbing her belly. She has never been more beautiful. Our fourth is due in two weeks. *David if it's a boy.*

David if they win, I tell her, knowing it's a stretch. *No team in baseball has ever won the ALCS after losing the first three games.*

I still believe, she says. *Maybe it's time for you to believe.*

I admire her conviction, but she doesn't know the Red Sox.

We could name the next one David, I suggest.

This is the last one!

You said that after the first one.

I mean it this time!

You said that after the second one.

I'm serious!

You said that after the third one.

I know, Kalin says, smiling. This is one of the patterns of our pregnancies. In the late months, her patience grows exponentially thin. That lasts until she holds our child in her arms for the first time, overcome with joy. Once they start sleeping through the night, and we've both caught up on our rest a little, she starts thinking about having another one. This time though, despite my playful teasing, I agree that the fourth will be our last.

Kalin kisses her hand and gently places it on Joy's cheek. She just turned two last summer. I double-check the monitor before we leave the room. In the kitchen, I watch Kalin getting the soda and ice cream for our root beer floats. We bought Ben & Jerry's for a while, but their obsession with politics took all the comfort out of our comfort food; people buy ice cream because they want ice cream. Tonight, we've got vanilla caramel swirl. I think of how much Grandpa would have loved to try it. He never got the chance—but I can. I have. And that's the thing: I get to see and taste and touch and experience everything they missed.

Not so long ago, new experiences haunted me; all I could think about was Grandpa not being there to try a new ice cream, Dad not seeing the sun rise at the station each morning, or Jim not gazing upon the stars. Now that

I'm older, with a wife and kids of my own, I've learned to appreciate the memories of those who have gone before, the ones who have passed.

Grandpa. Jim. Dad. They're always with me.

Not haunting, but watching. Guarding.

There are even times, like tonight, I can just see Grandpa try to flip that scoop of ice cream into the mug. He misses again, of course, but it's the fun we have along the way that matters. I smile as Kalin catches my reverie. *What are you thinking?*

Memories, I tell her. *Good memories. And maybe you're right. Maybe it is time for me to believe.*

Remember when Coach Belichick replaced Drew Bledsoe with Tom Brady? Kalin asks. Football has always been her favorite sport, going back to her days watching the Bison play at Gally. *We thought that was a mistake until the Patriots won two Super Bowls with Brady.*

Football is not baseball, I tell her. But I'm cautiously optimistic. New England is doing well enough this season to make the playoffs again this year. Maybe the magic hasn't left Boston just yet.

In perfect-pitch form, Kalin slides the foaming mug to me from across the table and smiles.

The next night, Game 4 becomes a nail-biter. The Red Sox climb ahead in the fifth only to give up two more runs as the Yankees take back the lead in the sixth. When the game goes to the ninth, I can't take it anymore.

During the commercials, I grab the remote and start flipping through the channels until I see a segment showing highlights from the Democratic National Convention this summer. I recognize the state senator from Illinois, Barack Obama, who gave the keynote address during his campaign for a seat in the United States Senate. It takes a moment for the captioning to catch up, but when it does, I remember the moment.

> I'M TALKING ABOUT SOMETHING MORE SUBSTANTIAL. IT'S THE HOPE OF SLAVES SITTING AROUND A FIRE SINGING FREEDOM SONGS; THE HOPE OF IMMIGRANTS SETTING OUT FOR DISTANT SHORES; THE HOPE OF A YOUNG NAVAL LIEUTENANT BRAVELY PATROLLING THE MEKONG DELTA; THE HOPE OF A MILLWORKER'S SON WHO DARES TO DEFY THE ODDS; THE HOPE OF A SKINNY

> KID WITH A FUNNY NAME WHO BELIEVES AMERICA HAS A PLACE FOR HIM, TOO.

I can't help but smile. It's the one thing I've always had—from that summer night seeing the original *Star Wars* at the drive-in theater through discovering my heritage and having a family, from the Deaf students who showed me who I could be during that historic week at Gallaudet to embracing my past, my family, and my identity.

It's the one thing, through it all, that no one can ever take from me.

The hope of America.

> HOPE IN THE FACE OF DIFFICULTY, HOPE IN THE FACE OF UNCERTAINTY, THE AUDACITY OF HOPE: IN THE END, THAT IS GOD'S GREATEST GIFT TO US, THE BEDROCK OF THIS NATION. A BELIEF IN THINGS NOT SEEN. A BELIEF THAT THERE ARE BETTER DAYS AHEAD

In the greatest darkness, the light endures. Hope endures. It is the one star we need to find our way. The sunrise we seek after a long, cold night. The lighthouse that guides us through our storms. It is the promise of life renewed every spring. And it is Dave Roberts stealing second fucking base in Game 4.

The Steal.

It's the one moment that turns it all around. The moment when an unstoppable force proceeds against an immovable object. The moment endurance rewards effort, and passion meets determination. When hope makes history. The one moment every soul craves.

In baseball. And in life.

Hope endures.

In the twelfth, David Ortiz obliterates a walk-off home run and the Red Sox live to die another die. The next night, Big Papi is the hero once again, lining a single to drive Johnny Damon home in the fourteenth inning. Boston takes it to seven games. I know it's over once Damon smashes a grand slam in the second.

The Red Sox set records with each pitch and every swing, winning eight straight games.

After the last out of the World Series, I sit on the couch crying tears of joy as the Red Sox celebrate their first championship since 1918.

Kalin sets her hand on my shoulder as I wipe my eyes.

We kiss. *I love you.*

Our fourth was born that morning. We named him David Jacob. My mothers smile, watching him as he sleeps.

I will tell my children, and their children, about this moment. And I will remind them that, in our darkest days, there will always be a moment when the night must yield to the dawn of a new day.

The sunrise of a new world.

Keep going. It gets better. I've seen it, lived it. And while it may get worse before it gets better, just remember—

There is always a moment.

Always.

CHAPTER THIRTY

SUNSET

KALIN TAKES MY HAND as we enter the Magic Kingdom. The morning majesty of Main Street amazes me. The classic architecture creates a whole new world filled with nostalgia yet laced with imagination. When I see Cinderella's Castle for the very first time, the magic suddenly becomes real. After all these years, we finally made it to Walt Disney World.

The crowds are always fierce in December, but we have reservations for an early breakfast at Cinderella's Royal Table, which allows us to get inside before Rope Drop. We stop before the statue of Walt and Mickey, and I wrap my arms around Kalin as she comes in close. Even with the Magic Kingdom to ourselves, we only have eyes for each other. We have been together nearly thirty years. We have plans to spend the week in New York to celebrate our silver wedding anniversary but wanted to get a head start with Mickey.

We kiss as the clouds roll in with the rising storm. The downpour begins, but Kalin suddenly keels over in a fit of coughing. My whole body aches as I lift her, but I defy the agony and carry her up the stairs. As we cross the threshold, I realize that we are outside Grand Central Station. I set Kalin down once she starts coughing again. When she hacks up a thick purple liquid, I know something is wrong—very wrong. Through her long, drenched hair, she looks at me with fear in her eyes before dropping to the ground.

My dream becomes a nightmare. I set her head in my lap and, with trembling hands, text emergency services to get an ambulance. Burning up and shivering, the pain in my muscles feels like acid in my bloodstream. I can't fucking breathe. As my body goes into shock, I collapse on the sidewalk beside her. The ice-cold rain pours down upon us, but people just keep walking, turning away or acting like we don't exist; to them, we're just another tangled mass of diseased flesh infected with a novel virus. They'll never know how much we love each other. The last thing I remember, just before passing out, is Kalin taking my hand.

In the hours or days that follow, I lose all sense of time and direction, forgetting even where I am. My dreams and memories and nightmares have all blended together, like a fog hovering through my mind. I wake up, aware, just as the nurses pull my wife's limp and lifeless hand from mine—watching, hopeless and helpless, while they cover her with a white sheet. The setting sun lingers through the windows as they wheel her away.

I want to scream but can't move; my energy is gone. They even put a tube down my throat to get air in my lungs. Instead, tears fall as my body fails. I try to fight, to resist. I tell myself that I have to stay, to be strong. I think of my kids, our family, but the rising darkness covers me like a warm blanket. The aches and pains are gone. I feel nothing but a soft floating sensation, like going to sleep.

With my last, labored breaths, memories and dreams pass through my mind like gentle winds. Walt Disney World is closing tonight; the magic is gone, and I'm in the hospital. I remember telling Ma, in a video call, that we were going to be a little late getting home; she was the one who told me about Disney and said that this is the same hospital they brought me to after I was born. We were both intubated the next day. It's fitting, in a way, that my life ends in the same place it started. After just fifty years, I've come full circle. I wanted more time, so much more, but it's too late for that now.

Too late for us. Far, far too late.

The kids aren't ready for this—no one ever is, really—but I know they will endure. Humanity will make it through this monstrous, merciless pandemic. My kids will survive. I take comfort in knowing how well they have done over the years. William is going to law school after he graduates while Faith is in her second year; they were both thrilled to meet Nyle DiMarco while he was working on a documentary about Gallaudet. Joy wants to play professional hockey for the Connecticut Whale. She practices every day after school and has been caring for Mom since her stroke a few years ago, cooking and cleaning, running errands, and keeping up on her medication. David, who inherited his mother's talent for math, does the books for the station; he has become best buddies with Ma. They remind me of me and Grandpa.

They're good kids—smart too. They'll be okay.

It seems like it was only yesterday that I was a kid. I remember Granny making breakfast while Papa would cook the bacon; I can still smell that bacon. I could always smell it. The scent now takes me back to the kitchen table at their old house in Philly. Granny hands me a plate filled with French toast and bananas, and Jim is so happy when Papa gets the blueberries for his pancakes. Dad and Grandpa return with the milk and juice and newspaper. When Kalin comes down the stairs, her hair damp from the shower, she gets the root beer and ice cream; Grandpa flips a scoop perfectly into the mug. After we're done eating, Jim gets up and opens the door, then follows my family outside.

I stand at the threshold with Kalin, her dry hair blowing gently in the breeze. The magnificence of the distant mountains stretches to the horizon as I gaze upon the deep blue sky and bright green grass before me. They are all waiting for us: Gershon and Miriam, Grandpa and Grandma, William and Dad, Granny and Papa, my aunts and uncles, my cousins, Jim and Craig, and all those who have gone before.

Kalin takes my hand. She has never been more beautiful to me in all my life. My true north, leading me home at last.

This, I know, is our moment. Always.

The end of the beginning.

As we cross the threshold, the look in her eyes makes my heart flutter one last time before it stops beating. I realize, now, just how much my grandparents love each other: once Granny passed, Papa lasted less than a day without her.

I know how he feels. And that's just the way it goes.

Sooner or later, that's always the way it goes.

All things considered, I think I did pretty well.

It was—

~30~

WHERE CREDIT IS DUE

Biesold, Horst. *Crying Hands: Eugenics and Deaf People in Nazi Germany.* Translated by William Sayers. Washington, DC: Gallaudet UP, 1999.

Bush, George H. W. "Remarks of President George H. W. Bush at the Signing of the Americans with Disabilities Act." The White House. Washington, DC: 26 July 1990.

Frank, Anne. *The Diary of a Young Girl.* New York: Bantam, 1993.

Christiansen, John B & Sharon N. Barnatt. *Deaf President Now! The 1988 Revolution at Gallaudet University.* Washington, DC: Gallaudet UP, 1995.

Gannon, Jack R. *The Week the World Heard Gallaudet.* Washington, DC: Gallaudet UP, 1989.

Halloran, Liz & Lyn Bixby. "The Casino Effect." *The Hartford Courant.* 28-9 November 1999, state ed.: A1.

Jankowski, Katherine A. *Deaf Empowerment: Emergence, Struggle, and Rhetoric.* Washington, DC: Gallaudet UP, 1997.

Jepson, Jill, ed. *No Walls of Stone: An Anthology of Literature by Deaf and Hard of Hearing Writers.* Washington, DC: Gallaudet UP, 1992.

Lane, Harlan et al. *A Journey into the DEAF-WORLD.* San Diego: Dawn Sign Press, 1996.

Mari, Jean-Paul. "The Chilling Aftershock of a Brush with Death." TEDxCannes, uploaded by TED. March 2015. www.ted.com/talks/jean_paul_mari_the_chilling_aftershock_of_a_brush_with_death#t-918400

Obama, Barack. "Keynote Address." Democratic National Convention. The Fleet Center. Boston, MA: 27 July 2004.

"Police Brutality Against Deaf People." YouTube, uploaded by Rikki Poynter. 26 Sept. 2016. https://www.youtube.com/watch?v=RFyW6Kob0c8

Sacks, Oliver. *Seeing Voices: A Journey into the World of the Deaf.* Los Angeles: U of California P, 1989.

Silvers, Ann. *Abuse OF Men BY Woman: It Happens, It Hurts, and It's Time to Get Real About It.* Gil Harbor, WA: Silvers Publishing, 2014.

Young, Stella. "I Am Not Your Inspiration, Thank You Very Much." TEDxSydney, uploaded by TED. April 2014. www.ted.com/talks/stella_young_i_m_not_your_inspiration_thank_you_very_much

If you would like to learn more about the Holocaust, please visit —

The United States Holocaust Memorial Museum
100 Raoul Wallenberg Place, SW
Washington, DC 20024-2126

Or online at ushmm.org

You can also visit the Auschwitz-Birkenau Memorial Museum online at auschwitz.org. The site includes updates and information for both in-person and virtual tours.

If you are struggling with suicide, help is available —

In the United States, please call the National Suicide Prevention Lifeline at 988.

For access to international suicide prevention hotlines, please visit online at suicide.org.

ACKNOWLEDGEMENTS

I WANT TO THANK my copy editor, Heather Sangster of Strong Finish, for her wisdom, guidance, patience, and insight as well her humor and humanity; and graphic artist extraordinaire, Danna Mathias Steele of Dearly Creative, for her patience, expertise, and professionalism when it came to design and formatting.

ABOUT THE AUTHOR

Michael C. Haymes came of age during the last great era of rock and roll, achieving his hereditary deafness just in time to miss the pop kids take over the stage. He loves to play with his beagle, Autumn, who sometimes shares the pillows. He lives in Portland, ME.

michaelchaymes.com

www.ingramcontent.com/pod-product-compliance
Lightning Source LLC
Chambersburg PA
CBHW050856130726
47900CB00013B/67

9780578907444